# THE
# NEXT
# CHAPTER

**Rebecca Ryan** is the author of *My (extra)Ordinary Life*, *The Philosophy of Love* and *The Next Chapter*, although she can't quite believe that she's written three whole books. She left a career in teaching to pursue writing full time, and now mostly spends her days making up stories, replying to emails from her children's school, or killing off brain cells watching reels on Instagram. Rebecca lives in Bradford with her three children, no small number of notebooks and an expansive collection of scatter cushions. And she wouldn't have it any other way.

You can visit rebeccaryanauthor.co.uk and follow her on Instagram @becsryanauthor and X @WriteBecsWrite.

### Also by Rebecca Ryan

*My (extra)Ordinary Life*

*The Philosophy of Love*

# REBECCA RYAN

# THE NEXT CHAPTER

**SIMON &
SCHUSTER**

London · New York · Amsterdam/Antwerp · Sydney/Melbourne · Toronto · New Delhi

First published in Great Britain by Simon & Schuster UK Ltd, 2025

1 3 5 7 9 10 8 6 4 2

Simon & Schuster UK Ltd, 1st Floor
222 Gray's Inn Road, London WC1X 8HB

Simon & Schuster Australia, Sydney
Simon & Schuster India, New Delhi

www.simonandschuster.co.uk
www.simonandschuster.com.au
www.simonandschuster.co.in

The authorised representative in the EEA is Simon & Schuster Netherlands BV,
Herculesplein 96, 3584 AA Utrecht, Netherlands. info@simonandschuster.nl

Simon & Schuster strongly believes in freedom of expression and stands against
censorship in all its forms. For more information, visit BooksBelong.com

A CIP catalogue record for this book is available from the British Library

Paperback ISBN: 978-1-3985-3879-5
eBook ISBN: 978-1-3985-3880-1
Audio ISBN: 978-1-3985-3881-8

This book is a work of fiction. Names, characters, places and incidents are either
a product of the author's imagination or are used fictitiously. Any resemblance
to actual people living or dead, events or locales is entirely coincidental.

Typeset in Bembo by M Rules
Printed and Bound in the UK using 100% Renewable Electricity at CPI Group (UK) Ltd

MIX
Paper | Supporting
responsible forestry
FSC® C013604

*For Vicky – always my first reader*

**Beyond Baton Rouge**
*Article*

**Beyond Baton Rouge** was an American pop punk band formed in 1990. For most of their career, the band consisted of vocalist Lola Starr, guitarist Ashton Vain, bass player Shawn Accrington and keyboard artist Prunella Sage. The band were managed by former music producer Jimmy Nickle for Universal Music Group.

Beyond Baton Rouge had several hits, including 'Storm Inside a Teacup', which sold over 100,000 copies and topped the billboard music charts. After their first album, *Don't Ask Me To Sing Softly*, went platinum, *NME* described the band as a 'completely fresh new sound'.

In total, Beyond Baton Rouge had seven top ten hits between 1990 and 1994. Their last single, 'Eyes Full of Wonder', was their only song penned by Starr herself. Released six weeks before the band split, it debuted at number one in the US charts and in five other countries to become their fastest selling single.

In March 1994 the band were due to perform in Vegas. Lola Starr never appeared on stage. She disappeared entirely from public life and was never seen again.

# Prologue

'Lily.'

I jolt upright. 'I'm awake. Totally awake. One hundred per cent not asleep right now.'

Dad's laugh is a soft chuckle. A shadow of the deep belly laugh it used to be. The machines *beep, beep, beep* around him. Fucking hell, I can't believe I fell asleep.

In a flash I'm out of the uncomfortable hospital chair, the type with the tall backs that are completely straight. I'm tucking in Dad's blanket, topping up his water. I'm not even fully awake yet, but I'm folding pyjamas like my life depends on it. Anything to distract me from the fact that Dad's breathing is this raspy shallow breath. The sort that sounds like it might give out at any second.

'Lily.'

Finally, I glance up at him. We don't look the same at all, for obvious reasons. But I've always liked the fact that Dad's eyes are slightly too big for his face, just like mine are.

Now, Dad's eyes are even bigger in his face. And there's a deep line between his eyebrows. Stupid line.

'You don't sound too good. Shall I press the button?' I ask him, my finger poised over the big red button behind his hospital bed. Me and that red button are very well acquainted.

The line between his eyebrows disappears. 'Sit down, Lily, love. It's okay.'

3

There's a beat where I don't move. I think about arguing with Dad that things are really not okay. In fact, okay is lightyears away, in some far-flung, distant galaxy. But you don't argue with people who are dying. So instead, I deflate and find myself back in the uncomfortable chair. I reach for Dad's hand as he takes a few shallow breaths.

'You know how proud I am of you?' Dad asks, and for a moment I'm too distracted by the feel of all the bones in his hand. The way his skin feels paper thin there. Like he's literally disappearing in real time.

'Course I do, Dad.' I'm not even pretending or trying to make a dying man feel good. Dad has been, by any definition of the term, a great dad. Both my parents were literally everything you'd want in a parent. Kind. Caring. Unfailingly proud. And oh, look now, I'm going to cry again.

'And your mum, too, I know she'd be so proud of you.'

Another hand pat. 'I know, it's okay.' Thinking about Mum doesn't do anything to stop the surge of tears; in fact, it sets them off with a vengeance. Mum died when I was eighteen and it's just been me and Dad ever since. Being my parent should come with a health warning: *side effects may include untimely death*.

'There's something I need to tell you,' Dad says, the background a symphony of beeping. His face is scrunched up in worry.

'Hey, whatever it is, it's fine.' I squeeze his hand again.

'Don't be angry, Lily.' Dad has to stop talking. I hold the oxygen mask up to his face while he catches his breath. I wait, trying not to fidget, until he pulls it away himself. 'Lola called.'

For a moment we're both completely still. It's as if I'm outside my body somehow, watching us both frozen in time. Can you have out of body experiences when you're still alive? Maybe not. But Mum, and now Dad and Lola too . . . it's just too much.

Finally, I speak. 'I'm not angry, I'd never be angry, but, er, when did . . . when did you speak to her? Recently?'

He shakes his head. 'Years ago. You'd just turned eighteen. She called. Wanted to speak to you.' Every word costs him.

There's no need to load up the calculator on my phone, or even have a go at doing the maths in my head, because Mum died two days after I turned eighteen. So, I know exactly when Lola called. Eleven years ago. It feels like all the air has left me, as if I'm the one who needs that oxygen mask resting on Dad's chin.

I mean, as deathbed confessions go, it shouldn't be all that shocking. To find out that the person who gave birth to you called hoping for a quick chat. But the thing is, it *is* shocking. Because I haven't seen Lola – my birth mother – in close to thirty years.

'Do you know where she is?' I ask.

Dad nods his head.

'There's a letter. It's with my will. Read it after.' Neither of us need to consider what *after* means. Dad coughs so bad that I cajole him into putting the oxygen mask back on. I tell him not to worry about any of this right now, that it's not important. It's hard to care about the woman who never wanted you when you're losing the last person who always has.

'I'm sorry I never told you. We were both going through a lot. But it was wrong. Everything I did was wrong,' he says through the mask. I won't lie, it has an air of Darth Vader about it.

'Shush. You didn't do anything wrong. Don't think about that now.'

The absolutely last thing I want is for Dad to have regrets.

'You should reach out to her. After,' he says.

That fucking after again.

'If that's what you want me to do, I'll think about it.'

He closes his eyes.

'I know you're lying.' Half his mouth is tilted into a small smile.

'I am not!' I protest. Even though I definitely was lying. I can't see any good reason for finding Lola, none at all.

'Just read the letter, Lily, promise me.' His eyes are open again. Bright blue, piercing in the way they hold my gaze.

I take a deep breath.

'Okay, I promise. I'll read the letter. Don't worry about that now. Just please, don't worry about anything.'

\* \* \*

**Six Weeks Later**

Dying is wild.

That's what I'm thinking as Dad's coffin disappears behind a set of beige curtains in the crematorium. It just doesn't make any sense. No sense at all. How can a person be here one minute and then in a box behind some drab curtains another?

They really are drab.

It's possibly an inappropriate thought to be having at your own dad's funeral. But focusing on the grim curtains is a useful distraction. Better that than to think about what is disappearing into them.

The curtains finally shut, and I can feel the eyes of everyone in the crematorium burning into the back of my neck. The place is packed – and I guess that is one of the benefits of dying young. Even if it is something of a pyrrhic victory, the fact that there's a whole host of people who are still alive and well enough to come to your funeral. Dad's friends are all here. Our neighbour, Mr Cains. Colleagues from school. Even the fucking window cleaner is here.

I think I'm going to be sick.

The music that Dad had picked for the end of the ceremony is still playing; it's one of the songs we'd had at Mum's funeral, too.

I'm not sure whether you get to call yourself an orphan at twenty-nine. Orphan makes me think of Oliver Twist and his bowl of grey gruel. It's just so strange to think that they're both gone, like I've become untethered somehow. Without either of my parents, it's just me, floating around in the world, all alone.

I wait while the last few beats strum out. The song ends and ... oh god, I'm still imagining myself bobbing about like a giant balloon in the sky. I think I'm having a breakdown.

'Lily, are you okay?' I turn slowly to Colin, my boyfriend, looking at him like I've never seen him before.

'Course she's not okay, dipshit, she's at her dad's funeral. Come on, you need a drink.' Seb, my best friend, answers for me. If I wasn't in some sort of state of suspended animation, I might register the flash of hurt that Colin tries to hide. But I think I've maxed out my capacity to feel bad. Like Seb said, I am at my dad's funeral.

'What do I do now?' I ask them both. They're on either side of me, in the front pew. Chief mourners because I don't have any family left. I'm not sure when exactly I started clinging to Seb, but he's half holding me up and I'm only just realizing it.

'Now we're going to the wake,' Seb answers. 'You've organized it all. You just need to move.'

I nod. Okay, wake, move, I can do this.

I try to steel myself for the rest of the day.

There's a creak from somewhere behind. It rattles through the almost silent crematorium, echoing off the stone walls. I turn, not caring that everyone will see how red my eyes are.

The door is open, just a fraction. It's only like that for a second before it closes again.

And maybe I'm just searching for meaning in an uncaring universe, but the door opening and closing like that feels important. It feels like the end of something, or else a beginning.

# Chapter One

**One Year Later**

*To Do:*

- Buy memorial plaque polish
- Meeting with Mr Vandergilden 11am
- Staff meeting 12pm
- Balloon arch order to chase
- Pay Elton vet bill
- Get on top of emails

Nobody wants to be forgotten. That's what this job has taught me. Everyone wants to believe that they've done something, anything, which transcends the confines of their own existence.

And in the case of Mr Chuck Vandergilden, that something is his proficiency with an M2 man portable, backpack flame thrower.

'And you're sure, absolutely sure, Sir, that you'd like to include all that in the memoirs?' I ask him.

'Now why the hell wouldn't I, missy?' he drawls in a thick Texan accent. 'What I did in 'Nam's the proudest God damn thing of my life.'

I pull at my collar. It's hot. I can feel a bead of sweat working its way down my spine. A combination of the heat and Mr Vandergilden's war crimes is making my skin prickle.

I draw a steadying breath.

'And make sure you get the death toll.'

'Death toll?' I ask faintly.

'That's right. There was no more effective killing machine than Company C 1st Battalion. Them there Viet Cong didn't know what hit 'em.'

He beats his chest. Actually beats it.

I mumble the words, 'Geneva Convention.'

Luckily, we're doing the interview over Zoom, so Mr Vandergilden, already hard of hearing, doesn't properly catch it. The Wi-Fi in the office really is pitiful and every now and then that works in our favour.

I try to force my face into a smile, but chances are I look like that crazed Joker from the *Batman* movies. 'Right, I think I have everything I need,' I say around my fake smile. 'Is there anything else you'd like to add?'

'Nah, that's everything, I reckon. When do I get the book?'

'I should have a draft of your memoirs for you in six weeks.'

'That should do it. Alrighty, then, I'll be seeing you, Louise.'

'It's Lily,' I tell him.

'What now?' He leans towards the computer screen.

'Lily, my name is Lily.'

'Huh?'

'You know what, never mind. Goodbye, Mr Vandergilden.'

I disconnect the meeting.

'Prick,' I mutter to myself.

'Lily Brown, is that you disrespecting a paying customer? I never would have believed it.'

Seb, my best friend and boss at Your Life, appears at my shoulder, the smell of nicotine making it obvious it's him. Must buy him some more Nicotinell gum on my lunch break.

Seb and I went to university together and when we left, he set up

Your Life. In the last nine years it's gone on to become a moderately successful personal memoirs company, a service for those who want their entire life memorialized into sixty thousand words or less.

Writing books designed for a readership that's almost exclusively close friends and family isn't exactly a business model that's going to lead either of us to riches and/or glory. But we normally do okay. Mostly because every now and then we get to ghost-write some celebrity memoirs. They're what keep us afloat. I love it here. It puts my history degree to some use. Admittedly not much use. But some.

'Mr Vandergilden's a war criminal,' I tell Seb. 'We should send a copy of his memoirs to the Hague.'

Seb raises a single eyebrow at me. Whatever the weather, he wears all black and has his dark hair gelled back. He looks like a cartoon baddie. 'Unfortunately, your wage doesn't allow for questioning the clients,' he says.

'I think wage is a stretch, don't you?'

'Well, you won't let me promote you,' he says breezily. 'Meeting starts in five.'

I don't reply that I don't want the promotion because I like working with the clients. I think of Mr Vandergilden. I like working with *most* of the regular clients. Seb already knows this; we've been over it plenty of times before.

Instead, I'm out of my chair. 'Let me get the muffins.'

I hurry towards the tiny kitchen. The Your Life offices are above a fish and chip shop in the centre of Manchester, so everything always smells faintly of vinegar. Hopefully the muffins I baked last night for our team meeting are still good to go.

I grab them out of one of the top cupboards and rush back, keen not to be late.

Seb, Clementine and Phil are already sat around the 'meeting desk'. Seb got all of the office furniture off Facebook Marketplace and quite frankly it makes a mockery of the ergonomics training we get new staff to do. Out meeting desk is basically a fake wood dining table that he paid twenty quid for eight years ago.

I take a seat facing Seb and open the Tupperware box, placing it in the middle of the table. 'Cinnamon and walnut,' I tell them. It's an unofficial, yet key part of my role here that I bring the baked goods.

Clementine and Phil dive straight in but Seb, who mostly substitutes food for cigarettes, just looks at me. 'Why the fuck are you making walnut muffins, you have a nut allergy!'

Seb has a unique approach to management. Even for him, though, he's extra prickly at the minute.

'Please.' I roll my eyes. 'It's not a *serious* allergy. And anyway, they're Phil's favourites.'

Phil, who is eating his muffin in a trough-like manner, holding it up to his face and munching straight through the centre, looks up and nods. He's the Your Life accountant. He has an open bottle of Gaviscon by his computer for a persistent stomach ulcer. It gets irritated by stress.

Clementine, our marketing officer and would-be TikTok star, launches into a story about an account she follows that shares medical advice, like CPR. I think she's trying to tell me that if I go into anaphylactic shock, she's got me covered.

I reassure them all that my allergy is nothing some latex gloves didn't protect me from. Mostly.

Clementine reaches over and brushes some muffin crumbs from Phil's shirt. They have an office alliance that nobody saw coming.

'Right.' Seb starts the meeting, 'Where's that agenda?'

I'm alert. I'm focused during the team meeting. You have to be. Clementine's minutes leave a lot to be desired. I refuse to be distracted by my phone vibrating constantly on my knee. It'll be WhatsApp. It's always WhatsApp.

I can't help but notice, though, that when we get to the bit about new clients, Seb goes all muttery and won't look any of us in the eye.

Plus, Phil has retrieved the Gaviscon from his desk and is swigging straight from the bottle.

Things have been rocky this quarter. Financially, I mean. There's no denying that. But stuff always picks up. And I know that Seb had a meeting with Kitty, the literary agent who sends some ghost-writing work our way, earlier in the week. It'll be fine. It has to be fine.

After some more muttering, the meeting is done. I shake off the niggle of worry. Like I say, it'll be fine. Fine! I gnaw at the end of my pen.

'Thank god it's almost the weekend.' Clementine stretches in her chair. Her arms and legs are long and tanned. I'm only mildly absorbed with jealousy about this fact.

I won't lie, I'm rarely thrilled about weekends. And yes, I'm aware that this makes me all sorts of tragic. But personally, I just prefer the working day. The more overwhelming and unachievable the better.

The thing is, to the unsuspecting eye, I probably look like I'm living my best life each weekend. Any descendants I manage to produce will look at my Instagram and think, *wow, there is a woman who knew how to have a good time.* I have a colour-coded social calendar and I'm in eighteen WhatsApp groups (cue aptly timed phone buzz) and really, my weekends couldn't be fuller. It's just . . . yeah, I feel aimless. Or maybe it's not aimlessness, but more that I feel lost somehow. Drained. As if I'm one WhatsApp 'what date can you make' poll away from a breakdown. And I'm not sure how healthy or normal it is to feel lost or drained like, all of the time.

Maybe I'm just feeling all aimless and drained because this weekend is especially bad.

It's been a year since Dad died.

But it's fine. I'm fine. Totally and absolutely fine.

'You're crying again.'

I've made it back to my computer.

My emails swim before my eyes.

'I'm fine.' I sniff.

'I did tell you to take the day off. Why don't you go home?'

'No!' Another sniff. 'I have to get through these emails. It's on my list. Plus, you're coming to mine tonight, right? Right?'

There's a definite air of desperation about my request. But Seb won't care. He gets it.

'Yep.' He pops the 'p', but he won't look me in the eye. 'Finish your emails and we'll head off in half an hour. Early finish, everyone,' he calls to the rest of the office. So just Phil and Clementine, who cheers like she isn't currently tweezing her eyebrows at her desk.

A new email appears in the corner of my inbox and even though I know that I should tackle the oldest ones first, that that's the most efficient method, I click on it.

'Oh,' I say, scanning through the text quickly.

'What is it?' Seb asks, peering over my shoulder.

'Daisy Flanaghan has died,' I tell him. Jesus. I'm going to cry again.

'No, how sad. What was she, ninety-eight?'

I hardly hear him. 'She was a hundred,' I say. And yep, here come the tears.

Tears over a little old lady who worked in the WAAF during the war and then went on to have seventeen grandchildren. Just feels as if it's everywhere these days. Death. Like people are dropping down dead left, right and centre.

'Her daughter has emailed. Apparently, she died in her sleep.' It's me talking, but it doesn't sound like my voice.

'Do they say anything about her memoirs? Surely, they'll still want it, won't they?'

Seb squeezes my shoulder, reading the email from behind me.

'They're cancelling. Fuck's sake.'

Seb stomps off while, through bleary eyes, I reply to Daisy's daughter.

It's not a particularly unusual thing to happen, a client dying mid-memoirs. It's basically a hazard of the job, since the people most likely to want their lives memorialized are those far closer to the end than the beginning of it.

So, I try to lock it away. I try not to wonder whether Daisy had done everything she wanted to do, achieved everything she wanted to achieve. Or whether she had things left unsaid or undone.

Obsessing about things like that, well, therein lay the path to madness.

'God, we need a drink tonight. Red, white or rosé?' Seb asks an hour later. I'm acting on autopilot and pulling on my raincoat while he waits by the door. It's July and it's particularly hot, but it's also Manchester, so it's fifty-fifty whether we'll get sunburnt or soaked.

'Rosé,' I say, aiming to sound like someone who hasn't been obsessing about the death of a centenarian she met twice. He flicks off the lights and follows me down the stairs through to the chip shop below. We pass Angus battering his fish behind the counter. A line of customers weaves their way out of the door.

'Night, Angus,' I call over the counter. See, I am breezy, cheerful. Unencumbered by thoughts of death and dying.

'Night, Seb, night, Lily love.' He pulls a long piece of fish out of some wet batter and sets it aside. 'Our Jenny loved that blanket you made for the baby.' Angus has to shout to me over the crowd. 'You didn't need to go to so much trouble.'

'It was nothing,' I call back, 'really quick to make.' I dig deep for a smile even though this isn't exactly true. The blanket had taken me three weeks and one online knitting course to pull together.

'She's a good egg, this one,' Angus tells Seb.

'Yeah, she's a real people pleaser. Tragically so,' Seb replies as we exit onto the street out front.

Bloody Seb.

'Come on.' Seb guides me towards the tram that'll take us to Dad's house.

My house.

Because it's mine now, this typical Manchester redbrick terrace. It's a two-minute walk from the park where Mum and Dad's memorial bench is. Argh, I still need to order the plaque polish.

I unlock the red front door and go through the hallway to the kitchen, Seb following behind. Elton, Dad's Persian cat, stalks out from somewhere and starts wrapping himself around Seb's feet, purring loudly.

Traitor.

I haven't redecorated since Dad died. Which really is a testament to how much I loved him. Because Dad had ... interesting tastes. He also had a completely unfounded belief in his ability to do DIY. Such is how I find myself in a chaotically colourful kitchen, where the cupboard doors are as likely to fall off as open. There's a whole bedroom filled with a mishmash of Mum's musical instruments that I avoid like the plague, and I've thrown an extra-large throw over the piano at the other end of the kitchen. Extra-large throws seem as good a coping mechanism as anything. At least I'm managing to keep Dad's house plants alive. I water them by rota and put them in the bath through winter.

I also inherited Elton, the geriatric cat Dad got a year after Mum died. Like I said, he's Persian, so there's just SO much fur. So much. Suffice to say, Elton has never forgiven Dad for dying and seems to suspect that I had a hand in offing him. He hates me on principle. Seb thinks I'm being dramatic, but I'm not. That cat has it in for me.

I peer down into Elton's bowl in the kitchen, sighing as I spot the two pills that I'd hidden in his food this morning. They're for a thyroid condition and come hell or high water, that cat is having those tablets. Not a chance that Elton is shuffling off his mortal coil on my watch.

'You're having your tablets, Elton,' I tell him. He's over by the radiator now, padding away in his deluxe, fleecy bed. He turns and shows me his bum as he lets out a particularly vociferous purr.

'I need this.' Seb has followed me into the kitchen. He's busy uncorking a bottle of wine with well-practised ease.

'Is everything okay?' I ask him, remembering the muttering of the team meeting. I lean against the countertop, looking away from the fridge. Yes, I am a person who tries to avoid my own fridge. Not for any weird reason. I don't have a fridge phobia or anything strange like that. It's just that on the fridge is pinned the 'Dad death admin list' that he'd left me last year.

I think he knew that an unfinished list would haunt me. And it does. I haven't ticked off the last item. 'Read letter about Lola.' So, like I said, it's nothing weird, or anything like that. Just your run-of-the-mill to-do list from my dead dad.

'Come on, let's go sit down and we can talk about it properly.'

I nod. Seb's poured us two glasses of wine already. Large glasses of wine, even though I told him we need to watch our alcohol intake. The government announced new guidelines and too often we're worryingly close to the recommended units.

We make our way through to the front room, which unfortunately didn't escape Dad's ambitious DIY attempts. He'd lived just long enough to see the return of wood panelling and so each wall has some fake wood halfway around it. All painted in different bright colours. Dad didn't believe in spirit levels, which probably tells you all that you need to know about how successful his efforts were. If I dwell on the wonky wood for too long, my heart starts to palpitate.

Still, I just can't bring myself to get a decorator in to fix his mistakes. It's like a really dull episode of *Black Mirror*: highly strung woman lives for ever in house where nothing even remotely matches.

I sit on the other end of the couch to Seb. He's staring at the wonky panelling under the window. I take a drink of my wine and try to ignore the sense that there's something he isn't telling me.

'Is it business?' I ask. 'Only we've had dry spells before.' I'm doing such a great job of giving the pretence that I'm fine. 'Plus, you had that meeting with Kitty this week, didn't you? I thought you did. It was on the shared calendar.'

Seb looks at me for a long time.

'You know that business has been slow this quarter,' he starts.

I reach over and squeeze the top of his arm.

'But are things really bad?' The business can't go under. It can't. It's all I have. Well, aside from Seb and Elton. It's all Seb has too.

Plus, how would I pay for Elton's vet bills? Or for his special food? The rest of my bills are cheap and the house is paid for, so I won't lose my home, but I might have to cancel my Spotify Premium. My podcasts, oh Jesus, my podcasts!

'What we need is some ghost writing work. Just one, like, big client.' Yes, I do always start to strategize in moments of crisis. 'Remember when we got that *EastEnders* actress. That memoir sold in actual shops. Kept us going for a year.'

'I remember, Lily.'

It really was a good year, 2018.

'We just need someone famous. Or better yet, someone rich. What did Kitty say?'

Seb's looking at me now and there's this feeling that the world is tilting. That things are coming to a head.

'She said there's a potential client.'

'Well, that's great!'

'But that it's all very hush, hush.'

'Did you tell them we're discreet? Did you mention our cast–iron GDPR policies?'

'Mm–hm.'

He's back to not looking at me.

'It would be huge, if we got the gig. It would solve all of our problems.'

'Okay, well, this sounds perfect. Why the stress?' I ask.

'It's Lola,' he says.

And for a second, his words don't register.

'Come again?'

'The person who wants their memoirs ghost-written. It's Lola Starr.'

# Chapter Two

'Eh,' I say. Profound.

'Sorry.' Seb pushes a finger across the bridge of his nose. 'Shit, I didn't want to say anything especially not today.'

He means, I guess, because it's been a year since Dad died.

I just blink at him while he keeps talking to himself.

'It's just that Kitty said she thought there would be lots of competition . . . and business has been tough . . . I thought I might have to let Clementine go even.'

That jolts me out of my daze.

'No, you can't let her go. Where else would she work while she waits for her TikTok career to take off?'

Seb is frowning. There's an actual line between his eyebrows. And kudos to that line, for breaking through the Botox.

'Hang on a second,' I say, trying to still my now whirling brain. 'What exactly has Kitty said?'

Seb twists his hands together.

'That's the thing, I don't even know for sure that it *is* Lola.'

He takes a deep breath. There's a weird buzzing in my ears.

'Kitty just said that she'd heard that there was someone super famous, who was maybe thinking about getting her memoirs ghostwritten. Said it would be the book deal of the year and there'd be a major payout for whoever got the contract to write them. Apparently, Lola, or whoever it is, wants to pick the ghostwriter herself. She didn't

say that it was Lola exactly, but then she started humming the tune to
"Eyes Full of Wonder". You know their last song, it's catchy as fuck.'

The song that Mum used to sing to me nudges through the ear
buzzing that I have going on.

It's all quite stressful, I won't lie.

'So, you think it's Lola?' I ask.

'I don't know. It sounded like that. And when I said, are you
talking about Lola Starr, she wouldn't confirm or deny it. Obviously,
I didn't tell her about you.'

My heart is beating really fast.

'But . . . but . . . if it is Lola, why, I mean, why now?'

'No idea. She's been missing for what, thirty years?'

I nod. 'A few months after she gave me up.'

'Shit. It's been going round in my head all week. No one even
knows where she is.'

'Most people don't,' I hear myself say. 'But Dad did. It's in a letter
she wrote me when I was eighteen.'

'OMG, the letter that haunts you from the unfinished to-do list
on the fridge? I've seen the look in your eyes when you look at that
list. I knew it was about Lola but not that he'd hunted her down. I
just assumed he'd written you a deathbed farewell.'

I shake my head. 'Hunted sounds quite predatory.'

Seb puts his wine glass on the old trunk.

'Lily, I can't ask you to do this. You've never even spoken to Lola;
you can't very well trot up to her now and pitch to ghost-write her
bloody memoirs. No, it's a terrible idea. Let someone else write it.'

That thought makes me feel vaguely ill. The thought that someone else might write Lola's memoirs. Dredge it all up again. Listen
while she talks about giving up her baby . . . People will find me . . .
everyone will know . . .

I'm sitting up straight now, perched on the edge of the sofa. I
wonder how it would feel, to be brave about this. It would definitely

help Seb, and the business. Plus, it's clearly what Dad wanted me to do. Maybe I could even help myself a little, too. Maybe I wouldn't feel quite so lost and drained.

Wondering feels like dipping my toe in a still lake and watching the ripples circle outward.

I take a deep breath. Close my eyes. Get ready to jump.

'What if this is meant to be, like, the next chapter? For us, for me, I mean?' I ask.

Seb is still frowning and muttering to himself. 'It's a bad idea, you might get hurt. You're already so needy. It'd be off the scale.'

'Just listen a second, will you?' I cut him off. 'You know Dad wanted me to get in touch with her, and it's a year since he died and then Daisy went and died, and I keep wondering if she had, I don't know, unfinished business.'

'She was literally a hundred,' Seb interjects.

'And now this with Kitty ... it just feels ... fated. Like maybe now *is* the time because everyone is dying all of the time and what if Lola wants her memoirs writing because she's dying too.'

I hadn't even considered that fact until I say it, but now it's a real-life worry.

Seb is looking at me like I've sprouted a third eyeball.

'Fated. Like in the stars.'

'No, not in the stars, just, I don't know, something that I need to do. Plus, the business needs the money and I hate, like really hate, the thought of someone else writing those memoirs.'

Another look from Seb.

'It's the unfinished to-do list, isn't it? It's eating you alive.'

'No ... well, yes, it is a little bit, but it's not just that. If I could do what Dad wanted *and* help the business, it could be a good thing. If she's going to write them anyway, it might as well be us. Perhaps I won't spend each night crying quite so much,' I say with the faux cheer of a budget Christmas elf.

'Okay, we're revisiting that at some point, likely with the help of a professional.' He pauses to have a drink. 'You really want to do this?'

I deflate a little. I did want to do this, a second ago, now I'm less sure. Decisive people really are life's winners.

'Maybe. I think so. We might not even get the contract, might we?'

Seb has another drink. Shakes his head. I think he's quite stressed. A couple of strands of gelled dark hair have fallen forward on his forehead.

'I already thought of that. The world and his wife will be pitching for this. If it's really her.'

We fall silent after that. I'm trying to picture how I'll feel, seeing Lola's memoirs on a shelf somewhere in a couple of years' time. Reading in black and white how she gave me up. Or maybe she'll leave it out. Maybe she doesn't even think of me as part of her story.

'There's one thing we know that the other companies don't, though,' I say, my voice louder than I expect it to be.

'What's that, then?' Seb asks.

'We can find out where Lola is.'

Seb laughs. 'What, so we can go pitch to her in person?'

'Exactly.' I smile. Possibly, I look demented.

'I'll go get my Lola folder and we can start from there.' I jump up from the couch and jog up the stairs faster than you could say, 'terrible idea'.

In contrast to the rest of the house, my bedroom is a haven of calm and order. The walls are white, and I've embraced the concept of minimalism with open arms. Every item has a place, which is why it takes me next to no time to locate the little manilla folder I have tucked away in my wardrobe.

It's impossible not to think about how weird this all is.

That I'm here, a year after Dad died, about to read his last message to me. Maybe that's why I've been putting it off. I've been delaying the ending. Lola and her bloody memoirs have forced my hand.

I slide out the folder and carry it carefully to the front room, feeling like a parent about to show off their newborn to a crowd. Except instead of a group of doting relatives, I have Seb and Elton.

'Here it is.' I inject some cheer into my voice for Seb, who is partway through taking a big drink of the wine, resting back against Dad's couch.

I sit at the other end of the couch from Seb and slide the folder onto the rusty, antique trunk that Dad used for a coffee table.

Seb leans forward. If he notices that my hands are shaking, he doesn't let on.

I slip open the folder and the letter's right there, resting on top of my adoption papers and my birth certificate. Plus, there's a bunch of magazine clippings, because that's what happens when you're a megastar who suddenly disappears from the face of the planet.

Which is exactly what happened to Lola Starr.

When I was younger, I was obsessed with Lola, with every article ever written about her. The ones from when she was in the band. By all accounts she was your archetypal mega rock star. Drink. Drugs. So many drugs. Glamour. YouTube clips of them playing in Madison Square Gardens to thousands of people, pictures of her stumbling drunk out of some LA club, in an orange dress so short you can see her black knickers underneath, the (uninventive in my humble opinion) headline, 'Is Lola Losing it?'

And then there are the ones from after she disappeared. All speculating about what might have happened to her.

I mean, could it be true that Lola became a leading scientologist? Or maybe she really did open an Ashtanga yoga retreat in the Himalayas. LA people are different to the rest of us, aren't they? In LA, it's perfectly normal to go from lead singer in a hugely successful band to Mongolian goat herder. No one questions these things out there.

I know all of the theories. I'd collected anything and everything that was written about her, gathering it all and storing it away in my manilla folder like a magpie with a sad little pile of treasure.

What hurts the most is that as a child I'd written to her every year on my birthday. Mum and Dad had encouraged it. I'd tell her stupid stuff about what I'd been up to that year and Mum and Dad had passed the letters on to the adoption agency to forward to Lola.

She'd never written back.

My curiosity had waned over the years. From journalists too. I guess they assumed that Lola really did not want to be found. I just figured that Lola wanted nothing to do with me. And then Mum went and died so I didn't want Lola anyway. I wanted my mum back.

It's not about the clippings or any of that stuff now, though. Now, my hands are moving towards Dad's letter, the white envelope with 'Lily' scrawled across the front.

I pick it up and rest it on my lap.

Look at it.

'No time like the present,' I say to Seb. He's been watching me this whole time. Waiting while I do a slow mo (and very dramatic) removal of the letter.

'That's what I've heard.'

'Okay, I'm going in.'

'Good for you.'

There really is nothing left for me to say after that.

If I don't do this now, I might never do it. I might never know.

I lift the flap of the envelope and shiver as I pull the letter out from inside it. There's another piece of paper, but I ignore that for now, too desperate to hear from Dad again.

I unfold it. His writing is instantly recognisable. Slanty and with the slight dip of someone who was left-handed.

Now that it's there, I can't believe I've left it this long to read it. My eyes start scanning before I can properly take in what they're reading.

# Rebecca Ryan

*Lily,*

*I imagine it's taken you a while to get to this. However long it's been, I hope you're doing okay. I hope you're not lonely.*

*I know you have Seb (I'm betting he's there, hi Seb), but hopefully you've broken up with Colin, you can do better (if he's there too, sorry Colin). And I know you have a lot of friends, but they're not the same as family.*

*That's why you need to go and find her. Find Lola.*

*She called once. Just after Mum died. I think legally she wasn't allowed to get in touch until you were eighteen and I don't know how she got our home phone number, but she did.*

*I'm so sorry that I never told you, Lily. She asked if she could speak to you and I was so mad at everything, at the fact that she was alive when your mum wasn't, I called her a bunch of stuff I shouldn't have done. I told her that you never wanted to hear from her and that she had to respect that and put the phone down. I told her that you hated her. I was terrified of losing you. I'm a coward for telling you this now, I know.*

*When I got the diagnosis and once I'd Googled it (stage four pancreatic cancer makes for miserable reading), I knew you'd need someone after. I hired a private investigator to look for Lola.*

*Anyway, I've enclosed their report.*

*I hope you'll consider finding her, Lily.*

*If you do go to her, you're going to find out some other truths I'm not proud of. I'm sorry about that, too. I hope you know that everything we did, it was because we loved you so much. You and your mum are the best thing that ever happened to me and I'm so proud of you.*

*Know that if I could have stayed, I would have done.*

*Love always, Dad*

\* \* \*

My face is wet by the time I read Dad's letter again. And again. Even Seb produces a tear when I read it out loud.

He gets up and marches to the kitchen, announcing, 'We need more wine.'

For once, I don't have the energy to worry about his poor liver. While he's gone, I unfold the second sheet of paper from the envelope. I had no idea that Dad had hired a private investigator, but now, I'm reading their report.

### DALTON AND SONS PRIVATE INVESTIGATORS
*Bronx, NY, United States*

Case number: 315-426
Account: \*\*7634
Date: 14th May 2022
Status: **FINAL REPORT**

**Summary:**
This report details information obtained via inland revenue and electoral registers into the whereabouts of one <u>LOLA STARR</u>. Lola is believed to reside at the address below:

Broadford Hotel and Water Sports Centre
Broadford
Isle of Skye
Scotland
IV49 9AB

After conducting extensive research into several unconfirmed sightings of LOLA STARR in the United States, our investigation concluded that one LOLA STARR has resided at the above address since approximately 16 March 1994, when she first appears on the electoral register of the UNITED KINGDOM under the name Lola Vain. According to deed polls, Lola Starr became Lola Vain in January 1994. Lola Vain is the same person as Lola Starr, the former lead singer of the pop punk band Beyond Baton Rouge. Our investigation concludes that neither Lola Starr, nor Lola Vain are registered as having been married. Lola Starr has no children beyond one, Lily Brown. The adoption order for Lily was finalized in March 1994.

As per our client's request, no contact has been made with the subject of this report. This information was correct as of 14 May 2022.

Please find attached our invoice. Payments can be made via bank transfer or over the telephone.

In something that feels close to complete and utter shock, I search for Lola's hotel on my phone, pulling up an image of a white building next to a lake.

I can't believe Lola lives there. Here. This whole time I'd been sure that there was a full-on gigantic ocean between us when she's been right here the whole time.

'Shit,' Seb says, reading over my shoulder. 'She was way easier to find than I thought she'd be.'

'I don't know if she was,' I tell him. I sound like I've been drugged. 'It says they looked in America first. No one expected her to be in the UK. She was American. Why is she in Scotland?'

I'm just looking between the letter and my phone.

My brain can't connect the image of Lola in my imagination with a Lola who lives in some secluded spot in Scotland. It's there in black and white. Lola was a party girl, a superstar. Lola in the band had more glamour in her little finger than I have in my entire being. I look again at the picture of her in the orange dress. Her hair is blonde and big. Not big in the way that mine gets big, which is entirely of its own violation. Big in a way that suggests it was meant to be like that. Her eye make-up is smudged, so I know there was a lot of it. Her lipstick is bright red. I don't know if it's weird to notice your birth mum's boobs, but she's wearing the push-up bra to end all push-up bras. We're just . . . very obviously different.

And that's before you even consider that she used to hang out with Bill Clinton.

I silently spiral while Seb sifts through some of the magazine articles that I have in my folder. Being gentle with them.

'Right,' he says. 'Let's sort this shit out. Start at the beginning. Tell me what we know about Lola already.'

I take a deep breath.

I don't like talking about Lola, but I do know many things about her. Apparently, it's a thing when you're adopted. They like kids to know about their birth mum because it saves them coming up with their own version of events, or else jumping to conclusions. Mum and Dad had told me a bit about Lola's early life, information the adoption agency must have shared with them.

Talking about Lola's early life feels a lot safer than thinking about that letter.

'Okay, so you probably know some of this stuff, I mean, it's on her Wikipedia page. Lola grew up just outside Baton Rouge, Louisiana. That's where they got the name of the band from, I think. She was really poor, from what Mum and Dad said.'

'How did she end up in the band, then?' Seb asks.

'It's one of those stories that no one believes could happen in real life, but Jimmy Nickel, you know their manager, he was on holiday there and heard her busking. She was only seventeen or something, crazy young. Anyway, he was putting a band together in LA. The label wanted to tap into the pop punk thing that was big in the nineties, find the next Gwen Stefani. He invited her to try out, and you know the rest. They were huge. More so in America, but big over here, too. It makes sense that she'd go a bit wild, when you think about where she came from.'

'He died a few years back, didn't he?'

'Jimmy?' I ask. Seb nods.

'Yeah, I think so. I haven't heard much about him for years, but he was like Simon Cowell famous when the band made it big.'

'So, Lola goes to LA and gets proper famous. What next – where do you come in? You don't know who your dad is, right?'

Seb must see me flinch.

'Your birth dad,' he clarifies.

'Nope.' I leaf gently through the stack of papers, pulling out my birth certificate and showing Seb the blank space where a dad's name should be. It's a space that I felt a lot when we did genetics in biology, or a couple of years ago when the GP asked me, 'any family history of . . . ' and I had to shrug and admit that I had no idea. It's not helpful to be thinking about that right now, though.

'Mum and Dad suspected her bandmate. The guitar player, Ashton Vain. According to the papers, they were very much on again, off again. I think he was from Scotland, too, so maybe that's why Lola is here. I always assumed she was in America. Plus, look.' I hold up the investigators' report. 'Lola took his name, his surname, I mean. Vain. It must have been him.'

Seb nods. 'At least *he's* still alive. I had a poster of him on my bedroom wall when I was a teenager. How weird is that?'

'Too weird to think about. He's been in various bands over the years. Smaller ones. Even now he seems to spend his life permanently on tour.'

'I didn't like his solo stuff as much.'

I have another drink and carry on.

'Lola was twenty-one when she had me. Maybe Ashton just

wasn't interested or whatever, but she was obviously on her own. I guess she thought that she'd have to quit the band if she kept me and go back to being poor. Giving me up for adoption was the right thing to do, if you think about it rationally.'

I try out a smile. Yikes, bad idea. I stare down at the unevenly tiled floor instead.

'Hard to be rational about being dumped as a baby.'

I roll my eyes. 'I wasn't dumped as a baby, it's not like she left me in the bin. She went through the proper channels, and I got so lucky. You know how great Mum and Dad were.'

Seb raises his glass. 'To the Browns.'

I cheers, swallowing past the lump in my throat.

Seb looks at the papers I've spread across the rusty coffee table trunk.

'So much of it doesn't make sense,' he says, rifling a bit. 'Why did she leave the band? If, like you say, she put you up for adoption because of the fame thing, why did she quit it a couple of months later? Right after they had their biggest, and best, single. It doesn't make any sense.'

I shrug. 'That's the mystery. No one knows why she quit.'

'And why would she want to go over it all? Why get someone to ghost-write her memoirs now?'

I make a movement that feels something like a shrug. My shoulders are up by my ears at any rate. I'm once again confronted by the thought that my birth mum is riddled with some sort of disease. That's what always happens. People get told they're going to die, and they want to write it all down. Make sure there's something left behind.

'Could quitting the band have had something to do with you?' Seb wonders out loud. 'It's too much of a coincidence, timing wise, don't you think? And no one knows about you, do they?'

I shake my head.

'Definitely not. No one knew that Lola was pregnant. Her management put out a statement to say that she was in rehab. It's in one of the articles speculating on where she went. Here.'

I pick up the article I'm talking about. It has a big picture of Lola in her tight orange dress down the side. 'Here,' I read aloud.

*Lola Starr, lead singer of Beyond Baton Rouge and all-round megastar, has seemingly disappeared off the face of the planet. Lola, known for her amazing voice, didn't make a scheduled appearance in Vegas, much to the disappointment of lots of Beyond Baton Rouge fans. We can't help but wonder where she's gone! Lola's no stranger to stints in rehab – her management confirmed she was there just last year. Is that what's happened here? Who knows? But if you're reading this, Lola, come back! We love you.*

'The shit these people write . . . honestly. Maybe she'd just had enough of them,' he says.

I laugh. 'Maybe. Either way, I don't know that me being born did have anything to do with Lola quitting. Because if she quit because of me, why didn't she answer any of my letters, or try harder to get in touch?'

'Well, this is all interesting, very interesting.' Seb drums his fingers on his wine glass. 'I mean, it'll make a great memoirs. No doubt about that. But could you stand to write it, even if we got the gig?'

I have another drink, to buy myself some thinking time.

'I don't love the thought of the story getting out. What if she tells them that she had a baby that she just dumped? Everyone will know she didn't want me then.'

I look down at Lola's address again and blink a couple of times when the words start to swim in front of me.

'Have you ever been to the Isle of Skye?' I ask Seb.

'Fuck no. It's like, a million miles away. You know that I loathe the outdoors.'

'This is going really well.' I sniff. 'How are you with water sports, then?' I ask him.

'Don't try to change the subject, Lily Brown! But since you asked, I'm not that kinky. For the right man, perhaps I'd give it a go . . . '

'Not *that* kind of water sports, idiot. Lola's hotel is by a lake, there's water sports there.'

'I see. Well, I don't have any desire to jet-ski. I did used to be a Boy Scout, though.'

'Of course you did.'

'But you're the one who's always exercising.'

'I'm not always exercising.'

'Last weekend, you did yoga for six hours straight.'

'That was a sponsored event. I told you, Chantelle, Sarah's best friend's cousin, is raising money for the polar bears of Nunavut.'

I do so many of these sponsored events that Seb keeps complaining I'm sending him into insolvency.

'Whatever, babe. All I'm saying is that you're much more likely to pull off Sporty Spice than me.'

He has a point. I've never even seen him in trainers.

'So, what, you think we just go up to this island in the middle of nowhere,' I ask, my heart racing hummingbird wing levels of fast, 'and announce that I'm her long-lost daughter who just happens to work for a business that would quite like to ghost-write her memoirs?'

I ask it like it's a question but at the same time, I'm dismissing the whole thing. It's a stupid idea. I might not know Lola, but I know what she's like. It's there in print. She's a famous singer who parties hard. She's the woman who left me as a baby, called once in thirty years and didn't answer any of my letters. She will not want to know me.

And then, if I march on up to Scotland and she rejects me as an adult too, well, that would be all sorts of nightmarish. I'd be in therapy for the rest of my life.

And yet, this image I have of Lola ... well, I never would have put that Lola somewhere like the Isle of Skye. Somewhere so quiet. In every single YouTube clip of her she's surrounded by noise. Music, fans, paparazzi. She's always smiling, too, like she liked it, all the noise.

It never made sense why she just up and quit like she did.

Deep down, I assumed she disappeared so that *I* wouldn't ever find her.

'Or,' Seb says, shuffling closer to me on the couch. 'We go up there, pretend we're on holiday, plead ignorance about knowing that Lola wants her memoirs writing and just play it off as a coincidence. If none of the other agencies even know where she lives, we'd have a massive advantage.'

'And what about telling her who I am?'

'You don't have to tell her. That's the beauty of it.' Seb has what I'd describe as his evil genius face on. An eyebrow is arched. 'You can get to know her a bit, incognito.'

'That's a lot of lying to my birth mother.'

'She did dump you as a baby.'

It's not a terrible idea. It's actually far from terrible.

My hands are working my phone, hitting keys with more force than is strictly necessary for a touch screen, as I pull up the booking form for the hotel.

I could finally get some answers. I could see her and maybe hear her side of things without ever having to confront her. I avoid any and all confrontation as a general rule. I could save the business.

I love saving things.

It's my favourite pastime.

'If we did go, we'd have to stay a couple of days.' I scroll. 'There're two cottages in the gardens of the hotel. One is booked up all summer, but the other one is free for most of it. We could spend a few nights there and let the memoirs thing just come up naturally while we're having a chinwag with Lola.' I look up at Seb. He's smirking. 'This is a terrible idea, isn't it?'

'Sorry, I was just thrown by someone under eighty using the word chinwag. Yes, it's a terrible idea. But now that we know where she is, can you imagine not going? Could you let someone else go and write this?'

I sit with the question for a second. I mean, I'm fine now. Totally fine. I have lots of friends. I have Seb. I have Elton. I only cry in the dark max one or two nights a week. And yes, there's the time I spend crying at Mum and Dad's bench to consider, but that has to be normal. So, I'm fine. I just thought I had time to deal with Lola at some other (far off in the future) point. But if she's planning to sell her memoirs now . . . well, that changes things.

Plus . . . that's what I thought about Mum and Dad, and Daisy Flanaghan, isn't it? I thought I'd have more time.

How would I feel if Lola is sick, and I didn't get chance to at least *see* her with my own eyes? To have one single memory that is real.

'I think I'd regret it,' I admit.

'Regret gives you wrinkles,' Seb says. 'And you never know, you might decide you quite like her and you want to tell her who you are. We could get Davina McCall involved.' He sits up straighter. 'Oh, I know, we could get a balloon thing like people use for those awful gender reveals. Or the cannons, the cannon ones are the best. We could fill it with a banner which says, "I am your daughter!" And fire it at her.'

Seb catches my eye.

'Or we could not do any of that.'

I take a deep breath.

'We're really doing this, then?'

Seb is gazing out of the window towards his car parked on the street. He loves that car. 'Maybe I'll finally find my lumberjack on the Isle of Skye.'

I know way too much about Seb's lumberjack fantasy to be within the parameters of a normal friendship.

'Thank you,' I tell him through glassy eyes. 'It means a lot. Not that it's about me. It's about the business. Obviously.'

He throws back the last of his drink. 'Obviously. Wow, I can't believe I'm going to meet Lola Starr. I grew up listening to Beyond Baton Rouge. I'm going to ask for her autograph.'

I throw a tassel cushion at him.

'Right, that's all the emotion I can take for now,' he says, throwing it back. 'For god's sake, book the cottage and put *Bake Off* on.'

'I'll have to ask Mr Cains next door to watch Elton and water the plants.'

'He won't mind,' Seb answers. 'He loves that cat.'

The hotel website keeps crashing. It takes an awful lot of jabbing at it to get the booking page to load and stay loaded.

'They have availability in two weeks.' I cross reference with my social calendar. 'I'm meant to be on a hen do then.'

'You're always on a hen do, they're all you do aside from the exercise thing. And then there was that time you did exercise on a hen do. Awful.'

I ignore him. 'I could cancel. I've only met the bride once.'

The thought sends an illicit thrill through me. I never cancel. Ever. Finding out about my long-lost Lola has sent me wild.

'Why the hell are you going on her hen do then . . . ? You know what, forget it. Just cancel and book the bloody hotel. Time is of the essence anyway if Kitty is already putting the feelers out.'

After another crash and reload, I click on the blue BOOK button, my confidence in the plan waning almost immediately.

Oh sweet Jesus, what have I agreed to?

'What have I done?' I ask Seb, wide-eyed.

'You're going to have an adventure, Lily Brown. And it's about fucking time.'

# Chapter Three

*To Do:*

- Balloon arch
- Pack for Skye
- Elton food and meds
- Research Skye
- Practise pitch for Lola memoirs
- Ginseng tea to order (next day delivery)
- Get on top of emails

I'm in my kitchen and I'm frozen with panic.

A sensible, well-balanced sort of a person in the lead-up to meeting their uber glamorous birth mum might have spent time undergoing a makeover type transformation. Like that woman in *Miss Congeniality* (Seb's favourite film) when she emerges from that bunker all shiny and fresh.

I don't do this. I think, if anything, ever since that night two weeks ago where Seb and I read Dad's letter, I've been going through an anti-metamorphosis. The heat wave has ramped up, wrapping us all in sweltering, sweaty hotness. The UK is just not set up for hot weather, we all lose our minds a bit.

My fringe, thick and troublesome at the best of times, is positively riotous. Like it's attempting to Great Escape my own forehead. It's the hot weather. And the stress. Stress and heat always send my hair batshit.

Plus, I have nothing that I need to survive in the wilderness of Scotland. All of my clothes have some sort of collar on them – cute little Peter Pan collars, big lacey collars, embroidered with flower collars. I've been watching a lot of YouTube survivalist videos and none of the survivors are wearing tops with decorative collars on them.

The fact that I'm regressing into a less good version of myself is the exact opposite of what I want to happen.

Even though Lola abandoned me, I still want her to like me. To think that I'm an unflustered sort of person who can deal with whatever life throws at them. I don't want her to know that the real me is strung so tightly that if I snapped, I'd catapult myself to Australia.

There's a knock at the door. 'Morning, morning, anyone ready to go meet the woman who birthed them?'

There's a squeak as Seb pushes past the balloon arch.

'Ah,' he says, 'I see we're having another nervous breakdown.'

I don't know what he means. I'm stood in the middle of the kitchen (facing away from the fridge) staring into space and breathing deeply. That's a normal thing to be doing, isn't it? My new neck fan lets out a low hum and sends a gentle breeze up towards my face.

'Can you calm the fuck down? Your stress aura is going to kill the plants,' he tells me.

I dart my head around, looking at the plants. I don't think plants require calm in the same way that they require, say, sunlight, but I try to relax my shoulders. Just in case.

'Why is there a balloon arch in your hallway?' Seb asks.

'I was in charge of the arch for the hen do I cancelled. It didn't seem fair that Charlotte missed out on her arch because I'm flaky.'

Cancelling my place on the hen do was a painful process for everyone unfortunate enough to be involved. I'd still agreed to provide the balloon arch. It's a ninety-six-piece balloon arch, because, you know, I felt guilty.

POP.

'Elton!' I call. 'Stop popping the balloons.'

POP.

POP.

I groan as Seb mutters something that sounds like, 'Give me strength.' At least Elton sabotaging my arch efforts has brought me out of my trance. I move over to triple check the 'Elton and Plants Guidance' I'd left for Mr Cains next door.

It's seven pages long.

Plus, I've left all of Elton's prescription food out, divided into days. Because last time I'd asked Mr Cains to cat sit, he'd given him some Sumptuous Salmon cat food and the jelly the sumptuous salmon was floating in gave Elton a kidney stone.

But Mr Cains genuinely likes Elton and always offers to have him. And Elton is much friendlier to Mr Cains than me, though that bar is admittedly very low.

POP.

'Elton!'

'You know that's why Elton hates you, right?' Seb nods over to the piles of weighed out dry cat food.

'What? He should love me. I want him to live a long and happy life. He's obese.'

'He's already lived a long and happy life. He wasn't even *that* young when your dad adopted him. Let him spend his golden years gorging himself on meaty jelly.'

I clutch the edge of the countertop at the thought of Elton dying. Which is a totally healthy response.

Still, I remind myself, it would be hard for anyone to kill a cat in three days. The hotel had a three-night minimum booking policy so we've taken today off work to drive up. I'll be back on Monday at the absolute latest. If we're successful with the memoirs pitch, we'll do the meetings online.

'I'll go and get my stuff,' I tell Seb, my voice higher than normal.

'You're not meeting your birth mum with that thing around your neck!' he calls after me.

'She won't know she's my birth mum, so it doesn't matter. And anyway, it's a fan, and I bought you one too,' I call back.

I jog up the stairs, slowing down when I realize that I'm breaking a sweat at the sudden movements.

Earlier in the week, I'd taken myself on a frenzied trip to Decathlon for some new, wilderness appropriate clothes. I've been reading all about Skye. There's an author, Noah Adair, and he's written a ton of books and articles about the island. It sounds wild. Not in the way that Lola's band days sounded wild, more lakes and mountains and just general outdoorsy stuff galore.

Apparently, it is one of Scotland's hottest destinations. Not in the temperature sense, more in that it's super Instagrammable. So, maybe it's not complete anathema, Lola living there. She's bound to be somewhere hip.

All packed. I'd had a moment of blind panic when I'd had a quick glance (spent hours draped over) the faulty website for Lola's hotel and realized there was a chance I'll have to take part in some water sports if we're going to be convincing in our, 'we're just here on holiday, oh, you're looking for a ghostwriter, what a coincidence' ruse.

It's one of the reasons that this is an absolutely terrible idea. I have a fear of open water. Not like a paralysing one or anything. Okay, it's a bit of a paralysing one. I'd just rather not swim in water where I can't see what's underneath me. If I'm going to swim, I like the body of water to be filled with so much chlorine that my eyes feel like they're going to burn right out of my skull.

So, the giant lake next to Lola's hotel is score one against this shit idea.

Secondly, I just don't know how I'm going to cope seeing Lola. I can't picture how it's going to play out in my head. Whenever I try to imagine meeting her, or worse, having to listen to her talking about why she left me, why she quit the band, maybe even letting on who my real dad is . . . the edges of my eyes start to go dark and I have a very Victorian urge to reach for some smelling salts.

It's just that I'm used to managing my sense of abandonment in small doses. Like exposure therapy. Every once in a while, I'll take out my little folder, have a sift through all my Lola stuff and then I lock it away again and move on with my life. But I can't pinpoint exactly how I'll fare coming face to face with the woman who abandoned me as a baby . . . who only called once in thirty years . . . who never visited . . .

I think I'm hyperventilating.

'Earth to Lily.' Seb's voice makes its way into my brain. He's followed me upstairs. 'I'd say you look constipated, but I know how obsessed you are with getting your five a day.'

That's me. A person who is obsessed with broccoli. And even if it is packed full of nutrients, fibre and natural anti-inflammatories, no one wants to be known as the number one fan of cruciferous vegetables.

Lola seemed to spend most of her band years living off vodka and adrenaline. And not the sort of adrenaline you get when you have a tricky email to reply to. The sort you get when you're performing for ten thousand people. In short, she's going to hate me.

'Lily?'

I think Seb's frowning. On principle, I've made a lifetime habit of never giving people occasion to frown.

'Sorry.' I force a smile. 'I was just having a minute.'

'You know we don't have to go?' he asks, eyeing me warily.

'We do,' I say.

Because I have to do something. It's like when you wear ankle socks with boots, and they roll down your feet and get all annoying. From the outside everything looks fine, but you know that it isn't. You *know* that it's a bit of a mess in there and you just want to do whatever you can to reach down and fix it. That's how I feel. This trip is me reaching into my boot and pulling my sock up. Or something like that.

'If you're sure? You know I'm grateful that you're trying to help.'

'I am. Let me get the rest of my stuff. It's in the spare room.'

Seb eyes the little suitcase by my bed. Objectively, I know that on its own it looks like a reasonable amount of luggage to take on a weekend mini-break. But I figure that this weekend is already going to be stressful enough, let alone trying to sleep on an unfamiliar pillow without my lavender diffuser and the white noise machine that I need set to volume seven if I have any chance of it not taking me three hours to nod off.

Plus, there's my products, because my skin goes blotchy unless I follow a meticulous five-step routine, my curling wand and my Frizzease, for obvious reasons.

Okay, it is a lot of stuff. I just want to be prepared.

Seb is back in the kitchen, waiting as I pile all my things at his feet.

I dump a third bag of stuff by my suitcase. It has my workout clothes in. Then I move to the top of the kitchen cupboards and start methodically filling the cool bag. I can feel Seb's eyes on me as I take it to the fridge, enjoying the blast of cold air as I pull out my probiotics. Lola's place looks pretty – read very – remote, and I don't know how readily available they'll be in the hotel shop – which I know she has because there is nothing I don't know about the hotel Lola owns and runs. I still just cannot picture Lola there. And that unsettles me, makes me think that I'm in for some sort of a surprise.

I hate surprises.

I'm the sort of person who reads the last page of a book before I start it, and I Google the endings to TV series before I watch them. That's how much I dislike the unknown.

At least I *know* that how I'm acting is insane behaviour, that's a really important point. It's only really weird if you think you're normal.

I already have my vitamins in the bag as I zip it up. They're the gummy ones because for about a year I've been feeding them to Seb on the down-low, pretending that they're sweets. I keep my back to him now so that he doesn't cotton on to my devious but motivated out of concern for his B12 levels plan.

Finally, I double check my rucksack for my water bottle, suncream, sunglasses, purse and phone, and make us some drinks for the car. The only thing left to do is say goodbye to Elton.

'Ready,' I tell Seb.

'Are you sure? We could dismantle the actual house and take that with us, if you like?'

I finally zip up my rucksack, giving Seb the finger as I do. It feels good.

Elton resists my attempts to give him a fond farewell in the hallway, leaving me with a shiny new scratch on my forearm for my efforts.

'And you'll remember his special food and his eyedrops? They're in the fridge.' I harass the eighty-year-old Mr Cains on the street outside the house, handing over the key. 'And if it gets over thirty-five degrees, move the window plants out of the sun or they'll overheat. The thermometer's by the back door.'

Mr Cains is dressed in a worn suit. He's a retired accountant who discovered magic when his wife died. This fact makes me feel a lot better about my own poor attempts to cope with my grief. I know that Mr Cains is going to want me to pull the handkerchief out of his pocket before we leave, it's something he got Dad to do all the time, too.

'Don't you worry about it, Lily. Me and Elton will have a whale of a time.'

It's probably best not to reply that I don't want Elton to have a whale of a time. I want him to have a nice, quiet, life-preserving time. But Seb is closing the boot of his car and declaring that we need to get going.

'Okay, thank you,' I tell Mr Cains. 'I really appreciate it.'

'You go and have a nice break, Lily. You deserve it. But before you go, would you like a hanky?'

I gasp in mock surprise as the handkerchief gets longer and longer.

'Well, look at that!?' I declare to Seb.

'Fantastic, truly.'

I'm still pretend laughing as I climb into the passenger side door.

Finally, we're ready. I'm going to see Lola.

Suddenly, I'm not laughing anymore.

\* \* \*

'Ginseng tea?' I ask Seb, holding out the flask I've made for him. We've decided to take his car, because he refuses to be a passenger. Apparently, I drive too slow and this is already an eight-hour journey.

Yes, eight hours. And I get car sick. Because of course I do.

Plus, Seb's car is some old red vintage thing with absolutely zero suspension. Like, zero.

His eyes dart to me.

'Some what?' he asks.

'Ginseng tea,' I tell him. 'I thought you'd like to try it. It's really nice.'

'Nicotine suppressant, right?'

'Well, er, n–not exactly,' I stutter. He's wearing a black T-shirt. If he was a bit taller, he could be a model, all pale skin and high cheekbones. Like a young Dracula. The roof is down on his car and his hair just lightly ruffles. Mine loses the plot entirely and stands basically on end. 'I just read that it can interfere with the dopamine receptors in your brain so I thought it might help and I had some in the cupboards already . . . '

Another look.

'Okay, I ordered some especially on next-day delivery—' I hold my hands up '—but it was no trouble and really, don't you think it's worth a try?'

'Why do you have to be so fucking nice all of the time?' he asks.

'I'm not *nice*,' I tell him, even though his words are music to my ears. I work very hard at being nice. I help myself to a seaweed thin and a travel sickness tablet.

Seb just huffs out a laugh.

'God, I really hope the person renting the other cottage is hot,' he says.

'I mean, that's not really what this weekend is about.' We're having to shout over the wind from having the roof down.

'Can we put the roof up?' I ask.

'Shush, stop ruining my fantasy. As if you couldn't do with a little summer of romance. Guys really go for your whole Zooey Deschanel thing, and it might loosen you up a bit, a good orgasm.'

'I'm loose!' I protest, now definitely shouting. 'I'm so loose.' I realize I'm sat ramrod straight in my car seat while my neck fan buzzes. I concentrate on slouching and the pile of travel sickness bags on my lap slips. I slink down a little further. 'And anyway, I only just broke up with Colin.'

'It's been nine months.'

'What?'

'NINE MONTHS.'

Seb relents and pulls over to put the roof up. Thank the lord.

'That's really quick to get over a break-up,' I say as we set off again. 'I thought he was the one.'

Another huff. 'He was too square. I still have nightmares about that time he showed me his Monzo account. All those fucking pots. Who saves a pound a week for "professional oven clean".'

'Er, I would do that, because I'm also square.' Colin was actually perfect for me. We were on the same page about everything.

And anyway, people like me, we don't end up with the sexy lumberjack types that Seb pines for. We end up with people who are in possession of lifetime saving ISAs and favourite mugs. We end up with a Colin. I'm not exactly sure what went wrong other than that I was too absorbed with grief for Dad to put any effort into a relationship. But when I'm feeling better, I'll be perfectly happy with Colin mark two.

'Your squareness is a coping mechanism,' Seb answers.

I stuff my mouth full of seaweed thins to stave off the sickness that's hitting me before we're even free of Manchester and also to avoid having to think too much about replying. It's cloying, sea-weed dust.

'Hey, what happened with that woman you met at the pottery class last week? The one in her nineties. Is she going to go for a memoir?'

'Nope.' He pops the 'p'. 'Her granddaughter had the bright idea of just setting up an Instagram account and flooding it with pictures. That way it'll be more "interactive and accessible" for them. Fucking social media. Instagram will be the end of us all.'

He grips the steering wheel so hard his knuckles turn white.

'That's the problem, isn't it?' he carries on, a conversation we've had a million times before. 'Who needs us to memorialize their life when they've already photographed every last second as it is? By the time all the socially awkward millennials start dying off, there'll be nothing left to record, and we'll be out of a business.'

I let him rant, but the thing is, we *do* offer a service that social media can't. Seb and I both have history degrees, and we pride ourselves on adding context to people's life stories. Plus, you get an actual book, not a load of disjointed posts.

Seb's great-granny was our first client and she'd lived this amazing life fleeing the Nazis and then fostering literally hundreds of children. If we hadn't written it down, there's every chance her story would have been lost at some point.

That's how I know the business means so much to Seb.

And it's why we can't let it go under.

We need to convince Lola to let us write her memoirs, that's all there is to it.

\* \* \*

'Wow, long drive,' Seb says, in my opinion, stating the bleeding obvious.

No, that's not fair. He's done all the driving. It's not like we could share it, what with my car sickness. The Skye Bridge connecting the island to mainland Scotland had been a particular low point. Like a rollercoaster if you ask me. And the bloody roof is down again.

I just hadn't imagined that my grand reunion with Lola would involve quite so much vomit.

'I know, I don't think I realized that anywhere in the UK was so far away.'

Eight hours. Eight long hours since we set off. My seaweed thins are long gone. And to think, when I'd found out that Lola lived in Scotland, I'd been surprised by her proximity. But honestly, I could have flown to New York quicker. Not that I'm a person who's flying to New York on the regular. Or ever. But you get what I mean.

At least it's been a beautiful drive. That does make a difference, vomiting by a stunning backdrop.

The satnav says that finally, finally, we're fifteen minutes away.

I click my neck fan back in place, earning myself a side eye from

Seb. But my nausea is returning, and for reasons unknown, I'm sweating an awful lot despite the car's air-con.

I force myself to breathe in and out. To stop staring obsessively at the dot as it moves along the blue line. To take in the scenery.

Lola's hotel is remote. I already know this from alllll of my Google Earth searches, but somehow being here, it feels even more secluded. Like we're at the end of the earth almost. That's how that author had described it at any rate.

That the Isle of Skye is like the edge of everything.

The single road we're on weaves along the coastal road, as if there's an invisible tether pulling me towards Lola and her hotel.

Fields with long grass stretch out before us, touching the feet of mountains. So many mountains. We've passed more than one sign for Broadford. The small town that Lola's hotel is near.

We turn, heading inland, away from the coastal town. According to the website, Lola's hotel is a couple of miles from town, set next to a loch, a fact I really don't enjoy. I just don't like lochs or lakes full stop. All eerie and still, as if you could drown and no one would ever realize. Looking at the satnav, there are little bodies of water hidden away in the mountains, too.

How does Lola live here of all places? Whenever I'd imagined her over the years, she was living in some ridiculous hotel suite, you know the sort that have their own dining rooms with chandeliers. Or at the very least, I'd pictured her in some country pile with a helipad on the roof. Not *here*. We're in the middle of fucking nowhere.

'Are you okay?' Seb asks. 'You can change your mind.'

I shake my head, having lost the ability to form any words.

Maybe it's the setting or maybe it's the fact that I know for sure that I'm closer now to Lola than I've been in the last thirty years, but I want to finish this. To see with my own eyes that she exists.

'I want to keep going.'

We round the final bend, and I can see the hotel just up ahead.

It's bigger than it looks in the pictures, more sprawling. We get closer still and I can make out that the white paint on its walls is chipped and crumbling. It looks like it might once have been a grand house. Out front there's a wide veranda with ornate white wooden pillars. A red, hand-painted sign that's hanging on by a single nail reads, 'Broadford Hotel'. Does what it says on the tin, I suppose.

My heart is drumming a persistent hard beat as we pull into the little car park out front, the tyres crunching over loose stones. I sit on my hands, not moving, just looking.

To the side of the hotel there's a wooden pier jutting out onto the loch, kayaks bobbing in the water next to it. On the bank, there's an enormous willow tree, its branches sweeping the ground. The lake, I mean loch, itself is huge and dark and still, with a pebbly shore where there's a big wooden shed.

Seb opens his door and on autopilot I do the same. The front porch has a string of bulbs wound around the two wooden pillars either side of the steps. It's taken us so long to get here that the sun is setting and one set flickers feebly to light as we watch. The other doesn't even try.

Once again, I'm struck by the fact that this is the last place on earth I'd expect to find Lola Starr.

'Is that a . . . ?' Seb's voice trails off as a chicken picks its way in front of the car. At least I think it's a chicken. It only has feathers on one side of its body and its eyes are shut. It's in an even worse state than Elton.

'Where are we?' Seb asks as the chicken stumbles its way to the other side of the car park.

'I don't know,' I answer, peering around. It's eerily quiet.

On the other side next to the loch there's the hotel shop. Another glorified rickety shed with an honesty box outside. It's all very, very surreal.

'We can leave our bags while we check in,' Seb says, and it's a good idea. I don't want to meet Lola carrying a cool bag full of probiotics after all.

Thank God this plan doesn't involve telling her who I am. I'd just explode from the stress of it all.

I nod, telling myself that I need to get my shit together.

We head over to the steps to the porch. It's still sweltering outside but the skin on my arms is pebbled, and it feels like my hair is full of static, as if I'm on charge somehow.

'Here we go,' Seb says, pushing the glass-panelled door to the hotel open with his shoulder and then bracing himself as it all but falls off on him. He gestures me through.

My feet are moving. I hardly notice the small reception area, the wood desk stacked with a mishmash of leaflets, the woman stood behind it, her long blonde hair in a thick plait slung over one shoulder.

'Welcome to Broadford Hotel,' she says as I stop dead in front of her.

\* \* \*

As I stand by in front of the desk looking at Lola, it seems impossible that no one has ever figured out that this is *the* Lola Starr, even if she is going by Lola Vain these days. She must be around fifty now, but it's the same face I've stared at countless times in magazines.

Her face is the only thing that's as I imagined, though, everything else is just *off*.

I expected ... I don't know that I expected high heels and big hair out here on the Isle of Skye, but I didn't expect green Crocs and dirt engrained hands. Gone are the sharp eyes half smiling at cameras in countless paparazzi photos. Here, Lola's eyes are soft, creased at the edges.

A barrage of emotions slam into me, fighting for dominance. Anger, because how can she have just been here, all this time?

Relief – we found her! Surprise, disbelief, happiness. The torrent renders me basically mute as I stare at the person who gave birth to me.

'Thank you,' I hear Seb say. 'We're happy to be here, aren't we, Lily?'

For a split second, Lola's eyes meet mine and I think the whole thing must be written all over my face because she looks at me intently. I should have gone with a different name! What if she knows my name? Mum and Dad said that they named me, but what if they let her have some say? I go to speak but she's turning her back to us, pulling some paperwork and a set of keys from a shelf on the wall there.

Seb gives me a 'what the fuck' look, tilting his head towards her.

Suddenly, I'm overcome by the urge to tell her who I am. Ask why she left.

It's not at all part of the plan. But I want to ask why she ignored my letters. Ask why she didn't try harder.

The questions I've had, this, now is my chance to find out the answers.

I take a deep breath and meet her eyes. This is my chance.

And I just . . . can't. Everything is wrong. Lola Starr looks nothing like the superstar I always pictured. Lola Starr, the girl in the orange dress, glamorous, famous and shiny – the person I'd pictured myself putting all these questions to – simply doesn't exist. The woman in front of me is wearing dungarees, for god's sake.

'Yeah, really happy,' I blurt. Lola's eyes are still boring into me. Oh god, does she know? Is she on to me? Is it the name thing? My heart speeds up, it's going impossibly fast as I crash headfirst into panic mode.

'I'm Lily . . . and this is . . . this is my twin brother, Seb.'

Seb's eyes go wide as Lola pulls her gaze away from mine.

I don't know what I'm saying, I just need to throw her off. Maybe

I imagine it, but she drops her head a little, giving it a small shake before she speaks again.

'That's nice. Well, y'all are very welcome. There's spare bedding in the cottage if one of you wants to take the sofa bed.'

'Good idea,' Seb says, still glaring at me. 'We shared a womb once, but we're not *Game of Thrones* close, if you get me?'

Lola laughs.

'You're all paid up for three nights,' she says. 'The cottage is a whole lot nicer than the bedrooms, just don't tell my other guests.' She does a soft chuckle. Her voice still has a faint American accent to it, the twang of the south, but it's being crowded out by Scottish more often than not. She's wearing a loose white shirt underneath her denim overalls. I pull at my fan collar, realizing that it's stopped working.

'This is the hotel timetable.' She slides a sheet of A4 paper towards us. It has a table on it with the days of the week at the top. I love a good timetable, who doesn't? I mean this one isn't colour coded, so it could be better, but it is pretty full. Kayaking, painting, hiking, yoga, skydiving . . . I do a double take. Skydiving.

It has never, ever made sense to me, why some humans throw themselves out of a plane. Sometimes, we really need to know our limits as a species. And if we were meant to fly, we'd have wings.

Lola is still talking. 'You're welcome to drive to town to eat if you like. It's just ten minutes back the way you came. They have some great seafood restaurants there or The Broadford Inn does the best neep and tatties if that's what takes your fancy. We serve a continental breakfast each mornin', seven through ten. Most folk like the porridge the best. And the cottage has a small kitchenette too. You'll have seen the shop out front.'

Seb peers down at the paper.

'Look, Lily,' he says, 'there's wild swimming Thursday mornings. It's a shame we'll miss that. It's her favourite.' He's smirking at me.

Knob. He knows how I feel about wild swimming. His remark does relax me enough to manage a small, 'thank you,' to Lola, as I take the timetable and fold it in half.

'No problem. If you need anything else, just holler.'

A blond Labrador comes out of what must be a small office behind the desk and starts panting at Lola's feet. She reaches down absentmindedly to stroke behind its ear. I watch the whole thing with rapt attention. 'I'm always around,' Lola carries on, oblivious to me gawping at her. 'And Noah's in the cottage next door. He knows the place as well as I do.' She shuffles some papers on the countertop, straightening them.

'This Noah you speak of,' Seb asks. 'Any chance he's a lumberjack?'

Something about the name Noah rings a distant bell at the back of my brain.

Lola laughs again. At least she and Seb are getting on well. I'm mostly just standing here with my mouth hanging open, having well and truly lost the plot.

'Afraid not. He's a writer. He'll be happy to help if y'all have any questions, though. Now you can go through the dining room out back to the cottage, or if y'all have luggage and what not, grab it and take it round the side of the house. Can't miss it.'

'Lola, have you seen my chaps? The leather ones. I can't find them anywhere.'

Seb and I twist around so fast that I'm surprised the top of my body hasn't detached from the lower half. Thumping down the wooden stairs from the top of the hotel is the man I am pretty certain is Ashton Vain. Aka Lola's old bandmate, aka my potential birth father. Now was a really, really bad time for my neck fan to cut out.

Ashton hasn't managed to stave off the aging process in the same way that Lola has. His face is tanned and there are some pretty serious wrinkles across his forehead. I have the beginnings of wrinkles there too. Do I get that from him? Am I looking at my future fore-head right now? His hair is black and a bit curly and sits just above his shoulders. Hang on, is *this* where I get my dodgy hair from? Wow, it is hard to breathe.

'Sorry, sorry,' he says quickly, arriving at the bottom of the stairs. 'I didn't realize you had guests.'

'Mm hm, meet Seb and Lily. They're staying in the cottage overnight.'

Seb, clearly overawed at being in the presence of two members of Beyond Baton Rouge, says, very effusively, 'The pleasure is all ours, honestly.' He's looking at Ashton like he's the second coming. I think he might break into a bow.

'The cottage is lush, you'll like it there.'

Seb throws an arm around my shoulders and almost knocks me over.

'Yes, we'll be super happy in there. Won't we, oh sister dearest?'

He squeezes my arm where his hand has landed and I'm forced to choke out, 'Yeah, super happy. What he said.'

There's a good chance that I've been confronted with both my birth parents and all I've managed are stuttered splutterings. Seb is never going to let me live this down.

'You still okay to take me to the station?' Ashton asks Lola.

'Course, let me get the keys.'

'Great, I'll grab my case and have another look for the chaps. Two ticks.'

It's becoming a bit weird that Seb and I are still standing here, watching them have a conversation, our eyes moving backwards and forwards between them.

'Right, come on then, twinnie.' Seb watches Ashton jog up the stairs before picking up the cottage keys.

I don't trust myself to speak. It's possible I've gone into shock.

That's not a thing, is it? On those reunion programmes you see on TV, one half of the people being reunited don't just stand there not moving. I want to watch Lola some more, but Seb is leaving again, so I'm forced to offer up a small smile and follow him back out of the front doors towards the car.

He's humming the tune to 'Storm in a Teacup'.

'Well, that went well! Couldn't have gone better. The business will be saved in no time! At least I got to meet Ashton Vain. My crush brought to life. Still does it for me. By the way, why did you tell her we were twins?' Seb angry mutters. He's talking so fast I hardly catch what he's saying.

'I panicked!' I angry mutter back, whacking my neck fan to try to get it back in action. 'I did just see my biological mother and maybe my biological dad for the first time in thirty years!'

'True. What did you think?'

'She's just not what I expected. I thought I'd be getting Meryl Streep in *The Devil Wears Prada*, not Meryl Streep in *Mamma Mia*.'

'I know, right, what was with those overalls? They looked older than me.'

'They were unexpected—' another whack '—plus my fan has broken.'

'Good, it looks ridiculous. Please take it off.'

'Ashton seems more aging rock star, though. I knew he was Scottish. Was he born round here?'

'Glasgow.'

'You really do know a lot about him.'

'I was sure I was going to marry him when I was about thirteen.'

We're still talking as if we're bickering, even though we aren't. We keep going as we pull all of our things out of the boot. I give my fan one final hit. It lands with so much force, I've essentially just smacked myself, hard, on the back of the head. I stumble back a few steps and crash straight into someone.

'Oh my god, I'm so sorry—'

I turn around and . . .

Oh.

'Sorry. I'm so sorry. My neck fan, it's on the blink.'

'Don't worry about it.' The man I bumped into smiles. 'No harm done.' He rubs a hand over the back of his own – decidedly fanless – neck. 'I'm Noah,' he says. 'Lola just mentioned that you're staying in the other cottage.'

Sometimes the genetic lottery really does play to win. Noah is wearing navy shorts and a white T-shirt that should be illegal. He has tattoos poking out from under his sleeves and his dark blond hair is long-ish, it curls around his ears.

He's like a Nordic David Beckham. And if I was a judgemental sort of person – which, clearly, I am – I'd say that he doesn't look like a writer. There must be something in the water up here.

Seb moves first. I'm pretty sure that given half the chance he'd throw me on the ground and trample over me in an effort to get closer to Noah.

'Nice to meet you.' He's shaking hands with Noah. 'I'm Seb and this is my twin sister, Lily.' He throws me a dirty look, like he's still not over having to pretend that we're related. 'Non-identical, obviously.'

'Nice to meet you both.' Noah takes in all of the bags sprawled at my feet. His accent is very Scottish. 'Do you need a hand with those?' he asks.

I say no at the same time that Seb says yes.

Deciding that on balance we probably do need some help, I agree that we'd really appreciate that. It's a good call because we get to watch as Noah picks up almost all of my bags at the same time. And even though feminist me should be offended, I can carry my own luggage thank you very much, feminist me has gone into hiding at such an overt display of raw, manly strength.

We follow Noah down the side of the house. Yet more kayaks are propped against the wall here. Seriously, how many kayaks does one dilapidated hotel need? There are also some life jackets and a couple of blow-up two-person canoe type things. I ignore them. There are animals everywhere. Cats sleep in the shade of the hotel walls (they don't wake up and hiss as we pass, so it's very much just Elton and not the entire feline species who hates me).

'There's a lot of animals here,' I say, stating what is completely obvious.

'Lola rehomes them,' Noah tells us, twisting round to look our way. 'If there's a waif or a stray out there, Lola will find it and give it a home.' He laughs a little self-consciously while I try and mostly fail to process this information.

I spot another two chickens, though this pair seem to have all of their feathers, and their eyes for that matter. And I'm sure there are more insects here than at home. More than one bee buzzes around me, though I've always thought they were overly attracted to my Frizzease. And the butterflies ... they look like they've taken steroids. Why are their wings so big?

Clearly, all those journalists got it wrong. Lola wasn't off swotting up on the art of scientology; she was up here prepping to man her own chicken-heavy version of Noah's ark. Complete with an actual Noah.

Past the hotel, the space opens up into the gardens, to patchy grass scattered with picnic tables. There are hammocks tied between the trees that line its edges.

'It's pretty nice up here.' Seb has stopped walking and is looking up beyond the tree line at the back of the hotel to where a mountain range rises from seemingly nowhere. They're all dark and shadowy in the evening light, with mist swirling around their tops.

Pretty nice doesn't quite cover it, I don't think.

There's an ethereal quality to Skye. It doesn't feel like it could possibly be a real place. Except it is.

'Most beautiful place in the whole world, I'd say,' Noah answers. We've all stopped to look at the mountains now. Noah begins pointing out the names of some different peaks and oh my god, Noah!

Writer Noah. That's why I remember his name. Is this the Noah who writes books about Skye?

'Are you Noah Adair?' I blurt out.

He twists around, his cheeks turning hot and red.

'That would be me, how did you, er . . . how did you know that?'

Okay, yes, definitely sounded like a stalker.

'I love your books on Skye. You write so beautifully.'

Probably best not to admit that I've studied his entire body of work.

'Thank you for saying so.'

He's redder than ever.

I don't have time to worry about the distress I've caused to the lovely Noah. I'm busy doing my best to concentrate on breathing like a normal person and also ignoring Seb cursing as he tries to drag his cabin-sized suitcase along the loose gravel path that winds through the gardens.

At the back, tucked out of sight of the main house by more trees, are two cottages sat just in front of a wooded area. The cottages are made of dark stone, but I'm guessing that the UPVC doors are not original. Each cottage has its own white plastic dining set outside the front, complete with two chairs.

'This is you.' Noah comes to a stop in front of one of the cottages. 'I'm right next door, so shout if you need anything.' Noah's cottage is very, very close to ours.

'We will do, thanks, mate,' Seb says, despite the fact that I have never in my life heard him describe anyone as mate.

'I'll be on the kayaks in the morning, helping Lola. You should check it out,' he tells us.

Neither Seb nor I are suited to kayaking. I have my fear of open water and Seb is, well . . . Seb. But I hear myself say that we'd love to.

How does a person say no to something they don't want to do at any rate? I've never figured it out myself. Though if someone suggests a nice spot of skydiving, I'll be giving 'no' my best shot.

Right, well, if nothing else, it's a way to spend some time with Lola and keep up the ruse that we're here on holiday. It's not like we could just rock up and ask for the rights to her memoirs all in one go. We need to, like, drop hints about what we do. Gradually lure her in. Possibly I'm evil now.

'Great, I'll see you both then.' Noah smiles and heads to his own cottage, three feet away.

Except when he gets to his door, he turns to look our way again.

Unfortunately, this means that he catches both Seb and I staring at the poor guy.

In our defence, he's lovely to look at. But it forces us to jump into action, fiddling with the lock to the doors.

The cottage inside is small, and if I'm being unkind, a bit decrepit, but cute.

In the living area there's a couch and a TV unit with some DVDs stacked underneath. There's a side table with a lamp and a welcome note on it and at one end of the room, facing the back of the cottage, there's a small kitchenette. It's only a single row of units with an under-the-counter fridge, but there's everything we'll need here.

I'm pretty sure there's a load of craft type people living on the Isle of Skye. I read about it. How it's a centre for that sort of thing. But all Lola's furniture looks like it came from IKEA. I'm not against IKEA, obviously their meatballs are excellent. It's just that IKEA doesn't exactly scream rich and famous, does it?

'I'll get your bags, don't worry,' Seb complains to himself, dragging my stuff in from outside. 'I'm your fake twin not your slave.'

He's busy piling my luggage down by the end of the couch so I walk into the other rooms. There's a compact bathroom and a bedroom with a double bed and a single set of drawers. Someone has put some red tulips in a jug on top of them. The walls are all the same – exposed stone painted white – and the floors are wood.

There's a window that looks across to Noah's cottage. That's probably his bedroom right there.

The cottage is quiet. Decrepit or not, if I were here on a genuine mini-break, it's the sort of place I might come to feel relaxed in. If I was a person who knew how to relax, that is.

I walk back into the living area. Seb has pulled the couch out into a sofa bed. It almost fills the place, the end knocking against the rickety TV unit. He's been forced to move the glass coffee table practically into the kitchen.

'Everyone is super-hot here,' he says.

I ignore him.

'I'll take the couch,' he says. 'You know I can sleep anywhere.'

There is tacit implication in that statement that I, on the other hand, could not sleep anywhere. I eye my hypoallergenic pillow, wondering if this weekend is already going to be stressful enough without adding in trying to sleep on a lumpy sofa bed.

'Okay, if you're sure.'

'I'm sure.' He peers over at my cool bag. 'Do you have anything other than seaweed thins in there?'

'Yep.' I smile, loving the fact that I'm being useful and prepared right now. 'I brought some breadsticks and dips and stuff.'

'Tell me there's wine.'

'Of course.'

'Perfect. I'm going for a cigarette.'

Seb slides back out of the double doors and I'm suddenly alone. I don't know how I feel about being alone right now. I move, taking my special pillow to the bedroom, eyeing up the note that Lola has left on the drawers.

*Lily and Seb! Welcome to Broadford. I hope you have a lovely stay. Lola x*

It's probably something she does for everyone staying in the hotel.

But it just makes me think, she can obviously wield a pen, so why didn't she write to *me* these past few decades? She's nicer to her hotel guests than she is to her own daughter.

And suddenly, it's all too much.

I slip out of the double doors and into the rapidly advancing evening. 'Just going to check out the woods,' I call to Seb where he's off at the edge of the cottage gardens. Thankfully, Noah is nowhere to be seen.

I don't give Seb chance to reply, I just march behind the cottage and into the tree line, stomping my way through the leaves and grass of the forest floor. Once I think I'm far enough away from the cottage, I look up at the tree canopy. It's darker in here still, cooler. My eyes fill with tears. Whether they're for myself, for Lola or the fact that this would all be so much easier if Mum and Dad were still here, I don't know.

I just stand there, then, my face still tipped up and cry. For Mum, for Dad. For me and how wrong I seem to have been about Lola all these years. I'm throwing myself the mother of all pity parties and I don't care, because it feels good to let it out.

There's a whisper of a breeze and I feel it across the wet streaks down my cheeks.

But I don't stop. I cry these great heaving sobs that make it hard to breathe in.

It's cathartic. Hopefully it's cathartic.

It's not stopping. It's causing havoc with my eye make-up, but it's still going strong.

Hopefully, it'll stop soon.

*Slurp.*

I open my eyes finally.

'Don't mind me.' A teenage girl approximately three feet away from me stands, drinking the last remnants of a bright blue drink. 'It's *meant* to be peaceful in here, but please continue to wail like a banshee while some of us are trying to enjoy some peace and quiet.'

She swallows the final bit of her drink, her lips now fully stained blue, and throws the plastic cup on the ground by her feet.

And that's bad, isn't it? Littering is always bad, but it's extra bad when it's somewhere lovely like this.

I look from her to the cup, my weeping mercifully dimming to small hiccups. The teenager has really pale skin and jet-black hair that's so poker straight it looks like it might snap. And at the risk of sounding ancient, her clothes seem to be hanging together by a couple of threads and sheer force of will.

'Would you like me to put that in the bin for you?' I ask, looking towards where the plastic cup is still strewn on the ground.

'It's a free country.' She glowers at me. I get the impression that picking up that cup would be tantamount to an act of war.

I don't move. I'm not going to leave the cup there forever, obviously. If I have to sneak back into the woods in the dead of night to get it, I will.

'I'm Lily,' I tell her.

'Why are you telling me your name, weirdo?'

'I'm here for the weekend.'

'I don't understand why you're still talking to me.'

Because I'm allergic to confrontation and convinced if I'm nice to her, she'll be nice back.

'How long are you staying for?' I ask, ignoring her snapping at me.

And anyway, the last question apparently appeals, because she rolls her eyes so dramatically that she could give Seb lessons and says, 'Seven fucking weeks, in this absolute shit hole. And I can't get my phone to work with the crap Wi-Fi.'

I mean, the beautiful island setting is likely no one's definition of a shit hole, but my phone buzzes in my hand and I look down. There's a WhatsApp from Mr Cains.

*The Next Chapter*

**Mr Cains:** Just sitting down to watch a Western like
real men.

There's a picture of Elton sprawled on the couch, his mouth turned down as usual and his admittedly large stomach on full display. I make a mental note to make a physical note about seeing the vet for some more of the prescription food that he hates.

I laugh, and then because the teenager is still looking at me, I say, 'My eighty-year-old neighbour is watching a Western with my dead dad's cat.'

Her eyes go wide. 'That's some seriously weird shit.' She sounds grudgingly impressed.

'Yep. Plus, it looks like my phone is working just fine.'

She leans towards me, some internal battle going on between continuing to talk to me and the promise of a phone with 5G. But then from just behind her Seb shouts, 'Lily, are you done crying? I can't find the corkscrew.'

The teenager takes off like a startled deer, turning around and darting back towards the hotel.

I pick up her plastic cup and head towards Seb's voice.

'Sorry, I just needed some air. I didn't think you'd be able to hear me.'

'You were ten meters away. Plus, look at you.'

There's no way that my face has returned to normal after all of the crying. I know fine well it'll be a patchwork quilt of mess, but Seb doesn't say anything else.

He just waits for me to follow him inside where I move to the cool bag and start pulling out the breadsticks I brought. I probably should go to the hotel shop, but honestly, I can't risk running into Lola again.

I leave the open packets on the kitchen counter for Seb to make up his own plate.

We sit on the sofa and for a while, we eat in silence. Both lost in our thoughts.

'So, what do you think, about Lola?' Seb asks eventually.

I shake my head. 'I don't know. She just . . . wasn't what I thought she'd be. She seems . . . caring. Like with all the animals and stuff. And it makes it even more confusing, why she never got in touch again. I know why *I* didn't, she never replied to my letters and after Mum died it felt like I'd be replacing her or something. But why didn't Lola try again? None of it makes sense. Plus, have you seen this place?'

He nods. 'It's a bit of a dump.'

'Do you think that's why she wants to sell her memoirs, for the money? At least she didn't look sick.'

Seb twists to look at me.

'I've been worried that she wanted to sell her story because she was dying.'

'Ah,' he says. 'I don't think sick people look sick the whole time, do they?'

'Not helping.'

Seb rubs at his temples. 'Maybe it is for the hotel, then. But she must get like royalties and stuff, mustn't she? They still play her songs on the radio.'

'Yeah . . . I don't know how it all works to be honest.'

There's no denying that the hotel is run down. And maybe a bit empty. I've seen two other guests so far. Noah and the scary teenager.

'I say we stick to the plan. Start dropping in tomorrow about what we do. Just be chill about it.'

I wrinkle my nose. 'I'm never chill. Ever. You know this. Do you think it's bad that we're lying to her?'

'Oh yes, because you've been nothing but honest so far, dearest sister of mine.'

'Yeah, but that was a one-off lie, not a long-term lie. There has to be a difference, in the sin stakes.'

Seb ignores me. 'Her memoirs might be worth even more money than we'd realized, you know. Who would have put her here, of all places? It's quite the story.'

'The business would be secure for ages.'

'Exactly. I think now that I've seen her, I'm even more desperate to know why she disappeared, aren't you?'

'Mm hmm,' I answer. 'I thought she was on to me for a second back there, I'm sure she was looking at me funny. I think that's why I said you were my brother, to throw her off. Obviously, she'd know that she didn't give birth to two people.'

'I guess that means we're kayaking tomorrow,' he says finally.

'I guess we are.'

'We'll get to see Noah in a kayak. I bet he really glides through that water. Do you think he has a kilt? Did you see his biceps?'

I pretend that I hadn't noticed.

'It's a pity Ashton is leaving.'

I scoff. 'Yes, please continue to use my family trauma for your lewd fantasies.'

Seb sighs, putting his plate down already. Honestly, he doesn't eat enough.

Suddenly, I'm exhausted. I unfasten my now redundant neck fan at last.

'Thank you, Jesus.' Seb eyes it as I yawn. 'Why don't you go and get an early night?'

Normally, I'm anti-early night. All that time when I could be being productive, it seems like such a waste to spend it asleep. But I am drained. Exhausted in a way that's not purely physical.

'Would you mind?' I ask Seb.

'Nah, go for it. It's been a day.'

I stand up.

'It really has. But thank you, for driving us here and you know, pretending to be my brother.' I say the last part in a strange comedy voice that I'll never use again. 'You're a good friend.'

'I know, I'm amazing. Best friend in the history of best friends. Now go to bed. I'll wake you up for our early morning kayak. Wow, there's a sentence I never thought I'd say.'

I stumble towards the bedroom, so worn out that I barely manage to turn my white noise machine on.

I don't even use my lavender spritz.

No, on the day I've seen the woman who gave birth to me, for the first time in thirty years, I collapse face first into my pillow and fall into a deep, dreamless sleep.

# Chapter Four

*To Do:*

- Pitch memoirs to Lola
- Survive kayaking
- Reply to WhatsApps
- Get on top of emails

The room is unnaturally light. It bounces off the white walls as I crack an eye open. I didn't pull the curtain last night and it's an absolute miracle that I've managed to sleep with the room like this.

There's obviously something about the country air that's wearing me out. Even if we haven't exactly breathed in much of it yet. Probably it's because I've spent the past two weeks not sleeping, I'm catching up.

There's a *thunk* from the living area, as if Seb's closing a cupboard out there. The smell of coffee starts to work its way under the door and if I'm going to go spy kayaking with Lola Starr, coffee is absolutely essential.

I've slept face down which means my fringe is basically pointing straight up from my forehead. Bloody thing once again proves to be more trouble than it's worth as I try to ineffectually get it to go down.

In a life first, I also didn't follow my complete skincare routine last night. I mean, I'd taken my make-up off, I'm not an animal, but I didn't use my night serum. I assess the damage in the mirror above the chest of drawers, pressing a hand to my fringe to keep it down. That serum is obviously worth the small fortune I'd paid for it because without it I look like a Victorian opium addict. I let go of my fringe and it springs back upright.

In the end, I do as much damage limitation as I can, the smell of coffee too alluring to keep me busy for long.

'Morning,' I call to Seb where he's over by the kitchen, looking exactly the same as he does every morning. 'Okay, how do you look like that?'

Seb is wearing outdoor clothes. But they don't look like any of the outdoor clothes I've bought. His are all slick and tailored and track the lines of his body. He looks like Timothée Chalamet in *Dune*. My outdoor clothes just have so much material in them. So much. I look like I'm wearing a tent.

'And your hair is all shiny.'

'Bad hair days are not in my DNA.'

I start drinking the coffee he's made in big gulps, hopeful that it might restore some sort of equilibrium.

'We should get down there soon,' Seb says, 'the schedule says that it starts at nine. That's twenty minutes away. Do you want some breakfast?'

The fact that I slept past 8am is a miracle that I don't have time to dwell on. Twenty minutes. I have twenty minutes to psych myself up for kayaking and seeing Lola again. And my fringe is vertical.

'No, I'll just grab a breakfast bar, thanks. I need to get ready. Do you need the bathroom? Or should I go in the bathroom? Had we better draw up a bathroom rota? I knew I should have brough my Sharpies.' Seb's hands are on the top of my arms. 'Get it together, Lily, it's okay.'

I'm nodding, still cradling my half-drunk coffee in my hands between us.

'Okay, good,' he says, talking slowly. 'Now, as you can see, I'm dressed. You need to go and shower and then get dressed. Got it?'

I nod, dreamlike still. This is what I need. Someone to manage my every move. Imagine how easy life would be, without the avalanche of micro stresses that comes with decision making.

In the bathroom, I have the speediest shower known to man. The shower is really small, and the water splutters out in fits and starts. It's also a bit cloudy, which I ignore. Panicking about Legionnaires' disease isn't exactly going to restore my equilibrium.

I get soap in my eye and bash my knee and then I have to try to pull my clothes on in the confined space, still mildly damp.

I pin my fringe back, having lost this battle, but vowing to win the war later with some heavy-duty hairspray.

Looking at myself in the mirror as I brush my teeth, I'm thinking that it's really going to be a toss-up which part of my cover story is the least believable today. The fact that I'm pretending not to know who Lola is or that I'm meant to be enthusiastic about kayaking. I feel green at the thought of the loch. Greenish hue or not, I am not a woman who looks like they might thrive in the wild.

I step out of the bathroom, followed by a plume of steam.

'What are they?' Seb asks, waving a hand at me.

'What's what?' I ask.

'On your legs. Why are they so big?'

'They're my new trousers. I don't know, they fit on the waist but they're massive everywhere else. But they do detach at the knee and turn into shorts.' I attempt a demonstration. The zip gets stuck at the exact moment Seb starts to laugh.

I hop about trying to force the snagged zip shut. Seb is now howling. 'Neither of us is exactly Bear Grylls,' I finish, finally reclosing the zip.

'True. Ah well, that's cheered me up no end. Thanks, Lily. Come on, we'd better get going.'

I inhale an all-bran breakfast bar and then stuff the (many) pockets of my half-short-half-trouser get-up with back-up snacks.

We step outside.

'God, my arse looks amazing in these trousers. Don't you think?' Seb admires himself in the reflection of the double doors, twisting round to get a good look.

'It does look pretty good, yeah,' I agree. 'Sort of more round than normal.'

'Morning,' Noah calls over, waving while me and Seb both act like we weren't just checking out his bum.

'Morning,' we call back, and Noah smiles. I think we got away with it.

Walking down to the loch together, I think that Noah doesn't seem to be quite as at war with the heat or the environment as me. He's wearing navy swimming shorts, a white T-shirt and flip-flops. His sunglasses are pushed to the top of his head. He looks like he should have a film crew following him around.

'A braw day to be out on the loch,' he says, glancing up at the already blue sky.

Braw means nice. I read about that already.

I couldn't disagree more, but I nod. 'Let's do this thing,' I reply. And there's a moment that'll be living in my brain for the rest of time. Popping up at unhelpful intervals to remind me how cringe I've been.

It's already warm as Seb and I trail behind him, making our way around to the front of the hotel. He leads us down to the wooden pier where there's already a small number of people waiting alongside some kayaks which, in my opinion, bob ominously.

Lola is there, too, her blonde hair in a plait again. She's chatting to a middle-aged couple, while the mostly bald chicken pecks around her bare feet.

I look down at my own Gore-tex shoes, the laces pulled tight, and wonder if that's one of the reasons she left. Maybe even as a baby there were signs that I'd end up awfully high maintenance and she didn't fancy dealing with it.

The closer I get, the more I'm realizing that the loch water is so dark it's almost black. If I fell in and drowned, no one would ever find my body.

We join the edge of the group as Noah goes to talk to Lola. The teenager from the woods last night is here, looking absolutely furious about the fact. She's stood with, but a little apart from, a regular looking couple. The teenager is dressed like she's about to go clubbing rather than out for a nice little kayak on the loch of doom. Her skirt is held together with actual safety pins.

A boy who must be about nine gestures to her to come over to where he's half dangling from the edge of the pier and I absolutely don't want to know what he's seen in there. I bet it's a massive fish. And there you go, giant loch fish, a new fear unlocked.

I expect the teenager to tell him to fuck off, that seems to be her go-to. But instead, she lets out a huff and says, 'What is it, Blake?', moving over to him.

'Careful Harper, careful Blake!' the man from the normal couple calls. The look Harper gives him is pure venom. Teenagers are literally terrifying.

'Right.' Lola claps her hands together and we all turn to look at her. 'I think that's probably everyone.'

I wonder if I'm the only person imagining a slow and watery death for us all. Those kayaks look very flimsy and if the *Titanic* sank, what chance do they have?

Lola asks whether it's anyone's first time in a kayak. I raise my hand like I'm seven and shouting, 'Miss, Miss, Miss,' during carpet time. The boy stood next to Harper, I think she said his name was Blake, puts his hand up, too, while Harper lets out a particularly loud, 'Oh my fucking god.'

'I'm raring to go, though,' I tell the assembled group. Because I cannot act like the catastrophe I am. That is group situations 101. You become the most amenable, least annoying version of yourself. You definitely don't ask to see a risk assessment, which is what I'd like to do.

Lola doesn't seem to mind, though, she just smiles really wide at Harper and says, 'Not to worry, we'll all be wearing a life jacket, and we'll stay together. I thought we'd go around the perimeter of the loch, and I'll point out some local landmarks as we go, if y'all like. Noah's here to help, too. The hotel is his second home.'

Course it bloody is.

Noah shuffles from foot to foot, looking like he'd really rather not have people come and talk to him.

Once again, I am struck by how obvious it is that this is *the* Lola Starr. Her accent is soft, but it's still there. All lazy vowels and rhythmic lilt. I look around, sure that at any second now, someone is going to point a finger and cry, 'You must be that singer who disappeared thirty years ago! I'd recognize you anywhere!'

But that doesn't happen. Instead, people are just wandering, casual as you like, over to the pile of life jackets behind Lola and picking one out.

'When have you been on a kayak before?' I whisper to Seb, because this sounds like the sort of question that a sister wouldn't have to ask.

'I told you I was in the Scouts.' I swallow. I'd been relying on the fact that Seb might be the only person less adept at kayaking than me to distract from how bad I'm going to be. I can't grill him about it, though, because I need to make sure I get myself a top-notch life jacket.

It's morning, but the day is already starting to heat up. Everything looks hazy and I watch Noah as he chats to Lola, wondering what their deal might be. They seem to know each other really well, but the report by the private investigators said that Lola never married and doesn't have any other children. I store the image of them laughing together away to analyse at a later point, preferably some place where I'm not having to face one of my biggest fears.

Harper catches me looking at Noah and Lola. She raises an eyebrow at me before returning to the life jackets. She's mostly kicking through the pile, scattering them across the deck.

'I'm not wearing one of them, they're all wet.'

She's right, the life jackets are all a bit damp. Hopefully, this doesn't mean that the last lot of people Lola took out ended up in the water. Maybe Lola just gave them a quick hose down earlier. Hopefully, she takes better care of the life jackets than she does the rest of the place.

'Harper.' Her mum says it like a sigh, as if this isn't the first time she's had to say it. Harper rolls her eyes but does eventually clip a life jacket on.

I go to ask her if she wants to row next to me, but before I can say anything, Harper tells me, 'She's not my real mum, we're just forced to live with them,' and suddenly, I understand Harper's anger. She's not just an irritable teenager who hates the world. She's in foster care.

It makes sense. Harper has jet-black hair and the couple look like they walked straight out of Sweden. Plus, the whole being angry at the whole world thing.

'Okay, thanks for telling me that, Harper,' I tell her, looking her in the eyes as I clip on my own life jacket and double, no, triple check that the straps are tight enough. 'I was going to ask if you wanted to kayak next to each other, seeing as neither of us have done it before.'

She narrows her eyes at me. 'Are you one of those paedos?' she asks.

'Harper!'

I can't help the inappropriate and totally unattractive snort that I let out. 'Nope, definitely not a paedophile.' Of course, Noah chooses this moment to walk past us. I lean in to whisper, 'I'm just terrified I'll drown.'

That seems to get her attention.

'You're nervous?' she asks.

'Deathly. The bits of grass poking up through the water make me feel sick.'

I don't know why I'm making so much of an effort with Harper. She's so frosty she'd give an Arctic tundra a run for its money. Maybe there's something about how obviously angry she is that appeals to me. Especially when I'm so good at burying my own anger. It's refreshing, watching it seep out of her every pore.

'Blake's coming with us, too.'

'Perfect.' Seb appears at my shoulder, somehow managing to look stylish in the life jacket he's clipped under his cape. 'Hi, Blake.'

Blake ducks behind what I'm guessing is his foster dad before sticking his head back out and waving at Seb.

'He doesn't talk,' Harper tells us.

Jesus, poor kid. I do my biggest smile at him, to let him know that it's okay. The humidity and no small amount of terror is making my hair frizz like there's no tomorrow and so there's a good chance I'm damaging him further. Still, he does a small smile back, so hopefully not.

'Let's head on down to the kayaks,' Lola calls to everyone.

I follow the group, dragging my feet as much as possible and only just stopping myself from agreeing with Harper who declares loudly that this is 'a stupid fucking idea'.

I come to stand in front of a kayak (or, as I like to think of it, coffin), the last in the line. It's . . . very small. I have short legs and I don't see how they're going to go in there. I look at Seb stood next to me. He'll have to fold himself in half.

A couple of people along, Noah has pushed his sunglasses down now that the sun is brighter. He's helping Blake tighten the straps on his life jacket in a way that's disarmingly sweet.

I make a mental note not to pay him one bit of attention while we're out on the loch. He's very distracting and I'll drown.

He catches me looking, meeting my eyes.

I'll definitely drown.

Instead, I focus on Lola, who is running through what I consider to be a very brief safety demonstration. It's hard to pay attention to what she's saying. I'm distracted by the fact that that's my birth mum. Right there! Standing barefoot on the edge of a worn wooden deck.

I zone back in as she assures us that we shouldn't go under, but that if we do roll, we'll pop back up the other side. I deduce from this that Lola has adopted the same cavalier approach to health and safety that she did to parenting and go about tightening the straps on my life jacket with a vengeance.

Once it's so tight that I can hardly breathe, I follow everyone else, my knees weak as I tug my kayak by a little rope to the edge of the water and make an awful job of climbing in.

Lola, already out on the loch, looks like she was born there. She's completely relaxed, bobbing just a little while she watches us all. All those articles about her singing voice, her partying, her stardom and not one of them mentioned her kayaking prowess.

Seb, too, seems to have no trouble. He's out on the loch before I even have a foot in my kayak, looking like he's in the middle of a Gucci shoot. Traitor.

I manage to get my legs in. Definitely coffin like. But once they're inside I'm beached on the pebbly shore. I try to bum shuffle, that's what people always did on the videos. Probably I'm not shuffling hard enough, because I'm stuck here.

'Here, I'll give you a hand.'

Noah, also already in the water, is tugging at the end of my rope and I'm moving.

'I don't know how I got stuck here!' I think I'm speaking too loudly.

I let out a sigh of relief as with one final tug, I start to float. I'd had some serious doubts that this glorified bottle could manage it, but the sudden feeling of weightlessness would suggest that I'm doing it, I'm bobbing on the loch.

I think I'm going to vomit. How am I meant to pitch the memoirs thing to Lola if I spend every day up here puking?

The loch looks still, so why am I moving? I look around, sure that other people aren't bobbing quite so much. Instead, everyone else is watching Lola as she demonstrates how to use the paddle. She's going round in a circle now and I didn't think that was a skill set we'd be needing.

Everyone else turns in a circle. Well, everyone except Harper. She's bobbing on the water, her paddle across her lap, looking positively thunderous. Blake is in a two-person kayak with his foster dad. He's smiling, a fact which seems to make Harper even angrier.

I'm frozen with fear.

'All right?' Noah is next to me.

'Perfect, thanks, raring to get going.' Noah smiles and looks at my hands where they're white knuckling my paddle, so it's possible he can see through me.

'Are we all ready?' Lola calls.

I get that it's not a question we're meant to shout, 'no!' to, but that's what I want to do. I haven't attempted one of those circle things. I daren't even look at the water. I already can't see the bottom and imagining all the giant fish that're underneath me is not helping my nerves one bit. I've seen *Blue Planet*. You know those fish that live at the bottom of the ocean with massive teeth and dead eyes? I bet there's one of them down there.

Breathing short little breaths and trying not to imagine falling foul of the dead-eyed fish, I manage to get my kayak moving, copying Noah. His paddles seem to be generating an awful lot less water than mine. Seb was right, his biceps are impressive. There's a vein running down the centre of one of them. Wow.

I can't get distracted by the bicep vein, though. Not when even Harper is now prowling through the water like a hungry crocodile, eyes focused on some unknown spot on the horizon. She's already abandoned our plan to stick together.

I mostly seem to be soaking myself. Every time I lift my paddle, half the loch comes with it, dousing my trouser shorts. I think it's because my arms are shaking so badly.

I try to zone in to Lola as she tells us all about the mountains, but looking up at them where they encircle the loch makes me almost topple over and so I resolve to keep my eyes firmly water level.

Lola stops paddling, floating a little while she points out some rare species of flora on the banks. We're basically a hundred metres from where we set off and I'm already drained. This isn't helping to answer any of my questions about Lola. If anything, it's just high-lighting the differences between us far more starkly. Lobbing them out there for the world to see. Even if we're not different in the way I expected us to be, we're definitely different.

'Isn't nature just totally, like, awe-inspiring?' Seb drawls like an American cheerleader, gliding up next to me and looking like he was born in a fucking kayak.

Objectively, it is beautiful. The sky is cloudless, and the local mountains rise majestically against its backdrop. Trees are scattered around the edge of the loch. It's gorgeous. Postcard worthy. Instagrammable. It's not just that, though. It's hard to describe, but Skye seems like extra wild somehow. I've been to the Lake District. I'm not completely unfamiliar with the natural world. But other places seem tame, compared to the wilds of Skye. Like the difference between seeing a tiger in the jungle and seeing one in a zoo.

'I'm more of a city person,' I whisper.

'Yep, me too,' he agrees. 'If it makes you feel better, Noah keeps looking at you,' Seb then mutters out of the side of his mouth.

I immediately swivel my head around to find him. He's talking to Blake and his foster dad. He tilts his head back a little and laughs at something their foster dad says.

'Ah!' I call as my kayak bobs violently.

'Please, be more obvious about it.' Seb steadies my kayak.

'He does not.'

'He does.'

'He's probably worried he'll have to rescue me when I go under.'

'Maybe. We should try to talk to Lola when we can.' Seb glides off, distinctly predatory.

I'll have to leave Lola to him for now, since my own efforts are probably best spent concentrating on not drowning. It's a lot trying to do that, while also taking in what your long-lost birth mum is saying about the local geology at the same time. I think I catch the words 'former glacier', but I can't be sure.

'That's Blà Bheinn,' Lola says, pointing up to her right at one of the taller mountains in the distance. 'Over two thousand feet of climb. But you'll not find a better view on a morning than from the top, 'specially if it's a clear day.'

Oh good, there's my vomit once more.

Noah hangs back again to check that I'm okay, and I have a sinking feeling that he's been dispatched by Lola to keep an eye on the woman straggling along at the back.

Seb is way off the mark about Noah looking at me. And anyway, I'm almost certain that my future husband will be into indoor sports. Colin had a squash buddy.

The only person seemingly having less fun than me is Harper. Every time Blake lifts his arms up like he's having fun, or smiles a big toothy grin, she looks like she wants to murder her foster dad with her bare hands. It's probably a good thing that there's a whole heap of loch between them.

With some effort and a fair bit of splashing, I make my way over to her.

'Everything okay?' I pant, annoyed that all the sponsored exercise I do doesn't seem to have made one iota of difference to my arm strength.

She side eyes me. We're bobbing again and I think Lola is talking about a secret loch somewhere behind a line of trees.

'You look like a drowned rat,' Harper says.

'Trust me, I feel like one.' She gives me a dirty look and paddles away.

'Sorry,' her foster mum, Sharon, I think she's called, mouths to me from the other side of the group. I wave it away because it really doesn't matter. And anyway, I don't want to admit that I'm drawn to Harper's overt hatred of everyone and everything. That would be exceptionally strange, even by my low standards.

We carry on. Lola's predictions that none of us would fall in turn out to be right. Even when I get a precarious wobble going trying to eat my second all-bran breakfast bar, I don't topple over.

I struggle along behind the pack, hearing maybe one word in ten that Lola says about the local area and reminding myself that I'll never have to step foot in a kayak again after today.

I do notice that Lola has spoken to everyone in the group aside from me. That's the sort of thing you notice when you can't stop looking at someone. The whole time, I've been conscious of where she is, looking for some sign that there's common ground between us. Like, does she snort when she laughs sometimes? Or does her fringe have a mind of its own too?

So far, I've got nothing. I mean, Lola has a fringe, a blonde one tinged with grey. But it just sits straight and obedient, a little bit wispy. Nothing at all like the out-of-control frizz magnet that sometimes graces my forehead.

She's chatting now to the middle-aged man who's here with his wife. I know for a fact that she's already spoken to him once, I've seen it. At least Seb has managed to talk to her. I could hear him declaring loudly that we were the foremost personal memoir ghost writing business in the North of England. Which is true. We also happen to be the only personal memoir ghost writing business in the North of England.

'How did it go?' I whisper when he paddles over to me.

'Not sure. She didn't say much. Just went really quiet, actually. But I've planted the seed.'

I'm almost certain this is not what Dad meant when he urged me to get in touch with Lola. But the more I see of her, the more the thought of getting to hear her memoirs without her knowing who I am . . . well, it's starting to appeal. Like, a lot.

The truth of it is that now, I'm more curious than ever about Lola. All those questions I had as a child are back, but the answers I've spent a lifetime telling myself don't make sense anymore. I don't know how to feel about her. And I hate how messy it all is. I don't like mess, as a general rule.

Mercifully, we're almost done. I can see the shore by the hotel up ahead. I power my arms, praying that they don't give out on me now. Not when we're so close to dry land.

'You're really getting into the swing of it all now.' Lola's voice takes me so much by surprise that my kayak rocks dangerously with all of the flailing I've got going on.

She reaches out a hand to steady me and for a moment I'm obsessed with that hand. I want to photograph it and compare it to mine, but later when no one's around to see how weird I'm being.

'Thanks, I've had a really lovely morning.'

I feel very proud of what I consider to be the first sane sentence I've ever muttered to her, but Lola just chuckles, like she knows I'm lying. Which I am. It's been traumatic.

'If you like to read, the hammocks in the garden are a good place to go,' she tells me. How does she know that I like to read? Some weird genetic-based telepathy? Or just the fact that my performance this morning screams 'BOOKWORM'?

'I'm reading a really good book on J. Robert Oppenheimer, actually,' I tell her, and she nods, like this might be something she already knows. 'You know, the guy who invented the atom bomb. They just made a film about him,' I say, thinking please God brain, shut up. 'They think he didn't say the whole "I am death" line after that initial test. It's fascinating.' Lola frowns. 'It's not that I'm, like, into weapons of mass destruction or anything, I'm the opposite, probably a pacifist, to be honest, though who isn't these days?'

I'm out of breath by the time I come up for air. The chances are, if I announced to Lola right now that I'm her daughter, she'd think she made the right call all those years ago.

We aren't moving anymore. We are the only two people floating as everyone else makes their way back to shore.

'I'm a pacifist too,' Lola says. And then she's pushing away with her paddles, leaving me behind. I obviously know that Lola is a pacifist. It's on her Wikipedia page that she protested against the Iraq War. In the grainy photo of her there, one of the last before she disappeared from public life, she's in front of the Washington Monument with a 'choose peace not war' T-shirt that she's wearing as a dress.

She glides smoothly onwards. Did she quit the band to take up kayaking?

Seb circles back for me as everyone else starts to drag their kayaks out of the water.

'What did she say?' he asks quietly, lining up next to me as I begin a slow paddle.

'Nothing important,' I reply, thinking that really, it was a bit of an unusual first proper conversation to have.

# Chapter Five

Having hauled my kayak, which seems seven times heavier than it had been a couple of hours ago, out of the water, I resolve to spend the rest of the afternoon in a hammock with my Oppenheimer book.

'I think I might take a nap,' Seb tells me back at the cottage. 'That drive yesterday killed me. Can you manage a few hours on your own? I want to work on Lola some more tonight.'

'Course.' I wave him off with the calm of a woman who hasn't been having a prolonged breakdown all morning. 'I'm going to do some reading.'

He looks at the massive tome that I have tucked under my arm. And okay, maybe it's not your standard holiday read, but Dad always loved history and he got me into it. Now I can't even see the word Stalin without thinking of him. Plus, it's hard to feel sad or lonely when you remember that there's been billions of humans before you, all going through the same thing. That's what I tell myself anyway.

Seb, having eaten half a cheese sandwich (and complaining loudly about the rye bread, I might add) and chain-smoked three cigarettes, unfurls his bed and lays down to close his eyes.

'Hey, did you notice on the hotel schedule that Lola runs basically every activity, except skydiving?'

I have obviously committed the hotel timetable to memory already. I enjoy the thought that even when we leave, I'll know what Lola is doing at set points in the week. It's creepy yet comforting, like long distance stalking. Anyway, I reply, 'Yeah, I did notice that. Do you think she has any help? Aside from Noah.'

'Doesn't look that way.' Seb's eyes are still shut. 'Must be why this place is a bit of a dump. It's a lot to run on your own.'

'Yeah, it's a pity. It could be amazing, you know, with the scenery and everything.'

'Yep. Still doesn't make sense. If Lola is a total loner and hiding up here, why the fuck does she want to sell her story?'

'No, I know . . . No idea beyond the money. Or the sick thing.'

'I know what I said yesterday.' Seb opens his eyes briefly. 'But she doesn't look sick. Must be the money thing. Either way, should we go to the karaoke tonight?' he says sleepily.

I wrinkle my nose.

But I'm just not ready for the off chance that Lola will sing. Heck, I don't sing. Not since Mum died. It had been a thing we did together, we were in the local choir. And on an evening, we'd play piano and sing. It was as wholesome as it sounds. But ever since she died, I just can't. I can't sing without Mum.

I think I've always been worried that if I sang, I'd like it a little too much. I'd find out that I was like Lola.

And anyway, even if I could sing, I think that really might be a bridge too far, watching Lola do the thing that she loved more than me.

'I don't think I can,' I tell him. 'Can you go on your own?'

He heaves a dramatic sigh.

'I can stick it out for a bit.'

I feel bad. It's not exactly like I'm doing a stellar job of helping Seb lure Lola into signing up for a memoir with us.

'No, it's fine, I'll come. Or actually, no, I don't want to. Or maybe I should. Argh, I don't know.'

'Wow, your ability to spiral is unrivalled. Stop panicking, it's fine,' Seb says. 'Now let me rest.'

'Okay, thank you, thank you. I'll see you later.'

I leave him to nap, heading outside in search of a hammock. It's another hot afternoon and I've unzipped the bottom of my trousers, really living life on the wild side.

I find a hammock in the shade around the perimeter of the gardens and have a good go at getting myself in. It's not pretty. My massive book throws me off balance more than once. A couple of times I manage to get in, only to roll straight out of the other side, landing in the dried dirt. I start to wonder if hammocks are worth the effort it takes to actually get into them. At least no one but the blind chicken is around to watch.

Finally, clutching my book to my chest, I manage to launch myself in and stay there. My bottle of water is still on the floor, but there's no way I can reach it. I resolve to just be thirsty for the afternoon.

I'm facing towards the back of the hotel and for a split second, I'm sure I see some movement in one of the upstairs windows. Probably I did. There are about ten people staying here. But whoever was there didn't linger, which is just as well. I don't really want anyone to witness quite how at odds with everything I am here.

Of course, now *I'm* thinking of how at odds I am.

I just don't fit.

Not in Lola's life then and not in Lola's life now. And it's me, that's the thing. I'm the one who doesn't fit. God, even Seb is better on a kayak than me, it's so patently obvious that I'm the odd one out, the anomaly.

Depressing realizations about my lack of belonging make it hard to concentrate on Oppenheimer, even if it's one of the things I've always liked about history, just how resolutely depressing it is. It's hard to feel bad about things in the here and now when confronted with the past. I mean, annoyed that you're not feeling well? Let me tell you about the Black Death circa 1381. Think our leaders are dodgy? Here's a guy called Pol Pot. It takes serious effort to be miserable about the state of the world now when in lots of ways, we have things so much better than people from the past. Proper mattresses didn't even exist for millennia, people had to sleep on straw.

Maybe humans are just born to suffer.

But actually, this isn't helping. I don't feel better knowing that other people have had it worse than me.

I'm not even pretending to read now. I'm just laid in my hammock, the sky all blurry in front of my eyes.

I feel exhausted again, definitely something about the island air. I close my eyes for a second, ruminating on how we can get Lola to let us write her memoir and when I open them again, two hours have passed.

There's movement to the side of me, Noah walking through the gardens.

He's looking my way, so I close my eyes. I don't know why I do this. But I do. And when I chance opening my eyes again, he's walking away.

Argh, come back, Noah.

'Afternoon!' I call from my hammock.

Noah stops again and comes towards me.

'Hi, Lily, I'm so sorry if I woke you up,' he says. 'I didn't realize you were asleep.'

The patches of red on his tanned cheeks are back.

'I was reading,' I tell him. 'You just saw me in the middle of a long blink.' I do another exaggerated blink for some reason. It feels awkward, laying down while Noah is stood next to my hammock, so with all the grace I can muster (not an awful lot), I roll myself out of it, avoiding sprawling in the dirt at his feet but by the grace of God.

I stand up with my water bottle. 'Thirsty,' I tell him, having a long drink.

Be normal.

'Have you had a nice afternoon?' I ask, my head still fuzzy from the nap. I never nap. I quietly *judge* people who nap. I blame the fresh air.

'Yeah, just got back from a hike.' Noah gestures over to a picnic bench, like he wants us to sit there.

Honestly, how Noah could have been good to go for yet more exercise is beyond me. We literally spent the whole morning moving.

I don't exactly know what's happening, but I follow him over. There's a small tabby cat curled underneath the bench and when we sit down it jumps onto Noah's knee and starts padding. Lucky cat.

The bench, I notice, has a massive hole in the middle of it and the broken wood around it is jagged. It has 'tetanus' written all over it.

'I know I said yesterday, but I really do love your writing.'

'Thanks.' He looks at the ground. 'It's the travelling I want, so much as the writing.'

Not sure why I hadn't realized that Noah would be a travel writer since he wrote actual travel books about Skye. Of course he wouldn't just write about one island. Travel writers really are the cool kids of the writing world. The tattoos, the hair, the shy sex appeal.

'Wow, how amazing. You must have been all over.'

'Pretty much,' he agrees. 'I love being away. But I always come and stay with Lola if I'm in Scotland. I'm doing another piece on Skye for Lonely Planet.'

'I'm surprised there's anything left for you to write about here, you've done so much already.'

'Ah, the island has a lot of secrets. Lola knows that as much as I do.'

I don't want to ask how he knows Lola, it seems strangely personal. And I also don't want to admit that I find holidays to be peak stress. I can't imagine going on holiday for a living. I'd absolutely hate it.

'I'm a writer too,' I tell him instead. He probably already knows this. Chances are no one at kayaking missed Seb talking about our jobs. But Noah plays along.

'No way, what do you write?'

'Personal memoirs. Say if someone wants their history writing down, that's what me and Seb do.'

'That sounds really interesting. It's so cool that you work with your brother.'

Yes. Right. Everyone here thinks that Seb is my twin brother.

'Yeah, it's great.' I've started to sweat again. I wish my neck fan wasn't broken. 'We're good friends. What's your piece on?'

'Those secrets I was telling you about. Hidden Skye.' He reels off what must be the title of his article.

'That's exciting,' I answer.

'Yeah,' he agrees. 'Though I grew up here, so it's hard to see it through the eyes of someone visiting for the first time.'

'That makes sense. I've never been before. I've been to Scotland, I mean, to Edinburgh a couple of times. It feels starker here, more remote.'

Noah looks at me for a second and then nods. 'That's why I love it here. Lola too.'

I can't think of anything to say to that. Maybe *that's* why Lola never got in touch. Because she liked it out here too much.

'Look.' Noah's voice, all deep and manly, pulls me out of my depressing spiral. 'Tell me to get lost if you like, but do you fancy coming on a hike with me in the morning? I don't know if you heard Lola say that Blà Bheinn has amazing views. I'm going to go first thing. It's one of my top five and I'd really appreciate your take on it as someone who's never been before and a fellow writer.' The red on his cheeks is back with an absolute vengeance.

I look at the mountain Lola had pointed out on the loch. Looks high.

I'm momentarily stunned. Obviously, Noah hasn't asked me out in a girlfriend/boyfriend type way. Even if he had, I'm only here for two more nights so at most we'd manage a quick kiss.

My tongue seems wholly on board with that idea. It's like it's trying to leap out of my mouth and down Noah's throat rather than helping me to form actual words.

'Seb could come too, if you'd feel more comfortable that way.' He puts his hands on his knees and then takes them off again. I think he might be fidgeting.

This is very interesting. Very interesting indeed.

I haven't said anything in too long.

'I'd actually really like that. Not Seb coming, he doesn't have the lung capacity for a mountain, but I'd be happy to help with your research. Thank you for asking me.'

He smiles. What a smile. Think peak David Beckham. 'No problem. I'd better go and have a shower, but I could knock for you in the morning. Is eight okay? It's a bit of a pull up there.'

Walking is not kayaking, I tell myself. I can definitely walk. Maybe there's still a chance I can impress Noah with my athleticism.

'No problem, great. I love a challenge. Anything in the name of adventure. And eight is perfect, I'll be ready then.'

'See you, Lily.'

'Bye.'

I wait a respectable five minutes to give him time to get back to his cottage before I hurry back to tell Seb of the latest development.

'And I said anything in the name of adventure!'

'And what did he say?' Seb asks. We're sat next to each other on the sofa bed, an open packet of seaweed thins between us, though I'm pretty sure that I'm the only person eating them.

'I don't know. Everything went hazy after I said that I love adventure.'

Seb cackles. 'Lily Brown, you're a liar!'

Possibly it's true. And a compulsive one at that.

'I know. He's just so handsome, it muddles my brain! But it's not okay to lie to Noah, is it? It's not like Lola, he didn't dump me in a bin as a baby.' Did I mention that there's an open bottle of wine between us?

'No one dumped you in a bin.'

I have another gulp of wine and a thin.

'Should I cancel on him? It's not like he asked me out, he wants help with his article. And we're only here for … ' I count on my fingers ' … two more nights.'

'Please, he definitely asked you out. The article thing was just his in.'

'You think?' I say, not bothering to hide the hopeful edge to my redundant question.

'I told you I kept catching him looking your way when he thought you couldn't see. I was watching him the whole time because, you know, biceps. Men like him really go for the preppy librarian thing. He's all strong and silent like the mountains – god, my mastery of the English language is wasted on memoirs! You're prissy and uptight. He's going to ruffle you up big time.'

There's potentially something pretty fucked up about getting ruffled when you're meant to be getting to know your long-lost birth mum. Potentially.

'I don't know if I want to be ruffled up.'

'When he looks like that, who the fuck cares? We're only here for another night after tonight, I say have some fun. You can get back to finding Mr Sensible and Boring once we're home. You know what they say about the Isle of Skye?'

I've had a fair bit of wine, but I don't think they particularly do say anything about Skye. Not in the same way that they do about somewhere like Vegas.

'What do they say?' I ask, as Seb tops up my wine again.

'The people here are proper horny. It's because of their primitive lifestyles. They get bored, so they shag all the time. That's why men don't wear anything under their kilts.'

'That . . . cannot be true.' I laugh.

From somewhere down the side of a sofa bed cushion, Seb's phone vibrates. He fumbles around for it.

'It's Kitty,' he tells me, unlocking the screen.

'On a weekend?'

'Literary agents never sleep. They're a different breed, honestly. Fuck.'

'What is it?'

Seb shows me the message.

> **Kitty:** Just heard that the deal we definitely didn't discuss this week is off. Client has pulled it apparently.

In the distance, the karaoke starts up. The music is faint, we can only hear the beat, but I have to resist the urge to hide under the sofa at the thought of Lola over there.

'Shit,' I say. 'If we don't get Lola's memoirs, all that kayaking will have been for nothing.'

I feel like it's helpful for us to maintain that we're here for the business and the business alone. Feels less complicated than any other motivations that we could possibly have. Like finally getting to the end of Dad's death admin list. Or seeing Lola in the flesh for the first time in thirty years.

Seb is frowning at his phone.

'Maybe I came on too strong earlier. I should have realized she was jumpier than I expected.'

'Nooo,' I tell him, even though he was laying it on a bit thick. 'You're brilliant at getting clients. What should we do?'

'I don't think we should give up. It would be a brilliant memoir.'

I do a nervous laugh. The thought of Lola having it all written down, even if we're the ones writing it, is terrifying.

'Noah might tell me more about her. She's definitely . . . different to what I expected. Or, I know, he might help us persuade her even!'

'It's not a bad idea. I'll try again tonight. Take a more softly, softly approach. She can't know that Kitty would message me. Speaking of which, I'd better go. Time and tide, or Lola's Saturday night karaoke at least, wait for no man.'

'Have fun touting for business with my birth mum!' I call as he gets up from the creaking couch. 'Hey, at least this means that Lola probably isn't riddled with cancer, if she's changed her mind.' It's a faint silver lining to the thought that we might have driven all this way for nothing, but it's a silver lining, nonetheless.

Seb rolls his eyes.

'I'll see you later, sister dearest.'

'Knock 'em dead,' I answer. 'Not actually dead, though. You know what I mean.'

Seb, halfway out of the door, turns back and looks at me.

'Wow, every moment of the day really is a trauma for you, isn't it?'

And you know what, he's not wrong.

With Seb gone, the small cottage feels distinctly empty. Still in a way that suggests I get to be alone with my thoughts when I'd really rather not be alone with my thoughts. They're all jumbled up and messy, and like I said already, I hate mess.

I turn on my laptop, thinking that only *Gossip Girl* can save me now, but instead of loading up Prime, I'm Googling Lola Starr again, thinking that there has to be something I missed. Something that explains how this Lola is *the* Lola.

There's nothing.

It's just the same articles I've read a thousand times already. Reams and reams of them. I've read them all. The newest ones all wonder where Lola the party girl went. Join the club.

It occurs to me then, that I *do* now know more than I did all of the other times I searched for her.

Excited, and wondering why I didn't think of this already, my fingers fly across the keyboard. *Lola Vain*, I type, *Broadford, Skye.*

There are fewer hits this time, only three, in fact, that look relevant. But still, three new articles! I'm giddy with excitement.

They're all from the local newspaper, *The Broadford Echo*, about the hotel. One, from 1994, saying that Lola is the new owner. There's a short Q and A with her where she says that animals and the outdoors are her passions, alongside music. It uses the word nurturing, which is a real kick in the teeth. But onwards I go. Another short piece says that she'd had planning permission to build a barn in the gardens. I guess she never got round to it.

The third article is about a midsummer fête in the town. There are pictures, people! It's from seven years ago and Lola is there, her hair and her dungarees, and nothing has changed. Except she's smiling in both the pictures she's in. In the first one, she's dancing around a maypole, a flower in her hair. In another, she's standing next to a man. He's much taller than her, wiry with dark hair streaked with silver. I read the caption underneath: *Local business owners Lola Starr (Broadford Hotel) and James Duncan (vet) smile under the midsummer sun.*

And Lola is smiling. I'm not sure I've seen her smile like that in any picture I've ever seen. All unguarded. She looks happy.

I'm more confused than ever. I think all of this time, I assumed that giving me up, whatever her motivations were, made Lola sad. But perhaps it really didn't. Maybe it's straightforward. She had a baby she didn't want, so she gave me up and moved on with her life.

And that realization . . . well, not even *Gossip Girl* and wine can save me from that.

# Chapter Six

*Tap tap tap*

  *Tap tap tap*

'Lily, there's a Viking here for you.'

I wake up with a start to Seb's voice on the other side of the bedroom door and attempt to launch myself out of bed. I hate the feeling of being asleep when I should be awake. My stomach rolls, whether from the booze or the misery or the feeling that I've over-slept, I don't know.

Why does this keep happening here?

The process of launching doesn't quite go to plan. Mainly because I was face down horizontal on the bed and so all I manage is to roll myself up in the duvet and knock the bedside lamp off the little table with my foot.

'What the fuck are you doing in there?' Seb sounds rough.

Last night comes back to me in horrifying increments.

Thinking about Noah and wondering whether people who herald from Skye are extra horny.

Googling Lola.

Laughing loudly, *really* loudly, at *Gossip Girl*.

Seb coming back and saying that Lola had avoided him all evening.

Announcing that Lola didn't love me.

I think there was weeping after that. So much weeping.

Seb whacks the bedroom door.

'Lily? What should I do about the Viking?'

I scramble around, pulling on clothes, and push past Seb. 'Morning!' I pull open the patio doors to find Noah on the other side of them looking as calm and collected as an FBI agent. I hold up one finger.

'Just give me a few minutes and I'll be ready for alllll the hiking.' I aim for chirpy and come off deranged.

A pause. The guy looks fresh as a daisy. And he's smirking a tiny bit. It's disarmingly sexy.

'Are you sure?' Another smirk.

'Just give me a minute,' I say through a gritted smile.

'Do you want to come and get me, when you're ready?' he asks. 'I'll wait in my cottage.'

I only have my head poked out through the door.

'Perfect, won't be two ticks.'

I shut the door in his face before he has chance to reply, rounding on Seb.

'Why did you let me have so much wine?!' I ask him.

'It was you.' He's rubbing his forehead with his hands. 'It was all the crying you were doing. Just tell him you can't go.'

'You're the one who kept telling me to climb him last night! No, I'm going. I'm going to ask him about Lola. It took us eight hours to get here. This trip cannot be a waste of time!'

Hangovers make me prone to hysteria.

But I'm determined. I will hike up that mountain this morning if it kills me.

I throw back two paracetamol and glug water like I've been trekking through the desert for days and just happened upon a watering hole.

I gather up my walking gear. Some sick comes up when I bend to pull fresh socks out of my suitcase and I have to pause a second, one hand on the edge of the bed until it passes.

I make my way to the bathroom and chew on my toothbrush.

As per my rota, technically, it's hair wash day. I in no way have the strength for that, so I just go overboard with the dry shampoo. I'm basically held together by the stuff when I emerge back into the living area.

Seb has laid down again. 'Don't hurry back,' he mutters as I pass.

I've taken max five minutes to get sorted, but I feel awful for being late for my hike with Noah as I knock on the door to his cottage.

'Good morning,' he says, brightly. 'How's the head?'

Noah must have some dark tendencies, because he's clearly enjoying this. He's happy that I'm suffering.

I open my mouth, hopefully to bring him down a peg or two with some quick wit, or else to puke on him, I can't quite be sure.

'We missed you at karaoke.' He smiles, stepping aside so I can follow him into his cottage. 'Seb was pretty into it.'

'Wait, what exactly did he sing?' I ask.

'Just a couple of Queen songs,' he says. 'It was good fun.'

'It's Freddie Mercury,' I rush out. 'He gets really emotional at "Rocket Ship".'

'Yeah, there was some crying.'

Noah smiles again and moves further into his cottage.

I follow him, realizing that it's almost identical to ours. He doesn't have a sofa bed taking up most of the living space, though, so it's all very neat. There's a small pile of notebooks with Post-it note tabs on his glass coffee table. They look like they might be colour coded. Well, that's hot.

'Do you write by hand?' I ask him, eyeing the notebooks, hovering just inside his doorway.

'Initially, yeah,' he tells me. 'It's just easier than carrying a laptop or whatever all the time. Plus, I like notebooks.'

'Oh my god, me too. They have a stationery expo in Manchester every year. I'm pretty sure that's what heaven looks like.'

'I'll have to check it out. Do you want a coffee before we go? There's still some in the pot.'

Stationery and coffee. At this point it's a miracle that I don't just turn into that meme which says, 'and then she was pregnant'.

'Please.' It comes out like a beg.

I scuttle across to the coffee, taking up his offer of a cup and then, when he nudges a jug of milk and a bag of sugar towards me, I think sod it, adding a ton of milk and way too much sugar. This weekend has already thrown all my carefully laid nutritional plans out of the window. I'll be able to get back to my nice, ordered existence once I leave. I drink the coffee like it's the elixir of life and then pour another cup. I'm halfway through draining it when I remember that Noah's impression of me won't be helped by my having to go for a nature wee up the side of a mountain.

With regret, I pour away the last half.

'Oooh, is that more of your books!' I notice a couple of paperbacks stacked against the other side of the kitchen countertops. There's a picture of a snow-capped mountain on the one at the front.

Noah groans. 'I should have hidden them. But yeah, they're mine.'

'Wow, that's seriously cool. Can I have a look?'

'If you want.'

I ignore his attempts to be self-deprecating. There's no getting that past me, I'm the master of it.

This one is called, *Discovering New Zealand*.

'How long were you in New Zealand for?' I ask.

'A year in the end. I got stuck there through the pandemic.'

'Shit, no way!'

He lifts his shoulders. 'There are worse places to be stranded.'

I think of New Zealand on a map, floating all alone in the middle of the vast ocean. Plus, aren't there like a ton of volcanoes there? I can think of better places, I won't lie.

My phone buzzes in my pocket. I smile at what I see, putting the book down but thinking that as soon as I'm back later, I am downloading that bad boy.

'Good news?' Noah asks.

I show Noah the picture from Mr Cains. It's of Elton out for his morning walk.

'Is it normal to walk a cat?' Noah asks after a pause.

I heart the message. 'He has a special lead. Elton has a problem with his thyroid that makes him prone to weight gain.' I repeat what the vet had said to me. They'd seemed really sad about Elton and his thyroid problem. And then they'd handed over a bill for £800. 'He hardly ever lets me walk him, though,' I tell Noah. 'He hates the leash. But he has to wear it because he's a bit deaf – if he runs off, he's a total goner.'

I can tell that Noah is thinking that with all his health problems, it is probably no bad thing that poor old Elton might not be around much longer, but at least he doesn't say so.

I notice, unhelpfully, that I have eighteen unread WhatsApps. Always so many. Now generally, I pride myself on being a fastidious replier. Need some dates for when we can meet up? Just give me two ticks and I'll send you ten. Want paying for the joint new baby present we're buying, I'm all over it. Normally, I get a real thrill from being so good at friendships like that. But now, I just feel drained. Like there's nothing left. And the ten pictures from the hen do I missed are liable to make me feel more guilty than anything else.

I vow to set aside time this afternoon for replying. I can't let my entire life go to shit just because of one incognito mini-break to visit the woman who birthed me.

'Are you ready?' I ask Noah, thinking that it's now or never.

'I've been awake for two hours, I feel pretty strong,' he says smugly, stretching his arms out over his head and revealing a few inches of tanned stomach as his T-shirt rides up.

Not today, Satan.

'Come on then, let's go,' I say with far more enthusiasm than I feel. I've done extreme sporting challenges, I did that marathon yoga thing. I know it's about your mindset more than anything. With the right mindset, you can do more than you ever thought you could. There is still time to turn this weekend around. Maybe Noah will tell me something about Lola that doesn't make my heart hurt. I can do this.

* * *

There is grass *everywhere*.

I know what you're thinking. It's a mountain, of course there's grass. Grass is a fairly innocuous part of the natural world. But see, it's not just any grass, it's not regular grass, it's super long spindly grass that keeps wrapping itself around my feet and making me trip over. I read once how long grass is the preferred environment of the tick. Harbinger of Lyme's Disease. So not only is this long grass really annoying, it's also potentially dangerous.

Noah asked whether I was okay to take the 'adventurous route' up the mountain, which he described as much quicker. Quicker sounded good but it doesn't seem to involve a path. No, we'd gone straight past the nice, winding path that weaved up the side of the mountain. Instead, we're basically crawling up the face of it.

This is what I get for saying that I'm up for an adventure. I'm suffering karma for my lie. I should have said no. I don't like adventure. If anything, I'm anti-adventure. I'm a play it as safe as possible-er. But then I'd remembered the kayaking and that he'd had to wait while I drank all his coffee. Plus, the fact that he's asked me to come with him even though I'm quite clearly a liability in this environment.

My Fitbit tells me we've done 16,000 steps already and we're not even at the top. We're trying our best to make small talk as we breathe heavily and continue to scale the mountain. Needless to say, I haven't exactly asked him about Lola. My thighs are screaming and I'm trying to ration my water to avoid an adventurous pee, but really, I want to douse myself in the stuff. The only good thing is that we're walking up the side that's in the shade. I think if we were on the sunny side, I'd just lay down and die.

I try to take in our surroundings as much as possible. Not because it's beautiful and I want to appreciate nature's majesty. No, because I want to be able to relay as clearly as possible my location when I inevitably call Mountain Rescue and wait for them to helicopter me back down to ground level. They'll probably wonder what the hell we're doing clambering up the face of the mountain when there's a perfectly good path to the side.

As it is, I'd say we're about three quarters of the way up. It's very high. Like seriously high. I feel like I should be wearing some sort of harness. The loch stretches out in the valley bottom behind us, the water almost black from this vantage point, and the trees around the edges are like little toy figures.

'Not much further.' Even Noah is breathing heavily. He wipes his forearm across his head and then has a drink from the metal flask that he has in his backpack. I'm holding the bottom part of my trousers in my hand.

Noah is managing to be significantly more upright than I am, and Seb was right. I catch him watching me a couple of times. I'd be pretty pleased about this if I wasn't so intently focused on maintaining three points of contact with the mountain at all times. I have both feet and a hand touching it. If this gets any steeper, I'll need to crawl.

'It's just a bit of a scramble to get to the top,' he tells me, re-screwing the top on the water.

I've not been letting myself look up. Because the one time I did, about two hours ago, I realized that we were closer to the bottom than the top and it had taken me a good ten minutes to recover from the fact.

But now I do look up. I'm pleased that the stupidly long and grabby grass seems to be coming to an end, but I'm dismayed to discover that it looks like it's about to be replaced with a load of massive boulders, boulders that I'm meant to somehow climb over. And fucking hell, is that snow? Do I need an oxygen mask?

'I'll help, don't worry,' Noah adds, clocking my expression. Because it goes without saying that I've not exactly blown him away with my athleticism this morning. The bit where I had to stop to dry heave by a bunch of pissed off looking sheep was a particular low point.

'It's just really high, isn't it?' I peer behind me down to the loch, almost immediately realizing that I've made a mistake. Heights and hangovers are no match made in heaven.

'Well, it *is* a mountain.'

'I know, I just didn't think that it would be *that* high. It's not the Himalayas, is it? Though obviously, I'm having a lovely time.' I try to smile. If I was here with Seb, we'd have killed each other by now. But getting to watch Noah's muscles bunch as he climbs is perhaps the only positive to this walk. Plus, I can't moan too much lest I become an inconvenience to Noah. Being an inconvenience is the stuff my nightmares are made of.

In the end, the boulders turn out to be more distracting than the grass. There's a hairy moment, when I almost lose my footing, and it turns out, when you're sure that you're about to fall to your death in the loch that you suspected would get you in the end, you forget all about the hangover pounding behind your eyes.

'I've got you.' Noah's hands are on my waist. They're big and firm and I could just rest here a second. Seb was right, he is like a mountain. So steady.

They're still there. Warm, as if they're burning a path through my clothes.

His eyes meet mine.

The jolt of *something* that I feel is so intense that I pull away. It's alien to me, jolts of things when it comes to men.

Jesus. I can't go lusting after Noah. He's Lola's pal and I'm her secret daughter. I'm lying to her and trying to kind of exploit her just a tiny bit.

I'm lying to him at the same time.

Well, there goes the lust.

Noah's turned away from me. Probably he just doesn't want to carry me the rest of the way. 'The top is just over this one,' he tells me.

One final scramble and mercifully the ground underneath my hands and knees is flat. Beautifully, wonderfully flat. I just stare at it where my head hangs between my arms for a second. Okay, maybe more like several minutes.

'Lily, look at this.'

I lean back on my knees and blow up to my fringe, which not for the first time in its troubled existence has decided to plaster itself to my forehead. I look up and oh my goodness, it really is something up here. There are mountains everywhere, mist swirling around their summits. The sun is out and you can see for miles in every direction. The ocean, the mountains . . .

I'm still on my knees and now I have the ridiculous urge to cry. Maybe I could pass it off as relief at having summitted an actual mountain. It's just that looking out like that, across the other mountains on one side and the ocean on the other, it's all so vast. And how are we meant to control very much of anything in the face of so much vastness?

Noah's hand lands on my shoulder.

'Do you need a hand up?' he asks.

I nod, still not trusting myself to speak, and then his hand is in mine, and I'm being pulled up and we're so close I can feel his breath on my forehead. 'Come on, let's go and sit on the other side,' he says.

I follow him and we sit on the side of the mountain that's in the sun, because now that we've stopped moving, I feel the chill in the air ever more keenly.

'It's so beautiful here,' I tell him. 'You should definitely include it in your top five ... Just tell people to take the path.'

He laughs. 'I forgot how much of a pull it is up. Worth it once you're here, though. It's one of my favourite spots,' he says.

'It really is lovely ... and a bit humbling.' God, I can't get emotional now, Noah will think I'm certifiable.

He nods, still looking out. 'That's what I like too. The world is so big, nothing we do really matters when you think about it.'

I agree with the sentiment, I just don't like to confront the reality that what we do doesn't count.

'Have you always been a travel writer?' I ask him.

'Pretty much. I was never very good at staying in one place. How about you?'

'Oh, I love staying in one place. I hate the thought of having no roots. It's a big deal for me, to leave home.'

Noah looks my way and then laughs, his head between his arms where they're resting on his knees.

'I meant about being a memoirs writer.'

'Right, course you did, not the roots thing.' I can feel my face heating up. 'But yes, I've always worked at Your Life. I love it, actually. I find people so interesting.'

'I find them a bit scary. Prefer a good tree.'

I burst out laughing at that, but seriously, just when he couldn't get any sexier, he throws out there that he's a bit shy.

After that, we sit quietly for a while, enjoying being the only people up here, while I process all the things I've learned about Noah.

I mean, even without the lying thing, he is absolutely awful for me. In every way. Which makes the pull I feel towards him even more inexplicable.

That's not why I'm here, though. I think of my Google search last night.

'Have you known Lola a long time?' I ask, venturing into dangerous territory.

Noah nods. 'Since I was eighteen. I, er, got into a bit of trouble and she helped me get sorted. She's really special.'

Oh.

'And how old are you?' I ask, as casually as I can muster.

'Thirty, why?'

'No reason.' I shrug while really, my mind is whirling. Lola was being all nice to Noah around the time she called Dad to ask to talk to me, then. I don't know how to process that information, or to reconcile Noah saying that Lola is amazing when she's been anything but to me.

Anger lights up inside of me.

'Between you and me—' Noah leans towards me '—I've got a bit of an ulterior motive for staying the whole summer.'

'You do?' I ask, thinking that Skye must be synonymous with ulterior motives.

'Yeah, you've probably noticed that the hotel is a little . . . er . . . '

I presume Noah is digging around for a polite way to say dump.

'It has a sort of charm to it,' I answer.

'Aye, it does that. But Lola, she won't ask for any help. Tries to do it all on her own and I thought I'd try to fix the place up, without telling her, like. She's so stubborn.'

Noah laughs like this is a good thing.

'That's really kind, Noah,' I tell him, meaning it.

It looks like Noah is going to say more, but then his eyes flick to behind me, surprise registering in them.

'Lola,' he says.

'What about her?' My brain is scrambled from his revelation.

'She's here.'

103

'Where?'

I don't even have time to school my reaction properly as I twist around.

'Lola,' I say, sounding more winded from the sight of her than the climb up the mountain. 'What are you doing here?'

# Chapter Seven

There's an awkwardness as the three of us stand motionless, staring at each other. Lola's wearing a floaty white shirt, with leggings that have giant sunflowers all over them. They're the sort of clothes that you can't help but admire someone being brave enough to wear.

I go to say something, anything vaguely normal to my birth mother, at the same time that Lola tries to talk.

'Y'all came,' she tells us, looking out at the view. Which is stating the very obvious. Maybe oxygen really is in short supply up here.

'We did. And you were right, the view is amazing. I was just thinking about how meaningless life is in the face of it, actually.'

What am I saying? Noah laughs, while Lola twists to look at me. Her eyes are such a deep, dark blue.

'You know, I think I agree.' She takes a deep breath and then turns her face to the sun.

We're all so still. Like no one wants to shatter whatever is happening up here on the top of the mountain. I have to remind myself that I'm still angry from everything I've learned in the last eighteen hours.

We know that Lola loves it up here, she was the one who told us about it. And now here she is interrupting what could have been a useful bit of intel gathering.

I swallow down the irritation with well-practised ease, fixing a smile on my face.

'It's really beautiful,' I say, only having to work a little at keeping my voice even.

Lola looks at me. 'I can show y'all the way down if you like?'

I mean, the path is right there. And I have every intention of using it. No more long grass for me.

And there's no good way to tell someone that you want to walk down the only path in existence separately because, actually, you're their daughter and being in their company makes you question everything about who you think you are. That's a bit much on any day of the week, let alone a Sunday morning with a hangover.

Instead, I just say, 'Sure, that would be nice, thanks,' and then when Lola asks if we're done and we assure her we are, we're following her across the summit to the path and setting off down it.

The whole thing is very, very strange. I have a ridiculous urge to lean on Noah. Or hold his hand. But as it is I need to put both my arms out to help my balance down the steep path, which isn't as sturdy as I thought it might be on account of the fact that several of the stones are loose. I'm having to concentrate hard, which does at least take my mind off the whole Lola thing.

Lola and Noah are not, incidentally, walking with their arms out. They're as sure-footed as mountain goats.

'Seb was telling me about your work, Lily, it sounds mighty interesting,' Lola says, actually jumping over a gap in the path.

Noah helps me over with a hand and I mouth a 'thank you' to him. I remember Kitty's message, saying that Lola had pulled the memoirs idea and wonder why she's bringing it up again now.

Still, I'm not daft enough to look a gift horse in the mouth. I don't have Seb's pitching skills, but I know I need to give this my best shot.

'Oh,' I say, not particularly adept at talking and walking. 'Yeah, the personal memoirs business we run, er, together. I really love it. It's a ... um ... real privilege. Having people tell you their story.'

Like I said, my 'bringing in new clients' spiel is not half as polished as Seb's.

I need to get my shit together.

'There's just something really special about it. There's always something we don't know about a person. Like, however well we think we know our family, we can't know or remember all of it. But it's there, recorded for whoever they want to know their story,' I say.

Lola is looking at me. I think I have her attention. I plough on.

'We started the company with hardly any money,' I clarify. 'Seb's great-granny – our great-granny – escaped Nazi Germany, while half of her family were killed in the Holocaust. It's an amazing story, you know? We do ghost-writing too. I tend to take the lead on those and they end up being properly published. But even the more ordinary ones are cool to do. The ones that are only ever for families. I love old people.'

'It's good, to find work that you love.'

Hopefully, I'm at least earnest. I nod. 'I really do. It's special, getting to hear about someone's life and giving them the chance to control how their story is told. I like that once it's written, it's always there. Plus, you hear a lot of the same things, it's . . . comforting, I guess. Thinking that we're all in this together.'

It sounds like a sales pitch, and really, it is a sales pitch, but it's all the truth. Every single word that I'm saying. I love my job.

Lola is looking at me and I think I might have her. The thought thrills and terrifies me in equal measure.

I try an encouraging smile, trip and fall over.

The wilderness hates me.

When I'm righted again, the moment has passed, and I don't know how to get it back. Lola asks where I went to university (Manchester), and where my parents live. I get all tight around my ribs when I mumble Manchester, because I'm not about to tell her or Noah that my parents are dead.

Hopefully they'd understand – my parents, I mean. They always understood. And anyway, I'm here because Dad wanted me to be. I'm doing what he asked. Sort of. He didn't mention using Lola to save the business, but still.

Lola seems to relax after that. She keeps talking all the way down the mountain, becoming more animated, waving her arms around and bobbing up and down with energy.

I can see it, then, lurking beneath the surface. Lola the star. The Lola people gravitated to and wanted to be around. She's warm, fun, interested.

It's nothing short of a miracle that she hasn't been figured out by now. Maybe it's just that no one would dream that Lola Starr would be someone whose choice of footwear seems to be Crocs with socks. Even I don't wear Crocs with socks and I'm patently uncool.

She asks if I have a partner and my eyes dart to Noah before I admit that no, Colin and I broke up nine months ago.

She tells me I'm young, that if I ever want to find someone, I have my whole life ahead of me.

It's not how I see myself at all. I feel older than I am, if anything. Not in the sense that I'm an old soul (though I'm probably one of those too), more just that I feel worn out. Ground down by it all sometimes.

Underfoot, the ground starts to level out. I don't have my arms out anymore because the path here is less treacherous. None of these things make me as happy as they should do.

I don't know if I've done enough to get Lola to change her mind. And time is running out. We're leaving tomorrow.

The thought makes me walk even slower, and I stop completely when Lola starts talking about the biodiversity of the region. Never in my life have I been so interested in heather. Don't get me wrong, I like heather, it's all nice and purple. But now, I'm obsessed. I hang off every word that Lola says about the stuff because she's obviously so caught up with it all. She's talking faster than I've heard her, her accent getting stronger and stronger.

'The bees like it real nice,' she finishes.

'Who doesn't love bees? Better than wasps anyway.'

'You know,' Lola says, 'wasps only get aggressive when their queen makes them redundant. They don't do so well, without a purpose.'

And of course, Lola is a fan of the wasp. Though maybe I have more in common with them than I realized.

Talking and walking are two skills which when attempted in combination are apparently beyond me. I stumble constantly over loose stones, only managing to avoid landing flat on my face again by Noah's hand on my shoulder. Lovely hand. When I look up, both he and Lola are looking at me, their heads tilted to opposite sides as if in a mirror.

I carry on walking to break the strange tension I sense. And trust me, I can spot tension a mile off.

Though out here, I'm not sure I trust my senses. Noah and Lola follow behind, chatting normally again, so maybe I imagined it all.

When we emerge onto the road leading back to the hotel, I'm not at all sure how I feel about the walk ending.

Should I mention the business again? It's a fine line. If we go too heavy, we'll give ourselves away.

I swear, it's like someone stuck my brain in a tumble dryer and set it on spin.

Lola follows us all the way through the gardens. She's moved onto talking about the hotel now. How she wants to do it up properly, grow the business. About how there aren't enough hours in the day for everything that she wants to do. How she needs a magic money tree. I wonder if Lola had some sort of catastrophic brain injury after she quit the band and gained a whole new personality.

We come to a stop just a little way from the cottages.

It's too late.

Lola doesn't want us to write her memoirs.

The business will fail.

I'll never hear her story.

'Listen, Lily, I wanted to ask you something,' Lola says while I spiral. It takes a second for my brain to catch up to the fact that she's addressing me directly. With her accent, she misses the 'g' so it sounds like 'somethin'.'

'Okay,' I reply. The beginnings of panic flutter deep in my chest. Has Lola figured me out? I flip back quickly through the conversation we've just had, thinking about what might have given me away. There's no time for the sort of deep analysis my brain normally excels at, because Lola is still talking.

'You know what you said earlier, about writing personal memoirs and ghost-writing and the like? Well, I wondered . . . I was thinking, see . . . ' She takes a deep breath. ' . . . that maybe y'all would want to write mine.'

Noah and I just stand there. He's probably letting Lola speak, but I've definitely moved into gawping territory. I . . . just . . . I didn't think my pitch had worked. And I know that this is exactly why we're here, but I thought our chances of success were low. Like Hades low.

I wonder now if maybe I was using the memoirs thing as an excuse this whole time.

Nope. No. Not helpful.

She's still going. 'It's something of a coincidence, but I was looking for a service like the ones y'all offer. Been thinking about it for a while, if I'm honest. The money, see – I can't lose the hotel. Not ever.'

She's hardly talking in full sentences and she's out of breath, but she's still doing better than me. I'm not talking at all. 'It'll require um . . . delicate handling, the things I've got to say. But if you wanted to stay, I could move some bookings around to free up the cottage for the summer. No charge, of course, while we work on this, but I'd be more than happy for y'all to stay there. Seb too. Noah's here for the six weeks. I think it could be beneficial, financially, I mean, for us all.'

Six weeks.

Lola wants me to stay for six more weeks. Six. Seb too. And Noah will be here.

Oh. My. God.

'That's ... very generous, Lola. We'd ... I'd have to check with Seb. And I wouldn't want you to be out of pocket.' It very much sounds like the hotel finances are in the same state as the rest of the place, so Lola's in no position to be offering a freebie.

Lola waves a hand at me. 'Nonsense.'

'Lola hasn't been so good at remembering to make money from this place,' Noah adds, making them both laugh. I join in, though my laugh sounds forced and loud. So loud.

'I need one of those business plan things y'all keep talking about.'

My brain is short-circuiting, leaving me capable of only one-syllable words.

'Seb, I need to ask Seb,' I say.

I think there's a plan. Maybe a bit of a plan.

'Course, whatever y'all need. I'd need some assurances, before we begin. But we can talk about the finer details later, once y'all have decided.'

I gaze at her some more.

At this stage, the prospect of interviewing Lola seems almost ridiculous. Half the time, I'm rendered mute in her presence.

'Seb,' I force out.

Lola, too, looks like she wants to say more, but I can see something shifting in her, almost like a shadow passing over her face. She's returned to quiet Lola already, the bubbly, chatty version going back into hiding. She nods. 'Y'all know where to find me.'

She turns and leaves, walking back through the gardens to the hotel. It's just me and Noah then.

'Do you think you'll stay?' Noah asks.

'I don't know,' I babble, injecting a potent dose of false cheer into my voice. 'I'm behind on Mr Vandergilden's memoirs and I just don't know if Seb will be able to spare me. Plus, there's Elton, I need to get back for Elton. Cats get separation anxiety too, just like babies. But, well, I mean, I would like to write Lola's memoirs, I think. And it's, you know, money.'

'She's had a pretty interesting life,' Noah replies. 'Hard at times.'

Interesting. I add this information to the box in my brain labelled 'LOLA'.

'But for what it's worth, I'd like you to stay.' Noah doesn't meet my eye and he works his bottom lip between his teeth. I think we're flirting here. And a better woman than I might be able to resist that, you know, because he's an adventurous traveller and I'm about as adventurous as a glow worm.

'You'd like me to stay?' I ask, my brain still tripping over the prospect of writing Lola's memoirs. However, from what I can gather, flirting involves a lot of asking the other person a question you already know the answer to but in a slightly seductive way.

Noah nods, slowly. Peak flirt. 'I really would. You could help me with more of my research.'

Oh. Maybe that's why he wants me to stay. For research not ravishing.

'I'll talk to Seb and come back to you,' I tell Noah, thumbing behind me to my cottage and breaking the maybe-flirt by talking about my fake brother.

'Well, let me know what you decide. I, er, I'm not surprised that Lola asked you to write her memoirs. I mean, I'm surprised that she wants it all written down but not that she asked you. You're really passionate, when you talk about it.'

'I feel passionate about it.' I can't tell if we're veering back into flirting territory and anyway, I need some space. A chance to clear my head. I manage to say 'bye' like a vaguely normal person but then stand and watch as Noah puts his hands in his pockets and walks back to his cottage. Me watching like that is possibly slightly less normal. Taking a deep breath, I pull open the doors to my cottage.

Seb is sat on his bed, the theme tune to *America's Next Top Model* playing out of my laptop. We always turn to nostalgia TV when we're hungover, stressed or in today's case, both.

'Lola wants me to stay and write her memoirs,' I tell him, my back against the doors.

Seb shuts the laptop.

'Ohmygod, you did it!'

'I know.'

'I don't want to be dramatic but ohmygod.'

'*I know.* She wants me to stay for the summer.'

'Ohmygod.'

'I know.'

'You have to stay!' he says. 'I can't believe our evil plan came off!'

'Hang on, is it evil?!' I'm pacing up and down the living area of the little cottage, looking around and trying not to panic. I'm doing a rubbish job of that by the way. 'You never said it was evil. I can't stay! We should do the meetings on Zoom. Same as we do for everyone else. I'm behind on Mr Vandergilden's memoirs – I'm not happy with the chapter on his fourth divorce.'

I'm talking at a hundred miles an hour. 'And the game hunting stuff won't write itself. Plus, Elton needs me, he's probably already wondering where I've gone. I've never left him for this long already! How can I stay?' I'm the human equivalent of an exclamation mark at this point.

'Relax,' Seb says, then laughs as if the idea of me relaxing is completely ridiculous. He's not wrong. 'I'm in the group chat with

Mr Cains. I've seen the pictures. Elton is showing zero trauma from the separation. Seems happier than ever, in fact, and you know Mr Cains loves to have him. He's lonely on his own. They're probably both better off without your whole stressy vibe.'

I purposefully unclench my hands.

'And this isn't any old client,' Seb says, 'this is fucking Lola Starr. You have to stay.'

'But six weeks here.' I try to bring the conversation back to the reasons why me staying is a bad idea. 'I never go on impromptu holidays. I had an itinerary ready for two months before we had that day in London last year.'

Seb taps a finger against his chin.

'The way I see it, it's only six weeks. People survived in the Gulags for decades. And you can come home at any point in that time if it all gets a bit much, right?' I nod, trying not to recall the eight-hour vomit marathon that was my journey here. 'And you'd probably regret it, if you didn't hear her out.' I nod again, knowing that he's right. At some point this weekend, things have changed. I've been confronted with a totally unexpected version of Lola. And I want to know more, because right now, the whole thing is making no sense. 'Plus business,' Seb finishes. 'That's why we came up with this whole evil plan. Okay, she doesn't know who you are, but you get to hear the whole lot and if at the end of it, you like her, you can tell her who you are. If you think she's a bit of a knob, well, then you can slink back off to Manchester and never grace the shores of Skye again.'

'You said evil plan again.' My mind is whirling. Everything Seb has said is right, though. It would give me chance to get to know Lola in a safer way.

'Okay, we should stay,' I tell Seb.

'I mean, *I'm* not staying. I need to get back to the office. I'll come back for you in six weeks.'

'What?!' I almost shout and then remember that Noah could hear us. 'What?!' I ask again as an angry whisper. 'You expect me to stay here on my own? You're abandoning me?'

'It's cute that you think everything is about you. I've spent the whole weekend pretending to be your brother, you've used all your best friend tokens. And anyway, it'll do you good to have some time on your own.'

I disagree with his last point, but he's right. He has gone above and beyond. I close my eyes. 'I don't know if I can do this.'

'I have absolute faith that you can. Now come and tell me about Noah. What did he look like going up the mountain?'

I move to sit next to him on the sofa bed.

'Really fit. He just propelled himself up it with thigh power alone. It's hard to tell, because he gets shy, but I think we're flirting. Like, he said he wanted me to stay. But then he mentioned his research and, I don't know, maybe he really does just want help with his article.'

'You could be an adult about this and ask him.'

'Please, no one does that.'

'True. Just remember, you have more to offer than you give yourself credit for.'

I give Seb a look.

'But when you're at home. Yeah, out here, god knows what he sees. What has happened to your hair?'

I burst out laughing. I look like I've been electrocuted.

'I'm kidding. You're a dark horse and we both know it. Hey, remember when I found those handcuffs in your bedroom drawer.'

I groan. 'We promised never to mention that again! I told you, me and Colin were trying to spice things up.' Not that Colin had been on board with this suggestion, he seemed to think I was some sort of sexual deviant. Needless to say, they haven't seen the light of day since then.

Seb pfts. 'Please, a punnet of Scotch bonnets couldn't make Colin spicy. I bet Noah has his own handcuffs,' Seb ponders aloud. 'Just think of all the no-strings holiday sex you can have over the next six weeks. I'm jealous.'

'I don't think that is what's going to happen.'

'Not if you keep wearing those things on your legs, it won't. Just don't ruin it before it's even gotten started.'

That does sound like something I would do.

For something to do that isn't thinking about Lola or Noah, I pull out my phone, wincing as I realize there's now an angry red thirty-seven next to my WhatsApp. They'll all want something. I just know it. No, that's not fair. It's none of our faults that we're like this. My head is just all over the place.

Get it together, Brown. Okay, won't be calling myself by my surname in my actual head again.

It's just that if I'm really doing this, I need to get on top of my messages and rearrange everything in my diary for the next month and a half.

Six weeks. Do I even have enough stuff with me for six weeks? (Chances are, I brought enough for a six-month expedition.) And there's a washing machine in the hotel. It's on the information sheet with the schedule.

Maybe being here longer term will help me feel a bit more grounded and not in one long out-of-body experience.

'Seriously, you don't have to do it,' Seb says finally, 'but I think it would do you good.'

I get up and walk to the kitchen, just to keep myself busy. I start pulling out more cheese … and extra cheese (I really do need to go to the hotel shop), because after the morning I've had, nothing else will do.

'I think I want to. It's just confusing,' I answer honestly. 'I don't know how to feel. I built Lola up as this monster, almost, in my head. Like, who abandons a baby for fame? But now she's here, decidedly not famous, probably a bit poor, and I wonder if I've got it all wrong.'

Seb hums but doesn't say anything. I'm slicing brie with such concentration, Heston Blumenthal would approve.

'But then the thought of going over it all,' I carry on, 'because I guess Lola will include the baby she had but didn't want in her story, it's terrifying. What if she says that she had me, took one look and thought, nah, not for me?'

I've stopped slicing now, I'm just gripping my knife, staring down at my white knuckles.

Mum and Dad used to say that it was okay to be angry about the whole adopted thing. I always tried *not* to be angry, though. Because it wouldn't have felt fair, to be angry that I got a life with them. So as a rule, I'm the opposite of angry. I'm no trouble ever. I smile even when I don't feel like smiling.

And deep down I'm worried that this time with Lola might change that. I already feel like my control is slipping. It's the wildness of it here on Skye, it's taking me apart piece by piece.

I shiver, goose bumps working their way along my arm.

'I have always wondered why she left the band. It never made any sense why she left six months after she had me if it wasn't *for* me,' I say.

Seb stays quiet.

'I'm going to do it,' I tell Seb.

'For what it's worth, I think you're making the right call.'

'Thanks, I hope so. Now, I really need some brie.'

# Chapter Eight

*To Do:*

- Start Lola memoirs
- Call Mr Cains
- Stop lying so much
- Food shopping (vegetables!!!)
- Message all WhatsApp groups
- Get on top of emails

This seemed like a much better idea yesterday.

'You're going to be brilliant.'

I think I'm going to be sick.

Seb is in his car; the engine is running and the roof is down. We're saying goodbye. But also, he's not driving off because I'm clutching the door through the open window. I'm not exactly sure what my strategy is. Force him to stay with my brute strength. That seems ridiculous, I could hardly lift a kayak paddle.

'It feels like you're abandoning me.'

'One abandonment and you think everyone's at it.' Behind his (very reflective) sunglasses, I'm certain that he's rolling his eyes. I look around to check that no one has heard the abandonment thing, but the only sign of life is the bald chicken.

Seb puts a hand over mine.

'You can do this.'

'I really can't.'

'You can.'

'Do you think?'

'I know. You've been employee of the year for over a decade.'

'Yeah, but our other employees are Clementine and Phil.' Still, I won't lie, I do love the certificate Seb prints for me every year. 'Argh, I'm going to do it.'

'That's the spirit. Now let go of the car before you change your mind again.'

I reluctantly release my grip.

'And call me every day.' I might be mistaken, but there's a slight hitch to his voice.

'Of course I will.'

'Love you, Lily Brown. Good luck.'

There's a lump in my throat making it impossible to speak.

Instead, I watch Seb do a three-point turn out of the car park ready to make the trek back. I try not to concentrate too hard on the fact that without his car, I'm basically stranded here, eight long hours away from home.

I take a deep breath in and out. Count to five and swallow around the lump as his car disappears through the hotel gates. I offer up a final wave.

Another breath.

My first session with Lola is in ten minutes.

It had all happened so quickly last night.

After I'd decided to stay, Seb had all but shoved me out of the cottage to let Noah and Lola know. I think he was worried that I would back out. It was a good call, I still feel like backing out.

Noah had promised to keep me company and even though he was just being nice and friendly, I still felt hot all over. A state of being that had quickly dissipated once I'd told Lola that Your Life would take her on as a client and that I'd stay for the summer. She'd suggested that we get started right away. As in the next day. As in ten . . . no, wait, five minutes from now.

I'm still breathing deeply and staring at the empty car park where Seb's car has disappeared from.

I need to move. I hate being late and I'm at a real risk of it if I don't move right now. Here I go. Moving right this second.

I take a final, calming deep breath and walk back towards the cottage for my phone. If we're doing the interviews online, I normally just get a transcript of the session, but whenever we get a local client, I use software on my phone to make sure I don't forget anything important.

Harper is in the gardens, by one of the picnic tables. She's holding her phone up to the sky.

'Hi, Harper,' I call to her.

She looks up, squinting her eyes against the sun as she sees me and ignores me.

Well, that's that, then.

Phone in hand, I'm walking through the gardens towards the back of the hotel, breathing in warm summer air. The grass under my feet is patchy, filled with weeds. It looks frazzled. I know how it feels.

Lola and I have agreed to meet in her office, once the breakfast rush is over, though personally, I feel that rush is a stretch. There are, like, eight people staying here.

The hotel isn't big. I find Lola in the dining room, piling empty bowls of porridge on a table. Like all of the rooms, in here, it's mostly wood. The walls are pine, and the floor is stone. There are worn wooden tables in various sizes and Lola has pinned the Scottish flag along one wall, along with a blue flag with a white cross on it that must be that of the Isle of Skye.

Seb and I haven't mixed much with the other guests this weekend, but now that I'm on my own, I'd better make more of an effort to be friendly. I wave hello at a young couple sat nursing cups of tea.

'Hi, Lola,' I say to her back. She stops wiping and turns to face me. 'I'm ready whenever you are.' I smile. See. I am calm, collected. I don't know who I'm trying to convince, but I'm going with it.

'Right-o,' she says, and I get it, she's nervous too. It's normal. Sharing your life story with someone is daunting. This isn't fiction, it's someone's actual life, the only one they get. That's one of the reasons I love this job, it's such a privilege to hear a person's history. She turns to the couple still eating. 'Y'all can just leave those on the side here, I'll get them later.'

'No problem, Lola,' the man says with a Scottish accent.

'Follow me, then,' she says to me. So I do, my own nerves ramping up as I follow her through to the entrance where we arrived on that first night. This time we pass the leaflets and wait outside a door by the entrance while Lola pulls a ring of keys out of her dungarees pocket. Today, she's wearing a tie-dye green and white T-shirt underneath and she has Crocs on her feet.

Lola wiggles a key into the lock and pushes the door with her shoulder.

'After you.' She waves me through.

Lola's office is the tiny office of a woman who is running a ten-bedroom hotel on her own. I think there's a desk under the pile of papers by the small window, but I can't make out any of the actual desk. The ends of my fingers twitch with the urge to sort.

The Labrador is here, sprawled asleep on the floor. Doesn't try to move as we tiptoe around him.

'He sleeps through anything,' Lola tells me and she's right, he doesn't even stir. I didn't expect to be carrying out the interview over a huge furry dog, but there we go.

'It's, er, organized chaos,' Lola says, moving papers off the chair by her desk. 'Heavy on the chaos.'

There's a guitar propped in the corner by the desk and the window, half buried under overhanging papers. My eyes keep darting to it. Over and over. I'm no guitar expert, but it looks old.

Outwardly, however, I am committed to professional indifference and so I stomp down the fact that the universe is presenting me with yet another difference between Lola and me. She is obviously someone who thrives in chaos, and I am just not. Instead, I say, 'It's nice and cosy,' as Lola finally frees the chair from its paper prison. Then she unfolds a small stool from the corner and sits on it.

'You take the chair, please.'

'I don't mind the stool,' I say, blatantly checking out the office. I think there's a long cork board along the wall opposite the door. Like the desk, however, it's been swallowed by a mountain of paperwork. This woman needs a to-do list like humans need oxygen.

'Don't even think about it.' Lola plonks herself down on the stool and I tentatively take the chair. It looks old, with a faded green seat cushion that has a rip across the middle.

'Okay.' I sit down, feeling strange about the height difference between me and Lola. It's almost like I'm a primary school teacher reading to children sat cross-legged on the carpet. Except in this instance the child is actually my mother, and she's wearing dungarees and Crocs. It's a pretty fucked up scenario.

I clear my throat, stalling for time.

I notice that she has a Greenpeace banner across one wall. 'I really care about the environment too,' I blurt out. 'I get these washing tablets delivered. They have, like, fifty per cent less packaging, and I stopped using that facewash with the little beads ages before it was properly banned. You know, the ones that killed the fish. And I was the secretary of the anti-fracking committee for a while.' I babble on, thinking that I really need to stop talking right about now.

'That's good, Lily,' Lola says. She's quiet Lola today. Not cheerful like she was up the mountain. She's pensive and calm. The woman has more layers than an onion.

'So how this normally works,' I say, bringing us back to the task at hand, because I can't think of how to stall anymore; I make a show of placing my phone gently on top of a pile of papers, 'is that I'd ask you to start at the beginning, or wherever you want your story to start. I'll try not to interrupt, unless I need you to clarify something. Mostly, I'll record it all on here.' I gesture to the phone. 'Once we've done all of the interviews, I'll type up my notes and we can start working on forming a draft. I've, er, signed the non-disclosure agreement you emailed over. Seb too. We sent it back to you this morning.'

'I appreciate that, Lily.'

I feel a smidgen of pride at the fact that the plan worked because Lola trusts us.

'I got the contract you signed too.' It had arrived in my inbox at gone midnight last night. When Lola Vain officially became a client of Your Life. The contract states that she pays us a flat fee, plus a cut of whatever book deal she might get. It's a standard contract, but I think Seb's right, this could be the answer to all our problems. So long as nothing goes wrong, that is.

The dog's tail flaps up then down as Lola squirms on her stool. 'I trust y'all to follow the rules.'

'Absolutely. It's all in appendix three of the contract.' I smile, nodding, feeling calmer. Because is there anything better than good appendices? I'd been the only person at Your Life excited about the new privacy legislation. Seb had made me GDPR lead. A promotion that came with zero pay rise, obviously.

And then before I can chicken out, I say, 'Shall we get started, then?'

Lola shuffles again but nods. Quiet Lola makes me a bit nervous.

To distract myself, I press record.

'Try not to worry about it recording,' I tell her. 'Just say whatever feels natural to you. It'll help me get a sense of your style. And don't worry about being too specific, we can go over dates and stuff at the end.'

Lola nods again and then takes a deep breath. Visibly swallows. But then, she begins.

* * *

*My ma said that I was born on the coldest day of the year. Which is saying something. Because down in Greenwell Springs, Louisiana we never got cold weather. But that year, 1974, there was a freak storm. Ma said the walls were rattling with the wind and rain was coming through the windows and she really hoped that I'd stay put a little while longer. 'Cept I didn't. Da was singing, playing his guitar to distract the others when Ma felt the first twinge. Apparently, she knew then that I'd be trouble.*

*'Cause of the storm, the midwife couldn't get to them. Greenwell Springs was a half-hour drive from Baton Rouge, though if anyone ever asked, that's where we always said we were from. No one ever heard of Greenwell Springs, after all.*

*Not that it mattered so much, about the midwife being stuck in the city. Ma had four babies by then, all under six. So, I guess her body just knew what to do. Not even two hours after that first contraction, I was here. Pa said that I screamed so loud that I drowned out the howling wind. Ruined the bedroom rug too. It was Ma's favourite and I'm not sure she ever forgave me for it. For being born in a storm or the rug either. All's I know is that right from the off, I was in the way. Inconvenient.*

*Like I said, I was baby number five. Two more came after. Real quick. All born on bright sunny days like we were used to. There was so many of us, we all got labelled with one thing or another, you know?*

*Stevie was the clever one.*

*Molly was the one who looked after us when Ma and Pa were busy. Everyone said she was the kind one. That's what she got for being the eldest, I suppose.*

*Jessie was the cute one. The baby of the family.*

*And me? I was the difficult one. The one born in a storm.*

*I didn't mean to be a problem. I was always just under Ma's feet, in the way. And if we were all playing, I'd be the one to fall and rip my dress.*

*Pa wasn't around a lot. He was a singer so he went where the work was. Did a few stints in prison too. I sometimes wondered how Ma managed to have so many babies, seeing how much time she spent on her own with us.*

*There were some happy times too, course there was.*

*Ma had this garden at the front of the house that was real beautiful. Pa used to say that she'd grow a flower from a stone given half the chance. Sometimes, she'd let me help her. That's when I didn't feel in the way so much. When me and Ma would plant in the garden together. Growing flowers from tiny little seeds.*

*But it was hard too. I think we all felt like the walls of the house might fall down at any time. It was this rickety old thing. Down a path that got so dusty in the summer. It's not like here, where houses are built of bricks or stone, solid like. The wood was nailed together for a wall, and here and there you could see the outside through it. It had been in Ma's family for decades. They'd been farmers and it was the old farmhouse.*

*Pa was no farmer, though. I reckon Ma's parents thought him a right flighty thing. He had these big ideas about how the world should be, but he never bothered so much with all of us in the farmhouse. The world at home. I know that now, looking back. At the time, I think I blamed Ma for driving him away. For never smiling when he came home and always nagging at him to fix this or to get a proper job. It got to the point where all they did was argue.*

*I guess that's why he started coming home less and less.*

*I think I was about twelve when he stopped coming home at all. He didn't even take his guitar with him. One day he just got up after supper and walked out of the door.*

*Didn't look back.*

\* \* \*

'Do you mind if we stop there?' Lola asks and I jolt.

'Of course.' I reach to turn off the recording, finding it harder than I should to look Lola in the eye.

It's just . . . sad. I'd known that Lola's family were poor, you can find it out on any internet search of her: *'Lola Starr grew up in poverty on the outskirts of Baton Rouge, Louisiana.'* But hearing it brought to life . . . It makes Lola more real than I was prepared for.

'It's nice that you come from a big family,' I say, even though we're not really meant to pass comment on what the clients have revealed. My eyes flicker to the guitar again. I wonder if that was her dad's?

'I don't know, all those little 'uns put me off babies for life.'

It's a throwaway comment, but I feel it sting like a slap to my cheek.

Lola must realize that she's said something to upset me because she says, 'I'm not trying to make anyone feel sorry for me.' I have to look at her, then. She's clasped her hands together, linked her fingers so tightly that her knuckles are pulled taut.

'I know, don't worry,' I say, forcing myself to relax. It's not like I don't already know that she left. It's hardly a surprise to hear that she doesn't like babies. 'This is your story,' I tell Lola, because she still looks troubled, shifting around on her stool, hands still tight. Even the dog seems restless, he's twitching away in his sleep. 'It's your recollections that we're noting down here. We can work it however you want.'

'I want it to be the truth.' She looks at me then with piercing blue eyes. Like she's willing me to believe her.

'The truth,' I agree.

Heck, it's not always the case. Chances are, in most instances, people might tweak things to make themselves look better than they really are. And I get it. Who wants to come across as anything but the hero in their own life story? Even when people say they want the truth, they don't mean it. That's our job. To give people a starring role in their own lives. But something tells me that when Lola says she wants the truth, she means it.

'Well, I'll work on typing this up,' I tell her. 'There should be enough here for a first chapter. If it's okay with you, I'll add some context. Describe Baton Rouge in the seventies, that sort of thing?'

Lola nods, standing up. 'I've got a picture of us all that you can see, if it would help?' she asks.

'Absolutely.' I aim for professional, thinking that it comes off far too breathless. Lola doesn't seem to notice. *I'm going to see more of my family!* I think, my palms suddenly clammy. My insides squirm as Lola pulls out a black, worn notebook from underneath a pile on a bookshelf and thumbs her way to the back page.

'I think it's in . . . ah yes, here it is. Y'all can keep it for a while if it would help.'

Holding it between her thumb and forefinger, Lola passes me the picture. It's in colour, but that sort of watered-down colour that makes it seem like everything in the past took place in sepia.

There they all are.

Stood in front of a one-story wooden house, with long grass pushed up against the front and a window shutter hanging on its hinges, there's Lola's family.

'I think I must have been about six,' Lola says, and I spot her as a child. She's closest to the man who must have been her dad. He has his arm around her, smiling wide. Lola is half hidden behind him, squinting at the picture, her hair as long and blonde as it is today. Over his other shoulder is a guitar. It *is* the one in the corner. I'm looking at a family heirloom.

In the picture, around Lola and her dad, there are the other children, all at various heights. Jessie, her youngest brother, is still a baby, balancing on his mum's hip.

I wonder what happened to all of my aunties and uncles. Surely most of them are still alive. They'll only be Lola's age, some slightly older, some younger. They all have Lola's wispy hair. Her small features. Obviously, I must get my looks from my birth father. Maybe I can ask Lola what happened to them in a later session and claim it as research. Maybe she'll tell me willingly without even asking. Because I can't deny that this session has thrown up a lot.

'Pa had just got out of jail, I think,' she tells me. 'He hadn't been in long, but long enough to know he didn't want to go back.'

I nod, clocking a tall, wiry man with long hair and a moustache. It's Lola's mum that I zero in on, though. Perhaps it's just what Lola told me about her that's affecting my perception, but she looks exhausted. She's holding Jessie and her other hand is resting on her hip. She's thin. Her hair, which is just like Lola's, long and blonde, is straggly. She's smiling, but it looks forced. I think of the difficulty I have keeping Elton and Dad's plants going and then look at all of those children her mum had before she was even my age. No wonder she was exhausted.

'Is your mum still alive?' I ask, before I can help myself.

Lola shakes her head.

'We lost touch, after I left home. But my brother Jessie wrote to say she'd passed thirty or so years ago.'

Thirty years. I'm thirty. Lola's mum died the year I was born.

Suddenly, I'm hot all over. It's like my skin is stretched too tight over me. I don't fit. The walls in the office seem to get closer, trapping me. I need to get out of this crowded little office and go someplace to think.

'I'm sorry for your loss,' I say. It sounds like the platitude that it is, because the truth is, grieving parents who were total top tier, gold star parents is really hard. But I have a feeling that grieving one when things were more complicated is even harder still.

Lola nods.

We do an awkward shuffle as I try to manoeuvre around her and the giant dog to get to the door. My arms and legs don't seem to be working as well as they usually do.

'So, if it's okay with you, I'd like to do another session this week?' I'm back to brusque, business like, trying to ignore the weird tight skin sensation. 'We're a little short on time. It won't compromise on quality, though, don't worry. I've done it before from time to time.'

I mean when people are dying and they don't think they'll have six weeks left. But I don't tell Lola that.

She nods. 'That's good for me. How's Wednesday after breakfast, same time?'

'Perfect.' I smile. I just need to keep my shit together for a few more minutes. 'If we could finish up your earlier childhood in that chapter, that should work nicely for chapter two.'

'I'll see you then, Lily,' she says.

'Not if I see you first.' I have literally no idea why I said that, but Lola leans back and laughs and like before, she looks ten years younger. As if the shadows which hang around her sometimes just disappear, floating off into the stratosphere.

I do an awkward wave and step back into the corridor, letting my breath out once the door to the office is closed behind me.

It's impossible not to feel like the ground has shifted somewhat. Before I got to know Lola, she was just a figment of my imagination. And even if that figment was a fame hungry, drug-addled egomaniac, it was never more than two-dimensional.

But it's like every moment I spend with the real Lola, she becomes more fleshed out, and hearing her history is only making it more so. I just don't know how to feel.

Heading back towards the cottage, I wonder how on earth I'm going to survive the next few weeks.

# Chapter Nine

It's closer to midday by the time I'm opening the cottage doors. Noah is nowhere to be seen and as I'm literally stranded here, I decide to make a start on the first chapter of Lola's memoirs while it's all fresh in my head. Plus, the chance to think about everything she said without an audience holds a lot of appeal.

I send off a quick email to Seb to say that I've done the first session and that I'm working on chapter one today. He replies to say that Kitty is putting the feelers out to editors at publishing houses and that she'll need the first three chapters from us before she makes a deal.

It's the same process we've been through before, but even the thought of someone reading what I've just heard makes me feel unsure. Lola has been so private; I don't understand how she could possibly want this now.

I open the patio doors wide, pleased to find that I can just about stretch my laptop cable outside if I pull the white plastic furniture closer to the doors. I make a drink and a sandwich from my ever-dwindling food supplies, then get set up thinking that it really is a shame that no one's around to witness how brilliantly normal I'm being.

It's very hot. How is it so hot? Skye is meant to be unpredictable weather wise. The Inner Hebrides are not known for wall-to-wall sun. They're the sort of place true crime documentaries are filmed.

It is an unspoken law of this land that as someone who heralds from the UK, I am meant to maximize time spent in the sun. But as the glare of my laptop almost blinds me and my legs stick together and to the plastic chair, I think, actually I don't love it sunny. For one, there's all the chafing. So much chafing. And there's just so much pressure to be enjoying yourself in the sun. Probably, admitting this out loud would see me stripped of my citizenship and driven out of the country so I keep my sun aversion to myself.

I plug my headphones in, ready to listen to Lola talk through the early years of her childhood again. I know what's coming now, can brace myself for hearing that Lola was the black sheep of the family, according to her own mum. I mean really, being born in a storm, like a baby can help that. I was born on a Wednesday, and no one ever held that 'full of woe' thing against me.

'Do all old people talk to themselves? Or are you just extra weird?'

Harper is stood a few feet away, on the edge of the forest, looking like that dead girl from *The Ring* when she climbs out of the well. She's watching me from the perimeter of the gardens between cottage and hotel. Scowling.

I pause the recording that has literally just started and pull out an earphone. 'I was muttering to myself. It's totally different. And I'm not old.' I laugh to cover the fact that maybe it isn't that different. Harper scowls some more. Despite the heat, she's wearing her ripped skinny black jeans and a black long-sleeved hoodie. Her hair, as usual, is poker straight and covering a fair bit of her face.

'Is everything okay?' I ask. Because I notice that she seems angrier than usual, which is really saying something. Her hands are balled into fists that hang by her side and her lips are pressed into such a tight line, they're almost invisible. It's as if she's vibrating with rage. Which means she doesn't answer me.

'Do you want to come and sit down?' I gesture to the other chair, closing my laptop to show her that I'm not too busy. 'I can make you a drink.' I extend my final peace offering.

She eyes the chair like it's personally wronged her and doesn't move. 'I still don't trust you,' she mutters.

'Okay, but remember, you came to find me today. You're pretty safe if you want to sit down.'

I hope she knows that I mean not just in the sense that I'd never do anything dodgy. I once lost a whole night's sleep after I accidentally forgot to pay for a cabbage in Sainsbury's. It hadn't had a sticker and I'd meant to speak to a cashier about it at the end but forgot. I'd gone back the next day to pay, but the whole night I'd been convinced that I'd end up with my own spot on *Crimewatch*. I annoy myself sometimes.

I'm wondering about relaying any of this to her when she snaps, 'Fine,' storming over to the other chair without committing.

'I'll go and get some lemonade,' I say, standing up as Harper continues to glare straight ahead.

I move back into the cottage, pouring some of the fancy lemonade I'd brought from home into two glasses.

Heading back outside, I'm pleased to see that Harper has actually decided to sit down.

'Here you go,' I tell her, passing her a glass.

She takes it but doesn't have a drink. I have an urge to feed her, which is odd. She's just so thin. 'Do you want this sandwich?' I ask her. 'I can make another.'

Her face morphs from anger to outright disgust. She wrinkles her nose and recoils away from my lunch.

'What even is it?' she asks.

'Hummus and rocket, it's really good for you.'

'Grim.' She pretends to puke on the grass. That settles that, then.

We sip lemonade for a minute, neither of us talking. My mind is still reeling from everything Lola said. And now Harper. And Noah.

This little patch of Scotland might be secluded, but it certainly brings its fair share of drama.

'Is everything okay?' I ask Harper after a few minutes. She's looking off into the forest that surrounds the cottage on three sides.

She shrugs and I think that's all I'm going to get until she says, 'Blake's gone for a walk with *them*.'

I remember that Blake is her brother. 'He's gone with your foster parents, you mean?'

She nods.

'Okay, how did that make you feel?' I ask her, ridiculously out of my depth. I think again about how even Elton doesn't respect me and reckon that my chances of getting Harper to open up are slim to none. I won't know what to do if she does.

Another shrug. But this one seems less angry. Even if she's still facing towards the forest, her shoulders are starting to slump. To curve forwards. 'You wouldn't get it,' she says.

'Try me.'

Something about the way I say it must ring true, because Harper turns to face me then with some sort of question in her wide eyes. I resist the urge to look away.

'I just feel so fucking angry,' she says, finally defeated. I figure that now isn't the best time to pull her up on her using the odd fuck or ten. Plus, pot, meet kettle.

'With Blake?' I ask.

She shakes her head. 'Nah, with Mum.'

I realize that we aren't talking about Harper's foster mum here.

I don't say anything, hoping that she'll keep talking.

She does. 'If she'd just laid off the booze, we could've stayed with her. She wasn't even bad or anything, not like they made out. I could have looked after Blake. It's not fucking fair.'

Harper takes some deep breaths. God, parents mess their kids up, or at least some of them do. I guess that it's the only job in the world where there are no prerequisites. Any old Tom, Dick or Harry can have a baby.

But I do know what it's like to feel all confused, to wonder why the person who is meant to love you most in the world just doesn't.

'I think anger's good,' I tell her, after we've both been quiet for a little while. I'm a complete hypocrite. I don't do angry myself. I hate angry.

'You reckon?' she asks.

'Absolutely. If you feel angry, you're angry. Whatever you feel is how you feel.'

'Blake's not angry,' she tells me. 'He's younger than me, though. It's hard to talk about.' She starts to study the dried grass by her feet. 'I just want her to be a better mum, you know?'

I nod again.

'I get it,' I say. Harper looks at me. 'I mean, I don't get it, but I get some of it.'

Generally, I try not to tell anyone what happened with Lola. Even Colin hadn't known the whole truth of it. Because who wants to be like, 'Date me! Marry me! I'm such a catch my own mother abandoned me!' But I do want to tell Harper more and wish I could. It's just that everyone here thinks that Seb is my brother, and if I spill that I was adopted as a baby and it gets back to Lola, she'll definitely be onto me.

And then she might work out that she's telling me her life story under false pretences. It's a bit of a dick move. But then she did abandon me, so you know, hopefully we'll be even after this.

'Wait, you actually do get it,' Harper says, and I realize that she's watching my face really intently. I make a conscious effort to unscrew it.

'Are your foster parents going to be wondering where you are?' I ask.

She shakes her head. 'Told them I was going to sit in the garden.

They've gone for a walk around that massive lake. It's not like I can escape from here, it's like that prison. Alcatraz.'

Teenagers are dramatic.

'Can I play music through your laptop?' she asks. There's a very good chance that we've now arrived at the real reason Harper has come to find me, like a teenage moth to a laptop with passable Wi-Fi flame.

'Sure,' I tell her, loading up Spotify and abandoning the idea of getting any work done for now. I go and get a bowl of vegetable crisps. 'Here.' I prop them on the table in front of her to yet more sounds of retching.

Music starts to play through the laptop. It's not the sort of grunge screeching that I'd imagined Harper would like to listen to.

'It's The Smiths. You won't have heard of them, but they're my favourite.'

I have of course heard of The Smiths. I'm basic, but I'm not that basic. But Harper looks pleased with herself, so I let it slide. Plus, it makes sense that Harper would be drawn to Morrissey, kindred spirits and all that. 'Do you play an instrument?' I ask her.

Another head shake. 'Not well. I want to learn guitar, though.'

'You should speak to Lola, I'm sure she'd teach you. You could do the karaoke on Saturday nights.'

'Fuck no.' Harper has her eyes closed, listening to the song. 'It was bad enough listening to Jake and Sharon singing that thing from *Grease* on Saturday night. The duet one. Made me want to pull my own ears off.'

I laugh. The song ends and another starts with a similar feel. We don't talk anymore, though. Instead, I think about what Harper said, about how she wanted her mum to be a better mum.

Harper's mum, Lola's mum, Lola. Maybe it's just that none of them knew *how* to be a mum. Because it's a bit of a myth, isn't it, that as women we're all born knowing how to look after kids.

The thought of hearing in Lola's own words how she didn't want to be a mum, for whatever the reason, sends this deep rolling swell of unease through me, like I'm on a train that's going to crash with no way off. And even if there was a way off, I don't know if I'd take it. Because now I'm on it, it's like I need to know how mine and Lola's . . . how our story ends.

\* \* \*

'There you are.'

I jolt at the sound of Noah's voice. 'I wasn't asleep or anything,' I tell him, trying to rearrange my limbs into a position that's slightly less sprawling in nature.

'You totally were,' Harper pipes up unhelpfully, 'you were snoring and everything.'

Great. He caught me semi asleep. Again.

Probably not the time to reveal that in all other settings I have low key insomnia. No one would believe me anyway. On Skye, I'm halfway to narcolepsy.

Noah laughs softly as I squint at the clock in the bottom corner of the laptop. Jesus, two hours have passed since I last looked. Maybe I did take a nap, just a short one that lasted several hours. It's all this island air.

'How was your morning?' I ask.

'Good, thank you. I made a start on the article. It's not due till the end of summer so there's plenty of time.'

Noah doesn't look like he's been sat inside working all morning. But then, I bet he's the sort of person who looks refreshed after a plane journey, not dehydrated and achy like the rest of us.

'I need to go for a walk to check out another hidden gem tomorrow, if you're still okay to help with the article?'

Hm. Confusing. Is he asking me out, or asking for help with the article? Because it sounds like the latter, but then he did just push his hair back where it's flopped in his eyes. And Harper is mimicking sticking her fingers down her throat.

I ignore her.

'Yeah, course, I'd love that! So long as I wouldn't be imposing or anything. It's totally fine if you change your mind. But if you don't change your mind, then, yes, I'd like to come. Thank you.'

'Fucking painful, mate.' That's Harper.

Noah smiles, which is a very generous reaction to my unprovoked outburst.

'Do you have any Pringles?' she asks him. 'All she has is rabbit food.'

Noah looks down at the little spread on the table.

'Are those crisps made of vegetables?' he asks, outraged but slightly flushed.

'I know, right,' Harper once again unhelpfully interjects, before coughing and saying loser at the same time. 'Earlier she tried to get me to eat a grass and hummus sandwich. And this lemonade doesn't taste like Sprite at all. It isn't even fizzy.'

I can't help but notice that Harper is being far friendlier with Noah than she's been with me, and he hasn't even shared his Wi-Fi yet. It's the whole slightly shy and disarming thing he has going on. We're all powerless in the face of it. Even Harper.

'It was rocket,' I say, smiling through gritted teeth because I don't want Noah to think I'm the sort of person who is mean to children. Especially ones who look so desperately in need of a friend like Harper does. 'And it's still lemonade.'

'I did get some Pringles from the hotel shop,' he tells her.

She lets out a groan of delight. 'Lifesaver.'

My stomach drops a little. It's not like it's exactly a prerequisite to a relationship, is it? That you have the same taste in crisps. Not in the same way that, say, living in the same country and not lying to each other might be, but still, it would be nice to have one tiny little sign that I'm not the black sheep around here. Especially when it comes to Lola and Noah.

Noah goes to retrieve said stomach-falling Pringles, passing them over to Harper, who clutches the tube close to her chest. I add Pringles to the shopping list of food that I need. I want to be prepared in case she comes again. Like I would if she were actually a stray cat.

That feeling where my skin becomes too tight and my arms and legs get jittery comes over me again. It's the point at which, if I were at home, I'd write a really great to-do list. Except, I've already done that today.

'I've had an idea, for you know what.' Noah says, looking at me.

My brain isn't working properly, I've no idea what he's talking about. Forming cohesive thoughts is like trudging through sludge.

'You know what,' I repeat back to him like an idiot.

'My summer plan.' He drops his voice, but Harper is deep in Pringle bliss. 'I was looking in the archives. You know, the hotel used to host an annual race around the lake. Way back in the day.'

'Wait, the hotel has archives?' That does jolt me out of whatever trance I was in.

'Mm hm, it's pretty old. Early nineteenth century. The original owners kept decent records.'

I look again at the hotel just through the gardens. It is old. Not like Tudor old, but still. I love a good archive.

'A race could be a cool idea,' I tell him.

'Apparently, people from the local town would dress up as Scáthach, even the men. Scáthach was a mythical warrior queen who had her fortress on Skye, in case you're wondering.'

'I was, I was wondering. Wow, that sounds great. Why did the race stop?'

Noah shrugs.

'I can't see any record of it after the Second World War, so maybe that, I don't know. But it would be a cool thing to bring back. Do you want to check out the route with me?'

What the hell am I meant to do with the information that Noah is kind, hot and interested in mythical warrior queens?

Thankfully, Harper comes to my rescue.

'You should definitely go on the warrior run,' she says, standing up. Noah and I just look at each other. 'I can't believe forty-year-olds run for fun, though. Tragic.' She wanders back towards the hotel, the crunch of Pringles getting quieter as she walks.

'Do you think she'll be all right on her own?' I ask Noah.

He nods. 'I saw her foster parents out front, think they're back from a hike. The warrior run, though; I like that.'

'Me too.' I pause. 'But for the record, I'm not forty. I'm thirty. Not one bit of me is forty. I did one of those "what age is your heart" quizzes on the BBC website and it said I have the heart of a twenty-eight-year-old.'

Noah laughs. 'I never thought you were forty. But I bet you'll look just as hot at forty.' My brain deems this the perfect time to embark on a full body flush.

'Okay, right, great. You too. I bet you'll look brilliant. At forty.' Looking at Noah makes me struggle to form human words. 'So shall we get . . . ' I gesture back towards the cottage and then realize it sounds like I'm propositioning the poor man.

'RUN. I mean shall we get ready to run? Or you could go your way and I could go mine. I could purposely run in the opposite direction from you, and we could see which way is best for the hotel run, if that's what you'd like to happen. I'd just need to know your route.'

I chance a look up at Noah. The edges of his mouth are twitching. I think he's trying not to laugh at me.

'We should go together and compare notes at the end.'

'Excellent plan. Two ticks! ... Wait, do you think there'll be ticks?'

I dart inside. It's only a degree or two cooler in here, but being away from Noah makes it much easier to breathe.

There's a text from Seb to distract me. He's telling me that he's back at the office and found Clementine putting shellac on her toenails. There's a picture of the LED lamp on her desk.

> **Seb:** Gen Z are fucking useless.
>
> **Seb:** Did you send an out-of-office notice to your WhatsApp? Who does that?

> **Me:** She's not that bad. I don't want people to think I'm ignoring them. I'm going to be too busy out here to keep on top of things. I'm going on a run with Noah in a minute. Part of his save the hotel plan. I'll explain later. There are archives here!!

> **Seb:** You really do not know how to take a holiday, do you?

> **Me:** It's a working holiday. I'm ghost-writing Lola's memoirs, remember.

I feel a pang of guilt at the fact that at this point, I'm basically lying to everyone. Including, and worst of all, probably myself.

> **Seb:** The WhatsApp thing is definitely going in your eulogy.

> **Me:** It's fun that you think I'll die first.

**Seb:** My nana smoked thirty a day and lived
till ninety.

        **Me:** That's an anomaly! It's not the norm. I
        sent you the Reddit post about how a
        sample size of one isn't a sample size,
        remember? Try that gum, please. I've got
        to go, this race idea could really help Lola.

**Seb:** LILY BROWN, DO NOT, I REPEAT DO
NOT TAKE ON A HOTEL MAKEOVER THIS
SUMMER. YOU HAVE ENOUGH ON!

I ignore him. Of course I'm not going to try to save the hotel. That
would be ridiculous. Plus, it looks to me like Lola just needs a good
business plan . . . I do love business planning . . . But no, Seb is right.
I have enough on maintaining my web of lies.

I quickly pull on my running shorts and a strappy top. Don't get
me wrong, I'd rather wear leggings or, better yet, a sleeping bag to
run in with Noah, but it's hotter than the surface of Venus out there.
It'll be like running through soup as it is.

Skye is meant to be the misty isles, that's what I'd read in Noah's
book. But I haven't seen one bit of mist yet. Just the baking sun.

I grab my suncream and step out of the cottage at the same time
that Noah leaves his. He's changed too and now he's wearing shorts
with a light blue loose-fitting sports T-shirt. Full coverage would
have been better, for obvious reasons. But I don't want him to die
of heat stroke. That would be unfortunate. I'll just have to keep my
ogling to a minimum. It's hard to run and ogle as it is.

I start absolutely dousing myself in suncream.

'Are you happy to set the pace?' Noah asks while I'm mid-dousing.
I nod.

'That's a lot of suncream,' he comments.

'I've been in the shade all morning and you can never be too careful when it comes to skin cancer,' I reply. 'Want some?'

'Okay thanks.' The edges of our fingers brush as I hand over the bottle. I don't look up in case I give myself away, but I catch him stealing glances at me while he puts a few splodges of the factor fifty cream here and there. Possibly because I am very much enamoured with him applying the cream. What can I say? I find his dedication to protecting his skin from the sun's UV rays very sexy. Very sexy indeed.

I do a few more covert stretches, mainly to distract myself. Noah seems good to go, straight off the bat.

I set off, heading down towards the loch, taking it steady. I might not be able to scale mountains with any sort of finesse, but I can do this. I usually do this, three times a week.

The path starts out fine. A little narrow maybe, and it's not a nice bit of tarmac like I'm used to, but it's decent enough for a fun run.

'I think head left and go round that way,' Noah says from behind me. I can hear his footsteps *thump thump thump* onto the ground. There are a few people down by the edge of the water, on its pebbly shore. I see Lola there, talking to a man I vaguely recognize. I raise my hand at them as we turn to run with our backs to them.

Underfoot, the path changes. It's now a thin strip of depressed grass that I stick to like glue, falling into a rhythm as I hear Noah behind me, breathing steady.

I'm tempted to accept that running here in Skye, where I'm not dodging trams or careering around bikes, I can relax into it.

It's beautiful. I think Noah's idea for the race would be a good one. Lola could charge an entrance fee. She could offer drinks after. If she did need money towards the hotel repairs, this could be a start. I mean, I would come, if I didn't live a million miles away.

I focus on the sound of our feet hitting the ground. I'm slow, I've accepted I'm slow. So, I can just be. Concentrate on putting one foot in front of the other, albeit at a steady pace, and just get out of my head for a while.

Of course, this doesn't happen. Instead, I'm zeroing in on my slowness. So slow. Noah must have expected me to be crap, surely. I wonder what he's thinking right now and whether it's about how slow I'm being.

I focus on his breathing in the hope that it'll give something away. It doesn't.

Come on, head, be quiet.

We round the top of the loch. Looking behind me, I can see the hotel in the distance. It's still so weird to think that's where Lola lives. Like, that's her home. I couldn't have got it more wrong.

The run-down hotel by the loch and the handmade clothes I hadn't factored at all. I have to say, the real Lola is far less terrifying than the Lola in all those magazine articles. The Lola in the orange minidress. It's hard to be angry at someone who stitches daisies into their own dungarees. But without the anger I feel lost, unsettled. Far from being quiet, my head is a cacophony of noise.

Soon, mercifully, the heat starts to make it difficult to concentrate on anything else. There's a rustle behind me and I turn around to look and whoa, big mistake. Noah has taken his T-shirt off and he's running holding it in one hand. I whip my head forward so fast my neck clicks. That's going to hurt later. That's what no one tells you about being thirty. One sudden movement and you've got yourself a deep tissue injury.

Still, at least the pain in my neck distracts me from the thought of Noah running behind me, with his T-shirt off. Not that he's super stacked or anything, he's just so tight. With my legs, there are certain parts that are absolutely superfluous to requirements. My legs would work fine without that lump or bump. But the way his muscles all slot together like a jigsaw. Well, there are no lumps or bumps, put it that way.

And now I know that the tattoo that I've seen peeking out under his T-shirt sleeve curves around his shoulder and down past his collarbone and what the hell, I've never had a thing for tattoos before. Colin was resolutely anti-tattoo and I mostly agreed with his sentiments.

But I'm a big fan of them now. A super-fan, you could say.

I only got a split-second glimpse, but I definitely saw a compass.

Thinking about Noah shirtless and all tattoo-y is not doing anything to help me regulate my body temperature. I'd tied my hair out of the way back at the cottage, but the bits that have escaped have welded themselves to my neck and forehead.

I push on, my only hope now to get back to the cottage and take a cold shower.

Noah's breathing picks up.

A very cold shower.

'Lily,' he calls, and I come to a stop. I have to rest my hands on my knees and take a few deep breaths as I reconcile the fact that I've broken into a sprint trying to outrun Noah and his six pack.

We're on the other bank of the river now, opposite the hotel. This is the side covered in forest and to the left of us, the mountains bank steeply uphill, dense with evergreen trees.

'Everything okay?' I ask once I've caught my breath and had a drink. I keep my eyes trained on Noah's face.

He nods and wipes his forearm over his head. I have a strange and possibly slightly perverse urge to lick him.

'Wow, you're fast.'

I don't mention that I was trying to outrun his abs.

'That infinity pool that Lola mentioned is just up here.' He points towards the trees and a small opening through them. 'I might include it on the hidden gems list. I thought it would help bring business to the hotel. Do you want to see it? You don't have to go in,' he tacks on the end, no doubt noticing that my eyes have gone wide with fear.

There's a number of things I could fixate on here. Like my fear of open water. Or the fact that Noah paid me a compliment. But I'm still stuck on the fact that Noah wants to show me something. Me.

'Well, we are meant to be circumnavigating this run,' I say, when really, I've spent the whole time thinking about Noah running behind me.

'I know, just a little detour, then we can get back to checking the route.'

I'm still not sure that I exactly trust myself.

'How far is it?' I ask, remembering my last trip uphill with Noah.

He peers into the trees. 'Not far. It's pretty steep, but after about ten minutes it levels out. We need to follow the water. I think you'll like it.'

Looking closer, I can see that there's a trickle of water coming through the gap in the trees. It cuts across in front of us and then disappears into the loch, too small to even be a stream.

'Okay, why not?' I tell him, earning myself a smile. 'I am always up for an off-the-cuff adventure.' (Lies just come so naturally to me these days.)

Noah does a soft little laugh. God damn it, he's onto me.

'Come on then, adventure awaits.'

He takes off through the gap and this time I let him lead. With no one around to catch or judge me, I take in his broad back. The way his muscles work together as he climbs, like a game of sexy Tetris.

It's possible that operating at a higher altitude than what I'm used to is scrambling my brain's ability to get a read on people. Or maybe like Lola, Noah is just a bit of an enigma. I *think* he's quite shy, he goes red a lot (which for the record, I'm a huge fan of). But then at other times he's more confident. Like the way he's taken charge here. What my brain isn't failing at, is coming up with other scenarios in which Noah could take charge. It's readily supplying those, no problem.

'Just a bit further,' he calls as we climb. My leg muscles are protesting now and I'm back to using my hands too. I wonder if every trip out with Noah is going to end with me crawling around on the floor.

'It's here.'

Noah suddenly stands up and I move to join him, pushing through a final thicket of branches that have knitted together between two trees.

The view steals my breath.

The tarn is about half the size of a regular swimming pool and sort of an oval shape. The water is clear blue. At one side, a smooth rock juts out of the mountainside, a small stream of water trickling over the edge of it. Noah's right, it's exactly like an infinity pool and looking out over the craggy mountains. It's absolutely stunning. Behind us, we're pretty much surrounded by trees.

'Lola doesn't want me telling people about this place,' Noah says from behind me, causing goose bumps to run down my arms.

'I can see why.' I look around. It's so beautiful, a hidden oasis among the trees, I have to wrestle against a ridiculous urge to cry. On Skye, I'm an emotional wreck.

'Cool, right?' Noah asks.

'Very cool.' I sniff and smile at the same time. If Noah realizes that I'm having a moment, he doesn't let on. 'I think I might put my feet in.' I just need a second of space so I'm already kicking off my shoes, pulling off my socks. The ground is mossy underfoot.

'You could go all the way in? You know, since you're always up for an off-the-cuff adventure?' Noah asks, still from behind me. I think he's taking the piss.

I twist around to see him smiling.

He's definitely taking the piss.

'I mean, I am. Obviously.' I peer at the edge, move a little closer. 'It's just … all the water … and the fact that it's hanging over the edge of a mountain.'

'This is like a glorified puddle.'

'It's definitely not a puddle.'

I reach the edge away from the infinity part of the infinity pool and feel the cool water lapping at my feet. It's delicious.

Noah has moved to stand next to me. 'It could be fun.' I look at him again. The flush of red across the top of his cheeks is back. I'm an idiot for that flush of red.

Wild swimming isn't even close to my definition of fun. And okay, the small loch isn't a big scary loch. At worst, there's probably a stray tadpole in there or something. Maybe proximity to a shirtless Noah is short-circuiting my brain, making it feel like it wouldn't be a *completely* terrible idea to get in the water.

'We don't have any swimming clothes,' I tell Noah, feeling like I must be going insane to even be contemplating this. I'm very hot, fevered almost. And the water is so very, very cool between my toes.

Noah raises an eyebrow at me as the goose bumps take over my whole body. Before I can reply, he's splashing forward, storming into the centre. Any poor little tadpoles in there have just gotten a rude awakening. Noah turns round and walks backwards with his hands out wide and do you know what's more distracting than a semi-naked Noah? A semi-naked wet Noah.

'But it's so nice!' he calls.

He walks further back and when the tarn gets deep enough kicks off and floats on his back. He's still wearing his running shorts (thank heavens for small mercies and all that) but all in all it's a visual which makes my impossibly blushing skin even hotter.

So much so that the need to cool off becomes a desire, a want.

Without really thinking, I sit down. I'm on the very edge of the tarn so I mostly have a wet bum but at least the backs of my legs are cooling down.

I don't take anything off, but I shuffle forward another inch. Then another. Like I'm being pulled by some invisible force to the edge of the water.

Nothing disastrous happens.

Before I know it, the water is lapping around my waist. My whole bottom half is in.

Yes, I'm basically frozen, alternating between warding off cold hard panic and warding off the actual cold. Because this water is freezing. As if he's reading my thoughts, Noah says, 'It's glacial water round here.'

My teeth chatter.

'Makes sense.' I start to swim.

Noah rights himself and then smiles at me before ducking his head under.

He comes up again and shakes his hair off and I have such a solid image of Ariel from *The Little Mermaid* flinging herself up on that rock that I can't help but laugh.

'What's so funny?' Noah asks, treading water.

'Just thinking you'd make a great Ariel,' I tell him, also treading. 'I think you'd really suit the purple bra.'

He looks down at his chest. So of course, *I* look down at his chest. 'I don't wear enough purple.' I can't help but laugh. Plus, now that it's less creepy to look, I can see that his tattoo is part of a map, with a compass in the middle, right on the meat of his shoulder. It's the reminder I absolutely don't want right now. Noah is an explorer through and through. If I were going to get a tattoo, it'd be of Dad's house. Complete with Elton in the front window.

'Why don't we check out the edge?' he asks, meaning the overhang part.

I'm either going to have to get out or move some more before I seize up completely.

'I'm all over it,' I tell him, amping up my adventurer charade.

He's coming towards me then. He's a killer whale and I'm a baby seal, trapped on a small iceberg on one of those nature programmes. The baby seal never comes out on top. But did we ever consider that it's so taken with the strength of the killer whale that it just thinks *what's the point in trying to fight this* and flops willingly into the water to die?

Noah is holding out a hand then, his legs floating out behind him. He's so like Lola, I think. In this setting, out here, he makes more sense. He's more at ease.

'Don't worry, I've got you. I won't let go,' he tells me. I get the sense that my wild adventurer charade is not quite as solid as I'd like it to be.

I test out putting my hand in Noah's and let him guide me slowly, ever so slowly, to the edge of the tarn.

'What the fuck was that?' I jolt, absolutely sure something brushed past my leg. I look down, flailing around, fully expecting to see an octopus, or something else with tentacles. A sea snake! I bet it's a sea snake.

'Just that bit of bark, don't worry,' Noah says. We're almost at the edge of the tarn now, both of us treading water.

It's so incredibly beautiful, almost like we're at the edge of the world. At the edge of everything.

Something brushes my hip and I jolt again, only stilling when Noah puts both of his hands on my waist. 'Is this okay?' he asks, and fuck me, his eyes are blue.

I nod, struggling to speak. Be it out of fear, lust or hypothermia, who knows at this point? To do something with my hands, I put them on Noah's shoulders. His skin under them is impossibly warm. And then we're just there, treading water, looking out at the view.

149

I'm not even worried about what's happening in the murky depths beneath me, because I'm finding it hard to concentrate on anything that isn't interchangeably the view or Noah's face.

And kudos to my body for managing to summon a hot flush at these temperatures.

While he's looking out, I study Noah's face, doing my best to work out what he's thinking. It's the sort of micro analysis I normally excel at, in that I can tell if someone's annoyed at me from a hundred paces just by the set of their mouth.

He turns his head then and the polite thing would be to take my go at appreciating the view. I can't look away from him, though.

He doesn't look away either. Instead, he's studying my face like he's about to be tested on it and when his eyes drop to my lips, I lick them.

He doesn't move.

I really want him to move. Preferably towards my mouth.

This isn't me. I'm not this person. But the wildness of this place is stripping me bare.

'What's happening here?' I ask, my voice really quiet. Noah's thumbs have started to move at my waist, over my clothes. Rubbing back and forth.

'I'm no good at relationships, Lily. The long-term thing . . . '

I nod. Appreciating his honesty.

However, I do, do relationships. I've had a steady string of long-term boyfriends since college. These last nine months without a Colin have possibly been the longest I've ever been single.

'It's just that I move around so much. But . . . well—'

'I understand,' I cut him off, because there's only so much time you can spend listening to someone explain why they don't want to be your life partner. 'I think . . . it would be tricky anyway . . . the distance . . . '

Noah nods, but he looks more troubled. He pulls his bottom lip between his teeth and grips my waist tighter even though we just said that this was a crap idea. We stay locked together like that for a few more moments. I'm thinking about what would happen if he just closed the gap between us, terrible idea be damned. Or what if I did it? How would it feel? What might happen after?

And if you're wondering whether I always do a benefit versus cost analysis before I kiss someone, the answer is very much yes.

Here, the benefit is that I'd get to kiss Noah. He might even let me touch a muscle or two. It's hard to think of a cost. Well, aside from the fact that there's absolutely no future for us and we both just admitted as much.

But as he leans forward, just a touch, I think who cares about the future? Futures are overrated, surely. Because here on Skye isn't real life, it's an alternate reality where I know my birth mum and swim in tarns perched on the edge of the world.

Finally, *finally*, Noah reaches up and brushes my bottom lip where I'm biting it between my teeth.

'Lily.' He closes the rest of the distance. I'm moving too, heading towards his lips like they're my very own North Star.

The first brush is soft, like a flicker.

But then I'm so pent up that soft is just not going to cut it.

With as much purchase as I can manage treading water, I wind my hand around the back of his neck. The move makes him bob down in the water which also lets him deepen the kiss. And almost drowning him aside, now we're talking.

The slide of his tongue is like heaven.

His hand on my scalp makes me shiver.

I'm a bundle of nerve endings and they're all lighting up. There's a good chance I look radioactive right about now.

We're a clash of lips and teeth and tongue. Treading water and kissing is actually not as easy as romance movies would have us believe, but we're A-star for effort.

I'm unleashed and I should be terrified about how good the press of his body against mine feels.

Then, there's a pain like lightning down my calf. I yank my mouth away from Noah's. 'Fuck, cramp!' I tell him. Every time I move my leg the pain gets worse, lancing through my muscle like a hot poker.

This. This is why I have a healthy fear of open water. One wrong move and you drown. This is it. I'm going to die in an oversized puddle on the side of a mountain.

I panic some more. Swallow icy water. It makes me cough and splutter. Oh god.

Warm arms wrap themselves around my middle and I'm floating backwards towards the mossy banks.

I will my breathing to go back to normal.

Not today, Death.

There's a chance I said that out loud because Noah laughs.

Well, that's one way to ruin a good kiss.

We're at the edge now, and even though I can absolutely walk, Noah hauls me out and I let myself be dragged like a ragdoll. We land on our backs, and I just stare up at the tree canopy above us. Breathing hard.

'Argh ... ahhhh.' Noah's hands are on my calf.

'This should help.' He rubs the sore muscle. And even though I'm pretty sure that rubbing has zero impact on cramp, I am not about to turn down a leg rub from Noah.

Still, I don't want him to feel obliged to do it for hours, so after a respectable amount of time, I say, 'I think I'm good now, thanks.' I can't look him in the eye.

'We should probably be getting back,' I tell him, all the reasons that kiss was a bad idea hurtling back into my brain now that we're no longer kissing. 'I need a shower.'

He nods and kneels up, pulling his trainers towards him.

I sit up too, realizing that half the forest floor is stuck to my wet back.

I wrestle wet socks onto wet feet and push them into my trainers with an audible squelch.

We agree to walk the rest of the way back, on account of the cramp.

What do we do now?

With Colin, we'd been talking online for so long before we met, it was obvious what we both wanted. A life partner. Someone to split the council tax bill with. But this with Noah, like everything out here, it's just so completely outside of my comfort zone.

'I can actually hear your brain, you know?' he says as we emerge onto the depressed grass path that winds around the loch.

And an impromptu swim is all well and good until you have to walk home all soggy with bits of branches in your hair. Then the whole thing loses some of its shine.

'I'm not thinking that hard,' I tell him.

He laughs like he doesn't believe me. And really, this level of thinking is nothing. A drop in the ocean. He should visit my consciousness while I'm trying to get to sleep, that's when the magic really happens.

Luckily, we'd done most of the run before we detoured towards the pool, so it doesn't take long for us to reach the hotel again. We go around the side as usual, through the gardens.

'So, the path is great for a run,' I say like a woman who doesn't have half a tree tangled in her hair.

'Really great,' Noah adds, also with faux cheer.

'I'll pull together an action plan.'

'Excellent idea.'

Harper, who I'm quickly realizing is almost always on her own, is sitting at one of the picnic benches on her phone.

She watches us pass. My clothes are stuck to me. My white vest

153

top has gone see-through, like I'm taking part in my very own wet T-shirt competition. Though thankfully, instead of my boobs, all you can see is my blue sports bra.

'Not one word,' I say to Harper as she opens her mouth to say something. She closes it again and smirks at us instead. At least she's smiling.

# Chapter Ten

'Er,' I start and stop outside my cottage. Noah stops too. 'I'd love to talk to you some more about ideas for the hotel,' he says. 'If it's not too much . . . you're already helping with the article.'

Didn't expect that. But I'm rolling with it.

'Okay,' I answer. 'I'd be happy to. Maybe later on, then?'

I'm itching to see more of Noah. Not in a naked way, though this too would be very welcome indeed. There was just *something* up in the pool.

But I know I shouldn't. I'm not a fling person. I've nothing against people who are. I admire them, in fact. I just can't, when I know there's no future.

'But just to discuss ideas for the hotel, right?' I clarify, hoping that the question is doing some serious heavy lifting when it comes to conveying my wishes.

His smile drops, though just a touch.

'If that's what you'd like, I'd really appreciate it.'

'Right, that's great. Is seven okay? I was going to make dinner for then, so I could make extra, if you'd like to eat too.' It's close to four now. I'll have to find some way to get to a bigger shop and then I can't put off washing my hair for another day. So, seven is a stretch, but if I eat too late, I won't sleep. Food is up there alongside alcohol, caffeine, cortisol, too little or too much exercise and existential anguish as one of the things that stops me from nodding off.

155

'Seven works for me. That would be nice, I'll bring a notebook.' Another full body flush. 'See you later, Lily.'

Noah disappears into his cottage.

Inside, mine feels empty now that Seb is gone. I don't particularly want to be alone with my own thoughts, so I make quick work of showering. I don't even dry my hair, I just plait it, and pin my fringe back, a decision I will no doubt live to regret. I realize that despite my very thorough efforts with the SPF, I've caught the sun across my nose. It's pinker than the rest of my face and dotted with freckles. Before I can even think about how I don't look like me, I'm out of the door again.

I'm dressed in a white maxi dress and calling a taxi from the parking lot of the hotel.

'Shit!' I mutter, as I'm informed that they can pick me up in an hour or so. God knows why anyone would want to live here, even getting food is a pain in the bum. The nearest shop is four miles from the hotel. It's a Co-op, so it has to be better stocked than Lola's glorified food shed and honesty box.

'Fucking shit,' I say again, just for good measure, jabbing at Google Maps.

'Everything okay?' Lola appears out of the hotel shop, the half-bald chicken following her around as usual. The shock of seeing her renders me momentarily speechless. It would be really helpful if she could wear a little bell, or better yet, have a town crier pre-announce her arrival.

'Fine, totally fine!' I call. Chances are Lola has just heard me swearing up a storm but I'm not about to start offloading on her. It's not her fault Seb abandoned me here without a car. 'I'm just about to walk to the shop in town,' I clarify, holding up the front of my phone like an idiot. I have the four-mile walk loaded.

Lola's gaze tracks down my front, past my white dress to the sandals which offer zero ankle support. Maybe I'd better nip back and put my zippy trousers and walking boots back on.

'I'll run you over there, if you like?' Lola says. It's no wonder most of the 314 hotel reviews mention her by name. She really does offer a personalized service.

Lola's dog, the blond Labrador, presumably hearing the word 'run', comes bounding out of the hotel. Lola rubs behind his ears. 'You want to come for a drive, eh Scout?' Scout is gazing at Lola like she's the second coming.

Obviously, an affinity with animals is not a genetic trait in the same way that, say, eye colour is (not that Lola and I are matched there either, mind). Here Lola has a whole harem of animals who adore her.

Elton sort of tolerates my presence, as opposed to actively adoring it.

I've now not spoken for too long, too busy mulling over our many differences. But then time with Lola always unsettles me, which I guess is normal. I probably shouldn't be willingly submitting to more of it. It's just that I really do need to eat . . .

'Okay, if you don't mind.'

'Y'all are fine. Hang on a sec.'

She really is just . . . nice. Or that's how she seems at any rate.

Lola disappears back into the hotel while I stand awkwardly in the parking lot. There's a motorbike there. Death-trap.

I'm not at all surprised when Lola reappears and heads towards the battered looking blue truck in the corner. I follow her in, sitting across a bench seat that could do with a good hoover. I try not to think of my white dress. Or the fact that the van appears to have heralded from a pre-seat-belt era.

None of these things surprise me, because I realize that at some point over the weekend, what I think I know about Lola has shifted. It's just not a shock that this heap of metal is her car, or that she has to give it a couple of goes, 'because the ignition is shot,' before it shudders to life.

Scout jumps into the back of the truck and we're off. Winding down the bumpy track away from the hotel.

It's a short journey and Lola turns the radio on, twisting the knobs until some country song starts to play. It's not a song I've heard and it's not the type of music her band were famous for. Lola seems to like it, though. She hums along tunefully and even though it means we don't have to talk, it's still uncomfortable. Like the guitar in Lola's office, it's an unwelcome reminder that this Lola is the same one who left me all those years ago.

It's been years since I tortured myself over it. Wondering what it must have been like for me as a baby, lost and confused and not in the arms of the person I'd expected to be with. It's a dark path to go down, and not helpful. And since Mum and Dad died, there have been plenty of dark paths without adding to them.

But now as I listen to her hum, I can't help but venture back there. How I felt, how she felt. Was it a straightforward decision for her? Did she agonize about it? Or was it as easy as swapping a handbag you changed your mind about?

By the time we pull up in front of the small shop, I've worked myself up into a panic. I've barely even taken in the scenes out of the car window. The houses, dotted along the thin stretch between mountain and the pebbly shores of the sea. The fact that on Skye, every direction seems to be picture postcard worthy, it's overwhelming.

'I'll wait outside,' Lola says, cutting the ignition as we park up in front of a small Co-op.

It's an old building, but the blue Co-op sign is like a beacon of civilization.

I practically dive out of the van, needing space and almost crashing into a group of cyclists. They all call a hello to Lola as they pass. I hurry onward in my quest for vegetables.

Inside, the shelves are stacked high with food. It's cramped and disorderly. Pasta sits next to loo roll. I'd have expected better from Co-op. How do people here live with such chaos?

There's a middle-aged woman behind the till. The self-check-out has a handwritten 'out of order' sign stuck to it.

'Afternoon!' I call over, the edges of my voice frayed, just like the rest of me.

'Hmm,' she says in answer.

So, she's not the friendliest of sorts. I'm having a hard time meal planning as it is without the woman tracking my every move. In the shop window, there are several posters, all of which read things like 'Tourist GO Home' and 'Save Our Shores'.

Ah. I did read that there's a lot more tourism on Skye these days. Something about it appealing to the Instagram generation.

I grab a basket and make my way up the first mini aisle.

I get pasta, even though there's no wholemeal. And pesto. I decide to make a risotto for Noah, mainly because I can make enough to do me some lunches too. I basically clear the place of any and all fruit and veg. Seb was right, I am way too excited by the prospect of broccoli. I dither in front of a small fridge full of ready meals, unhappy about the salt content. But then starvation also holds little appeal. I pick up a couple. By the time I drag my basket towards the tills it's overflowing. I don't exactly know everything I've got in there, but hopefully it's enough to keep me going for a week at least.

And even though chicken and mushroom risotto isn't exactly what I'd have liked to make Noah, the Co-op manager already hates me for being a tourist, so it'll have to do.

I adopt my politest, most pleasant demeanour while I pay. It doesn't seem to go down particularly well and isn't helped by the fact that the card machine takes three goes to get signal. I curse my ill preparedness in not having cash.

I carry the bags back outside to find Lola still in the van, chatting to the same man I saw with her on the shores of the loch earlier.

Now I remember him, he was in that article about the summer fair. He's the vet. A silver fox vet, I might add.

Lola has the driver's side window down and she's resting her elbow on it, chatting away.

'Lily, this is James, he's the local vet here in Broadford.'

I smile and make out like I hadn't already gleaned this information during a late night Lola stalk.

'Nice to meet you, James,' I say.

'And you, Lily.' His accent is thick. 'I'd better be getting going, though, we've had word that there's a sheep trapped in a fence down the way.'

I don't ask how or why a sheep would be in a fence.

'Mcleary's farm again?' Lola asks.

'You know it. I'll be seeing you Lola, Lily.'

James sticks his hands in his pockets and marches towards a pickup truck that's in an even worse state than Lola's.

Before he gets in, he gives Lola another wave.

I feel ... I don't know, angry? Yes, I think it's that. It's the fact that, at times, Lola seems so happy and content in a way that feels impossibly alien to me. It's definitely anger. Irrational or not.

'Did y'all get everything you need?'

'Yes.' It comes out sharp. Lola doesn't say anything.

I take a breath, relax my shoulders, stamp the anger down because it isn't helping anyone. 'I think I got enough for now. Thank you for bringing me.' I climb back in, balancing the paper bags with all my food in by my feet.

'I'm cooking for Noah tonight,' I tell Lola for absolutely no reason. 'Risotto,' I finish like an idiot, thinking that if I just keep talking, it'll stop me from dwelling on the anger.

Lola starts the engine again. 'I'm sure he'll appreciate that, Lily, he likes risotto, and did I see y'all running around the loch earlier? Noah has always loved that route.'

I resist the urge to whip my head around in a very dramatic WTF moment. Noah definitely didn't say that he'd been around the loch a lot. In fact, he made out like we were going to figure it out to see if it would work for a fun run. Though he did know that little infinity pool was there, which should have maybe given him away.

Not the time to be thinking about the infinity pool.

Wait, did he lie as an excuse to spend more time with me?

'My mum said that when I was a teenager, all I ate was carbs,' I tell Lola just for something to say and she laughs.

'Are your mum and dad retired?' she asks.

I swallow and shake my head. I don't want to tell Lola that they've died. It's like I'm betraying them to admit it. Though that makes zero sense. Or maybe it feels too close to the painful reality of it all. Skye isn't real life. Instead, I talk as if they're still here.

'Mum's a piano teacher. Had me in music lessons before I could talk by all accounts,' I tell her, 'and Dad works in the local secondary school. He's a history teacher.' The façade is slipping, on my alternate reality. It's incredibly hard, talking about your parents as if they're here when they're not.

'They sound like good people,' she says.

'They are, the best,' I tell her.

'I'm ever so pleased to hear that, Lily.'

We're both quiet the rest of the journey back. Me, lost in memories of my parents. Of how different it would be if they were still here. I wouldn't be in this car with Lola right now, that's for sure. I don't know what Lola's thinking, only that she *is* thinking hard. She pushes her lips together and tugs at the bottom one with her teeth. She seems to be driving on autopilot, and by the time the gravel crunches under the truck's tyres, she looks shocked.

'Thanks again for the lift,' I tell her, struggling to balance both the shopping bags in my arms.

'No problem, Lily. Y'all have a nice evening now. I'll see you soon.'

'Yeah, bye Lola.' I feel a shimmer of unease as I leave down the side of the hotel to the cottages. Running over what I said in the car. We hardly talked and when we did, I definitely talked about Mum and Dad. Probably it was just Lola being Lola. It's like she can be fine, but then she goes all quiet and intense. I resolve to try to ask Noah about her some more later.

Speaking of Noah, he's going to be here in an hour. And this risotto isn't going to cook itself.

* * *

'My arm is killing me!' I complain to Seb. He's on speaker, my phone propped on the small kitchen worktop.

'Risotto is never worth it. All that effort for soggy rice. I don't know why you bother.'

'It's a staple meal!' I protest, holding my stirring arm up with my other one. 'It's exactly the sort of thing you'd make for a business meeting but also to say thanks for stopping me drowning today.'

'Yes, well, nothing says thank you for saving my life like rice.'

'I've made a salad too.'

'Never doubted it. Anything else to report from up there?'

'Not really. I did see Lola with some vet, though. I think they might have a thing.'

'I can see her with a vet,' Seb muses. 'What about Ashton, though?'

'What about him? If Lola was in love with him, she's waited long enough.'

'True. So what's this business meeting you and Noah are having?'

'I told you, he wants to try to help Lola out this summer. He's already writing the article to bring business her way and he has this idea for the fun run. He just wants to chat about some other ideas.'

'I can't believe you went up there with the intention of meeting your birth mum and now you're single-handedly saving her hotel. This could not be more you coded if you tried.'

'I'm not single-handedly saving the hotel. You're so dramatic. I'm just helping Noah to help Lola. In secret. Because apparently Lola is too proud to ask for help.'

'And you're doing all of this without her knowing who you really are. It's like a movie . . . what could possibly go wrong?'

'It's not like a movie.'

'Playing devil's advocate here: what happens if you just tell her who you are?'

I think while I stir. Seb's half right. The sensible thing to do here is to tell Lola who I am. Carrying on the lie is frankly ridiculous. I can't see Lola kicking off or being mean about it. I doubt she'd throw me out. She seems to collect waifs and strays, if anything. And while I'm neither waif nor stray, as a highly strung orphan, I'd fit the bill.

It's just I can't picture myself saying it. It's like a cliff I need to jump off for my own good, but I can't see the bottom. I don't know what'll happen if I jump, but it feels scary and potentially quite messy. Lola not knowing who I am is safe. I can learn about her. I can study her. I can hear all about why she did what she did, why she quit the band, in this nice safe little cocoon.

'It gets messy and awkward,' I reply, finally. 'I hate messy and awkward.'

'When you get therapy, make sure you mention the fact that you dodge confrontation.'

'I do not appreciate the "when" not "if" in that sentence.'

'Everyone needs therapy, there's no shame in it. Now let me sit in my deep-seated need for vicarious pleasure . . . tell me about the kiss again.'

I groan loudly, already regretting telling Seb.

'I told you already, it was great, and then I got cramp in my leg and ruined it.'

'Sounds like you need a do-over.'

'I do not need a do-over. There is absolutely no future for me and Noah. Continuing down this path would be insanity.'

'You could jump him after the risotto.'

'What? Are you listening to me? Even if there was a future with him, and there isn't, I've only known him three days and we've kissed once. I made Colin wait a month before we did it.'

'There is so much I could say about that. But according to you, you don't have that sort of time with Noah. I vote for jumping him.'

'Of course you do.'

'I mean it, you know you like it really.'

Seb's right. I do like it. It's like the swearing. It might not be in my MO, but sex takes me out of my own head, just like running.

Good sex, I should say, the sort that distracts me from thoughts of dead relatives watching on.

There's a knock at the cottage doors.

'Shit, he's here. What should I do?!'

'You've been stirring that risotto for decades. Let the poor guy in so you can eat it.' There's a pause. 'And then shag him.'

'Seb!'

'Er, just letting you know that I can hear your conversation,' Noah calls from the outside.

Seb must hear enough of what Noah says to start cackling. I end the call mid-cackle and pull open the door to Noah, my face absolutely on fire.

'We're having risotto?' he asks, half his mouth pulled into a smile.

'Ohmygod, I'm so sorry that you heard that. I don't . . . I never . . . ' I draw a blank. Whether through shame or the fact that Noah is wearing a soft grey shirt, I don't know. His hair looks wet, and it's pushed back for once. He has a notebook in his hand. It's a good thing that I am mortified, otherwise there's a chance I really would jump him.

He starts to laugh. 'Don't worry about it, Lily.' He smiles a full smile now. 'You look nice.'

He's probably just being polite. I get that. Especially since I don't feel nice. I feel unravelled, and as predicted, my now dry hair is frizzing up with gusto.

'Thanks, you look ... ' Edible. That's weird that I think that, right? Luckily, I manage to stop my brain from spouting it out, settling on 'nice' too. It's bland, but also less Armie Hammer.

'Come in.' I step aside and let him pass, only doing the shallowest of breaths as he does. I don't *want* to know that he smells clean and kind of earth-like. But I can't be held responsible if I just happen to breathe in some of his smell. We all need to breathe.

'I hope risotto's okay?' I ask, going back to stirring to give me something to do. Seb's right, this is a lot of effort for wet rice. 'I made a salad too.' I'm the embodiment of lame.

'Great, thanks.' Noah sits on the sofa. 'I'll eat anything.'

I've put a bottle of wine on the little glass coffee table that's now back in front of the sofa since Seb isn't here anymore. I'm suddenly very, very aware that every single thing I've done screams DATE instead of BUSINESS MEETING. Like at all. Oh good god, I lit a candle. I look over at him.

'You're panicking again,' he says.

'Nooooo.' I draw it out. 'I'm not panicking. Just, er, recalibrating. Like yes, we have wine. But we don't have to drink it, you know, because this is about Lola and the hotel. I have water, obviously. Everyone has water. Fresh water from the spring ... couldn't be fresher. Shall we make a point of that, erm, somewhere? Or some more of that lemonade that Harper hated. We can have whatever you like.'

'Do you always put so much thought into what you have to drink?' he asks.

'I feel like the answer you're looking for is *no*,' I venture. 'But the honest answer is yes. I overthink everything. Seb calls it the millennial curse.'

Noah laughs.

'Well, how about this. I'm not great with . . . people. Too complicated, you know? So, honestly, if I don't want wine, I'll just say so. I don't think too much about things.'

Interesting. Very interesting.

Imagine not thinking about things.

'But as it is—' He's talking pretty fast. '—I'd really like wine. Thanks very much. I'll open it, if you like. You seem to have your hands full.'

I actually can't think of a reply to what he's saying.

Honesty sounds refreshing. It's just obviously not something I can offer him back. No matter how honest we are, I can't tell him who I am or why I'm here.

It takes some of the shine off the evening.

Still, I can't openly admit to not wanting to be honest either. He'd run a mile.

'Okay, honesty. I like that.' I just keeping talking as Noah moves to the kitchen drawer by my hip to get the corkscrew. 'I read this thing once, about radical candour. Basically, it's where you just say it as it is. Seb sent it to me, I think. I liked it in principle, but I find it hard, you know, practically.'

Can you over-stir a risotto? I've sped up despite the persistent arm ache.

'You want people to like you,' he says simply, like it's not my whole reason for being, my worst and best quality all rolled into one.

'I really do,' I admit. He's looking at me again and my breath catches in my throat. 'This is nearly ready.' Chances are, I'm about to stir this rice into oblivion. Noah pops the cork out of the wine.

## The Next Chapter

I ladle the chicken and mushroom risotto into two bowls and get the side salads I've already chopped out of the fridge.

'This looks amazing. Thanks for cooking for me,' Noah says as I spread it all out on the coffee table.

'Oh, it's nothing, honestly. You showed me the secret pool,' I reply, arm ache long forgotten.

'I don't think I've ever had so many vegetables on one plate.'

I realize here that he's taking the piss.

'Let me guess, you live off cheeseburgers and look like that. What a cliché.'

That makes him laugh.

'Look like what?' he asks.

'You know.' I take a prim mouthful of risotto. Seb was wrong, it's definitely not soggy rice.

'Cheeseburgers are delicious, though,' he finishes. Now isn't the time to get into the correlation between red meat and incidences of bowel cancer.

Keen to move the conversation away from Noah's looks or my slight obsession with keeping everyone around me alive, I think of some of the pre-prepared questions I thought up earlier.

I started doing this after Mum died, when I became acutely aware that awkward silences had become especially awkward. Enter stage left, preconceived talking points. They've been a lifesaver on many a Bumble date.

'Do you know what you'll be working on next?' I ask Noah. 'After the stint in Scotland, I mean. Or is that not how it works? Do you not get to plan?'

Noah swallows. We're twisted so that our knees are pointing towards each other.

'Sort of,' he answers. 'You can't plan too far in advance. Normally how it works is that I get commissioned a couple of months ahead. So, I know I have a month in Italy after Skye, working on a piece for Intrepid.

After that it's a bit up in the air. I don't like to plan too far ahead, I like the unpredictability of not knowing where I'll be in six months.'

Sounds like my actual living nightmare. Still, I can't say that so instead I say, 'Wow, Italy sounds amazing. I've always wanted to go.'

Noah has a drink of the wine. 'So why don't you?'

He makes it sound so simple.

'I'm more of a home body. My ex said I was hard work on holiday.'

'Fair enough. Though for the record, you don't seem hard work to me.'

'That's because you've only known me, like, three days.' I laugh. 'And Colin was all right. He could be hard work as well, so we were probably too similar. Did you never want to settle down and stay in one place?'

This was not one of my pre-arranged questions. *Stick to the script, brain.*

'Sometimes,' he admits. 'There are a lot of travel influencers now so commissions can be harder to come by. I pitched for the one on Skye, though don't tell Lola that.'

'Seb says that Instagram will be the end of us all,' I tell him.

Noah laughs. 'I've been offered a steady gig with the *Guardian*, actually.' He keeps his eyes on the rice. 'I'd still get to travel, but shorter trips. It's one of the things I'm thinking about for after Italy. I don't like the thought of staying in one place.' He is still zeroing in on that rice. 'I'm used to moving around a lot. But it's fine. I like my job. It would be good, though, being closer to Lola. I could help more.'

I've been eating the whole time he talks and when he's done, I have a whole mouthful of salad so we both have to wait while I finish.

'In secret?' I ask.

'Probably.' He laughs. 'Lola's too ... '

'Stubborn?' I offer.

'She doesn't like the thought of being a burden,' he answers. 'But

I know how much the hotel means to her. She thinks she needs money, to do it up properly. I guess she's not wrong . . . '

That has to be it, then. Lola's selling her story for money for the hotel. I wonder why she's so enamoured with this place. Majestic beauty aside, obviously.

'So that's what you're doing this summer. The article, the repairs, the thinking of ways to bring in business, they're all for Lola. Like a three-pronged plan?'

Noah doesn't answer. Instead, he puts his bowl on the table and opens his notebook. His writing is all spidery, but it's right there in black and white: 'The three-point approach.'

And okay, a three-point approach isn't exactly word for word the same as a three-pronged plan, but they're still freakishly similar. He has bullet points and everything. Everyone knows that it's not a real plan until it's committed to page via bullet points.

'That's . . . so funny,' I say, feeling a bit freaked out. Noah and me, we couldn't be more different in so many ways, but we obviously have *some* similarities. Mainly those based around stationery and planning, but they're pretty big ones.

I scan my eyes over his 'Save Broadford Hotel' plan. It's broken down into the three things I suggested.

1. *Increase footfall.*
   Underneath, there are things like 'increase marketing' and 'involve people from the island more (run?)'

2. *Guest experience.*
   Repairs to hotel, consider timetable – fit for purpose?

3. *Pitch article.*
   Hidden gems of Skye? Focus on Broadford and surrounding area. Broadford hotel at centre?

There's a big tick next to number three.

'Wow,' I say.

I have to, once again, resist the urge to jump poor Noah. A ticked off to-do list will absolutely get me going.

'You have a whole business plan almost.' My voice is full of wonder and awe.

'I don't know what I'm doing really.'

'It looks great . . . but does Lola . . . is the hotel really struggling?' I ask.

'Maybe. But it's not just that. Lola, she can't keep going like she is. She wasn't well, last year. Nothing serious.'

Noah must see me almost jump out of my own skin.

'But she had a chest infection that turned to pneumonia, and it took her a while to recover. I just want to help, if I can. Get her to a point where she can maybe hire someone.'

I nod. So much nodding while I try to process.

I wonder if Noah knows that Lola plans to sell her memoirs to a publisher. They're both trying to do the same thing, save the hotel, they're just coming at it from different angles. It really is a tangled web of deceit up here on Skye.

'You mentioned that Lola helped you out when you were younger?' I ask, hoping that Noah doesn't realize how desperately I want to know about all of this. Maybe it makes me a bad person, using this thing with Noah to gather quite so much intel on Lola. My need to know her overrides any feelings of guilt, though.

Noah nods. 'Yeah. It's a long story, but I moved around a lot as a kid. You know how it can be.'

I don't, actually, my upbringing was incredibly stable. But Noah is still talking.

'I up and left home when I was eighteen. Got as far as the train station before I realized that I had no money and nowhere to go. I'm not proud of this, but I pickpocketed the wallet of some guy. Lola saw the whole thing. I thought she was going to call the police, but she didn't. She handed the guy back his wallet, said he'd dropped it. She'd just finished doing up the cottages in the hotel and let me stay on. Gave me money with the pretence it was to write a tourist information leaflet about the area, which gave me something to do. That's how I got into travel writing. I'll always be grateful that she didn't turn me in. That's not why I come back, though. Lola's pretty special, once you get to know her.'

Even though we're the same age now, Noah at eighteen seems so much younger than I was at that age. When I was eighteen, Mum had just died. It ages you, losing a parent. I'd always been a sensible child but even more so after that. I never wanted to give Dad any reason to worry, things were hard enough.

Noah has stopped talking, but instead of silence, there's a ringing in my ears.

'Lily, is everything okay?'

Chances are, I look like I've been drugged. It's just so confronting. My parents. Lola. Clearly Lola *now* is fine, a nice person. I'd get that from her affinity with animals if nothing else. But what Noah's saying makes it seem like she's been a nice person for ages, like she really tried to help him. But she hardly tried at all with me. Her own flesh and blood.

The urge to start wallowing in self-pity is strong.

I really have to work at the smile I set on my face.

'It's no wonder that you want to help her out so much now,' I say, wanting to be genuine and less conflicted about this.

'Yeah, she's the only family I have really.'

God, this is some fucked up situation I'm in. Noah's still talking.

'So, you think the plan for the hotel is decent? And pointers? You're running a successful business with Seb, you must know your stuff.'

'What? Oh yes, we're super successful.' I make a show of looking

171

down at the list again and not mentioning that chances are I'm now entangled with not one but two struggling businesses. 'Fairy lights,' I say finally, 'fairy lights go a long way.'

Noah is nodding. 'Got it. You know—' He taps his pen on the list, our risotto long forgotten. 'Point two.'

'The guest experience,' I interject.

'That's right. You could always let me know what it's like to stay here, as a guest.'

I really should be working at becoming less, not more embroiled in the affairs of Lola and Noah. The more I involve myself, the bigger the betrayal will be if, no when, they find out who I am.

'Er . . . ' Again I'm stumped. How are we meant to say no?

'I know you're already helping with the article; I don't want to put on you . . . '

'I wouldn't have to do all of the hotel experiences, would I? I'm not too good with planes but . . . ' *Shut up, Lily. I'm not good with planes. Or throwing myself out of planes. Or throwing myself out of anything really.*

Noah laughs. 'It's not Lola offering the skydiving, she has an agreement with Skye by Sky. I've already done it.'

'Well, it's just such a shame that one of us has already done that. Because I would have loved a good bit of skydiving. I'd have been all over it,' I say, smiling a huge smile of relief.

'It was a long time ago, though.'

'Still, done. Checked off the list.'

He laughs again.

'So, you'll help?'

I shouldn't. I know I shouldn't. It involves more lies. More deception. To Noah but also to Lola. How does one say, *Hi, I'm your daughter and also the person who has been involved in low-level subterfuge regarding the saving of your hotel?*

The thought makes me start breathing fast.

Plus, there's the fact that Noah probably doesn't know that Lola's planning to sell her memoirs to the highest bidder to raise money for the hotel. He doesn't even need to do all this stuff.

But then, I think of how uncomfortable Lola had been at our first session. How much she has shied away from the limelight ever since her Beyond Baton Rouge days. Maybe if the hotel was doing better, she wouldn't need to ...

The thought process makes me realize that a part of me does want to help Lola. Lola as I know her now deserves the help. And the building, its history, I want them to thrive too.

'Okay,' I tell him. 'I'll help. But we'll need a proper business plan. Something that we can present to Lola formally.'

I'm imagining a boardroom type scenario here. Chances are that the three of us wouldn't all fit in Lola's office.

'We'll have to do costings, and projections and planning. So much planning.'

'Sounds exciting, Lily.'

It does sound exciting. It's also the exact opposite of what Seb told me to do, but I can worry about that tomorrow. For now, I'm high on the thought of an action plan.

This is a terrible idea. This is a brilliant idea; I'll learn more about Lola. I'll get to spend time with Noah. Ah, no, that's bad. Bad brain. Stop it.

'What are you thinking?' Noah asks.

I'm thinking too many things at once. My mind is positively racing.

'I'm thinking that I wish I could just not think for a little bit,' I answer honestly.

'You're a writer, we all think hard.'

'You've no idea. Sometimes I feel like it's overheating. I want to detach my skull and let it air.'

And isn't that a lovely visual that I've given us both – my decapitated head.

'I get it. It's like that for me too sometimes. Describing places can be frustrating. I see all these little details, how they all fit together to make a whole. Like the top of Blà Bheinn, it's so beautiful up there. It can be a challenge, getting it on the page in a way that seems real. Once I start writing it helps, though.'

I'm back to wonder and awe.

'Writing helps me too,' I admit. 'The details of people's lives. I find them comforting. I used to play piano and sing a little, to help me relax, but I haven't done that in a while.'

'I'd like to see that. Lola has a piano here, you know.'

'Does she?' I ask.

He nods. 'It's in the corner of the breakfast room.'

'I didn't see it. It doesn't matter, though; I don't sing or play in public.' Not since Mum died.

I don't know how it's happened, but Noah is closer to me than he was a few minutes ago. Maybe he too gets turned on by action plans. His hair has dried and parts of it are falling over his head now. It's giving Brad Pitt when he was with Gwyneth Paltrow – nature was having an absolute riot the day it made Noah.

And though I hate to be that girl, I have absolutely no idea what he could possibly see in me. Maybe it's like Seb said and he wants to unruffle me. I want to be unruffled. Or more unruffled than I already am at any rate.

He's somehow closer still.

'Can I kiss you again, Lily?'

I should say no. I know I should, there are so many reasons why this is a bad idea. *No future,* I say to myself. It's going nowhere. Nothing. Zip.

But I'm a ball of tension, taut and brittle, ready to shatter.

And this night feels full of bad ideas.

Maybe I can just get him out of my system. Just this once. I've read about it in books. It always turns out exactly as they're hoping it might.

I snap.

'God, yes, please do.' It comes out as the plea that it is. I'm nodding my head, so when Noah's lips actually meet mine, it takes me a second to still.

At first, our lips are closed. It's chaste, not enough to unravel me fully.

But then the slide of his tongue against mine is heaven and I lose myself in the push and pull of it all. I sigh into his mouth, pulling him tighter towards me.

I could cry with relief as my thoughts are crowded out by lust. I just need more.

The kiss turns feral and it's because of me. I'm clawing at him. Pulling at his T-shirt. I just need to forget.

'Lily, I . . . '

No. No. I don't want to talk about this anymore. I don't want to have to think about talking. 'Six weeks,' I say. I don't know why I'm saying it. I'm unravelling. 'I'm leaving in six weeks. And you . . . Italy . . . So . . . just . . . this . . . once . . . '

Six weeks stretches out before us like forever. I've never had a fling. I've never wanted one before. But the Isle of Skye operates on a different plane to everywhere else. Here, I just want my brain to shut up and for Noah to kiss me. No, it's not a want, it's a need.

I can feel Noah's heart beating hard under the flat of my palm under his shirt.

'Once?' He pauses before he answers me. He's stopped kissing me and that will not do.

I nod. 'That's all.'

It's the truth. Noah and me, we would never work. I can list the reasons we wouldn't work.

1. He loves to travel and most days, I have to psych myself up to leave the house.
2. He's leaving in six weeks.
3. I'm leaving in six weeks.
4. I'm lying to him about Lola. About Seb. About who I am.
5. I've told him more than once that I love adventure when the reality is that I get excited when my favourite toothpaste is on special offer.

No, all this thinking is bad, we don't want thinking.

Noah pauses for another moment, his eyes meeting mine. 'Okay, then.' He's kissing me again and it's escalating. My hand is moving again under his shirt, his body hot beneath my palm.

I'm lost to it as I climb onto his lap and wriggle out of the straps of my maxi dress. I'm not myself. I'm fevered and frenzied and I'm going to die if he stops trailing his mouth along my collarbone.

'Please,' I say, pressing his mouth against my chest. I don't even know what I'm asking for. Except my brain is quiet and I don't want this to stop.

I don't want it to stop when Noah stands up, taking me with him. His shirt is open, and my dress is bunched around my waist.

'Bedroom?' he asks, stumbling around the coffee table.

'Yes, definitely.' See, there are some benefits to having short legs, it makes you easy to carry.

Noah gently drops me on the bed and I reach for him when he stays standing by the side of it.

'Do you have a—?' he asks and my mind is so off that it takes me a second to realize that he means a condom.

No. No, I don't have a condom. It wasn't on my list. How have I brought a lavender diffuser and no condoms?

'Don't worry, I'll be back in a second.'

Noah darts from the cottage and I just lay there, a picture of debauchery.

He's back, with a small black wash bag.

'Come here, please,' I half beg him.

Finally, he lowers himself on top of me, his body pushing me into the bed, the solid weight of him perfect.

We're moving as one and for once, everything in my head is still.

# Chapter Eleven

*To Do:*

- Google one-night stand etiquette
- Three-pronged plan to save hotel
- Lola memoirs chapter two
- Cover design for Mr Vandergilden – carcass or guns?
- Get on top of emails

'Why are you calling me? You know I cherish my alone time in the morning.' Seb's voice down the phone is harsh.

'Shhh, you're so loud, you're going to wake him up,' I angry whisper, looking back at the bedroom door that I'd pulled closed but not shut properly.

I'd woken up very naked, an equally naked Noah next to me on the bed.

'Wake him . . . oh my god, Lily, you did jump him!' Seb cackles down the phone and I have to put my hand over it to muffle him.

'Are you done?' I ask when his laugh finally tails off to a gentle chuckle.

'I think so,' he answers. 'But if Noah is in your bed, I have to say I'm impressed. I didn't think you had it in you. But why the fuck are you talking to me? Get back in there,' he orders.

'It's not as simple as that.' I pull my summer dressing gown tight around me. It doesn't exactly feel like the protector of my virtue I might need it to be. 'You know I've never done this before. What's the etiquette? Do I make him a coffee? Do I shake his hand and bid him farewell?'

Seb starts to laugh again. 'Please do that last one. Film it for me, would you?'

'You are no help. How do I get rid of him?'

I start to pace.

'Get rid of him? Was it bad?'

'No, not bad. Amazing, actually,' I tell him. 'Plus, before, I agreed to help him save the hotel. We have a three-pronged plan!' I'm whispering hysterically.

'Wow, your saviour complex knows no bounds. Impressive. I'd slow clap you, for the sex, not the saviour thing, if I wasn't holding my phone. Good for you, my short-legged friend. I told you a good orgasm would sort you out.'

I make a non-committal hum. It really was a good orgasm. No, I can't let my orgasm distract me.

'Seb, there is no future between me and him. None at all. He's going to fucking Italy in September. You know where I'm going? Salford. Plus, there are all the lies I'm telling and the fact that I've given him the total wrong impression of me,' I tell Seb. 'He thinks I'm all wild and adventurous. Especially now.'

'Please tell me you got the handcuffs out?'

'What?! No, of course I didn't even pack them. I was just ... freakier than usual. I kind of lost it a bit.'

A completely X-rated still from last night presents itself clear as day in my mind's eye. Not helpful.

'What do I do?!'

Seb thinks for a minute. 'Look, if you don't want to do it again, you don't have to, you know that, right?'

'I know, I just ... I thought I'd get it out of my system. But Seb, the people in books, they're lying, that is not reality. It makes you want to do it more!'

It takes several minutes for the laughing to stop.

'Get it out of her system,' he finally finishes. 'Look, are we done here? I can go back to bed for half an hour. Let's just say I've unearthed some of my old pictures of Ashton and you're not the only one who had a long night.'

'Did not need to know that. But yes, we're done. You're still going to check on Elton for me today?'

'Yes.'

'Make sure he's only having the dry food. You know what Mr Cains is like.'

'Got that.'

'And you promise to try those patches I got you?'

'I promise, dear.'

'And you got the draft of the opening for Lola's book that I sent?'

'I did. And exhausting as this is, I have some thoughts about the book I need to share. Will the Wi-Fi there hold for a Zoom meeting, do you think?'

'I reckon so. Harper managed to play Spotify for three hours yesterday.'

'Good, I'll set one up. Keep me posted on how you're getting on up there. Call anytime.'

'I will, thank you.'

'But not before 7am again or I'll block your number.'

'Fine. Bye, Seb.'

'Morning.' I twist around to find Noah in the doorway of the bedroom. Mercifully, he's put his boxers back on, because even him shirtless is a lot for this early.

I flail and drop my phone.

'Morning.' There's a very good chance I look like a startled deer. My eyes, already on the big side, are wide and fixed very determinedly on Noah's face. Even though I fear that after last night, this is something of a moot point.

I clutch my dressing gown ever tighter.

'Coffee?' Noah asks, walking past me, seemingly oblivious to my particular brand of startled panic.

'It's okay,' he says, stopping before me to plant a kiss on the top of my head. Maybe not so oblivious, then. I should have Googled the etiquette thing over calling Seb. He was useless. And I really didn't think that morning head kisses were within the parameters of a fling. But then what the hell do I know? I decide to follow Noah's lead.

'Yeah, I bought my own. It's in the top cupboard.'

Noah moves around the kitchen, filling up the percolator and boiling the kettle. I watch him with the kind of rapt attention normally reserved for children and zoo animals.

'Milk and sugar, right?' he asks, no doubt remembering the coffee that I drank at his cottage two days ago.

Trying to maintain a semblance of control, I add my own milk and half a spoon of sugar and then breathe it in, hoping that I at least look like the cool, calm and collected person I aim to be.

'So should we revisit our plans for the hotel or ...?' Noah lets the sentence hang.

I mean, first of all, how the fuck is it only Tuesday? I feel like I've lived several lifetimes already on Skye. And secondly, it's almost ridiculous to think that I'd bail on a plan. Plans are life.

'Yes, definitely.' I start talking at pace. 'Let's recap. We have a three-pronged plan of attack.' I don't even stumble over all the p's. 'Step one, we do what we can around the place to help Lola out. Step two, I live the guest experience and report back, and step three, we make your article as amazing as possible. As a subsidiary of step two, a step two b, if you will, I'll look to consider a new marketing plan for Lola. Something with some real wow factor. I did an MA in marketing a couple of years ago. Just for fun.'

Noah appears momentarily lost for words. Seb does say that I get a little giddy when I'm forming a plan.

But this is excellent. I'm going to be busy. So busy. There'll actually be no time at all to carry on this little ill-advised tryst. I'll hardly have time to write Lola's memoirs and keep on top of my other work with it all. It's brilliant. What I'll need is a robust weekly timetable.

'Er, Lily, is everything okay?'

It's only then I realize how flustered I've become.

'Yes, fine, why do you ask?' I try to get some of the sweat off my forehead. Styling it out as a yawn.

'You just look like you did last night, you know when . . . '

He trails off. It's all the confirmation I need that I equate weekly timetables with orgasms.

Noah's leaning back against the kitchen worktop, his long legs crossed at the ankles. Distracting, very distracting.

'Right, I'd better get to it. What's on at the hotel today? No time like the present.'

'It's painting today.'

'Brilliant,' I lie. I hate painting. 'Who doesn't love painting? I think I'll go and sign right up.'

I'm like Roadrunner, zipping around the cottage. Focusing on anything that isn't Noah. While I zip, Noah says, 'And if you're free this weekend, I was thinking of checking out another hidden gem for the article.'

So far, Noah's hidden gems have involved no small amount of physical pain. But standing in just his boxers like that, he could ask for a kidney and I'd cut it right out myself.

Plus, it's part of the three-pronged plan.

'Yes, excellent idea,' I answer, aiming for businesslike as I attack last night's risotto pan. What was I thinking, not leaving it to soak. The leftover risotto has basically welded itself to the bowl. It looks like cement.

The tap fits and spurts out water. Probably, we need a plumber.

'Penny for your thoughts?' Noah asks.

'I was just thinking that risotto really is not worth the effort it takes to make.' I chance a look at Noah. 'And also, the plumbing in the hotel is shot.' I'm being weird and I don't want him to think that I didn't have a good time last night.

'Can I see you again later?' he asks.

'Yes, yes, it'll be good to regroup after my painting day. I'll take notes. We can mind map.'

I make it sound like a business transaction and Noah frowns. Don't love that.

It's just, I have no way of telling him that I can't do this. I don't want to get involved if there's no future, and there isn't. Plus, Noah . . . Well, he only likes the Isle of Skye version of me. The one who hikes up mountains and has wild flings with intense orgasms. Skye me has sugar in her coffee without even uttering the words 'insulin resistance'. No wonder he wants to keep seeing me – he isn't getting the real me at all.

I open my mouth to articulate all of that, it's just that nothing comes out.

I want, so badly, to be the sort of person who is wanted by someone like Noah.

But it's always been like this. Like there's this vast chasm between the person that I am and the person that I want to be. And I've never, ever known how to cross that chasm.

'Cool. I'll . . . I'd better get off. I always write better in the mornings, so if I don't do some work now, I never will.'

'Me too. I'm sure my brain shuts down after lunch,' I hear myself say. 'My favourite time to write is in the mornings before anyone gets to the office,' I tell him as he disappears into the bedroom.

'Same,' he calls back. I can hear him rustling around, putting his clothes on while I nurse my coffee close to my chest.

Noah reappears, dressed in last night's clothes. Him walking back to his own cottage dressed like that feels illicit and thrilling all at the same time.

He kisses me and I momentarily forget all of the reasons why this really is a terrible idea.

\* \* \*

Here are the reasons why I dislike art.

No, that's not fair. I like art, as in, it's nice to look at. I can feel things when I look at art. I'm not a monster. And Mum was super arty.

It's just the practical application that I struggle with.

Art was the only subject I was actively discouraged from pursuing at school. My art teacher said I was A* for effort, which is code for 'struggles with stick people'.

I think the issue is, there are so few rules with art. And beautiful art is subjective.

Which is why, when Lola calls from behind her own easel that we should 'paint what we feel', a little bit of me dies inside.

Don't get me wrong, there's no doubt about it, the backdrop is beautiful. There are shimmering lochs and dark craggy mountains for as far as the eye can see.

Plus, the loch, with the mountains reflected in it, it's just beautiful. No wonder Noah worries he won't capture it in his writing.

And no doubt about it, I'd rather be painting the loch than actively on it. Or worse, skydiving over it. Lola's hotel can crumble to the ground, a burning pile of financial ruin, before I throw myself out of a plane.

I remind myself that I'm here to gather intel on the guest experience, and that it doesn't matter that my trees look like a three-year-old has painted them.

It's all about the guest experience.

And so far, the guest experience has involved us driving a mile or so away from the hotel in the rickety hotel minibus, standing in a field and being instructed to paint. A little bit of extra guidance wouldn't go amiss. It was the same with kayaking. Lola maybe needs to realize that most people are trying this stuff for the first time.

'That's an interesting perspective, Harper.' Lola is doing the rounds. There are only five of us here. Harper and her foster family, and me. Lola definitely needs to be doing a bit more marketing. No reason that people from town couldn't come to this. There are loads of artists on Skye. It's that sort of place.

Harper is next to me. She's painted the whole thing in black and red. It's like a massacre on canvas. On my other side, Blake has painted Spiderman. Or what I think is Spiderman. The watercolours have sort of run together so he looks to be melting. Whatever it is, it isn't a scenic mountain vista.

I plough on, doggedly determined to produce one noticeable feature of the landscape.

I swish the paintbrush across the bottom of my canvas, flooding it with blue. It's more turquoise than the deathly dark blue of the loch. It looks like I'm painting a tropical bay.

'You could concentrate on adding more of the reflection, see there, how the trees are mirrored in the water?' Lola points to the distance, over my shoulder.

I do see it, the trees reflection on the lake. It's lovely. Really beautiful. But Lola must be out of her mind if she's looked at my painting and thought that I'm a person capable of replicating that on a canvas. My sun has actual yellow beams coming off it.

'I'll give it my best shot,' I say, through gritted teeth, thinking that once again, a little more instruction wouldn't go amiss. Maybe Lola could get an actual artist to run the session.

Lola nods and goes to move on, but before she can I say quickly,

'Just checking that you're still okay for another session tomorrow morning?' I drop my voice in case she doesn't want anyone to hear.

'Yes, Lily, that's fine.' She looks away.

'Great,' I say, jabbing my brush at the canvas in an attempt to create a tree reflection. It looks shit. 'I'll come to the office, shall I? Usual time?'

Lola nods and moves on.

It's only when she goes that I realize how fast my heart is beating.

\* \* \*

I'm waiting for my second session with Lola.

It could be that my limbs are just puddles of goo and I can't quite summon the energy to be stressed, but a part of me feels less tense than the first time we met. I don't know what I'd expected, but hearing about Lola's childhood definitely made her seem less scary.

This morning, Lola is ready, waiting for me in the lobby. That's good. I don't need to be hanging around thinking. Thinking is bad. Given thinking time, I might relive last night with Noah, which was strained and a little awkward.

We had at least produced a programme of work for the hotel.

Programmes of work might be my idea of foreplay, but they're no one else's. We've planned out everything we can fit into five weeks. Noah, who seems to be able to turn his hand to basically anything, is going to do most of it. Then, I'd shaken his hand and practically thrown him out of my cottage. At the time, it had felt like a win. This morning, not so much.

'Breakfast is done.' Lola interrupts my thoughts. Today her dungarees are khaki green. She's wearing a loose purple shirt underneath, her hair in its usual long plait. I catch a glimpse of the pair of us in the mirror that hangs on the wall opposite the reception desk. She's so tan compared to me. We're like chalk and cheese, the tanned and pasty version.

I follow Lola into the back office, not even protesting when she sits on the stool again. At least there's no giant dog this time. I pull out my phone. 'Same as last session, if that's okay?' I ask her.

She gives a little staccato nod. It's reserved Lola today, then.

Now that I'm here, I realize that I'm desperate for her to start.

'Whenever you're ready,' I tell her, hitting record. 'Just pick up where you left off.'

Another nod.

She sits on her hands.

And starts to talk.

* * *

*I was about twelve, the year that Da left. Almost ready for high school. I think for about a year, Ma didn't accept that he'd really gone. Sometimes, I'd catch her in the garden, looking down the path like she expected him to come bumbling along it like he used to. Except he never did.*

*It was a hard time for Ma. She had all these kids and I don't know that she was that fond of any of us by that point. Six kids is hard work for anyone. Six kids when you're dirt poor and on your own is extra bad. At first, she started selling stuff just to get by. I thought for sure that she'd sell Pa's guitar, though she never did. After a while there was nothing left worth selling so she got a job fixin' people's hair in a salon in Baton Rouge. Long shifts and an even longer bus to get there. She wasn't around much and when she was, she'd look at us all, even Jessie, like she didn't know how she got to be here in this crappy house stuck with all of us.*

*It was the 1980s then and it felt like the whole world was changing around us. I started high school and learned about all the things Pa had cared so much about. Civil rights, nuclear war, that sort of thing. Except sometimes I wondered if the world had forgotten about our family, left us behind, like. I started to hate everything, and I don't know, maybe that's the way of* teenagers, but I was just so angry all the god damn time.

I started to get in trouble at school, fell in with the wrong crowd. Other kids would pick on us because our shoes had holes in and rather than turn the other cheek like they'd taught us at church, I'd get into fights. I remember once, Ma got called into the principal's office and while I was waiting outside I heard her tellin' him that I'd always been difficult. That I was born in a storm.

Needless to say, I spent a lot of time in detention. But rather than makin' me see sense, it just made me angrier and angrier. It's not healthy living with so much anger, it makes a person bitter. I needed some outlet for it or else I was going to explode, least that's how it felt.

I can't remember what started it, but one-night, I must have been about fifteen, me and Ma got into this blazing argument. We never did the gardening together anymore, all we ever did was bicker and snap. I think looking back I blamed her for Pa leaving, for keeping us in this rubbish house that the rest of the world forgot.

So, we're having this enormous argument and callin' each other all sorts of bad names. I'd learned a lot of new swear words from the crowd I hung around with and I felt real grown up to use them. Well, one of the names must have been bad enough for Ma to finally lose it because she told me to get out, said that I couldn't stay there anymore. That I'd always been trouble and now I'd gone too far.

I didn't even think about the fact that I had nowhere to go. I just up and grabbed Pa's guitar. It was covered in dust. I took it and I walked out of the house.

I vowed then that I'd never rely on anyone again. Thought I needed to make my own way in the world, away from the Ma who never seemed to want me.

I never went back there again.

'Could we stop there?' She breaks off suddenly. 'It's a lot, you know?' Her eyes glisten with unshed tears. It might be hard to get a proper handle on Lola, but I'm almost certain that if she cries, she only does it in private.

'I'm so sorry,' I tell her. 'I can't believe your own mum threw you out.' It's completely unprofessional to pass judgement on what a client has just told us. It's not about us, after all. But the boundaries between me and Lola are blurry at best, even if Lola doesn't quite realize it. I just could never picture my own mum doing that. She wouldn't have done.

Lola shrugs. 'Some people just aren't cut out to be parents.'

It's impossible not to wonder whether Lola is talking about herself. I guess she must be.

'I've heard that,' I tell her slowly, hating that my voice has a little wobble to it. 'My parents are amazing.' I scrunch up my eyes at how insensitive I'm being. 'Sorry, I don't know what's wrong with me.'

'It's okay, Lily.' Lola has her head tilted slightly to the side. 'I'm glad you have that.'

I stand up suddenly. This is not what I'm meant to be doing. We're not meant to sit around and swap life stories with the clients.

'I think I'd better go,' I tell Lola, even though I'm already stood up and holding my phone. 'We don't need to meet again until next week. There's plenty of time left yet. I scheduled sessions, for the summer, I mean. I'll send them to you. Or just tell you them. When I see you.'

'Course, Lily. Y'all just let me know when you're ready to meet again.'

I nod. 'Of course. It'll be good to have a couple of days to work on the material you've given me so far anyway.' And I need a break, I think but don't say.

'Alrighty, then. What do you say if the weather's nice still, next time we do this outside? It's awful stuffy in here.'

Outside seems like a bad idea. I don't like the idea of Lola feeling all free and easy and getting to say things like *some people aren't cut out to be parents* whenever she feels like it. But then what choice do I have? That's not a valid reason for saying no. And as I remind myself for about the millionth time (this whole episode is making me very egotistical) this isn't about me.

'Sounds good to me,' I say. There, I'm breezy. So incredibly breezy. I'm just going to breeze on out of here and then go find a stiff drink. Or ten. 'See you, Lola.'

Before she can reply I'm out of the office and through the back door of the hotel. I'm across the gardens and because it's only 11am, I'm not cracking open more wine, but I am adding extra beans to the cafetière. I realize my hands are shaking. Have they been shaking this whole time? I've no idea.

I pour a drink and then take my laptop outside. At least I have some designated work time for the rest of today. I need that. To get on top of work feels safe. Plus, it's peaceful and still out here. It's just me and my overactive brain running a constant loop of Lola saying that some people aren't meant to be parents, while trying to tackle my mountain of emails.

She *must* have meant herself.

Her mum too, obviously. Possibly it's a hereditary defect. I mean, Elton hates me, doesn't he? Maybe I have anti-maternal instincts oozing out of my every pore.

But then if I think about myself with a child – I think I'd love it. No, I know I would. I've always wanted a family of my own. It's why I don't do flings. Because I want something serious. I'm desperate for it. My parents showed me how great it could be, marriage, kids, the whole thing. I hope they wouldn't think me being here with Lola is trying to replace them. Dad wanted me to come, but did he want me to stay for six weeks?!

All I know is that I want what they had. I want a family, it's one of the reasons that I'm keen to nail down another Colin. With me and Mum and Dad, it felt like us against the world, and I want that. I want to give a child that.

I start work on Lola's second chapter.

At some point in the afternoon, Harper appears from the forest. She doesn't even ask, she just leans over me and clicks on Spotify. We sit in silence for a while until she asks, 'Are you okay?'

It's like an accusation almost, as if I'd better be okay or else. I don't even know why she's asking until I realize that I've been crying a little bit. Okay, maybe a whole lot.

'I think so,' I tell her. 'Or I will be at any rate.'

'Life's shit.' She shrugs. 'But it's probably a bit better than being dead.'

# Chapter Twelve

'How was the session with Lola?'

Noah finds me in the garden, hunched over my laptop, typing hard. Harper had left at about the same time as the Pringles I'd bought had run out.

Despite what I said about my brain dying off in the afternoons, today it's working overtime. And even though, as per my timetable, I should be prioritizing Mr Vandergilden's cover design, it's Lola's memoirs that I'm desperate to write.

'Really good, thanks. Lola's a great storyteller, it just writes itself.'

It strikes me, then; I don't know how much Noah knows about Lola's past. I mean, he must know that she's *the* Lola Starr, but I can't ask him about it, not until Lola tells me.

My chest tightens at the reminder that I'm basically lying to everyone here.

I hit the full stop key with more force than I need to.

'Right, I'm done for the day,' I tell Noah. 'I think I'll go for a run.'

I need to do something to escape the jittery feeling.

'Mind if I join you?' he asks quietly.

'Be my guest.'

\* \* \*

Over the next few days, my weekly time plan really comes into its own. It goes some way to calming me the fuck down.

192

Early mornings, I sit outside and do some work, forcing myself to make a little more headway with Mr Vandergilden's memoirs. I owe him a draft this summer and something tells me that informing him that it'll be late while I gallivant around the Isle of Skye and reconnect with my long-lost mother will not go down well. He has a whole chapter dedicated to the anti-woke movement, after all.

After the first day, Noah had come to sit outside too. He works at his little white picnic table; I work at mine. It's all highly civilized.

On Friday, I do yoga with Lola on the pier. Happily, my yoga-thon for charity means that I excel at this activity at least. I notice that once more, Lola is running the session herself. I wonder if she's one of those people who doesn't sleep. Like Maggie Thatcher. Or vampires.

The last few evenings have been tricky. I hadn't thought to plan for the evenings. So, I don't know what to do when Noah appears. Harper too, under the guise that she wants to use my laptop. She mainly ignores us, but she does eat an inordinate amount of Pringles each night.

I'd checked with her foster mum that it was okay that she'd been demolishing so many, only to be told that so long as Harper's eating, that's all that matters. I couldn't help but notice that Blake, Harper's brother, was sat with his foster dad, being read to under the shade of a tree.

I'd gone and cleared the hotel shop of Pringles after that.

Nothing else has happened with Noah, not since that Tuesday night. For the past three nights, we've kept it strictly professional, working on his piece on Skye. I'm equal parts relieved and bereft at this.

It's for the best, I remind myself for the millionth time.

Absolutely, it's for my own good.

I don't know why, then, I'm re-reading his books on Skye. Why I read them late at night when I'm on my own.

Or why I feel so sad that I only got that one-night with him.

* * *

*The Fairy Pools are a must-see on Skye. Known for their crystal blue waters and set at the foot of the Black Cuillin range, the pools make for the perfect place for a swim. The history of the pools is entwined with no small amount of magic. Local legend holds that the pools were once the preserve of a fairy princess, forbade by her father from marrying the mortal man she had been handfasted to.*

I have to stop reading Noah's book, even though I don't want to, because I'm meant to be meeting him in the car park for our next scouting trip right about . . . now.

I grab my rucksack and tighten my shoelaces and rush through the gardens to find Noah waiting by the motorbike. His motorbike. Because obviously the motorbike in the hotel car park belongs to him. Why should it be that the man who writes beautiful prose is also into motorbikes I'll never know.

'All ready?' he asks.

'Yeah, but just to be clear here. You want me to get on the back of that while it's in motion. I mean, moving.'

'I'll drive carefully,' is all he says in reply.

I peer again at the motorbike. It's just, there's nothing over you, is there? No roof. If something goes wrong, you're very exposed. It's not exactly like the emergency services are going to be on hand out here. Not when it's a half-hour round trip for a loaf of bread.

'I can ask Lola if we can borrow her van?' Noah offers. Obviously, I'm not doing a very good job at hiding my alarm, which just will not do. I'm meant to be wild and free Lily, that's the deal here. Not Lily who is frozen with abject terror.

'No, don't worry, this looks great. I've actually always wanted to go on a motorbike.' I take the helmet Noah is holding out and pull it over my head (my hair will make me regret this later). Noah swings a leg over with ease and I clamber on behind him with much less ease. My knuckles are white where they grip the seat behind me.

I want to message Seb, to tell him that if I die, he can have the house so long as he looks after Elton, but I also don't want to let go of the seat. Even not moving, the bike feels precarious. There are only two wheels!

I grip onto Noah's sides through his T-shirt. He at least is solid and warm. It's calming. He puts his hand over mine where I'm clinging on to him so hard several G forces couldn't dislodge me. Noah squeezes. 'I've got you.'

I try to match my breathing to his. In, out. In, out. How bad can this be?

The engine revs to life and I scream. We haven't even set off.

'We should get the van,' Noah calls. We're stationary in the car park. I've screwed my eyes shut.

'No, just go.' I cling on even harder. 'I want to try.'

'Okay?' Noah calls back to me. 'It isn't far, try to relax.'

Fat chance of that.

We turn around in the car park and I don't fall off. Excellent.

'Here goes.'

I scream again as we set off properly. This one muffled into the back of Noah's T-shirt.

I'm sure we're going faster than the speed of sound. We zip through the lanes, Noah completely at ease, me the very opposite of that. Is it normal for your life to flash before your eyes while you're still alive?

I've glued myself to Noah's back. My arms are wrapped so tightly around him, it's a miracle that he can draw breath.

'Almost there!' I hear him say above the noise of the wind we're creating. My eyes are still screwed tightly shut. Because if I'm about to go careering to my death, I don't want to watch it play out.

Finally, we slow down. We've been stopped for quite some time before I chance opening my eyes to see Noah standing at the side of the bike, looking down at me. That at least makes my heart cease and desist its efforts to batter its way out of my own chest. It settles on a nice simple swoon instead.

I smile, even though my mouth is super dry from the ride. It's a strange sensation, that of your own lips being pulled back across your teeth.

'We could have taken the van.' Noah helps me off with my helmet and tucks some hair behind my ear, where it stays for approximately a nanosecond before springing right back out. He has another go and then gives it up as the lost cause that it is.

'You know what, I think I enjoyed that actually.' I hop down, my sentiments undermined somewhat by the fact that my legs are like jelly and I have to prop myself up with a hand on the motorbike seat.

Noah looks suspicious. His frown has lessened, but it's still there.

'So where are we?' I ask, looking around. As per, we seem to be in the middle of fucking nowhere. Just the usual fields and mountains. I'm a bit over fields and mountains.

'Camas Mor,' Noah answers, pulling his rucksack out of the bags over the back of the bike. 'Come on, it's about a twenty-minute walk. This way.'

I catch up to Noah as he sets the pace across a field, pleased to see that we seem to be walking across as opposed to up today. Zero elevation and the beautiful clifftop walk towards the ocean is exactly what today needs.

We walk quietly for a little while, still heading towards the edge of the cliffs. The landscape here, a mere ten minutes away from the hotel, is different. It's expansive and bare, full of open fields. We're mid-field when I say, 'Wherever we're going is definitely a hidden gem.' I'm pleased that I opted for my walking shoes today. The sole is so cushioned, it's like walking on air. 'There wasn't even a car park!' We'd left the bike at a small indent in the road, next to a fence. Imagine a land where you're not paying £2.50 an hour to park a car. It's like Narnia.

'We're going down there.' Noah has his sunglasses on again. Those things should be illegal. He nods his head towards the cliff edge.

And oh no, is he going to make me scale a cliff? It looks steep. So very steep.

'It's something I didn't consider when I pitched for the commission, how maybe it would be better if these things remained hidden. I wonder if one day there'll be nowhere left for us to discover. Especially with climate change, you know.'

As someone with zero wanderlust in their body, not a single dose of the stuff, nowhere left to discover doesn't seem quite the tragedy to me as it does to poor Noah. Not that I want the planet to burn or anything. I wash out my glass jars like we're meant to. But for Noah, it sounds like it would be a disaster. I guess because the man does have a compass tattooed on his shoulder. He's obviously a very committed explorer.

'I get what you mean,' I say, trying to look to the edge of the cliff for a path down. 'It's like you say in your book, it's all a lot more fragile than we hope it might be.'

He groans and goes red, and I'm delighted with myself.

'I still can't believe you're reading that.'

'Why not? That's the whole point of writing a book, Noah, for people to read it.'

'Not people I know!' he protests.

'Especially people you know. We can cheer you on. I'll buy a copy for everyone I know for Christmas.'

He laughs. 'Okay, well, in that case, thank you, Lily.'

I hum. 'You're welcome. Actually, it's a little bit like history really. Not having anything left to discover. We know so much about modern history, it doesn't hold the same mystery as, like, the

Middle Ages. But then, I think that we can never know history fully, because we can't ever go back there. And anyway, people who were there experienced it differently. So maybe it's like that. Even if there's nowhere left to discover, it'll still be a discovery for new people who go there, because they'll see it different to other people.'

He stops walking to look at me.

'That's actually . . . really profound.'

I grow a couple of inches taller and smile at Noah's praise, I'm sure. And also, I did sound quite profound. Possibly it's the leftover adrenaline from the bike ride. Everything is heightened when you've just narrowly escaped death.

'Have you always liked history?' Noah asks.

'Yep, I studied history at Manchester. Dad got me into it.' Thankfully, I don't recount the same Oppenheimer tale I'd told Lola in the kayak.

'That's cool. I was more of a geography man myself.'

'Well, that's just blasphemy.'

Noah laughs. There's a moment of silence as we set off walking again, which I of course aim to fill by just continuing to talk.

'I think I've always been interested in, like, where we come from. Do you ever think that a hundred, or even a thousand years ago there might have been someone walking across this very field? And somehow, we're connected to them, even though they don't know us, and we don't know them? Because I think about that a lot.'

Noah looks around as if he's expecting to see neolithic man stomping across the field, maybe with a spear.

'I never thought about it like that before, but I will from now on. What do you think our hypothetical historical counterparts were doing here, then?' he asks.

I look around. The ocean is perfectly still. 'Maybe fishing,' I wonder aloud, 'or coming to relax in the fields and enjoy the view. Maybe they were going wherever we're going. Someone must have discovered it first. Ooh, I know, are we going to a burial site? I love them.'

My history chat is desperately unsexy. Which is fine, since this is a business outing. But Noah smiles and makes some agreeable sounds. We're at the cliff edge, looking out over the ocean. There is a path. Hallelujah. However, it's a steep path with a big 'danger when wet' sign in red at the top. Not ideal. It isn't wet but it is steep. I'm on my bum. Essentially sliding down the cliff top. The crash of the waves on the shore gets louder as we descend, until finally, Noah announces that we're here.

It's not a burial site.

It's a cave.

It's a . . . gold cave.

'Is this cave made out of gold?' I ask. The rocks around the entrance jut out of the ground, glinting at us.

'That's exactly what it is,' Noah answers. 'The cave of gold.'

'It really does feel like we're discovering it for the first time,' I tell Noah, stroking a finger down one of the rocks. It's smooth and cold under my hand.

'Come on, let's go take a look. We can't go inside, but we can explore around the cliff face.'

The entrance to the cave is almost like a door cut into the cliff, the jagged gold rocks around the edges.

'Oh my god,' I say, peering inside. It echoes and dances off the walls. 'I can see why they call it the cave of gold.'

'It's the lichen growing on the rocks. In the sun, it looks gold,' Noah tells me.

I almost can't believe that this place is real. Just outside the cave a band of sunlight pokes straight down, like the light that might come through a church window. A strip of sunlight so bright it's hard to look away from. It lands on a particularly gold piece of rock, making it glint and glimmer where it ripples in the light.

I'm weirdly emotional. It's so beautiful, so unlike anything I've seen before.

I don't want Noah to see how overcome I am, so I look around some more, running my hands over the jagged rocks, tracing what looks just like gold in them.

Noah, I notice out of the corner of my eye, takes his notebook out of his rucksack and leans back against the wall by the entrance to make some notes. It's like someone conjured up everything that I might possibly find sexy in a person and rolled them into one Noah-shaped package. I really do have a thing for notebooks.

'It's beautiful,' I tell him once I've made my way all around the edge. I'm standing just next to a shallow pool of sea water, directly in the beam of light, letting the sun warm me up again. 'It feels, like, weirdly holy.'

'Are you religious?' he asks.

I shake my head. 'No, but it's like the history thing. I can imagine other people here. I imagine that they would know that it's a special place.'

Noah moves towards where I'm standing by the entrance.

'I like hearing you talk about history.'

Possibly it's the vaguely ethereal nature of the cave, but it's like Noah and I could be at any point, any moment in time and it wouldn't matter. I try to remind myself why I can't have this thing with Noah. I think that there was a list. Possibly. I can't remember any of its points.

'How about you, religious?' I ask as he looks up, right into the sun. I look at him, so also like looking at the sun.

'Nah. For a long time, I didn't even believe in the good of *people*.'

'That's sad,' I tell him. Even with all the awful stuff that has happened in the past, is still happening all over the world, I've never stopped believing in the good of people. If we don't believe in that, what's the point in it all?

'Do you believe in the good of people now?' I ask.

Noah steps back and unzips his rucksack again, pulling out a picnic blanket. It screams DATE! He spreads it just by the entrance. We look out at the ocean again.

'I think so. But then I don't spend a lot of time with people, so I'll reserve judgement.'

'How can you travel all the time and not talk to people?'

He shrugs. 'It's easy. I just watch.'

I think as I kneel down to help him that I don't like that thought. The thought that Noah might just be a little bit lonely. But admitting as much is so far away from one-night only terri-tory, it's not even funny. Maybe when I've left, I could set up a WhatsApp group with him and Lola. I don't think I'd find that one quite so draining.

'Shall we eat?' he asks. 'I brought things you like.'

He means vegetables. Or salad. Or possibly vegetables with salad.

'Sounds good.' I kneel next to him on the blanket, right there on the floor, looking out on the ocean. It's possibly the greatest ever setting for a business lunch.

Noah has brought little boxes of salad and chicken in a cool bag (cool bags, another thing I find ridiculously sexy). He unpacks it alongside drinks and some cutlery and we tuck in, sharing the boxes of food between us.

I'm cross-legged on the blanket. My shoes, while delightful to walk in, seem to make sitting a bit of a challenge. My feet feel huge.

'You said you don't do relationships. Is it because you don't think that people are good?' I ask Noah, feeling my heart pound. Why on earth I've ventured down this line of questioning, I don't know. My aversion to silence will be the end of me. 'Or am I not meant to ask about that? You know, because we just had a one-night thing. Feel free not to answer, there's no pressure from me.' Why? Why am I asking these things when we'd moved so seamlessly from fling to friend? Well, Noah has made that move seamlessly. I'm reading his books in the dead of night and pining after him.

Noah chews for a moment and looks like he's thinking.

'You're fine, Lily,' he answers finally. 'Mum and Dad just ... encouraged the worst in each other, so I never saw relationships as a positive thing, you know? Plus, I'm always leaving. It's hard to make friends that last, let alone anything more.'

I nod along, trying to look unmoved but really eating up all this intel and setting it aside to analyse later. 'Well, for what it's worth, you're really good at the friend thing, Noah.'

I mean because of the salad, and the lean protein, and the gorgeous cave picnic. Noah looks at me for a moment and I think *look away, you crazy woman!* But after breaking my gaze he starts to gather up the Tupperware. 'Yeah, maybe.'

'Are you done? Or do you need more time to make notes?' I'm talking really fast and also gathering Tupperware, slamming the boxes into the cool bag with intent, annoyed that I made it weird.

'I'm almost done, I just need to take some pictures.'

He isn't looking at me properly and his voice sounds flat.

Urgh. It *is* awkward and weird. I've ruined our trip to the gold cave.

I need to get us back to where we're meant to be. What we're good at. Sort of friends and allies with a three-pronged plan.

He stands up and holds his hand out for me. My rise is much less graceful. Stupid huge shoes.

Noah takes a couple more photos on the perimeter of the cave and we head away. He's not frowning anymore. He's not smiling. It's more a thinking crease that's between his eyebrows.

We look back and Noah speaks into the cave as much as he's talking to me.

'I like you, Lily.'

And oh dear, I'm totally and completely fucked.

# Chapter Thirteen

*After Ma threw me out, I walked all the way into town with that guitar. Those first few weeks I slept on friends', if you could call them that, sofas, always lugging the guitar with me. I never played it. Got into more trouble at school till eventually they found me a place in a home of sorts, for kids with nowhere else to go.*

*It was run by a devout couple, the Merrywells they were called. They really believed in that saying that cleanliness is close to godliness because they always wanted us to be real clean. And the place was bare, not that I minded those things. It was just different, a lot quieter than home had been. The Merrywells were sure that if we prayed hard enough and really believed, God would come to our rescue. Save us from our unfortunate circumstances.*

*That was the first time I played Pa's guitar, sat on this single bed in a row of other single beds, looking at a cross on the wall. I didn't feel anything when I looked at that cross. No matter how hard I prayed, I didn't think there was some god who was coming to save me. I guess when I realized that, I felt lonely.*

*I don't know if it was muscle memory, but it was like my fingers just knew where to go. And all the songs I used to sing with Pa came right on back to me. Pa had only ever played country music then, and I played those songs, but I started trying new things too. And singing, I'd never really sung before, but it just came so easy to me.*

*Soon, the other kids would come and listen to me every night and it felt* good to be good at something, you know? Till then I'd only ever been in the way or in trouble, but here I was, doing something that folk liked. It made me want to get better and better. So, I practised, and even the Merrywells, who didn't much go in for music so much, thought I was good. They thought it was god's intervention working through my fingers.

I joined the school music group and learned more new songs, ones that were different from what Pa had taught me. The teacher helped me with new riffs and I loved showing off to the other kids what I'd learned that day. You weren't allowed to be in the band unless your grades were all right, and mine hadn't been. I started working harder at school. It sounds real cheesy, but right then it felt like music was saving me, and I didn't want to let it go.

It took a year but I'd gotten pretty good. I didn't see Ma this whole time but most of my brothers and sisters were still at school. They said that Ma had started drinking and that I should come home, that she wouldn't care if I came home now. And I probably could have done. But me and Ma were as stubborn as each other, I didn't want to be the one who backed down. Plus, I was happy for the first time.

I started busking down in the old town on a Saturday to make some money and even though it probably didn't seem like much to other people, I'd never had so much cash in my life. I hid it in my socks because the Merrywells didn't approve of that sort of thing.

But underneath it all, I still felt angry. Not that I knew it at the time, hindsight is a wonderful thing, but it was always there, simmering away. Towards my parents, mainly. It took a long time, to deal with that.

Maybe eventually, I would have gone back to see Ma. I was almost ready to graduate high school and I didn't really have a plan past that. Just get a job, I suppose. College wasn't really an option for me, my grades weren't ever that good and anyway, I didn't have any money. You only got to stay with the Merrywells while you were at school, that was one of the rules. I was hoping that Mikey who ran a record shop in town might take me on, seeing as I spent so much time hanging around in there. I never nicked anything from him either, not like I did other places.

So maybe I would have gone back to Ma and made up if I hadn't met Jimmy and his wife.

I was busking one Saturday. By then I was close to eighteen. I noticed this guy kept walking past. Over and over. He just looked like a regular middle-aged man with a moustache, everyone had them then. The first time he and his wife passed he put $20 in my guitar case, so I tried extra hard when I saw him coming back again. And again. He didn't put any more money in, though. He waited until I finished a song and then he and his wife came right up to me. He had the biggest smile, it made him look completely different. His wife was smiling too. I remember thinking that they looked really happy, that maybe I'd never seen folk look so happy.

I stared at them, even more so when Jimmy said that he was Jimmy Nickle, some music producer from London, and that if I wanted to talk to him, they were headed to an ice cream place round the corner.

I knew the place, like I did everywhere in the old town. Course I was worried that he'd be a bit dodgy, I knew enough about boys then to know that they weren't good for much, but Jimmy's wife was there too, and she was real pretty. And maybe I was naïve, or desperate, I don't know, but I decided to trust them.

I didn't want to seem too keen, right, so I finished up my set like I planned to. I always think that people give more money when they see there's already some there, so Jimmy's $20 meant that I had a good day by the time I was done. Maybe I walked a bit quicker to the ice cream place, because for the first time in my life, it felt like something was happening.

Jimmy was right where he said he'd be, at the counter with his wife. I looked at the back of them while I could. They both looked so refined to me, especially his wife. She wasn't like Ma at all. Jimmy saw me and they both smiled so easy. They had these accents that I thought were mighty posh. I'd have probably done whatever they wanted me to.

Jimmy explained that he was a music producer from London and that he was putting a band together. It took me a long time to realize what he was asking.

*He had to really spell it out for me. 'I want you to come and try out with the band, Lola.'*

*And what's that phrase they say? That's it. The rest is history.*

\* \* \*

'I've been talking a long time, am I all right to stop there?'

'Of course, good place for a break, if you ask me.' I sound more composed than I am. In reality, I've spent the last twenty-five minutes in some Lola-based trance. Her storytelling has a weird, hypnotizing quality. There's a very good chance that I've just been gaping at her this whole time.

'Was that, er, the real Jimmy Nickle, the man who heard you busking?'

Lola doesn't make as if she's about to get up, so neither do I.

Like Lola suggested, we've moved our sessions outside, down by the loch.

Two weeks have passed since the trip to the cave of gold. Skye, I'm sure, operates on a schedule all of its own. Nothing much happens, but the arrow of time flies faster here than anywhere else, I'm certain.

We're sat in the shady shadow of the willow tree, a concession no doubt made with my skin tone in mind. I try to ignore the row of ants marching across the picnic blanket we're sat on.

'That's right,' she says, looking at me. She doesn't seem bothered by the ants. They're getting closer to me, though. Her eyes are a different colour to mine, but they seem familiar in some deep-seated way that I can't quite explain.

This close to her, I can see the faint lines in her face and how dark the skin under her eyes is. It's the first time I've thought that she looks tired. Worn down, almost, by it all.

Or maybe I've just lost the plot.

We're skirting closer and closer to Lola's time in the band. Jimmy

Nickle was their manager. People said that Simon Cowell learned everything he knew from Jimmy Nickle. I know from my research that he died a few years ago. Heart attack.

'So, you were in a band?' I venture, shifting my weight, because one of my legs has gone numb, and also to dodge the ants, which I'm sure are now personally targeting me. I'm wearing a T-shirt and denim shorts. Denim, I decide, is not particularly forgiving in the heat. Me and the hotel washing machines have a long overdue date this afternoon.

'That's right. Beyond Baton Rouge, they were before your time.'

'I've heard of them,' I rush out.

'You have?'

I nod and let out a nervous giggle.

'I thought it might be you.' I do my best to play the part of someone who's been unknowingly confronted with a megastar. 'Ashton being here the day me and Seb arrived kind of gave you away.'

Lola squirms, she looks uncomfortable. Maybe I'm playing it too well.

'They, *you* were really famous. My mum loved your music. She taught me one of your songs, "Eyes Full of Wonder". We played it together all the time.' I talk fast, hoping that Lola doesn't cotton on to the fact that I just described Mum in the past tense.

'That song means a lot to me, I'm glad your mum likes it,' Lola says.

And suddenly, it's as if there isn't enough air under the willow tree, like my oxygen deprived brain can't compute of a world where Lola and Mum coexist.

I often feel like Mum is here with me somehow, but under the willow tree with Lola, it's as if I can feel her. Right there. It's comforting and heartbreaking in one fell swoop. And it makes it all so real.

Mostly, when Lola's telling her story, I can imagine that all of this happened to someone else, someone who isn't me. It's worrying that I don't feel ready for this to be real yet.

But also, ants.

I jump up, almost falling over – my leg is still dead.

'Shall we pick this up again later in the week?' I wave a finger between me and Lola, adopting the personality of a highflying New York CEO. 'I've got you down for a Tuesday, is a Tuesday good for you?'

'Course, Lily. You know, if you wanted to play, we have a karaoke on Saturday nights. It might help Harper to come if you do. She's taking a liking to you. I know her foster parents are keen for her to get involved. I can probably coax Noah along too.'

I get that one part of the three-pronged plan is for me to get involved in all the stuff on offer to guests. But just, no. I can't. Not yet at least. Three-pronged plan be damned.

'No! I mean, maybe. I mean, one week I'll think about it. Probably just not this week. Or next. I have a timetable.' I sound like I've just got back from a run. 'Anyway, got to dash. I need to do some washing, it's on the timetable.'

I know that here I'm meant to be a version of myself that just goes with the flow. A super chilled, grab life by the horns version of me. That version probably *would* rock up to karaoke with her birth mother and the man she wishes she was having sex with for the summer.

But that's not me, not really. It's all pretend. And I can't have the lines between real me and pretend me blurring. That just won't do.

And anyway, at least I'm over whatever unsettling Noah thoughts I'd had back at the cave the other week because obviously we'd just been to a beautiful ancient cave. You'd have to be dead inside not to be a little moved. But it's fine now. I remember about the whole no future thing. I remember my list. I'm over it.

I'm mostly over it.

'Whatever you like.' Lola smiles. I wonder if all her smiles are tinged with sadness. She hasn't got up, so I think she must be staying there. It feels weird walking away while she's just sat there. I hook a thumb over my shoulder. 'I'm just going to . . . washing . . . ' I finish feebly, walking backwards. I get tangled in the leaves of the willow tree. Willow trees, it turns out, should only be entered face first. At least I've tied my hair up and pinned my fringe out of the way. I'm not sure I'd ever escape otherwise.

Lola watches on while I go full *Apocalypse Now* with the long swoopy branches and lets out a quiet little laugh when I finally emerge victorious.

'See you later!' I call from the other side of the tree, doing a speed walk up to the hotel. I'm through the gardens and in front of the cottages in the blink of an eye. Noah is sat outside at his little table, typing away on his laptop.

'Lily, Lily, is everything okay?' It takes me a second to realize that my hands are shaking. I'm trying to work the door on my cottage, but I can hardly grip the handle.

Noah's body is right there. 'Here, let me help.' He's not wearing a T-shirt because it goes without saying that it's still fucking boiling. Obviously, someone in the universe has decided that today will be the day I get to profoundly suffer.

He follows me into the cottage.

'Sit down, I'll get you some water.'

Oh. No. No. No. I can't have Noah being all extra nice and caring to me. One considerate glass of water and I'll fall right in love with him for sure.

We have less than three weeks left together. I try to remember my list. About him leaving the country.

But I also can't do anything other than what he tells me, so I sit on the couch and take a sip of the water he brings me. As he sits next to me I put it on the coffee table, wiping at my eyes with the back of my hands.

'Did you know that Lola was in a band?' I ask him, my voice shaky.

He nods. 'They were pretty big back in the day. Lola doesn't advertise it, but most folk around here know.'

'I just don't get how she could go from being in a super famous mega band to here, living on her own like she does. It doesn't make sense.'

Noah must be wondering why the hell I care. I should call Seb and talk to him about this sort of thing.

'Lola told me once that something went wrong, when she was in the band. She liked the music, she's a brilliant singer when she does it. And with her guitar too but, I don't know, something happened. She never told me what. I always got the impression she was running away, though. I think that's why she didn't call the police on me, because she got what it was like to need to escape. Or that's been my take on it all these years.'

Is it me? I think. Was I the thing that went wrong? Or was it something else, not related to me at all?

I slump back against the couch.

God, I can't dump this on Noah.

'Sorry,' I tell him, 'I don't know why I'm letting Lola's story affect me.' It's a barefaced lie. Another one. And it doesn't make me feel good about myself.

Noah moves closer to me; I can feel the heat from his body across my side. He brushes a couple of strands of escapee fringe off my forehead. It's such a sweet move, my eyes fill with tears. He must think that I'm unhinged. I am unhinged.

'Lola's had a really hard life,' he tells me. 'It's normal to feel something about it.'

It's so far away from what I'm feeling, but I appreciate the fact that he's giving me an out. I also appreciate that he's basically – there's no other word for it – cuddling me right now. I've wrapped an arm across his stomach and my head is on his chest, I can feel his heart-beat under my ear. It's steady and sure and it's worrying, because I can't have this with Noah.

But it feels like exactly what I need.

# Chapter Fourteen

'Tell me everything about you and Noah, I want all the details. Actually, not all the details . . . just the sexy ones.'

'Shhh.' I look around wildly, double checking that Noah isn't around to hear Seb ask for the details of our non-existent sex life. Noah must already think that me and Seb are weirdly close for siblings, even if he's never said anything about it.

I'm sat on the patio table in front of the cottage for a Zoom call with Seb, nominally for a work meeting, but when Seb shared the agenda, point one was 'gossip – specifically, getting dicked down by Noah'.

'I've already told you everything. Several times now. It was only that one-night, and this is being recorded!'

'You know that. But you're the only person who reads the transcripts,' he counters.

'I want to make sure that I don't forget anything.'

'Yes, that would be the stuff of the world ending right there, if you forgot one tiny little thing.'

I shuffle around in my seat, because that's how uncomfortable the thought of forgetting something makes me.

'How are things your end?' I ask. 'Any new business?'

Seb shrugs. 'A couple of leads, maybe, but I'm just wrapping up the Templeman memoirs. Kitty emailed to say that Lola has made it clear that she wants to sell this thing to the highest bidder. Maybe

Phil's stomach ulcer will finally settle down. And Clementine had a TikTok that went semi-viral, so she's been in a good mood.'

'The morning routine one she did?' I say, ignoring the bit about Lola selling the memoirs to the highest bidder. 'I saw that, one of her best, I thought. I can't believe she gets up at 4am every day for Pilates and affirmations, though.'

'She doesn't,' Seb answers. 'It's all made up. Most days she doesn't even get to the office for nine. She's driving me mad.' Seb rubs at his temples, same as he always does when Clementine is mentioned.

I laugh, but looking at Seb on the other end of the call, I'm hit by such an intense bout of homesickness, it makes my head spin. I miss them all. I've been away for three weeks and I miss my life in Manchester. I miss my routine and always knowing what's happening. I miss not worrying whether the grass is full of killer ants every time I sit down. I have no idea how Noah does this for his whole life.

'Your great-granny would be proud, you know?'

On the outside, Seb is as warm as a slab of concrete, but I know that the reason he cares so much about Your Life is because of people like his great-granny. Deep (deep) down, he's like a marshmallow.

'Thank you for saying so, sister dearest.'

'Can you help me FaceTime Elton again later?' I ask.

Seb rolls his eyes.

'We're talking about FaceTiming your cat like it's a totally normal thing to do now, are we? I know you're dodging talking about you and Noah.'

I look around again, checking that he's not about to appear. He'd said this morning that he was going to repair the fence around the other side of the hotel, the side by the loch. It's on the business plan I drew up when I'd had a spare couple of hours at 2am ten days ago. But knowing my luck, he's absolutely going to emerge any second now, declaring that he heard the whole thing.

I drop my voice to an angry whisper.

'There is no me and Noah . . . '

Seb levels me a look.

'Wow, you are stubborn.'

'I'm not! I'm realistic. There's no future me and Noah. There can't be. Even if he takes this job which means he's home some of the time, he's still some free-spirited wildling and I'm . . . '

'Anally uptight?'

'I was going to say "me", but thank you, for filling in the blanks in such a positive and life-affirming way.'

'My pleasure. But let's circle back to the thing you said about Noah potentially staying here.'

'It's nothing,' I say, still hunched over my laptop to whisper. 'He just mentioned that he had the chance to go for a position which would mean shorter trips and more time in the UK. He's not sure whether to take it and I'm not going to try to sway him either way. Even if we did give in to this thing and have a summer fling, everyone knows that summer flings don't last. The key is in the title – summer, as in, over by autumn.'

'But you like the guy, right?'

I think about Noah. How at first, I'd thought he was just nice to look at. And he is, don't get me wrong. The man doesn't have a bad angle. But that was shallow. *I* was shallow. Because there's a lot more to him than that. He's sexy, sure, but he's thoughtful and kind too. Like the fact that when I went to top up Harper's Pringle stash from the hotel shop I couldn't because Noah had already bought them all.

Sigh.

'You get that I'm still here, right? Your tongue is lolling out of your head.'

'It is not lolling. But please, it really doesn't matter whether I like Noah or not.'

Seb lets out a groan. 'See, admit it, you're incredibly stubborn.'

I'm outraged! Or vaguely irate at least. 'I am not stubborn!'

'At least admit that you like the guy.'

'Fine, I like him.' My voice is getting louder and louder. 'I'm madly in love. I'm obsessed. I want him to wife me up right now. There, are you happy?'

Movement in the corner of my eye causes my head to snap up.

'I'd just come to see if you had any Pringles, but I'll, er, come back later.' Harper is smirking at me.

Is there no privacy to be had on the Isle of Skye?

'Yes, that would be great, Harper, if you don't mind. I'm just on an important work call.'

I can hear Seb laughing through my laptop, but I feel like it's important to maintain eye contact with Harper. Like you're meant to if you come face to face with a bear. I link my fingers together on the table and smile at her, hoping that she isn't about to run back to her foster parents and tell them that some crazed maniac is living in one of the hotel cottages.

'See you later.' She's still smirking as she turns to leave.

'Oh my god.' I wait a couple more minutes until I'm sure that Harper has gone before I scuttle off inside, back to angry whispering. 'Why is it that every time I talk to you something bad happens?'

'Can't answer that for you, babe.'

'What if she tells Noah that I'm in love with him? When I'm not, I'm not!' My voice is getting higher and higher.

'Don't worry about it.'

'Oh yeah, that's completely me. When have you ever known me to not worry about something?'

'True, true. Though I have to say, it's refreshing that you have something real to worry about this time.'

'Are we done here?' I ask him. 'This work meeting hasn't exactly involved an awful lot of work and I need to get on with Mr Vandergilden's memoirs.'

'I read a couple of chapters of that, by the way. Good job. I think you really captured his anti-gun regulation ethos.'

'What a compliment!' I sound sarcastic, but actually, I'm storing away Seb's nice words because it's the sort of affirmation I need on a daily – okay, hourly – basis.

'We both know you love it,' Seb answers. He really does know me too well. 'I did want to talk to you about something, though.'

'Okay.' Seb is being more serious than usual. Which is, admittedly, a low bar. My mind goes immediately to the worst-case scenario. Elton has cancer. Seb has cancer. I have cancer and for some reason, Seb has been informed before me.

'It's about Lola.'

Lola has cancer!

When she seemed like such a beacon of health to me. Having three parents die on you has to be some sort of sign that you're cursed, doesn't it? Not that Lola is a proper parent, but she's in that general remit. If I was doing a Venn diagram of my family, she'd be on there.

'Stop panicking for a short minute, will you?'

I realize that my heart is beating very fast. I close my eyes for a second and will it to chill the fuck out.

'You said that Lola had told you who she is, about the band now?' Seb asks.

I'm confused. 'Yeah, that's right. She mentioned it on Saturday after we'd finished recording. We haven't covered it as part of her memoirs yet, though.'

'That doesn't matter. I just wondered if now might be a good time to tell her who you are.'

'What? Why?'

'If Kitty is getting closer to a deal, and you're halfway through your time up there, this is all going to come out soon, Lily.'

It takes a couple of seconds for Seb's words to fully register.

Of course, what he's saying makes sense. I should tell Lola who I am. I've gotten so used to lying to her and Noah that I hardly even register it anymore. And as for the thought of her memoirs coming out . . . I can't even . . . I just can't.

Plus, I'm still all over the place with her. Sometimes, I think I'm *fond* of her. More than that even, it's like I admire her. For going through what she went through and surviving all of it and building this place. I had a stable upbringing and I'm a mess. Yet here Lola is, surviving her childhood and still growing her own carrots.

Other times, I can't see past how angry I am. How unfair it all feels. That she did what she did and still gets to live this life. That she's here and Mum and Dad aren't.

I look at Seb.

'Oh good,' he says, 'you're done.' It's probably best not to share that the back of my neck is damp with sweat.

'Okay, I'll think about it, I promise. But before we go, I just wanted to say – you know if anything happens to me?'

'Another death conversation. Excellent.'

'You'll like this one. I want you to have the house. And Elton. Maybe you and Mr Cains could work out a joint custody arrangement or something. I'll get a will, when I get back.'

Seb frowns at me, his dark eyebrows moving closer to the centre of his forehead. 'What's brought this on?'

'I was on the back of Noah's motorbike the other week.'

'God, to be a straight woman.'

'And I definitely thought I was going to die.'

'Standard.'

'And I don't know, I just realized that I don't really have anyone to leave all my stuff to.'

'First of all, thank you, I would be honoured to be Elton's guardian. Though if the geriatric cat outlives you, something has gone seriously wrong.'

My shoulders drop somewhat at Seb's words.

'But you do know you'd have plenty of people who'd be willing to help. You're busier than any person I've ever known. You have a personal discount code for the balloon arch place, *that's* how many balloon arches you order. You get that that's not normal, don't you?'

'I know I have a lot of acquaintances . . . ' I start, struggling to put into words what I mean. 'I've just – I don't know; I haven't missed many of them.'

My WhatsApp hiatus is possibly the only thing I don't feel guilty about. It's an absolute revelation, not being quite so easily contactable.

'Ooh, I saw a reel about this. Apparently, your thirties are when your friendships get really meaningful. You've got to ditch the hangers-on.'

'But who would that leave me with? You, obviously. Maybe Mr Cains. Phil and Clementine. I can't have four friends!'

'Why not? I only have you. Though you're very needy.'

I roll my eyes.

'I'm not saying ditch them all. Just don't put so much pressure on yourself. These things should be about balance.'

'Who are you and what have you done with Seb?'

'It's all the therapy I'm having.' Seb has been in therapy for as long as I've known him. 'I've had to double my sessions since we hired Clementine.'

His eye twitches.

'You didn't tell me what she's done this time?'

'I had a call from the crematorium, apparently she's been touting for business at a couple of funerals.'

It's so inappropriate, but I burst out laughing. 'You're the one who decided to pay her on commission.'

'Yes, but as I had to explain to her, once people are actually dead, they aren't really in a position to buy the fucking diamond package, are they?! She's turning me grey.'

'Well, kudos to a grey hair if it makes its way through all of the Just for Men.'

'Please.' He runs a hand through his hair. 'This is completely natural. I reject that entirely.'

I can't help but laugh.

'I miss you,' I tell him, serious all of a sudden and fully expecting him to take the piss.

'I miss you too,' he says. 'What are the chances of you leaving us all to go gallivanting around the world with Noah? You get that that's how this *should* end, right?'

Should it?

'Slim to none.' Of that, I'm certain.

'I'd be happy for you, you know. I wouldn't even sack you. You can do our job anywhere.'

'I know you wouldn't.' I sigh. Honestly, I am starting to wonder how incompatible Noah and I really are. He has a favourite mug, for instance. It's blue and it says 'it's a hill, get over it' on the front. Plus, aside from the cramp in the pool and the crawling up the mountain, I've enjoyed our adventures together so far. He's tapping into my as yet untapped adventurous side, and I don't hate it. I like it. It still doesn't change the fact that he's leaving for Italy at the end of summer, though, and on however many other adventures after that. I want to settle down with Colin mark two, do my job well, have a couple of kids, see if I can get a white picket fence shipped in from somewhere.

I shuffle about. Because even though that's what I always thought I wanted, since I've been here on Skye, I'm just not sure anymore. Definitely something about this island air.

'What if another Colin won't cut it now?' I ask Seb, my voice quiet.

'Then we'd all thank the good lord for that. I had nightmares about his fingernails for months. Colin's, not God's.'

'They were fine, you're ridiculous.'

'They were too long! Never trust a man who has long nails, that's what I always say.'

'I've literally never heard you say that in your life. Anyway, I've got to go,' I say, 'I need to get the pizza in the oven.'

'Are you cooking for Noah again?'

I nod. 'We have a rota.'

'Okay, and I assume you've warned him that your pizza is not actually pizza.'

'Er, yes it is. And no, I haven't warned him of anything. He's eaten everything I've cooked so far.'

'That poor, poor man. That pizza you made for me didn't even have cheese on it.'

'It had cauliflower cream.'

'Exactly. In what realm is cauliflower a cheese? Wasn't the crust cauliflower too? Why are you obsessed with making cauliflower into pizza?'

'It's really good for you!'

Seb's eyes darken. 'You haven't made the cauliflower pizza for Noah, have you?'

'No.' I eye the small oven like it's about to betray me and reveal to Seb what I've actually done.

'Lily . . .'

'I added some spelt flour to the base, that's all!'

'And . . .'

'And a couple of vegetables to the topping.'

My pizza is more vegetable than pizza, but Seb doesn't need to know that.

'You know you're on holiday, right? You can relax a bit.'

'I'm not on holiday, it's a working break. Like a sabbatical. And when do I ever relax? I am incapable of relaxation, it's a fundamental flaw. We're going out to build a pagoda for Lola after dinner. She needs to make more of her outdoor space.' There's a chance my voice has ventured into the realm of 'shriek' again.

There's a knock on the cottage door.

'Got to go,' I tell Seb.

'I see how it is. You just dump me as soon as he comes knocking.'

'We've been on Zoom for an hour and a half!'

'Fine. Bye. Message later if you want to FaceTime Elton.'

I slam the laptop closed and dash to the door with the enthusiasm of a woman who is doing a terrible job of keeping her wayward feelings in check. At least when I slide the door open to find Noah in a white vest and navy shorts it's easier to remind myself that it's an impossible situation. Because people who look like him couldn't do anything other than leave a trail of broken hearts behind them.

'Pizza might be a while still,' I tell Noah. 'Do you want to sit outside?'

Noah disappears and returns with a glass of wine for me. I leave it on the small counter while I get on with the cooking.

It's all very domestic. Too domestic, surely, for a fling? When I asked ChatGPT about it, there definitely wasn't much about dinner rotas or sharing pens. Noah said he had the perfect pen, a Dialogue 3 fountain pen that cost over a hundred pounds, and I have to say there's no accounting for the thrill of a high-quality pen. So no, none of those things are in the casual sex handbook.

I'm lost in my thoughts. Serving pizza on autopilot. I carry it outside on the little wooden chopping board I've found.

I catch sight of myself in the reflection of the doors.

I looked wrecked. I've taken to pinning my fringe back as par for the course every morning now, but parts of it have escaped and are stood on end.

But it's not just that. I don't look like me. I look like a version of me who's been forced to live in the wilderness for weeks or survive the zombie apocalypse. I'm on my way to being Tom Hanks at the end of *Castaway*. My cheeks are flushed, and I'm covered in a thin layer of sweat.

How can this have happened? I've been here three weeks. Three. And I have a shower (when it works) and a flushing toilet and everything.

Maybe all the lies are aging me.

I force myself outside, because standing there dwelling on the fact that I look like a woman whose life is falling apart is not a precursor to a productive evening.

'Pizza's ready!' I say with false cheer.

I plonk it down on the little white table, my arm shaking from carrying everything while I stared at myself in the window.

'Looks great, thanks for cooking.'

Noah always says thank you, even though we take turns. It's a travesty to womankind that he comes with manners and tattoos but an aversion to staying in one place.

'Oh, it's nothing, my pleasure. I'll go get the salad.'

'There's pizza?' Harper appears from behind us. I wonder if I should be worried about how much time she spends alone in the forest. At least we know how to lure her out. I guess we can add pizza to her calling card. Alongside Pringles and Spotify.

'I made plenty, help yourself.'

I go to get the salad, remembering as I'm heading back outside that Harper heard me and Seb on Zoom talking about Noah. How have I not panicked about that more? There's just so much to worry about here, it's making me miss stuff.

Either way, I need to get her on her own and warn her against saying anything.

I speed up, bursting out of the doors with a very enthusiastic 'Salad!' that makes Noah smile and Harper narrow her eyes.

'What the fuck is this?' she asks, turning to look at the pizza. We have three chairs around the table now, one borrowed from Noah, because Harper spends a lot of time here too.

'It's a pizza.'

'Where's the cheese?'

'Underneath the vegetables.'

I sit down as Harper takes a slice and starts picking the vegetables off the top, leaving them like a little vegetable mountain on the table.

'It's really nice,' Noah says around a mouthful. He hasn't picked any of the vegetables off his pizza. And maybe that's a thing we have in common, alongside the pen thing. Pens and vegetables. Pity I've never heard either of those things mentioned in a wedding speech (and I've been bridesmaid nine times. Obviously having never said no to an RSVP. I can recite that love speech from *Captain Corelli's Mandolin* by heart).

'You should count yourself lucky,' I tell Harper. 'I could have made cheese out of cauliflower like I do at home. But I didn't. At least you're digging towards real cheese.'

'You're sick in the head.'

I don't disagree. Instead, I take a big drink of wine and pile salad and pizza on my plate. All the while, I hold Harper's gaze, tilting slightly to Noah and then shaking my head with wide eyes. Hopefully, the movement acts as some sort of code for *don't tell Noah you heard me declaring that I love him earlier.*

Harper just smirks, which is worrying. Very worrying indeed.

Still, she doesn't say anything. Instead, she launches into a fifteen-minute monologue about the fact that her foster parents thought that it would be nice to take one of the row boats out on the loch today. I'm not sure I've ever known anyone to have such strong feelings against row boats. They've always seemed like one of the more innocuous members of the boat family to me. But Harper really seems to hate them, as evidenced by the fact that she's swearing up a storm.

At least she talks a bit more now.

I'd hoped that I could maybe have a positive impact on her, seeing as we've been through something similar, even if Harper doesn't know it. But as she gets ever more sweary, I do wonder if I'm actually corrupting her further.

She finishes, ' . . . and then they asked us to take a selfie.' Her voice is dark. Selfies are obviously up there with row boats and vegetables in the list of things that Harper hates. We've eaten all of the food.

'What have you got against selfies?' Noah asks.

'Nothing.'

Harper looks down at her vegetable pile. It's not the selfie she had an issue with.

'I get that it must be weird, feeling like you're playing at happy families.'

And I do understand playing at being happy. Sometimes I think I deserve an Oscar for my acting skills. Or if not an Oscar, one of the lesser acting awards. The equivalent of a British Soap Star award, maybe.

Harper pulls at a black thread from her hoodie. 'Yeah, that's it,' she says.

We all sit quietly for a moment then, until the silence starts to get uncomfortable. For me, at least.

'Well, I'm going to take these plates in.' I go to stand up.

'I've got it,' Noah interrupts. 'You cooked. We can manage it, can't we, Harper?'

God, if they're alone, she will definitely tell him about the 'wife me up' comment.

But I've got nothing. Instead, I'm forced to watch as Harper and Noah carry everything into the cottage and strain my ears for words that sound like 'obsessed' and 'married' while they're doing the washing up.

I don't hear anything but sit silently stressing about the whole thing, just to be on the safe side.

'All done. Shall I put some music on, just for ten minutes?' Noah asks. 'We should let our food settle before we start work.'

He's not looking at me any differently. Maybe Harper really is going to do me a favour and not say anything. She plonks down in her chair as Noah passes over his phone to her so that she can scroll Spotify. I'm not sure when exactly it was decided that Harper would have dictator levels of control over what we listen to, but that's the way it is. I don't mind, she has good taste.

She puts on No Doubt and her and Noah talk about music a bit. I just listen because No Doubt were one of the bands Beyond Baton Rouge were compared to. I notice that Harper never maintains the same level of vitriol for Noah that she does about almost everything else. I think it's because he's just so affable, it's hard to muster any hate towards him. It'd be like hating on a puppy, or a cupcake. But a cupcake that has this prominent vein running down the front of its bicep that I'm low-key obsessed with.

We drink and chat and when it starts to get dusky, Harper says that she needs to get back. I breathe a faint sigh of relief. She really did do me a favour. I make a mental note to source yet more Pringles tomorrow.

'I'd better leave you to it anyway,' she says louder than she's talked all evening and I'm hit with a dose of dread, deep in my stomach.

'Harper.'

'You know, because you're *madly in love* and she's *obsessed* and wants you to *wife her up*.' She uses air quotes and adopts a high-pitched voice whenever she's relaying my bits. 'Whatever the hell that means.'

I sink down in my chair, halfway under the table at this point.

'You're welcome,' she says to me, winking before she walks off.

I have a feeling that Harper thinks that she's done me a favour, so I can't even be irritated by this turn of events. Maybe I can just crawl right on under the table and run away. Noah has those long legs, though, so he'd definitely catch me.

Out of the corner of my eye I can see that Noah is looking at me, even though I am very determinedly not looking at him.

Maybe I'll just go swan dive into the loch of death and be done with it.

'I didn't say that to Harper,' I say, still not looking. 'She overheard me on Zoom to Seb, but it was a joke. He was winding me up. I'm not in love with you, I know there's no ... you know, future.' Why does my voice sound weak when it's the god's honest actual truth?

Noah looks ... oh god, he looks in actual pain. That's how bad the thought of me being in love with him is. He's rubbing the back of his neck and frowning.

I stand up. I need to do something. 'I'm going to have a quick shower; I'm literally covered in sweat.'

I make a run for the bathroom, thinking that the cramped little space is not the place you might want to be when you're having a mild nervous breakdown. It's claustrophobic enough in here without adding all of the heavy breathing I'm doing.

I turn the shower on and then turn it to cold when it splutters to life. Plumber! We need a plumber around here! I clutch the edge of the sink and look at myself in the small square mirror above it. I look like an animal trying to get out of a cage.

I just need a plan. Plans make everyone feel better.

What I'll do is stay in the shower so long that if Noah wants to flee, he can do so without me catching him in an awkward half in, half out of the door situation (this actually happened to me once. Seb still brings it up).

I'm in the shower now. It's not even a hair wash day, but I shampoo twice and then condition the ends. My skin is tingling and wrinkly by the time I switch the shower off, realizing that in my mad dash I didn't pick up any clothes.

Instead, I dry off and wrap a towel around me. My hair is soaked, running rivulets down my arms. I don't know why, but everything just seems so hyper focused here; my skin feels rawer than it ever does at home. There must be something in the water.

I pull open the bathroom door to find Noah sat on the couch, one ankle resting on the other knee. The cottage is dark, the heavy curtains pulled across the glass doors for once.

I think a part of me hoped that he'd still be here. That he wouldn't walk away. I needed him to not walk away. I don't know if the realization comforts or terrifies me.

He puts down his wine and walks towards me.

'Lily,' he says and I feel it deep in my bones. He twists a piece of my wet hair between the end of his fingers and I'm not thinking about how something feels different this time. I'm not.

'I don't know how to do this,' he says.

'We don't have to do anything, it's like I said, about the future thing.'

I try to get the words out with some gusto, but proximity to Noah is scrambling my brain.

'I want to try, though,' he says, ducking down to whisper in my ear, making my skin break out in goose bumps.

And oh god, how is it possible to get what you want and feel so conflicted about it? Because in this world, where Noah realizes that he wants to stay, where Noah figures out how to do this, I'm still lying. It's still ruined because he doesn't know who I am.

But when his fingertips trail across it at the edge of my tightly pulled towel, I kind of forget the whole ruined bit.

My heart is racing super fast.

'You want to try, like girlfriend, boyfriend try?' And who doesn't appreciate clarity at a moment like this?

He nods.

I feel like I'm losing my mind.

Especially now since his hands are working my towel, then tugging on where it's tucked in on itself. Then it's on the floor and he's kissing me. His clothes against my bare skin feel illicit out here in the open.

I don't want to think about how this feels different, I really don't. But I can't help it. It feels like I've crossed some sort of chasm that I didn't know existed.

'Take off your clothes, please.' I hardly recognize my own voice, it's desperate and needy and wild.

Noah pulls me towards the couch, and I go, willingly.

In some deep, dark crevice of my brain, the thought that I don't want to acknowledge pushes to be acknowledged.

How am I ever going to give this up?

# Chapter Fifteen

*To Do:*

- Truth reveal to Lola?
- Tidy cottage
- Amend timetable – when will we build the pagoda now?
- Next Lola chapter to write
- FaceTime Elton
- Get on top of emails

Looking at the long lines of Noah's back where he's sprawled face down in my bed, I'm forced to accept that in so far as not developing feelings for him, I've been a total and utter failure.

It's not even just the sex.

I like him. And that's somehow even worse.

But where will all of this get us? We didn't exactly hash out all of the details last night. You don't stop someone kissing their way down your stomach and ask them to hash out anything.

But I don't have time to dwell on it anymore this morning. We've overslept, and I'm due to meet Lola again.

'Noah.' I lean over him. 'It's eight thirty. I'm going to get ready to meet Lola. I'll see you later.'

He hmms and shifts a little, causing the white bedding to pull down. I'm out of the bed in a flash, I've no time for distractions.

Noah still hasn't emerged by the time I leave, thinking that I'll have to clear up when I get back. Clothes and towels are scattered to every corner of the cottage.

I pick my way round the side of the hotel and towards the loch, where I can see Lola under the willow tree. It's another hot day, but it's early and there's a faint breeze, so it's possibly the least flustered I've ever been here.

'Hi,' I say to Lola, sitting down next to her on the pink and white striped blanket she's laid out for us. She's staring out at the loch, inscrutable to the max.

'Morning, Lily. Sleep okay?'

Oh my god, does she know about Noah? I bet she knows.

'Great, thanks. I don't normally sleep well away from home. Not that I sleep well when I'm home most of the time. I think it's a me thing rather than a sleep thing. Anyway, last night was good.'

I think ... there's no other word for it: Lola's smirking at me. Not in a malicious way, more just that she thinks I'm mildly amusing. The edges of her mouth are turned up at the corners. How strange.

'Shall we get started?' I ask, uncrossing my legs and then realizing that there's no more comfortable a position to be had, so I recross them. It's all well and good having beautiful lakes and mountains up here, but there's a woeful shortage of chairs. I'm literally always sat on the floor.

At least it's too early for all the flies.

'All right.' Lola stills even more before she starts to talk. I didn't think it was physically possible for her to be any stiller than she already was, but I've noticed now, she always does this before she starts. She's like those crocodiles who slow their hearts so that they beat three times a minute or something. She's poised.

I set my phone between us and hit record.

'Ready when you are.'

* * *

*I thought I was gonna die on the flight to LA.*

*I'd never even been out of Louisiana before. And here I was in what felt like a tin can right above the clouds. I didn't like flying then. Still don't like it that much, if I'm being honest. I was seriously glad when those wheels hit the ground.*

*I left right after I graduated. It hadn't been a hard decision to go, even though Jimmy told me the label wanted to set up a pop punk band and I wasn't all that sure what pop punk was. I pestered the record shop to play Gwen Stefani over and over, though I couldn't imagine ever being anything like as glamorous as her. Jimmy said I'd pick it up and I trusted him.*

*I'd told my sisters where I was going and they must have told Ma, I suppose. But she never reached out to wish me luck. Probably she was annoyed that I'd managed to get something decent for myself, it ruined her idea that I was good for nothin'.*

*Jimmy was there to meet me off the plane. I remember thinking that he looked so happy to see me. I don't think anyone had ever looked at me like that before, it was . . . nice. He looked rich too, or richer than he'd seemed on holiday in Baton Rouge. I only had one bag filled with my thrift store clothes and Pa's guitar. I was half terrified. I kept thinking that someone was going to come and tell me that it was all some awful mistake, that they'd got the wrong person and I'd have to go straight home. My hand was shaking so bad I could hardly open my passport. But seeing Jimmy made me feel better.*

*The rest of the band were staying at this apartment in Silverlake and Jimmy took me right there to see them. They'd been put together by the record label, but they hadn't been able to find a lead singer yet and that's where I came in. It all felt more than a little surreal to be honest.*

*We took a car to the new neighbourhood, and it was like I was in a trance. Baton Rouge had been hot and dry and busy, but LA was a different beast. The air felt different. Like it fizzed and crackled with excitement. Already I thought LA was the place where things just happened.*

*I'd never cared so much about what I looked like. We all looked poor back home. Even my nice thrift store clothes weren't real nice. They were just better than something that had been handed down four times already. But on my way to meet the rest of the band, I couldn't help but wonder what they'd think of me. Every person we passed on the sidewalk looked real beautiful. I didn't think I looked much like a lead singer. I definitely didn't look like Gwen Stefani.*

*I started to worry that even if it wasn't a mistake, me being here, the rest of the band wouldn't want me. That they'd take one look at me and send me straight back on the tin can in the sky.*

*'Relax, Lola,' Jimmy told me when we got to this block of flats, 'you're gonna do just fine. You're special, I can tell.'*

*And when Jimmy told me to relax, I did, for a little bit at least. He had this way of making you do whatever he asked. The flat wasn't in a high rise or anything, just two floors. It looked new then, but I imagine it's dated a fair bit since. I followed Jimmy up some steps and waited while he banged on a black door.*

*When it opened, there were two people stood there. A boy and a girl, both smiling. They didn't look that much different to me, their clothes were tatty too.*

*'Say hi to Lola,' Jimmy told them.*

*'Hi, Lola,' they said, and I dared step inside after that.*

*'Is this everyone?' I asked Jimmy. Maybe it was daft not to have asked how many people were in the band before now, but I'd been so focused on just getting there, I didn't ask anywhere near enough questions.*

*'I'm Prune,' the girl said. 'I play the keyboard.'*

*'Shawn.' That was the boy. 'Bass.' He pointed at himself. 'Ashton is here somewhere. ASHTON,' he shouted, way too loud for the tiny flat.*

*And this Ashton, he came wandering out of what I guessed was his bedroom, rubbing his eyes. 'Jet lag is the worst,' he grumbled in a funny accent before he realized I was there. His hair was long and stuck up all over the place, where he'd been asleep.*

*He scratched his stomach, and his T-shirt rode up a bit. He was tall and skinny, like someone stretched him out. He moved next to Prune and Shawn and smiled at me too. I remember thinking that he had a kind smile and maybe this really would work out.*

*'That's all of you,' Jimmy said, looking around at where we were stood in a sort of circle by the door. 'We'll give you the rest of the day to settle in, Lola, but then you're all due down the studio tomorrow. We'll send a car, be ready for eight.'*

*I realized then that Jimmy was leaving, and I didn't want him to go.*

*'Wait,' I called when he turned to leave me. Us, he turned to leave us.*

*'Er, what're we gonna be called, the band, I mean?' I asked the first thing that came into my head.*

*'Beyond Baton Rouge.' Jimmy winked at me. 'And you guys are going to be stars.'*

* * *

'So, that's how you met Ashton?'

Lola nods. 'That's right, we stayed friends, after all these years.'

God, if Ashton's my biological dad, does that mean that Lola's been pining for him for all these years? Poor Lola. She tells me she'll be right back, and I don't know if she needs a moment, just like I do, because she disappears into the hotel, emerging a couple of minutes later with a glass bottle full of orange juice and two glasses. She sets them down on the stripy blanket. All I need is a parasol and it'll be like I'm being courted in the nineteenth century.

I think this might well be the first time I've ever seen Lola relax.

'Didn't Ashton do *Strictly* ages ago?' I ask, ending the recording on my phone. I'd watched that series with Mum, on edge the whole time. Seeing him had made the whole thing real and I'd been worried that someone was going to come and take me away from Mum and Dad.

Lola nods and smiles a little. 'He did. Came third, I think.' She pours some juice in one of the glasses and has a sip.

'He got knocked out with his rhumba.'

'They all do,' Lola answers.

'I know, right. So unfair.'

'He's from here,' she volunteers. 'Ashton, I mean. He grew up in Glasgow, but he had an aunt out here. So it was him who showed me Skye and I went and fell right in love with it straight away.'

Oh my god. It must be him, then. Ashton must be my dad. Shit. Shit. Shit.

'He did?' I ask, sounding like I'm dying of heat exhaustion. Which if this heatwave doesn't let up, I might well be.

'Mm hm. We stayed close after the band broke up. He comes to visit when he's in the country, but he spends a lot of time on tour.'

I can't reveal to Lola that I know he's currently in South Korea. How would I explain low-key stalking an ex-band member of hers? But this is all a lot. My head feels fuzzy, as if I've gone full Victorian housewife in need of some smelling salts because my corset's too tight.

'Is everything okay, Lily?' Lola is blurry, which isn't good, is it? Is it possible to have a stress-induced stroke?

'Just the heat,' I tell her, flopping back to lay down. 'I skipped breakfast.'

Before I even realize what's happening, Lola's hand is on my forehead. It's cool, I've no idea how, maybe she really is a cold-blooded reptile. She's peering down at me, closer than she's ever been.

And I should be panicking. That's my go-to reaction, I panic when Lola gets too close, worried that something might give me away. That she might realize that my nose is similar to hers, or I don't know, she might notice anything which shows me to be her baby. But instead of panicking me, her hand on my head calms me down. It's soothing.

'I feel better now, thanks,' I tell her, when it goes from being soothing to just a bit weird that I'm a grown woman who half fainted during what is meant to be a professional work session. Not to mention having the client (who is secretly my actual mother) sort me out.

'Just the heat,' I mumble, forcing myself to sit up.

'Have a drink.' Lola hands me my orange juice and I start to glug it.

But despite the funny turn, I don't have my usual desire to run for the hills. I guess hearing about how Lola went to LA like that, I can get it, a bit. How she might have felt, leaving home and everything she knew like that.

It was brave.

I've moved eight hours up the road for six weeks and look at me, I'm a wreck. So, like I said already, I admire her a little bit, for making a go of it. And every time I talk to her properly, I admire her a little more.

On top of that, the basic confirmation that Ashton is my birth father has made me realize how much I've reserved my anger for Lola over the years. I haven't thought much of the dad who obviously gave me up too, maybe because I never knew for sure who he was. He always seemed less tangible than Lola.

He wasn't even on my birth certificate.

But listening to Lola talk about the first time they met shifts some of my anger over to him. Showing someone the admittedly picturesque Isle of Skye doesn't cancel out abandoning them when they had a baby, does it?

'So, you said Ashton showed you Skye? Weren't there ... rumours that you were close?' I venture.

Lola has been staring off across the loch of death, as I privately refer to it.

And whatever I now think of Ashton (scum of the earth), I think he did a good job showing Lola Skye. She fits here, silent and still. Timeless, almost.

Jesus, one funny turn and I think I'm a poet. But it's true, I'm finding it increasingly hard to picture Lola anywhere but here.

'We were close. I'll always love Ashton.' She looks back towards the hotel. 'This was his aunt's house. He helped me buy it when she passed on and kept it all quiet, you know? I didn't want folks to know where I was.'

Seriously, could just one of my birth parents pick a side? Good or bad. It's not helpful, them both being so confusingly complex.

But if I needed any further confirmation, there I have it. Lola loved him. No, she's admitted that she *still* loves him, even though he didn't exactly stick around. Well, she wouldn't be the first woman to fall for that. Though I'd have hoped that older Lola would have had more sense than to pine for someone who clearly is never going to stay. I think of me and Noah – maybe Lola and I are more alike than I'd realized. Falling for the wrong person must be a genetic fault.

'It's cool that this used to be his aunt's house.'

Lola nods. 'It was run down by the time she passed, but it's one of the oldest hotels on the island. I was on my own, but that's how I liked it. And I was used to fixin' things from the farm. And then Noah arrived, and he helped me do out the cottages. It's getting harder, though, to keep on top of it all. It needs money spending on it. I can't lose it. I just can't.'

It's starting to make sense now. Lola needs to sell her memoirs to raise money for the hotel because it belonged to Ashton's aunt. And he's the love of her life.

I kind of hate that Lola's willing to put all of this out there, when she clearly doesn't want to, just for him. I vow to get building that pagoda later. Come hell or high water.

'You, er, seem to do everything yourself?' I say, knowing that she's leading a hike this afternoon. 'That must be hard.'

She shrugs. 'Noah helps when he's around. But, I dunno, folk think that when you're from a big family, or around people all the time, you must be good at it, but for me the opposite's true. I feel like I'm meant to be alone. I reckon that's why Noah and me bumped along okay. He's that way too. He's a travel writer because he wants to observe, not interact.'

I don't think it's true, that Lola and Noah are meant to be alone. I don't think anyone deserves to be alone. When people write their memoirs, they don't so much focus on what they did, as who they did it with. It's people. That's the stuff we really care about when all is said and done.

I realize that I'm sat talking with my birth mum about Noah, about a man. It's something I never got chance to do with Mum.

'I don't think you'd have to be alone, Lola. Not if you didn't want to be. I'm sure there are plenty of people who'd want to get to know you.'

Something that feels like shame settles low in my stomach at my words. Or it could be that I'm out of my probiotics and as predicted there's a scarcity of them up here. But no, I think it's shame. Because whether I don't want to admit it to either Lola or myself, I'm one of those people.

# Chapter Sixteen

I'm reading more of Noah's book. Again.

Yesterday, after the session with Lola, I'd gone on her mid-afternoon hike. There's no reason things like this couldn't be advertised more. Like on Airbnb, where they have experiences. It would be an easy way to bring in more business. It cannot be a good business model, Lola leading a hiking party of five for two hours.

At least my zippy trousers had gotten another run out.

The whole hike, Lola's words about she and Noah feeling alone even when they aren't were at the front of my mind. Now that she's said it, there is a lonely quality to his work, like he's the only person in the world somehow. My phone buzzes next to me, but I ignore it to keep reading. In the book, Noah is describing a hike around The Old Man of Storr, a high pinnacle of rock on the Trotternish ridge. It buzzes again as I finish my paragraph.

*Old Man of Storr was likely the result of lava flow and landslips, but legend would tell a different story, that of a giant, encased in earth after he fell and died while wandering in the area.*

**Seb:** You seriously think that this guy is your real dad?

I put down my kindle. Seb has sent a photo of Ashton from his most recent tour. He's wearing a black jacket that's covered in feathers and the leather chaps that he must have found. He isn't wearing a shirt, and his tan is of the mahogany variety. He's wearing more eyeliner than I've ever seen on a human.

> **Me:** I told you. Lola all but admitted it, she said she loved him.

I peer some more at the photo, even though I'm committed to believe that he's a wanker who has strung Lola along for decades. I zoom in on his hair. That has to be where I get mine from. His is sort of knotted. That's what mine would be like without my hair care plan.

> **Seb:** I love you, but you don't see me wanting to dick you down, do you?
>
> **Seb:** Just saying that made me sick in my mouth.
>
> **Seb:** But Ashton, I'd dick him down in a heartbeat. I think he'd like it too.

> **Me:** Bisexual people exist you know. And please can we stop saying dick down. It's 8am.

> **Seb:** All I'm saying is don't get ahead of yourself. Let Lola's story play out how she wants it to.

> **Me:** That's actually really good advice.

> **Seb:** I always give good advice.

**Me:** No, you told me I could pull off that half-shaved head look.

**Seb:** I was only saying that for the LOLs. You would have looked ridiculous. But my real advice is golden.

**Me:** How reassuring.

**Seb:** Got to go. I have a meeting with Kitty. She wants the first three chapters by the end of summer. Told her you're all over it.

**Me:** Yeah. No problemo.

Unease settles deep in my stomach. I'm still sure that given the choice, Lola wouldn't be telling anyone anything. But she feels like she has to for the sake of the hotel. Maybe Noah and I should help her more. We'd made a start on the pagoda last night. And you know what's wild? Building a garden pagoda in the dead of night. But even if the three-pronged plan was a success and Lola didn't need to sell her story, Your Life would still lose out.

I have my laptop open next to me on the bed having just ordered my business plan to be printed, bound and sent with a courier. Because at the point at which you're doing some mild construction work, it's time to present your plans more fully.

An email comes through from Mr Vandergilden. He's chasing me and becoming increasingly impatient, even though I'm exactly on schedule.

Urgh, he's impossible sometimes.

Speaking of impossible, Noah sticks his head around the bedroom door.

240

'You ready?'

'Am I ever!' I overcompensate with my levels of enthusiasm. 'Are you going to tell me where we're going yet?'

Noah makes a zipping motion across his mouth. Lovely mouth. 'It's a surprise, but I think you'll like it.' Noah said that about the cave, and I did like it. But just to be on the safe side, I narrow my eyes. 'It's not paragliding, is it?'

He laughs. 'Nope.'

'Okay, good. Obviously being the adrenaline junkie that I am I would absolutely be down for that, so just checking.'

Another laugh. 'Come on.'

We head to the car park at the front of the hotel. That vet guy, James, is there, chatting to Lola.

Lola looks a little flushed, if you ask me, which obviously no one is, but still.

'James has come to check on Bertie,' Lola tells us as we pass.

'Bertie?' I ask them all.

'The chicken,' James answers. 'He keeps walking into walls. I'll get him right, though.'

If this James can sort out Bertie, Bertie the bald, blind chicken, he's not a vet, he's a miracle worker.

'Okay, well enjoy!' I send a quick wave to them all. Lola has her tool belt around her waist. Right on time, Scout the Labrador, the daft chicken and a small pig come out of the hotel doors. It is very, very bizarre up here.

'It's a little bit of a drive, so get comfy.'

I use Noah's words as an excuse to hug his middle a bit tighter. I'm an old hand at this motorbike malarky now, so at least I'm not wearing a long dress. I'm in denim shorts and what I use interchangeably as a nighttime T-shirt. It's one that I got for taking part in some sponsored run. Basically, I've given up fighting the fact that Isle of Skye me looks like she occasionally lives in a bin.

We set off and the sweet, sweet numbness that comes from feeling like death is just a hair's breadth away takes over while I cling to Noah.

Fields and mountains blur around us as we pass them, the hills becoming slightly smaller in scale, greener than the dark, jagged mountains around Lola's hotel.

Eventually, we join a short row of cars waiting to turn into a driveway.

'Technically, this isn't a hidden gem,' Noah twists round to tell me. 'But I think you're going to enjoy it.'

We edge forward in the queue, and I see the purple sign by the entrance.

'Welcome to Dunvegan Castle.'

Now, some people get excited about boxes of chocolates. Flowers, jewellery even. Noah gets turned on by naturally occurring phenomena. But me, historical landmarks are my kryptonite. Nothing gets me going more than a good castle.

I almost fall off the bike, letting go of Noah to flap my hands around.

'I love castles!' I say. 'Like, seriously love them. I once had this idea about going around all the castles in the country. I made a map and everything.'

'That sounds like a plan I could get on board with.'

'I don't think you understand, Noah, you have to really love castles to commit to a plan like that. Seb came with me to three and then said that they were all the same. And he calls himself a historian.'

Noah laughs some more as we park up.

'Well, this castle has an extra surprise in store too,' Noah says.

It's then that I see it. Taking away from the majestic beauty of the castle, a little red plane with 'Skye from the Sky' painted on it.

Oh no.

'Er, what's that?' I ask Noah, leaning back on the bike because I don't trust my legs to support me.

'It's just that you went on and on about how it was such a shame that you wouldn't get to skydive, I thought I'd give you the chance.'

Noah must see what is, no doubt, sheer terror written all over my face.

'Obviously, you don't have to. There's no, like, obligation.'

I swallow.

This feels like punishment. For all my lying. But seriously, if one of my lies was going to catch me out, of course it would have to be the skydiving one. Couldn't have been any of the other lies, could it?

Possibly, this is a test as to just how deep my people-pleasing tendencies run. Will I throw myself out of a plane rather than admit to not wanting to do something and risk disappointing the lovely Noah? Unlikely.

But here's the thing. A tiny part of me does want to be the sort of person who does this. Who rocks up to a castle and embarks on an impromptu skydive. I want to be the person Noah believes that I am. A part of me wants to be the person I am on Skye. At least some of the time.

'I'll do it,' I say.

Steve, my tandem flyer, at least takes health and safety very seriously. He could tone it down a bit, if you ask me. He's very reassuring, though. Apparently, our chances of dying are 'negligible'.

I send a quick 'last will and testament' WhatsApp to Seb, just in case. Hopefully, it'll hold up in the coroner's office if it comes to it.

Noah is laughing and joking with his diver.

'It'll be fine,' Steve says. He's having to hold me up at this point. We're strapping ourselves into the plane. And isn't that a ridiculous thing to have. Seat belts in a plane we're about to leap out of.

'Excited, Lily?' Noah asks. He's positively glowing as we take off from a patch of grass, leaving the perfectly lovely castle beneath us.

I knew he'd look good on a plane. And he's filling out his jumpsuit very well. I look like a child in a sleeping bag.

This is Noah in his natural environment. I can see, now, the kick he gets out of travel. It reminds me how different we are and makes me wonder why exactly I'm about to throw myself out of a bloody plane to impress the guy.

'Sooo excited,' I answer feebly.

'That there's Loch Dunvegan.' Steve points to an open body of water to the side of the castle. Brilliant. More water. I've started to shake.

'And what do we do in the event of a water landing?' I ask, my teeth chattering.

'Nah, there won't be one of those, like.'

How reassuring.

We don't seem to be climbing anymore. In fact, the pilot is giving us an okay sign from the front of the plane. And that doesn't seem very technical, does it? How do they know we're at the right place? I think that they should think some more about it. Go around again, perhaps.

I open my mouth to say I've changed my mind. I want to go back down. I don't want to be the sort of person who does adventurous things. I want to be the sort of person who stays in bed with a book. It's a myth, we don't contain multitudes, we should just pick a lane and stay in it.

But Steve is saying that it's time to jump and the plane door is open.

How am I at the edge of a plane?

Don't they need to check that I'm sure for one last time? They asked a lot on the ground.

Steve is counting down. What happens next?

Oh my fucking Jesus, we aren't in the plane anymore.

The wind hits me like a wind tunnel turned up to the max. Steve has manoeuvred us so that I'm on my stomach, riding on the wind.

'Open your eyes!' he calls.

'No!' I call back, thinking that I'd be really panicked right now if I could actually draw breath.

Why is my mouth so wide open?

'Look!' he calls.

I open my eyes, thinking that whatever I look at might be the final thing that I see and I'm ... well, I'm blown away.

The loch is there in the distance, stretching out to the ocean. Everything is so small down there, so insignificant.

I can't cry. My eyes are too dry.

I see Noah and his diver in front of us. He actually waves. Lunatic.

There's a massive tug on the harness and we're flying upwards again.

I scream, but it's carried away on the wind.

The parachute is up and it looks like all of Steve's checks paid off.

I find the bit with the parachute up much more genteel. Giant wedgie aside, it's civilized, almost. Why we left it so long to get it out, I'll never know. I hang like a ragdoll off Steve and wonder why my cheeks are so wet when my mouth is so very, very dry.

I'm happy to report that I manage an excellent landing in the castle grounds. Steve taught me well. He tells me that it's one of his best landings this week, in fact.

When I'm detached from Steve, I fall to my hands and knees. Lovely grass. I'll never abandon you again.

'That was amazing,' I hear Noah call behind me. I'm still stroking the grass.

'It was ... something.' Like a religious experience, almost. I think that maybe I'm being dramatic, but I did just throw myself out of a plane.

'Do you want to head down to the beach, or we could go look around the castle, when you're, er, done,' Noah says. I desist from stroking the grass, sit back on my heels. My legs are still shaking.

'Let's go to the beach, that would be lovely.'

With some effort, I stand up. We say our final farewell to the Skye from the Sky team and turn away from the castle, heading towards the shore of the loch.

I expected to feel, I don't know, drained after the skydive. But instead, everything feels heightened. Like I'm looking at the world in high definition.

'It's really beautiful here.' I sit down (or rather my legs give out) on a small mound of sand close to the shore. The perimeter of the loch stretches out on all sides around us.

It's all so big. That's what I thought at the top of the mountain, from the infinity pool, from the sky. Everything on Skye makes it impossible not to feel inconsequential. It makes me think, who cares what rubbish you have going on, look how big the world is?

'It is.' We sit and take it all in until the afternoon sun gets hazy, then venture down the cliff and along the beach.

Neither of us talk much. It's like we shared something, jumping out of that plane. I don't even think about what the skydive did to my hair. Chances are, all the Frizzease in the world couldn't save me now, but I'm not thinking about that as I kick my sandals off and walk in the water so that the waves lap at my ankles. Noah holds my hand, the one not carrying my shoes, that is, and for the first time I truly let myself think about how nice it would be, to have more of this. Not just with Noah, but with Lola too. What it might be like to make space for her in some capacity in my life.

The thought of telling her who I am, of having her reject me again, fills me with dread. But maybe I could keep pretending and she need never know.

Maybe Noah will take that job, the one that means he could be around more.

'You're crushing my hand.' Noah laughs.

I relax my iron grip.

'Sorry.'

Noah tugs me to face him, then he's looking down at me intently and his features seem softer around the edges somehow. I'm sure we're about to kiss. We're on a beach and the sun is starting to set – it's the perfect backdrop to some gold star kissing. Except he doesn't kiss me, he hugs me. I bury my head in his shoulder, breathe him in and hug him back as if my life depends on it, as if hugging him tight enough will be the thing to keep him here.

When we break apart, he's frowning.

'Is everything okay?' I ask him as we turn and start to walk back.

'Yeah,' he says. 'Well, actually, just over there is a caravan park. I lived there with Mum and Dad for a few years. Coming back here always brings it back.'

'God, Noah, I had no idea. I'm sorry, we didn't need to come.'

'It's fine. I like it here. I used to escape down to the loch as much as I could.'

'Okay, good, okay. Do you, er, ever miss them?' I ask him, feeling like I should say something but not sure what.

'Sometimes.' He shrugs. 'I've seen them on and off. If they get wind that I'm in the country they pop up now and then, normally to ask for money.'

'That's so awful.'

'Yep. But it's just . . . addiction, right? It's not really them. Even when I lived with them, it was like being on my own. I guess I got used to it over the years and now it's just the way things are. Aside from Lola, I don't really have anyone.'

And well done me, for not ruining this beautiful moment of Noah opening up by screeching 'Me! Have me!' at the top of my voice.

Plus, I get it, what it's like to feel alone. It's one of the reasons I wanted to meet Lola after Dad died, because despite all the hen dos and weddings and gender reveal parties, I sometimes feel like Seb is the only person who really knows me.

'I understand that,' I say, squeezing his hand again.

'What are your parents like?' he asks, and my stomach falls a little, at them being described in the present tense.

'Great,' I say without thinking. 'The best really. They always just had so much time for me, you know? It meant that they put a lot of effort in. With all these traditions. Like every Christmas we'd get a new bauble each and have a competition about who could pick the worst one. I got a hot dog one from Paperchase that I loved. And every birthday we'd have birthday hugs instead of birthday bumps. Sorry.' I stop myself. 'I'm being insensitive.'

He brushes a thumb along my cheekbone, and I lean into him, just a little.

'You aren't. It makes me happy, that you have that.'

I do a slow breath out as we look at each other. In my head, I'm thinking that we're more alike in the parenting stakes than Noah could possibly know. The urge to tell him is there then, thrashing around in my chest. But how can I admit that I lied? What a mess.

I stamp the urge down. Noah must see that I'm wrestling with something because he says 'Urgh' and shakes his head, as if he's trying to actively dislodge the melancholic thoughts. 'I didn't mean to get all maudlin. Let's walk some more. Unless you want to get back?'

I want to drive on the back of the motorbike in the dark less than I want to get root canal work at the dentist, but I don't want to leave the beach. I don't want the day to end.

'Let's walk some more.'

It's a shame, really, that the story of me and Noah doesn't get an ending where we walk off into the sunset together.

# Chapter Seventeen

Seb had taken the news of my skydive as expected. He hadn't believed me, and I'd had to get Noah to come and confirm that I had in fact jumped and not been pushed out of the plane.

'You've changed, Lily Brown,' he'd said.

'Not really, I've just tapped into my adventurous side.'

'Like I said, you've changed.'

I'm confused. On the one hand, it seems that time has no meaning here on Skye. Or that's how it probably seems to everyone else. For me, time is galloping away at pace. I count down every morning. Every evening. I drive myself mad counting it down. At the start of summer six weeks felt like forever, a huge expanse of time ahead of me. But now, there's only one week left. One.

And I'm still lying to them all.

At this point, I'm telling so many lies, I'm convinced I'll trip up and give myself away.

I'm lying to Lola and Noah about who I am.

I'm lying to both of them about the fact that I knew who Lola was before I came up here.

I'm lying about Seb being my brother.

I'm lying to myself about what I want to happen when the summer is over.

At least the courier made it with copies of the business plan.

I've met Lola a couple more times and she's talked me through the first weeks and then months of the band. She'd gotten all breathless with excitement, talking about how the band had learned together. How Jimmy kept promising them that they'd be stars. How they all felt like they were on the edge of their big break. It's strange, hearing your birth mum get excited about the thing she cared about more than you. I don't think I've seen Lola so excited this whole summer as when she talked about the band's early days when everything seemed possible. She was pretty thrilled with a big cucumber she grew in her vegetable patch, mind.

Nothing she's said even comes close to hinting at why she left.

It's all muddled in my head because on the one hand, I can't wait to get home, to get back to everything being nice and ordered and calm. But on the other, the thought of all this ending, to go back to filling my days without Noah and without Lola, well, it fills me with dread.

I'm back under the willow tree, fidgeting with the edge of the picnic blanket Lola has laid out again. She's disappeared to help Harper and Blake's foster parents with something, so I've nothing to do but wait for her and think, wondering what she'll say today that'll reveal some part of my past without her even realizing it. I stare out over the massive black loch and watch as the sun dances flecks of gold across it, you know, for maximum drama.

'Sorry about that.' Lola's voice makes me twist around.

She's kicking off her worn Crocs and lowering herself onto the picnic blanket.

Today her dungarees are cut-offs, bits of thread hanging down. Her white T-shirt is covered in strawberries. It's really hard to feel anything but warmth for a woman covered in embroidered fruit.

'Everything okay?' I ask.

Lola nods. 'Blake can get frustrated. It's hard for his foster parents, but for some reason, I calm him down.' She shrugs. It's not at all hard to imagine Lola soothing Blake, talking to him steady and low in her lilting accent. It's then that I realize that the image I had of Lola as a drug-addled party addict just isn't there anymore. I don't mention that I think Blake's foster parents need to worry as much about Harper as they do about Blake. It isn't my place.

Bertie the blind chicken, the one that seems to have a sixth sense about where Lola is at all times, comes bumbling down the hill towards her. It gets close this time before it falls onto its side, its legs still moving as if it's walking.

Lola reaches out and picks it up, righting it as it clucks happily.

'You do seem to collect waifs and strays,' I tell her, watching as the chicken does a couple of laps of where she's sat.

Lola smiles. 'I feel an affinity with them all. Same with Noah, I guess.'

I nod and look down at my phone, which is ready to start recording. I'd half wondered if Lola was trying to make amends with all of her good deeds, but I probably need to remember that not every single thing in the universe is about me. And despite all the time we've spent together now, Lola has never, ever mentioned the baby she left.

'Shall we get started?' I ask, to cover the weird feeling. 'How many more sessions do you think we'd need?'

'Two, maybe?' she ventures.

I'm back to professional mode, totally professional. Not at all thinking that it's yet another countdown hanging over me.

'It's like therapy.' Lola smiles as the chicken finally flops down next to her, upright for a change.

'A lot of people say that. But I think that actual therapists get paid more. I barely make a living wage.'

Lola laughs.

'But if you're ready, let's start.'

\* \* \*

*'Jimmy's right, you're going to be a star, Lola,'* Ashton said when we finished in the studio that day.

He put his arm around me and I heard the click of a camera from somewhere. The label liked that, when we got pictured doing things like holdin' hands. They said it would help us get traction, if people thought there was a romance between us.

Our first single would be called 'Storm Inside a Teacup'. Someone else had written the words, all I had to do was sing them. Over and over and over again, I sang the same words, till Jimmy said that it was perfect and that me singing like that was going to make all of them a whole lot of money. No one mentioned how much it would make me and I didn't ask.

I worked harder than I'd ever worked in my life. Burnin' the candle at both ends, like. The label arranged for us to go to all these parties, to get us mixin' with the right sort of people, making connections, that sort of thing. And even though we weren't old enough to drink, or me and Prune weren't at any rate, no one seemed to mind very much that we weren't twenty-one yet.

Sometimes I'd catch a look at myself, all dressed up in some outfit that Jimmy thought was a good idea, and I'd hardly recognize myself, you know? Especially since I had all my thrift store clothes in a drawer in my room.

I'm not sayin' we didn't work hard. We weren't famous yet, even though there was this buzz around us. That's what Jimmy said. We were pipped as the next big thing.

I worked at everything, even the apartment. If something needed fixin', I did it myself. You don't live in a falling down house without learning a thing or two about sorting it out yourself. Ma wouldn't have ever called a plumber or anything like that.

One morning I was fixing the tap in the kitchen and when I sat up, Ashton was there. I must have been all red faced. Some days, I wondered that I was half in love with him, he was always making me laugh.

It was . . . a good time. I'd never been real excited for the future when I *was young. But I was now, for the very first time. I guess we were all caught up in it, in this idea that we'd be superstars.*

*When no one else was around, Jimmy would tell me that I was the special one, that the band would be nothing without me. I'd never been special to anyone, not in a good way, and I liked it, though it's shameful to admit it now. I liked being special.*

*Jimmy arranged for us to go on MTV the week our first single was released. They dressed me up in this orange dress that was so tight and short, I remember thinking that the Merrywells would have had a coronary. I hated that dress. There was glitter all over my face too, making my skin itch. I don't know that I was nervous, I think I'd gone beyond nerves. I was numb to it all. It felt like it was happenin' to someone else. I still felt like I was there by mistake, even then.*

*We'd practised so much that I didn't even have to think about what I was doing while I was on stage. It took me a few moments at the end to realize that everyone was cheering. Ashton was jumping up and down next to me, Prune and Shawn too. And the audience were deafening. The loudest thing I'd ever heard.*

*It's intoxicating, people clapping and cheering for you. Addictive. Anyone who says otherwise is lying.*

*It went quickly after that. We went from acting famous to being famous. Those first months it felt like we were the most famous people in the whole entire world. We never stopped moving, no matter how tired we got. There was always some other high to chase. I'd think jeez, I just met the president! And then the next week we'd see Prince Charles at a charity gala. We were always on display, always performin'.*

*I didn't know then what I know now. 'Bout how it costs you, performing like that. Living under a scrutiny of sorts. Or maybe it doesn't cost everyone. Some folks thrive off of it, I dare say. But it cost me. It cost me so much.*

Lola stops talking and I realize that she's done for today. This is what I expected to hear, stories about her performing, being famous.

'It sounds like a wild time,' I tell her.

'It was different to old town Baton Rouge, put it that way.' She smiles.

'Do you miss it? Or do you think you would if it hadn't . . . cost you?' I ask, repeating her words.

Lola thinks for a second. 'Sometimes. Or maybe what I miss is the feeling of possibilities. It felt like anything was possible then. Course it wasn't. I was still me, but it was a nice feeling. Plus, there's a lot I'm not proud of from back then.'

I pause a second, not entirely sure what to say.

'Things are still possible now,' I tell her in the end.

'Are they?'

I don't know what she's asking.

Or why the air feels so heavy all of a sudden.

'If you want to stay a moment, I could bring us some lunch out here. It's such a nice day,' she says.

I don't even think. 'That would be nice, thanks Lola.'

Lola stands up, dislodging the chicken who's fallen asleep next to her. Or at least, I think it's fallen asleep. I do wonder how anyone will know the difference between it being asleep and dead.

I take the chance to text Seb.

**Me:** Guess who's having a picnic with Lola!

**Seb:** If it's not you, that was a seriously
misleading message.

**Me:** It is me!

**Seb:** Such a nauseatingly uplifting tale.
Families reuniting. Warms my cold, dead
heart.

254

**Me:** Except Lola doesn't know that we're reuniting.

**Seb:** She still hasn't dropped the B bomb, then?

**Me:** Nope, no mention of baby me. She did say how much her and Ashton got along though again, and how she was half in love with him. It has to be him.

**Seb:** If you say so.

**Me:** Got to go, Noah and Lola are coming.

**Seb:** Sounds like you're working really hard up there.

**Me:** I am! I sent Mr Vandergilden a draft last night. He was emailing every day. Do you know how many times I typed the words 'and then I shot ...'

**Seb:** Relax! Jeez, I was kidding. I wish you'd work less not more. You highly strung people are so touchy.

**Me:** I really have to go.

**Seb:** Have fun with lover boy and Mum.
**Seb:** That sounded dark. Enjoy!

'Look who I found!' Lola smiles up at Noah with something that looks close to maternal pride. It makes my skin feel all itchy. Those bloody ants better not be back.

'I was trying to finish painting the bedroom,' Noah protests, being dragged down onto the picnic blanket by Lola.

'Ah, there's time a plenty for painting. I've never known you to turn down food.'

'That's true. Hi.' Noah smiles at me.

'Hi.' I can't help my stupid face from smiling. Lola hums.

'You should have seen him when he was eighteen.' Lola starts pulling food out of a wicker basket. We have affable Lola for lunch, then. 'Right scrawny little thing, I couldn't fill him.'

I look at Noah, with his lovely bicep vein. He's no one's definition of scrawny.

'He's actually the only person who eats whatever I cook without complaining,' I tell Lola.

'Well, once I ate tarantulas in Cambodia so Lola's right, I'll eat anything.'

'Hey! But also, gross.'

There might be many, many ways in which Lola and I are different. But if there's one thing that can be said to bond us, it's our shared passion for the humble salad.

Lola produces Tupperware full of different types and I pile up my plate.

'These radishes are amazing,' I tell her.

'Thanks, Lily. They're from the patch.'

'It really makes a difference. Is that the giant cucumber too?'

'Yep, seemed a shame to cut it up in the end.'

Lola's one step away from that character in *Encanto* who shoots literal flowers from her fingertips.

I think of the rota I have to water Dad's plants. Printed and laminated and pinned to the fridge. Lola probably just looks at a plant and knows instinctively that it's at risk of dehydration.

## The Next Chapter

Lola tells me stories about Noah.

'There was this one time I was caught kissing the vicar's daughter in the food shed,' Noah says.

'The vicar's daughter.' I laugh. 'Painfully clichéd.'

Noah holds up his hands. 'I was nineteen and she was … enthusiastic.'

We all laugh because Lola's funny. Not in the way that Mr Cains is funny, all in your face. Lola's humour comes from quiet observations.

'Y'all should come to the karaoke tomorrow night. You can play piano, Lily, isn't that right?' Lola asks. 'Noah mentioned something.'

'Yeah but, I don't know, I never sing in public. I'm not really a karaoke person. And I haven't played since I was eighteen.'

When Mum died.

Lola looks at me for a second longer than might be considered normal. I'm worried that my grief is written all over my face. I attempt a bright smile.

'I've been before, it's not too bad. You don't have to sing.'

I get what Noah's saying, but actually I reject the premise that karaoke people are fun people. I'm not sure that karaoke makes anyone feel good about themselves, ever. It's like an all you can eat buffet. Sounds great in principal, but everyone leaves feeling like they've lost a bit of their soul.

'You don't have to do anything if you don't want to.' Lola is stretched out on the grass. 'I just know that Harper's foster mum would really like her to take part in some more of the activities. When she does them, she always has fun. But she's still mighty reluctant to join in. I thought she might be more likely to come if you were both there. She seems real taken with you.'

Harper is still quite insulting towards me, though maybe less than she was originally. Whenever I've seen her around her foster family, she's always seething in silence. I can't help but feel like they're so preoccupied with Blake, no one seems to have realized that Harper isn't coping well either.

Anyway, there's no way I'll say no after that. Guilt is my primary motivator in all walks of life.

'Okay fine, but I don't think I'll play or sing. I'll just watch.'

'Course. Whatever y'all like.'

I relax again after that. None of us make a move to leave the willow tree.

Time stretches out and I think what it would be like if we could all stay here in this endless summer, this endless day. How nice it would be if I got to keep Lola and Noah like this forever, if this was my life. Where everything is relaxed and easy.

But that's the thing about holidays, they aren't real life. *This* isn't real life. It won't last. Real life is coming for us all and I'm just not sure how I'm going to cope with it.

# Chapter Eighteen

I'm drunk.

Okay, I'm tipsy.

But in my defence, I am about to go to karaoke with my birth mum. Karaoke on its own is bad enough. But throw in the birth mum who left me to be a singer and being tipsy is almost essential.

'I've never seen anyone get drunk off of two gin and tonics,' Noah comments as I stumble through the hotel gardens.

'I think stress amplifies its potency. Plus, I care about my liver. I want it to stay all pink and sponge-like.'

'I'm sure it appreciates your concern.'

Noah puts his arm around my waist, and I wonder again why we're going to karaoke when we could just stay in the cottage and get it on.

Super glad that that was in my head.

'Why are we going to this again?' I ask, looking up at him.

'Because Lola asked and you said yes.'

'Oh yeah, I did.'

'Harper,' he says.

'Yeah, Lola said if I go, it'll make her go too.'

'No, look, she's there.'

He's right, Harper is sat in her usual spot by the picnic benches, scowling down at her phone.

'Harper. HARPER!' I'm not sure how I'm managing to whisper and shout all at the same time.

Harper looks up and narrows her eyes at us.

'She looks angry,' I tell Noah, possibly quite loudly because Harper is stalking towards us then. And instead of anger, she actually looks full of something I'd describe as sinister glee.

'Is she pissed?' she asks Noah. Yep, definitely sinister glee.

'She's on her way. She had two gin and tonics.'

I'm not sure I've ever seen Harper smile properly. It's vaguely terrifying.

I make a sort of choking sound.

'Sorry, I was just sick in my mouth a bit.'

Harper's smile grows even wider.

'We're going to the karaoke, you should come along.' Noah is so smooth. Smooth like silk.

'Oh my god, she's stroking you, this is brilliant.'

I hadn't realized that I was rubbing Noah's silky-smooth arm. I stop immediately. 'It's because he's smooth like silk,' I tell them.

'Fuck yeah, I'm coming. She'll be singing, right?' Harper asks, walking with never-before-seen purpose towards the back door of the hotel.

I don't seem to remember promising anyone that I'd sing. Quite the opposite, in fact. I can't think properly.

It's not just the gin. The evening is close and sticky, suffocating almost. That sort of weather where you think it needs a good thunderstorm to clear the air. It feels like an omen.

Still, as I set off to follow Harper, I can't help but wonder what it's an omen of.

\* \* \*

'Tell me more, tell me mo-o-oore!'

There's scattered applause.

Unlike me, Harper's foster parents have absolutely no qualms about singing. None at all. I think at this point, someone is going to have to take one for the team and rugby tackle the microphones from them. They're doing the *Grease* medley. Again.

I wince as they get too close and the mics screech.

Karaoke at Lola's hotel is . . . not like anything I ever thought I'd take part in. I think it's fair to say that should any extraterrestrial life stumble upon us all gathered here in the breakfast room of the hotel, they'd think the human species were completely insane and flee to the nearest galaxy.

The breakfast tables have been pushed to the sides of the room and the chairs are scattered around the floor. Someone has closed all the blinds, I presume so that no unsuspecting ramblers happen upon us and have to witness this, but it might also be because Lola has a small disco set up and there are multicoloured lights flashing across the wooden floor.

The 'karaoke' is just a single mic plugged into Lola's laptop and she plays songs through YouTube, testing the hotel's Wi-Fi to its absolute limit.

And if I'd thought I was a bit drunk before I got here, I quickly realize that I'm not drunk enough.

'Fuck's sake, why are they like this?' Harper mutters as Blake runs over, smiling. Her foster parents start up a rendition of 'Everything I Do', the Bryan Adams version. From what I remember, it's about eighteen hours long.

'Shall we get a drink?' I ask Noah, who is watching the whole scene with a sort of bemused smirk.

I guess it's nothing he hasn't seen before.

'Yeah, come on, Lola has a bar over here.'

'Can I have some booze too?' Harper asks, her and Blake trailing behind us.

'No.' Me and Noah answer at the same time.

261

Lola seems to be both karaoke monitor and barwoman tonight. She's standing behind a table in the corner, swaying a little to the music. James the silver fox vet is standing next to her. Also swaying. I wonder if there has been another Bertie-based emergency.

I think it's possible that Lola's dressed up for the occasion because she's wearing a skirt, for the first time ever. It's long and black and it has crescent moons stitched onto it. Her hair is down. Limp and obedient against her tanned shoulders.

'I'm glad y'all decided to come. What can I get you to drink? We have wine, or there are some beers and soft drinks in the cool box.'

'Wine please, any colour,' I say as Noah laughs and gets himself a beer.

Blake and Harper get cokes.

We pay and Lola stores the money in one of those little money tins.

'It's busy,' I say, looking around the room, which is now only vaguely spinning. There are groups of people dotted about, most with their backs to the karaoke, as if that might help to block it out. Half of them are wearing kilts. Locals, then.

'There are folk from town here. We're not often full, even in summer. By winter, it's mostly the odd school group.'

'School groups?' I ask.

She nods again.

'Lola does a reduced rate for kids on free school meals,' Noah tells us. Course she does, bloody Saint Lola.

'How lovely.'

'It's nothin'.'

'This is nice and everything, but I thought you were going to sing. That's what I was told,' Harper butts in.

'I don't think I ever promised that I'd sing.' I start downing my wine with a vengeance.

'For what it's worth, you're a great singer. I heard her in the shower.' Noah completely sells me out. Traitor.

The piano is still pushed against the wall and there's no sign of Lola's guitar. So at least I don't have to confront the very particular trauma of watching her play.

'What about Noah?' I say, too loudly. 'Why does he get out of this?'

'Actually, it's my song next.' Noah has a drink.

Harper cackles.

I think I'm possibly the only person who realizes that this is a big deal for Noah, standing up and singing in front of all these people. He'd definitely rather be up a mountain somewhere; he has the blotchy neck of a man suppressing the urge to run to the nearest hill and climb it.

All thoughts of Noah fleeing the scene go out of the window as he takes up the mantle of the mic. Instead, I find myself rapt as I watch Noah self-consciously air guitar his way through a bit of Bon Jovi. He's not even particularly good, it's just . . . it's the air guitar. It's freaking hot.

'I still can't believe he's going out with you,' Harper says. I realize that most people have stopped what they're doing and are bobbing up and down, cheering Noah. I'm edging ever closer to where he's singing and when he smiles at me around the mic, I practically melt into a puddle on the floor.

I don't even have it in me to be insulted by Harper. Because, honestly, same. 'I know,' I tell her.

'I suppose you're quite funny in your own, strange way.'

I take another big drink of wine as Noah's song comes to an end. I'm so nervous that I don't even register that Harper was moderately nice to me there.

Noah finishes and there's a smattering of applause.

He takes a bow before walking quickly away from what is obviously the 'performance space'. The fluttering in my stomach that's always there around him becomes a persistent ache.

I have another (and another) drink. It doesn't make it go away.

Noah says something to Lola who takes the mic, looks at me and says, 'Sing for us, Lily Brown?'

I guess that Noah did tell her my surname after all. She doesn't seem to have freaked about it, though, so maybe it didn't ring any bells.

It's not what I need to be thinking about now. Chatter has broken out around us. Hopefully this means that everyone has gone back to their drinks, and they'll just ignore me.

I hand Noah the remnants of my wine. 'You were really good,' I tell him.

He laughs. 'Not my first karaoke here. What are you going to sing?'

'I don't know, do you have a list?' I ask Lola.

'Just whatever's on YouTube,' she tells me.

'Okay, how about "Love Story" by Taylor Swift? I've always liked that one.' I try to play down just how much of a committed Swiftie I really am (top one per cent on Spotify round-up). But I could sing this song in my sleep. Lola searches and despite my knowing all the words, I still think it'll be good going if I don't just puke all over them. Whether from booze or nerves, who knows. The last time I properly sang for anyone was before Mum died. And that was in the school choir.

But the song starts up and the mic is in my hand. So, it looks like I am doing this. At least no one's paying me any attention, aside from Noah, that is, and Lola and James. Oh and Blake, who's smiling, and Harper, who is also smiling, but in a much more sinister way.

I miss the bit where I'm meant to start so I decide to glue my eyes to the screen of Lola's laptop instead. It doesn't matter that the words are a tiny bit blurry because come on, as if I need the actual words.

I'm a bit croaky at first and I'm gripping the mic so hard there's a chance I'm going to snap it in half. But then I remember Harper's foster dad going for all the high notes in the *Grease* medley that they did, and I think the bar isn't particularly high here.

And actually, if everyone thinks I'm rubbish, it doesn't matter. The world won't come crashing to an end.

My slither of personal growth relaxes me a little bit, not that I take my eyes off the screen. It's not a song that allows you to breathe too often – Taylor must have really brilliant lung capacity – but I give it my best shot and when the song ends, I think it's probably gone all right, if truth be told.

What I absolutely don't expect to happen is to look up and see everyone sort of . . . gaping. Yeah, there's no other word to describe it. They're all gaping at me.

When I think back on this, or better yet, write it into my memoirs, I'll definitely insert a sort of slow clap, starting with Noah for maximum drama. In reality, it's everyone clapping together, but it'll sound much more theatrical as a slow clap.

'I can't believe you're actually good!' Harper says as Noah whistles at me.

'Do another one!' he calls out. And even Harper's foster parents shout in agreement, though they don't have a problem with mic-hoggers, being ones themselves.

Only Lola is looking at me with her head tilted to the side. As if I'm a puzzle she's trying to figure out.

I can't think about that now. Not when people are shouting out things like 'Sing more Taylor' and 'Do you know any Shania Twain?'.

Maybe it's the alcohol I have flowing through my system or the sheer relief that what I thought was going to be an out and out disaster has actually turned out pretty good, but after that, I get really into it. It's an excellent thing that as adults, we're allowed to change our minds about stuff, because I do a complete U-turn when it comes to the humble karaoke.

I sing 'This Charming Man' with Harper, who shouts all the words and Noah and I give 'Señorita' by Camilla Cabello and Shawn Mendes such a good go, it's practically pornographic. Just what I want in front of my birth mum and all these strangers from town.

And okay, my knee slide at the end of 'Don't Stop Believin'' was very much ill-advised. I'll likely have knee problems for years now. But other than that, people are dancing around me, and I can see it, then. I can see why Lola loved this, loved people cheering and clapping at her, at least at first. Making people happy is what I am for, always. Making them this happy is an addictive high.

This is what I always worried about. That I'd like it too much. That it would mean that I was like Lola. Singing with Mum was safe, singing because I liked the admiration, less so.

Which is strange, because the only person showing zero admiration is Lola. She's not smiling or clapping. In fact, she's retreated to the drinks table and from what I can tell, is hardly talking to anyone.

'I need a break,' I gasp at the end of a particularly energetic rendition of 'Bohemian Rhapsody'. I make my way over to Lola. I think I've sweated out most of the booze, but I'm parched.

'Do you have any water, Lola?' I ask her.

She rummages around in the cool box and hands me a bottle.

'You have a lovely voice,' she tells me. 'I'm surprised you didn't want to sing.'

I shrug, feeling the urge to squirm at the way she's looking at me, as if she's trying to see through me.

'I haven't really sung anything in a long time,' I tell her.

'Why is that?'

I'm not about to get into this.

I shrug. 'No real reason.'

There's a moment of silence and I think that somehow, I've given the game away. Though how could I have done? I've sung a load of generic karaoke songs. Lola takes a breath, and I think then that she's going to tell me that she *knows*, she knows who I am.

And ... I don't mind. At first, I just wanted the space to get to know Lola without this thing hanging over us. Then not telling her became the default, because I didn't want to admit I lied about knowing who she was. But now, I'm past that. I want her to recognize who I am to her.

I steel myself for hearing her say the words.

Except those aren't the words she says. Instead, she says, 'Lily, I don't suppose you'd sing with me?'

# Chapter Nineteen

'Okay,' I answer, way more nervous to sing with Lola than anyone else. 'Sure, why not?' I give the fakest nonchalant shrug in the history of fake nonchalance. My voice is unnaturally high.

'I'll go get my guitar.' Lola leaves, and I know that she's going to her office to get the guitar that she has hanging on the wall there.

I walk back over to Noah. He's leaning against the wall to the dining room, watching everyone else mingle.

'I'm going to sing with Lola,' I tell him where he's standing with James. Saying it makes it even more real.

James's eyebrows lift up. 'Lola hardly ever sings on karaoke night.'

'She doesn't?' I swallow.

'I think you'll sound great together.' Noah must be able to sense my nerves. 'Look, she's waiting for you.'

I twist around and sure enough, Lola's stood by the laptop, her dad's guitar strap over her shoulder, looking closer to Lola the star from Beyond Baton Rouge than I've ever seen her.

'Did you want to play the piano?' she asks. And at this point it's very much in for a penny in for a pound, because in a second, I'm pulling the piano out from the wall, opening the lid with a clunk. The whole thing is very sobering.

'It's been a long time since I played.' We seem to have agreed on what we're singing at least. Lola strums and I recognize the opening chords of 'Eyes Full of Wonder'. I suppose that I did tell Lola it was a favourite of Mum's. And Lola obviously knows all the words. She wrote them, after all.

She strums the guitar some more and fiddles with the tuning keys at the end. It's the most melodic of all Beyond Baton Rouge's songs. 'Pared back', I've seen it described as. Apparently, people went absolutely wild for it. It was their last single and it made Lola quitting seem even more inexplicable.

'You said that about singing.' Lola brings me out of my recollections.

I risk a glance out and see that everyone has moved to stand in a semi-circle around the front of the hall. At least some of these people must know who Lola is. So, they know that they're about to get a show from a real-life superstar, for free. I wonder if this is why more people seem to come to karaoke than anything else that Lola offers.

Lola starts to strum the opening notes again and I hover my fingers over the keys I'll need, hoping that muscle memory kicks in. It's all so painfully familiar to what I used to do with Mum. Something catches in my throat and the keys get blurry in front of me.

Lola's voice is, well, it's amazing. I've heard her before, of course. There are plenty of videos of the band on YouTube and I've probably contributed no small amount to their crazy high views over the years. But hearing her in real life is different. And it's completely at odds with the quiet, softly spoken Lola.

I join in after a second. I'm nowhere near as good as her, but we sound nice together. The words come back to me like I sang them yesterday and I'm sure my fingers aren't in any way connected to my brain. They dance over the keys like they've a mind of their own.

*With eyes wide in wonder, you looked at me and I think you knew.*
*That I was just no good for you.*

I've sang the words before, but I've never really thought about them. About what Lola was trying to say. Everyone assumed that she'd written the song about a lover, possibly Ashton after things went wrong between them. But what if it isn't a song about lovers? What if it's a song about something else entirely?

*And now you're gone, it's just too late.*

*How can what I'm living be my fate?*

We finish singing the chorus and this time there's no delayed reaction. I won't have to pretend that there was a slow clap in my dramatic retelling of this. It's instantaneous, people are clapping and cheering and I'm smiling and taking a pretend bow from where I'm sat at the piano.

I'm laughing along until I realize that Lola is looking at me. I feel it too, some unfathomable link between us. Between me and Lola and my mum.

Lola is speaking but she's being so quiet that I have to lean towards her to hear.

'I think I'd like to finish my story now,' she says.

And even though it's a Saturday night and I've been semi-pissed for half of it, I get it. The sense of urgency, that things are coming to a head. Except is it too early? I'm meant to have another week here.

I feel the panic rising in every fibre of my being. Swelling like a wave that doesn't crest.

Lola looks straight at me. 'I'll see you in my office.'

And then she turns and leaves.

I make my way over to Noah, who immediately pulls me into a hug. 'You were amazing.'

I hug him back extra tight, wondering if I could just stay here. Because I can't help but feel that if I follow Lola into that little office, everything might change.

'Lola wants to talk to me,' I tell him, watching as his eyebrows crease together.

'Now?' he asks.

'Yeah, she's waiting in the office.'

'Did she say what it was about?'

'No.' I shake my head, feeling guilty because even though Lola didn't say, I know why she wants to talk to me. I just do. 'I'll come back to the cottage after. Wait for me?'

'Course.' He smiles. 'I'll see you there.'

There's nothing left to do then except go to Lola and listen to the start of it all.

* * *

'Knock, knock,' I announce myself before pushing the door open to Lola's office.

I find Lola on her little stool, waiting. It's getting dark outside now, so she's turned on her desk lamp, making the room warm and glowing.

I take my own seat, just like that first time, though now there's so much more familiarity, it's hard to believe that it was only five weeks ago that Seb and I arrived.

Lola hasn't moved. She's tracking me with her eyes, though, like she can't take them off me. I make a show of getting my phone out, ready to hit record.

I clear my throat.

When I can't think of anything else to do and the silence is becoming oppressive, I say, 'So last time, you'd been practising with the band and getting close to Ashton.' Another throat clear. 'Did you want to just pick up where we left off?'

Lola closes her eyes and does a big breath in and out and I think for a moment that she's going to call the whole thing off. I don't know whether to be relieved or disappointed. But then, with her eyes still closed, she starts to talk.

*Like I said before, it all took off after the first single. We weren't maybe going to be the next big thing anymore, we were the next big thing. The single*

271

*went straight to number one. Then the second one did too, three months later. Then our first album went to number one – platinum.*

*We're talking about a time when there was little to no press regulation. Photographers followed us everywhere. The label worked us hard. We never knew where we were going from one day to the next. Most days it made my head spin, the pace of it.*

*But I loved the singing, and the music. I'll admit to it, I liked being famous. For the first time ever, people wanted to be around me. Men wanted to kiss me. Women wanted to dress like me. Or how the label wanted me to dress at any rate. I was like a doll. Even that orange dress that became a bit of a thing, well, I'd never pick somethin' like that for myself. It's like I was a whole different person. A better person, or so I was told.*

*We were playing other people's songs then of course, not that I minded that much. I didn't know anything about writing music. It felt like every time we played, I was proving something. I don't know what. Maybe I hoped that Ma or even Pa would call me up and tell me that they'd been wrong. That Pa had been wrong to leave, and Ma was wrong about me being bad luck because here I was, making something of myself.*

*The band members were my friends too. There were the usual rumours about in-fighting and us all being tempestuous and what not, but they were pretty much all started by the label, by Jimmy, the same way that they put out about me and Ashton dating. It wasn't true, none of it. I'd say that Ashton's the best friend I ever had, but he's like a brother to me, nothin' more.*

*Plus, there was Jimmy. He was with us almost every day, I remember thinking that we must have seen him more than his own family. Even late at night, after we were done doing whatever we needed to be doing that day, Jimmy would come into the apartment – we had a much nicer one by then, mind, but we still all lived together in LA – and sit around with us.*

*He always paid me extra attention. I thought it was on account of me being the youngest at first. I wasn't even twenty yet, but I'll admit to liking it a whole lot when he called me his little star.*

*I think that was about the only time that me and Ashton argued, come to think about it. He wasn't happy about how much time Jimmy was spending with me. I thought he was jealous. The label wanted Ashton to be careful, said a whole lot of things that wouldn't be allowed these days. Things are better now, or at least I hope they are.*

*But the truth is, when Jimmy said that I gave him something his wife couldn't, I believed him.*

*It's . . . hard to admit now. How I fell for all the things Jimmy said. How I got so swept up in it all when he'd lay next to me and talk about the future and all the things we could do together. He was so much bigger than me, broader. It felt safe there with him.*

*It was Christmas time, the first time he kissed me proper. We were in London to play on Top of the Pops and he'd come with us. There are not many places do Christmas like the British. I was so caught up in it all. Jimmy came to my hotel, said he couldn't keep away no more. It felt like somethin' from a movie. When he started to kiss me, I didn't push him away.*

*I'd heard Ma and Pa arguing about the other women Pa had and I remember hating them. I told myself we were different, Jimmy and me. I thought we were in love. I don't know what else there is to say about it really. He was older than me, and he had so much power. But he didn't force me or anything. I liked the attention, and I liked him. When I went to his bed, I went willingly.*

*Except when we got back from London, Jimmy didn't talk no more about our future plans. He went back to being the manager, all formal like, and I was . . . confused. I wondered what I'd done wrong. Ashton said that Jimmy was an arse and that we should tell some other folk at the label. But I didn't want to tell anyone. It was embarrassing, to be rejected again. I wanted to forget all about it. I started to drink more and more and the newspapers, well, they didn't have to work so hard at comin' up with things to write about me no more. I was becoming the thing they'd always painted me as, or something like that.*

*It took longer than it should have done to realize that something wasn't quite right. Like I said before, I was young really. Inexperienced. So, it was spring when I realized that I might be in trouble.*

*There weren't any proper symptoms. I'd feel dizzy sometimes, but we were working real hard and I just put it down to that. And I'd never been that regular. I didn't even look all that different.*

*But then one day, I saw some woman pushing a pushchair down the road. It was awful frilly, with ribbons and lace and stuff everywhere. And I just knew.*

*I told Ashton before I even did a test. He was shocked and the things he said about Jimmy coulda made a sailor blush. But he promised me that it'd be okay, that we could do whatever I wanted.*

*I know there are ways to be without a child. But I'd been raised in Baton Rouge, I'd gone to church my whole life and I couldn't ignore that, you know? I told Ashton that I wanted to keep the baby. Even though I knew that it would mean I had to tell Jimmy.*

*It wasn't easy even getting him on his own. I was five months gone and my stomach was a little round. When I finally did tell him, the spring was almost over. Jimmy went real quiet, then said that he didn't see how I'd be able to have a baby while I was in the band. Said that I'd have to go back to Baton Rouge.*

*I noticed that he never said we.*

*I was back to feeling like I'd done wrong by everyone, being a burden. Every night, Ashton told me that it'd be okay, and I tried to go along with it, to believe him. But when he was asleep I'd lay there and think about my own ma. About how much she'd struggled. I had no idea how to do a better job than her.*

*I started to show, and they had to find me clothes that would hide it. The whole time I just felt more and more guilty. About Jimmy and the label. About Ashton, for making his life harder than it ought to be. It's no wonder everyone thought we were together, we were never apart. And I felt bad on Prune and Shawn. They just wanted to be famous and here I was ruining everything because I was more tired now. I couldn't stand for twelve hours a day like I used to.*

*But most of all, I felt so guilty towards the baby. For getting me as its ma. It was overwhelming, the guilt.*

## The Next Chapter

The label pushed the release of our next single back until October. A month after the baby was due. Jimmy told me I had a decision to make. If I had the baby, I'd have to quit the band and go back to Baton Rouge. He made out like the baby might not'a even been his. But I knew it was.

I didn't know what to do.

Then my brother called, remember my youngest brother, Jessie? He told me that Ma had died. Right quick. A stroke, even though she was only young. I took it as a sign that history was just repeating itself, like by having the baby I was cursing it to a life of bad luck. Without the band I couldn't provide for it, I didn't know how to be a ma. I'd be sent back to Baton Rouge with nothing.

So, I did what I thought was best. I told Ashton and Jimmy that I wanted to give the baby up for adoption.

The label put out an announcement that I was in rehab abroad. When really, there was no hiding my stomach anymore. I flew to England and came to stay up here on Skye with Ashton's aunt. No one ever thought to look for me here. Skye wasn't up and coming like it is these days. There was no Instagram.

I was numb. Between the baby and Jimmy and Ma, I think I lost the ability to feel anything at all. I cursed myself for relying on someone again.

Ashton came with me, and he did all the work. He found me an adoption agency. There were local ones, but I wanted the family to be far away. I didn't want to think that I might run into them any day. I thought that would hurt too bad. We settled on one in Manchester. The agency asked me a whole lot of questions and finally they found me three potential couples.

They were all mighty nice, really they were. But this one couple in particular, I liked them a lot, right from the off.

I remember thinking that they were the sort of parents I would have liked to have grown up with.

Plus, she was a piano teacher and I thought it might be nice for the baby to know music, like it might be a link between us still. They cried when I told them I wanted them to have her. Big wracking sobs. They kept saying thank you. Told me they already loved the baby.

*Seeing that couple so in love, it felt like I was doing some good. More so than I'd ever done in my life. Like maybe I could break the cycle.*

*Giving birth was the hardest thing I've ever done. Not the physical part of it, though that was mighty tough too, but I knew that this was the last thing I'd do for her, for the baby. Even though I hoped that she'd see that giving her up was an act of love in its own way.*

*I wanted to call her Lola. If I'd have kept her, that's what her name would have been. Lola Starr, like me. Maybe it's a bit vain, I don't know. I just had this feeling that even then, this baby was all the good I might do in the world. I wanted her to have my name. Course, that was up to her parents, it wasn't my decision to make. But for those few hours we had together, she was a Lola to me.*

*There's nothing much can prepare you for the pain of giving away your child. It's against the natural order of things. I thought I deserved for it to hurt so bad.*

*The room was so quiet after she'd gone, even though she hadn't really made much noise to begin with. She'd been a reserved little thing right from the off, with big brown eyes. They were full of wonder, those eyes. I remember wondering how the right decision could hurt so bad.*

*It was the kindest and worst thing I've ever done. And it ate me up. I tried to go back to how things were before . . . I just couldn't. I drank to try to forget about it. I wrote her a song, 'Eyes Full of Wonder', and then tortured myself, thinking that she'd hear it and not know it was for her. Jimmy told me that I was ruining everything.*

*I did try to move on, move forward. I'd given up so much for the sake of the band, it didn't make sense that I'd throw it all away.*

*We were due to play in Vegas, and there were rumours that we might get a residency there one day. I don't know if y'all have ever been to Vegas, but it's an assault, on the senses. It's big and busy and I thought it would be the perfect place to drown out everything that I was feeling.*

*But it wasn't.*

*I missed my baby so much; I couldn't hardly think straight. I'd written* her the song, our biggest one, and that helped for a short while, but it wasn't enough. It didn't get easier, it got harder.

I was standin' there, waiting to go on and perform. The lights, the noise, everything was as planned, but I didn't know what I was doing. It wasn't what I wanted.

I just . . . walked away. Right before we were due to go on stage.

I walked away, got on the first flight back to the UK and called the adoption agency. I told them I'd changed my mind, I wanted my baby back.

It was the week after her parents had finalized the court order. I was too late. They told me I had to wait until she was eighteen to get in contact.

That there was the second worst day of my life.

Everyone was angry with me. The label. Jimmy. I didn't care. I didn't want to go back to the band anymore. The band was the reason I didn't have my baby. Or that's how it felt in my head. Ashton stood by me, though. He asked me where I wanted to go. We were so big in the States by then, it didn't feel like there was a corner of the country I could go to where someone wouldn't find me. Skye was the only place I could think of since the band started where I'd felt some peace and calm. Ashton's aunt had passed not a month before so his family helped me to buy it off them, off the record, even though I didn't know anything about running a hotel. I had some money, but not as much as people might've expected. It's not the same as it is now, the label had all the power.

None of it mattered to me.

I changed my name, I moved to Skye, I settled down for a quiet life in the only place I'd ever felt close to my baby. And I've been here ever since.

# Chapter Twenty

'When did you know?' I ask her.

'That you were my baby?' Lola answers. Both our faces are wet.

I nod.

'I suspected ... But I knew for sure when you sang tonight. Maybe something like mother's intuition, though I don't know if I've earned the right to call it that.'

'I felt it too,' I admit, thinking of that unfathomable thing I'd sensed. 'I'm sorry,' I say.

It's quiet between us then and I wonder if, like me, Lola is thinking about how completely random it all is. That she had me. That she picked my parents. That she was too late. But what she's said, it means that she wanted me. After all that, she did want me.

'I'm sorry about Jimmy,' I tell her.

Lola shrugs. 'I doubt I was the first girl to fall for him, I certainly wasn't his last. He died of a heart attack.'

She lets the words hang, neither of us acknowledging the fact that it means I'll never meet my birth father.

'Is that why you're writing your memoirs? To save the hotel?' I ask.

Another nod. 'For a long time, it's been the only thing that linked me to you. I can't lose it.'

It's quiet again as my mind whirls. I'm building up to saying the thing that I've wanted to say this whole, entire time.

'You never replied to my letters.'

Lola's forehead creases.

'What letters?' she asks.

I roll my eyes, because after everything she's told me, I didn't think she'd deny them.

'The letters I wrote to you every year.'

She's still looking at me blankly.

'Every birthday, I'd write to you. I was obsessed with you. All the clippings and videos. Mum and Dad passed the letters onto the adoption agency to give to you and every year I was so sure that this would be the year that you'd write back. Every year that you didn't, it felt like another rejection. Like you were making it clear over and over that you never wanted me.'

I stand up, needing . . . I don't know what I need.

'I swear I never got them. Did your dad tell you I called once?'

My head is spinning. 'Yeah, Dad said you called when I was eighteen. How did you even get our number?'

Lola is still sitting down, looking at the floor.

She nods. 'I remembered about your mum. Her piano lessons. I found an advert for them and called the number on there. I spoke to your dad. Your mum had just died, and I think he wanted to give me a piece of his mind.'

I go to interrupt, and she holds her hands up. 'Not that I blame him.'

'Well, he had just lost the love of his life.'

Lola shakes her head. 'I don't think that's quite true, Lily. Your dad obviously loved your mum, very much. I remember that about them. But that's what he said about you. That *you* were the love of his life, and he wasn't about to lose you. He said you hated me and that you never wanted to hear from me. It was . . . hard to hear that you didn't want to know me, even though I understood it. I felt like I should respect your wishes. That I owed you that at least.'

I'm only half listening. Instead, I've zeroed in on the fact that Dad was worried I'd leave him when Lola called.

'I never would have left him,' I say, partly to myself.

'They were good people.'

'I *know* that.'

'But I never got your letters, Lily. I swear it.'

'But . . . but you must have done. I wrote them. Mum and Dad said that you were getting them.'

Lola just looks at me. I know what she's thinking.

She's thinking that Mum and Dad lied, that they never gave her the letters.

But that can't be true. They'd never have done that to me.

Would they?

And suddenly I am furious with myself. God, how could I even think about doubting them like this? My wonderful parents who took me home and raised me when my birth mother – the woman standing in front of me – didn't. I feel such awful, all-consuming guilt. Especially when they aren't here to defend themselves either. What a shit daughter I am.

I can't do this anymore. I need to get away.

I leave the office, ignoring Lola calling for me.

I storm through the hotel to the outside.

I call the only person in my life who has never let me down or left me.

'If you're calling me at ten o'clock on a Saturday night to FaceTime your cat, we are going to be having serious words.'

'I'm leaving. I'll get a taxi. I'm coming back.'

'What, now?' says Seb.

'Yes, now.'

'You'll need to remortgage the house to pay for a taxi home.'

I hear him moving around. I stand in the gardens and look up at the stars.

'I can't stay. Lola told me the rest of her story.'

'I worked that bit out.'

'She came and stayed here, while she was pregnant, I mean. With me. She came back here because she felt close to me. That's why she's willing to sell her memoirs to save the place.'

'Shit, no way. And what about Ashton?'

'He isn't my dad. It was Jimmy Nickle. Their manager.'

'What? But he was old when Lola was in the band.'

'Yeah, he manipulated her. What great stock I come from! Oh, and Lola said Mum and Dad never passed on my letters, which can't be true. Why the fuck don't they have Uber up here?'

'I'm already in the car, babes. Get off the island and I'll come and meet you.'

'I'll find a hotel and message you. Thank you,' I finish.

The call ends and the urge to keep moving is back. I need to pack. I need to get back to the cottage and . . . Noah.

He's waiting for me on the couch when I come into the cottage, a beer in hand. There's music playing through his phone. Lola's song. My song.

He smiles when he sees me. 'I can't stop listening to this, you guys sounded great. Hey, what's wrong?'

My ability to stamp down my emotions has clearly gone haywire. I don't even need to look at myself to know that every bit of hurt I'm feeling is written all over my face.

'It's Lola,' I tell him, making no move to go to the couch and sit next to him. What would be the point?

'What about Lola?' He frowns. 'Is she all right? Is everything okay? You're freaking me out, Lily.'

'She's fine, don't worry. Well, except for the fact that . . . well, Lola, see, she's my . . . Lola's my mum.'

Lola isn't my mum.

'She's my birth mum,' I clarify.

Noah is staring at me like I've lost my marbles and honestly, it feels like I have.

'I don't understand?' he ventures.

'It's pretty straightforward when you think about it.' I laugh a hollow laugh. 'Lola had a baby when she was twenty and that baby is me. She gave me up for adoption ten seconds after she had me by all accounts, so even though she's technically my mum, she's not really my mum. My actual mum is dead. And my dad, for that matter. Also dead. My birth dad sounds like a bit of a sex pest and guess what? He's dead too!'

Now my fake laugh is tinged with mania.

Noah has stood up, now looking distinctly alarmed at the way I'm just throwing dead parents at him.

'And you've just found all this out now?' he asks, talking as if any sudden movements might set me off.

'No. I knew before I came here. That's *why* I came here. But Lola has just told me the whole story. I know you're super big on honesty, but I've been lying since the beginning. I imagine it's going to cost me a fair amount of sleep over the next few decades. If I live that long. Dying seems to be a hazard of being connected to me.'

Under his glorious, golden tan, I think Noah's paled somewhat.

I'm on a roll, though.

'And while I'm at it, Seb isn't my brother. He's my best friend. So, it's not as weird that I talk to him about our sex life. I think it's important to look for the silver linings in these sorts of occasions, don't you? Anyway, he's coming to meet me. I've called a taxi and it'll be here in—' I check my phone '—two hours, so if you don't mind, I'll get packing and then be out of your hair.'

Noah laughs like he thinks that I might be joking.

'What, you're serious? You're leaving?'

'What else am I going to do? Stay and play happy families with Lola?'

'I don't know, Lily, you've just come and said all of this . . . stuff. I don't know what to think.'

I take pity on him at that.

'I get that. And I'm so sorry I lied to you. I couldn't risk you telling Lola, see. Lying to you is absolutely going to haunt me, so rest assured I'll suffer. But we both knew this was going to end.'

Even as I say them, the words hurt. I don't want this to end, but it has to. Even without all the reasons we aren't suited, Noah comes with Lola. Lola, who is making me question everything I thought I knew about Mum and Dad. No. Nope. I can't do that.

'But I thought we were going to try?' he asks. 'I thought you felt the same?'

'What difference does it make how we feel? In two weeks you're going to Italy and in an hour and fifty-five minutes I'm going to be anywhere but here.'

I remember my list. All the reasons we wouldn't work out.

1. He loves to travel and most days, I have to psych myself up to leave the house.
2. He's leaving in six weeks.
3. I'm leaving in six weeks.
4. I've told him more than once that I love adventure when the reality is that I get excited when my favourite toothpaste is on special offer.
5. I'm lying to him about Lola.

Suddenly, so much of the list seems stupid now. Daft in a way that it didn't before. But it's the last one, the Lola one. I might not be lying to Noah about Lola anymore, but there's no denying that Lola comes with Noah. I can't have one and not the other.

And here's the thing. I want to forgive Lola. I want to be the sort of person who does that. Having her and Noah in my life would make me feel good, I think that it would. But knowing this and doing it are two different things entirely. I just can't. Or I don't think that I can. We don't owe anyone our forgiveness, surely.

'So, you've already made up your mind.' Noah runs his hands through his hair, pushing it back off his head. He stands up, and then looks around as if he's not sure what to do next.

'I can't be forced into having Lola in my life. It's okay for me not to want that.'

'I never said it wasn't okay!'

'Oh.'

My phone buzzes in my hand. I look down.

My taxi is on its way. Just a mere hour and fifty minutes to go.

'Yeah. I'm really sorry, Noah. This was never going to be more than a summer thing for me.' Even as I say the words, I know I'm lying.

I start moving towards the bedroom.

'I'm sorry too, Lily.'

He slips out of the doors, and I think at some point, I'm really going to feel this. But now, I'm acting on autopilot.

I'm in the bedroom throwing things into my case with absolute gay abandon. Nothing gets folded. I empty the bag for life I've been using for dirty clothes on top of the clean stuff. I have the suitcase version of complete mayhem. I have to put my full weight on the top of the case, just to get it to shut.

I leave the bound business plans on the bed, thinking how ridiculous this whole thing was.

I make a sad little mountain of my belongings in the main room of the cottage and then sit on the couch staring into the darkness playing the whole evening over and over in my head.

Wondering how it can be the same night as the karaoke party.

Thinking back over everything Lola had said about Jimmy, about me. Essentially, I've given my brain enough over-analysing fodder to keep it occupied for a couple of millennia.

Plus, should old age ever deign to strip me of some of the more heartbreaking of tonight's memories, I have an actual recorded copy of my birth mum talking about giving me up in the form of a song. A song, incidentally, that was my real mum's favourite. That's what you call winning at life.

Finally, I get a notification that my taxi is here, so I gather up my stuff (carrying my phone charger in my teeth, I might add) and trudge down the side of the hotel.

If Noah hears me going, he doesn't come out, and maybe this is better than some sad, sorry goodbye. A clean break.

I don't look back at the cottage.

It's only when all of my things are in the car and I'm closing the boot that I realize the light is on in Lola's office at the front of the hotel.

This time I do turn around.

Lola's there, watching as I leave.

I buckle myself in.

'Please,' I tell a very startled looking driver. 'Please get me off this island.'

# Chapter Twenty-One

*To Do:*

- Get life back on track
- Consider finding therapist
- Bond with Elton
- Pay off taxi
- Get on top of WhatsApp messages
- Get on top of emails

Seb picks me up in Fort William early Sunday morning. The drive home passes in a blur, mostly because I'm trying to sob quietly the entire time. At least the fucking roof is up.

I'm also back to puking.

'Do you want to talk about it?' Seb asks.

I shake my head against the window. 'Not yet.'

In a rare concession to my feelings, Seb doesn't push it. We're both exhausted so we're forced to stop and spend Sunday night in a Premier Inn. It's neat and ordered but it feels bare and clinical compared to Lola's hotel.

Finally, at some point on Monday, we pull up outside my house.

'Thank you, for coming to get me.' I sniff.

'You're leaving me a whole house when you die, it's the least I can do.'

'I'll see you tomorrow.' I open the car door.

'Tomorrow?' he asks.

'For work.'

That makes him laugh at least.

'Lily, you just sobbed and puked for a day and a half straight. Quite frankly, I didn't realize it was possible for someone to cry for so bloody long. You really think you'll be in a fit state to come to work tomorrow?'

I do another sad little sniff. My head is aching; quite possibly I've cried myself into a state of dehydration. I can't even settle on what exactly I'm crying about. Lola and everything she went through, Lola and her leaving me, Noah, Mum and Dad – it's all just one giant ball of messy emotion in my brain.

'You should take some time,' Seb finishes.

'No!' I might be completely confused about everything that's happened, but if there's one thing that I'm absolutely sure of, it's that the best thing I can do is to get back to normal.

Get back to my nice, normal, ordered life here. Hopefully, in time (and with possibly no small amount of therapy) what happened on Skye this summer will come to feel like a fairly potent fever dream. The sort of story I recount when I'm in my nineties and people tap my hand in a way that suggests they don't quite believe me.

'I don't want to take some time.' I think of my mound of washing. 'Or at least not much time. I want to dive straight back into it. I have a meeting with Mr Vandergilden on Wednesday, I can't miss that.'

'Well, that's bound to make you feel better.'

'I'll see you Wednesday,' I say firmly.

Seb rolls his eyes before getting out to help me unload the boot. I really can't ever let him die; I don't know what I'd do without him.

'Call me tomorrow if you need me?' he asks. I'm stood in the doorway, the detritus from Skye piled around my feet.

287

'I will, thank you. I think I'll sleep for a week after this.'

Seb nods. 'We can talk on Wednesday, but only if you're up to it. Please tell me you'll call in if you aren't.'

'I will,' I lie. 'I'm sure I'll be fine.'

He narrows his eyes at me. 'Rest up, Lily. Call if you need me.'

I must be giving off a seriously unhinged aura. I'm not sure Seb has ever been so consistently nice to me. Well, except for when Dad died that is.

'I will do. See you later.'

I shut the door and stand in the dark hallway on my own. I'm so bone tired by everything I trudge straight up the stairs, where I find Elton sprawled on my bed. I don't have the energy to worry that to the naked eye he looks to have gained weight. Or about the fact that he's squarely on my pillow, the only place in the house he's not meant to sleep.

Maybe he wanted to feel close to me while I was gone.

The thought of Elton missing me sets me off again. Seb's right, how can it be possible for a person to cry this much?

Tomorrow.

Tomorrow I'll get everything sorted out in my head. For now, I just lay down, careful not to disturb Elton, and fall into a fitful, disturbed sleep.

* * *

I wake with a pounding headache and a mouthful of cat fur.

Elton had been reluctant to share what I now presume to be his pillow. I'd woken several times to him, intentionally or not, suffocating me with his girth. Now he's flopping his tail with force over my face.

I roll away after another flop smacks me across my forehead.

Pleased to have more space, Elton spreads out. I check my phone. 6am. I've been asleep (if you can call it that) for four hours.

But you know what, if I'm going to start getting things back on track, there is no time like the present.

I need a plan.

Maybe a three-point plan.

Though that sounds way too much like the three-pronged plan I'd had with Noah. My time on Skye can't have taken planning from me, anything but planning!

I force myself out of bed. In the morning light I'm unfortunately unable to miss my reflection in the mirror above my dressing table.

I look like a victim of Dracula. How can someone spend so long in the sun and come back paler than ever? There are deep dark circles under my eyes. I think I might have actual foliage in my hair.

On Skye, I blended right in, but here, I'm all out of place in my white bedroom.

No, I'm not going to dwell on where I fit. Chances are, I don't fit anywhere. Instead, wrapping myself in my dressing gown, I head downstairs, deciding that it's now or never when it comes to tackling the mountain of washing that I've brought back with me.

Washing, it turns out, is an excellent distraction from fleeing your birth mum and the man you're pretty sure you were falling for in the dead of night and instead sleeping with your dead dad's cat who hates you.

I'm a woman possessed. There are piles of colour co-ordinated washing raring to go.

Of course today would be the day when the weather finally breaks and I can't hang anything out on the line.

Not to be deterred, I drag out my drying rack.

I add fabric softener and get a little thrill of pleasure at the fact.

I read an article once that millennials were abandoning fabric softener, fools.

The first load on, I think that I might as well clean the house and check on all the plants.

And that's how Mr Cains finds me at 8am. Scrubbing the wonky skirting boards in the hallway. Rubber gloves and dressing gown on and it's quite possible there's still tree in my hair.

'Oh hello, Lily, I didn't realize you were home.'

I smile at him from where I'm kneeling on the floor. 'Yes, yes, I'm back. Thank you for feeding Elton. I should have messaged, and now you've come all the way over here, I'm so sorry. But me and Elton, we have it all under control.'

Elton, the absolute traitor, comes thumping down the stairs to miaow at Mr Cains. So far, Elton has not deigned to recognize my presence. So much for us bonding.

'There's a good boy, Elton. Isn't it nice that your mum's home?' He strokes him behind his ear. I'd lose a finger.

'Elton's taking some time to readjust,' I declare grandly. 'But we'll be getting on like a house on fire in no time at all, won't we, Elton?'

Elton hisses at me as the end of his tail makes the slightest contact with my leg when he tries to get around me to move towards the kitchen, presumably in search of food.

'Is, er, everything okay, Lily?' Mr Cains asks. 'Only you don't seem quite yourself.'

It's because I haven't stopped scrubbing. Most people stop scrubbing when they have guests. I sit back on my ankles.

It's quite possible that I'm high on the fumes of all the cleaning products. The house is cleaner than it's ever been. It's almost enough to make me forget about everything. Almost.

The only thing I haven't cleaned is Mum's piano under the giant throw. I know my limits. Seeing Mum's piano is a hard limit.

I wave the bottle of bleach I have in one rubber-gloved hand at him. 'Course I'm fine. Why wouldn't I be fine? It's not like anything happened that could make me not fine.'

Mr Cains looks at me for a moment longer.

'Well, if you're sure you're fine . . . '

'Never in human history has a person been finer than me!' I say, in such an unhinged, manic way it undermines my sentiments entirely.

'Okay, Lily,' Mr Cains says cautiously, and if we still did it, there'd be a chance some men in white coats would arrive in the near future to drag me off to the asylum.

'Ooh, and before I forget, I'm going to get on with some food prep later. I'll drop some of your favourites off.'

'You know I always appreciate the sentiment, Lily love, but don't pressure yourself on my account.'

'I'm not, honestly, it's just really important that I keep busy. It . . . helps, you know.'

He nods. 'I felt the same after Amber died. That's when I really took it up a level, with my magic.'

Oh god, he thinks that this is all because of Dad.

I nod along. 'You've just got to do whatever you can, to get through.'

'You know I was there, the day your mum and dad brought you home?'

'You were?' I did not know this. Dad had told me how happy they were to bring me home, about how they'd bought everything you could possibly buy for a baby, and a ton of stuff that they never even got out of the box. But now, the imagined memory is tainted by the thought of Lola sitting in that hospital bed after she handed me over – how alone she must have felt.

Mr Cains nods. 'They were so happy to have you, Lily. Never seen two people happier.' He's trying to make me feel better, but he's just making me feel worse.

'I was really lucky,' I tell him. Unlike Lola, who wasn't lucky when it came to her parents.

There's an actual, physical pain then, somewhere around my middle.

I close the door on Mr Cains. 'Thanks again for looking after Elton. Okay, bye, bye, see you soon.'

I slam the door shut and slump on the floor in the hallway, overcome with no small amount of upset on Lola's behalf. How awful she must have felt when her dad left and then her mum wasn't bothered about her. How rejected she must have felt when Jimmy ignored her after they slept together. How bad she must feel now that her own daughter has left her. No wonder she won't go out with James the silver fox vet. She probably hates feeling like she's relying on anyone.

And here's the thing, I care about Lola and how she might be feeling.

I just . . . can't think straight.

Saturday night, it felt like the absolute right decision to flee. To get away from her and Noah.

This morning I'm not so sure.

I need to get everything sorted, everything straight in my head. Once everything is ordered and I can think clearly again, I'll come up with a plan. Not three but five steps back to normality. Or something like that.

I catch a glimpse of myself in the hall mirror.

Better make it ten.

I head upstairs to my wardrobe, not thinking too deeply about what I'm doing. I read Dad's letter again, the one he left me that told me to go after Lola. And what he said at the end.

*If you do go to her, you're going to find out some other truths I'm not proud of, Lily. I'm sorry about that too. I hope you know that everything we did, it was because me and your mum loved you so much. You and your mum are the best thing that ever happened to me and I'm so proud of you.*

Is that what he meant? Did he realize that I'd find out that Mum and Dad didn't send my letters to Lola?

If someone had suggested, before I met her, that my birth mum had been complicit in a deceit against her daughter, I'd have believed them in a heartbeat.

But I have met Lola. I know her now. I've heard as she's told me about the worst parts of herself. And so, in the cold light of day, it's hard to imagine that the Lola I know would lie about not getting them. Sure, it might make her look better, but I don't know . . . she really did seem surprised.

But then I'm here, aren't I? Living in the house that Mum and Dad created for us to be a family. It feels dishonest and ungrateful to doubt them.

It's all so messed up in my head.

I put the letter back.

Later. I'll think about it later.

\* \* \*

Replying to 213 WhatsApp messages is guaranteed to drive even a well-balanced person to an existential crisis.

After a very frenzied cleaning session, followed by an equally frenzied personal grooming session, I sit down to sort out my phone messages.

In six short weeks I missed two pregnancy announcements, three engagements, one divorce and one dead grandparent. People needed me and I wasn't there.

I go through and add my reactions, crying sad emoji, heart emoji, confetti emoji, careful not to mix them up.

It should make me feel better.

I should be relishing the organization. The ticking of things off a to-do list has always made me happier than is probably normal. But even as I glance at my new 'to-do list', putting a neat tick next to 'WhatsApp', I don't feel good.

I wonder what Lola's doing now?

I wonder if Noah misses me?

I knew it. I knew I wasn't cut out for a summer fling.

I make it into the office first thing the next morning, ready to take on the world of personal memoirs. Seb, however, takes one look at me and sends me home, claiming that I need some time and space to process (and also claiming that I look like someone dying of TB, which is, you know, rude).

I send an email to Mr Vandergilden rearranging our next session.

It's stressful, the thought of time off with nothing to do. But then, I remind myself of how productive I can be, with all my time. I clean the oven with the new top spec oven cleaner some influencer raved about online.

Who needs family when you have before and after pictures of your oven?

I get the ladder out and clean the outside windowsills. I've had this on my house jobs sub-list for quite some time and the thrill I get ticking that one off. Wild.

It's a shame that I obviously slept way too much on Skye because now I can't sleep, even though I'm scaling ladders during the day to tire myself out and I have all of my sleep aids to hand. I'm taking herbal Nytols like they're going out of fashion and wondering if the mountain air was the only reason I slept so well on Skye. Possibly it had something to do with the calm I felt up there. Of knowing I was close to Lola. Not wondering the whole time. Possibly that had something to do with it. Now I'm back to wondering. About her. About Noah. So much wondering.

Instead of sleeping, I lie awake, running through everything I said to Lola. My brain is tired but it's showing no signs of letting up. I think of Jimmy Nickle, the man I know for sure is my biological dad and who sounds like a complete arse.

I start to feel mad then, on Lola's behalf. Who even does that? Abandons someone when they need them?

I mean, I did that. But it's completely different. Not the same at all.

These happy thoughts whirl around my brain every night until around 4am, when I finally give in and get up.

The next morning, I beg Seb to let me come back to work after a week.

> **Me:** Please. I'm ready and I'm totally fine now.
> Spick and span.

> **Seb:** God help me.
> **Seb:** Fine, come back. But at least let me
> forward you my therapist's number. I'll get
> a refer a friend discount.

Come Monday, I'm the first person in the office.

I'm not even going to think about Lola's memoirs. I'm just going to clear my emails. Nice and easy to get me back into the swing of things. Plus, imagine the joy I'll feel, finally being on top of them. I'll have achieved the impossible.

'It's like watching a slow-motion car crash.' I hear Seb behind me. I don't look round though because I am flying through these emails, and I don't want to break my pace. 'Oh my god, are you eating a Mars bar? I'm staging an intervention.'

I take another aggressive bite of the half-eaten chocolate bar I'd picked up this morning.

'Good morning to you too.' My voice is strained. That's what insomnia and three cups of filter coffee on an empty stomach will do to a person. My fingers are flying over these keys.

'You need to take a break, Lily.' He comes to lean against the desk next to mine, looking down at me.

'What? No! I don't need a break. I only have seven emails left.'

'You just replied to Clementine with "Love you, Lola". One, pretty sure that's not your name, and two, let's stick with best wishes, shall we, for the sign off?'

I start frantically scrolling through my sent items.

'Are you checking my emails now?'

'You cc'd me into it. Same as you have every other email. I can't believe you pulled out an *as per my last email* to Mr Vandergilden.'

'He wanted to confirm when our next meeting was. Apparently, he has edits.'

I try to roll my eyes but clearly my eyeballs aren't working anymore. They feel like sandpaper. Probably all the caffeine. Wow, what a mess.

My phone buzzes on the desk.

**Noah:** I miss you. I want to talk. Call me?

I look away from my phone and then check again because I don't trust that I haven't hallucinated it.

Well, that's . . . that. Definitely not hallucinating. Imagining him thinking of me makes me warm in a way that's all nice and cosy and lovely. I miss him too. Like an ache that just won't let up.

I look at Seb, my eyes wide. 'Oh my god,' he says, 'you're going to ask me to drive you to Skye again, aren't you?'

I shake my head. 'No. Dramatic as that would be, there's no way we could execute a plan like that in the morning traffic. But I do think that maybe I need to resolve things a little better than I did.'

'What, not fleeing in the dead of night, you mean?'

'Yeah . . . ' I push my thumbs into the side of my eyes. 'God, it's all so messed up.'

The door to the office opens behind us and Clementine says, 'Hi Lily, we thought you weren't back yet.'

'I decided to come back early,' I tell her, turning round to smile.

She's wearing pink hot pants, even though the weather has (finally) cooled down. Never has a person been happier to see a black cloud as I was this morning. Let's be honest here, summer just isn't my season. Give me a pumpkin spiced latte over a mojito with a little umbrella in it any day of the week.

'Summer's over, I think,' Phil says.

Everyone hums their agreement.

'Did you bring us a present back?' Clementine asks.

Is that the done thing these days? Bringing your colleagues gifts from a working holiday? Five weeks on the edge of civilization and I'm all out of the etiquette loop.

'Er . . .'

'Don't worry, she won't have forgotten to bake something for the staff meeting. She's never missed one yet.' Phil goes to sit by his desk, opening a new bottle of Gaviscon. He once admitted that he gets a real thrill out of the crack that comes with opening a new bottle.

That's not what's distracting me, though. No, it's the fact that I *have* forgotten to bake something for the staff meeting. And it doesn't matter that I've had an awful lot on my plate lately, so much that my plate is now invisible under the mound of stuff on there. I'd never have let what was going on in my own life distract me from baking for the staff meeting before. Even the first meeting after Dad died, there I was with a chocolate tray bake.

'Well, the thing is, see . . . ' I start, the urge to say sorry so patently strong that I have to wrestle it down. Because I shouldn't be sorry for this, I don't think. Isn't that one of the things I learned on Skye? That I can do hard things. And anyway, me making baked goods each week is not what is keeping the world turning.

'I actually haven't had time to bake this weekend. Maybe we could start a rota where we each bring something in when we have a staff meeting?'

There's a beat of silence that feels monumental. That is, until Phil says, 'Good idea, Lily,' and Clementine says, 'I could pop to the bakery down the road for today.' Seb squeezes my shoulder and says, 'That was painful.'

But I feel lighter, like I've grown an inch or two.

'I'd better get on,' I tell Seb. 'I have that meeting with Mr Vandergilden in ten minutes.' I pull my headphones out of my desk drawer and begin the process of disentangling the wire, looking down at the notes I'd made ahead of our meeting.

Mr Vandergilden – final check list

- Statute of limitations?
- Does second affair add to narrative – Already established that you were a hit with the ladies.
- Trigger warning for hunting chapters?

I open the Zoom meeting, even though I really am too tired to deal with this today. My headache is so expansive that it's spreading down my nose, which I didn't think was a thing.

'Eat this.' Seb shoves half a croissant at me, and I wolf it down. I don't have the energy to worry about that reel I saw of a croissant being made and the shocking butter to pastry ratio.

The screen fills with Mr Vandergilden as I swallow the last bite.

'Laura, is that you?' His face is so close to the screen that I can see the broken capillaries across his nose, which make the end of it look super red. Like Rudolph.

I stifle a laugh at my own joke. 'It's Lily.'

'What?'

'My name, it's Lily.'

'Huh, I was sure that you were a Laura.'

'Nope, that's not my name.'

He mumbles something that's hard to make out under all the hair on his face. Probably a good thing.

'Anyway.' I draw it out, feeling vaguely reckless. 'Shall we get started?' I ask. He answers with more mumbled nodding.

We run through my checklist (don't worry about that, yes, no) and a couple of things that he's noted that aren't quite right.

He'd like me to expand on the chapter we've entitled, 'from the woods to the plate,' for instance. The result is a book that's hedonistic, completely immoral and totally offensive.

I'm slightly in awe of the fact that *this* is the legacy that he wants to leave.

'If you're happy with it, we can get it to the printers early next week and ship you your copies?' I ask him.

He coughs. 'That'll do nicely, missy. So long as I get it for my birthday, I'm gonna give everyone a copy.'

I nod. This has been the plan all along, to work towards his October birthday deadline.

'Normally, people give them out at Christmas,' I tell him, just making conversation while I type.

He coughs again.

'Nah, won't be here by then, not according to the docs at any rate.'

I stop typing and look up. Now that he's said it, maybe under all of his facial hair I can see that he looks a bit thinner around the jowls.

It's not a particularly unusual situation. Writing the memoirs of a dying man. Women tend to get theirs done earlier in my experience, but men often wait until they've had the final, 'get your affairs in order,' talk with their doctors.

'I'm very sorry to hear that, Mr Vandergilden.'

It's true, I am. I can think he's a bit of a knob and be sad for his situation at the same time.

In this job I realized a long time ago that bad people die, just like good people die. The thing that really matters is how we live. There's a choice to be made, every single day that we're alive. We all get to decide whether we're a force for good or bad. And maybe it won't matter in the end, but it matters in the here and now. It matters in the tiny moments that make up a life. And really, in the end, that's what counts, isn't it? The choices we make.

'Pah, I've had a good innings. Nothing to go getting your panties all twisted up about.'

I nod, because what else can I say?

'The thing to remember about all of this, Louisa—' I let the Louisa go this time, '—is that you've gotta take the bull by the horns.' I think we're talking about life here, though I can't quite be sure. 'You gotta do what makes you happy, even if it scares ya. Fuck the rest of 'em.'

If I were feeling less generous, I could point out that Mr Vandergilden certainly did his bit when it came to fucking people over. But it is making me think about Lola, about Noah and how much the thought of them both leaving scares me.

Even though they sounded like they wanted to stay this time, how can I trust them not to leave? Everyone leaves me.

Sometimes I wish I was braver. I wish I could move through the world freely, without resistance. Sometimes being me feels like one long battle through a wind tunnel.

'Thank you, Mr Vandergilden, I'll keep that in mind.'

'Make sure you do, missy. When you're scared, that's where the magic happens.'

I'm almost certain that he's referring to the story of when he almost got mauled by a bear during a particularly bloody hunting trip, but the sentiment rings true.

We say our goodbyes and then I just sit, staring at my screen as the office moves around me. I don't even take off my headphones, so the sound is all muffled.

Mr Vandergilden was right (and there's a sentence I never thought I'd think). I need to do the thing that scares me.

But there's one more thing that I need to do first.

I pull my headphones off.

'I'm going for a walk,' I announce to the office.

Clementine and Phil are playing chess.

'Fucking finally,' Seb says.

I head outside, ignoring the ominous rumble of clouds above me, heading in the direction that I've been in so many times before.

Neither Mum nor Dad wanted a traditional burial. They weren't religious and they both asked for that poem, 'do not stand at my grave and weep,' at their funerals. But after Mum died, Dad picked out a memorial bench for her and put it in Whitworth Park. It's where they met all those years ago. There's a plaque with Mum's name first and then Dad's next to it, the etching newer.

I march all the way there, the air cool and the rain spitting.

The first sob comes as soon as I clock the bench.

Sometimes, I think that Dad didn't choose anything bigger than a bench because he knew how much time I'd spend cleaning it. And even now, I'm proud of the fact that their bench is the best looking one in the park. The council didn't seem to mind when I revarnished it after the winter. And their new plaque is super shiny. That plaque polish I'd bought from Amazon really is the best in the business.

I sit in the corner of the bench, facing the plaque and wondering what I'm meant to do now.

Normally when I come, it's the weekend or after work. I bring a book. Just being here is a comfort. I've never before arrived in a fit of dramatics on a Monday morning.

The first splash of rain hits my nose.

'I can't believe you made me go find her,' I tell them, thinking that if now is the time that I start to talk to myself, at least there's no one here to witness it. 'But then, I guess you always knew what was best.'

The rain starts harder. I don't have an umbrella; I didn't even pick up my coat.

'The thing is, I really want to hate her. It was easier when I hated her. But now I like her and I'm so scared. What if she chooses to go again? What if she doesn't choose it but goes anyway? Leaving isn't always a choice we get. You both didn't want to leave.' Dad's letter. *If I could have stayed, I would have done.*

Obviously, no one answers.

'And then there are the letters. I wonder, did you keep them from Lola? I think you did. I'm so mad at you for that. And for not telling me. For thinking that I'd have picked her over you.'

I think back to how obsessed I'd been with Lola as a child. About what Mr Cains said about how happy Mum and Dad had been when they brought me home.

Maybe we've all just been scared this whole time.

I hate the thought of Mum and Dad being scared.

What would I tell them? What would I tell Dad when he told Lola that he couldn't lose me?

I'd have told him that they could never have lost me. That in this life and any others that there may be, they'll always be my parents.

I'm all out weeping then. My face is so wet it's hard to know where the rain ends and my own tears begin.

'I think I need to go back. Not to replace you both, she could never do that, but I don't think I can let being frightened stop me anymore.'

A man walking his dog under a huge raincoat gives me a wide berth. Probably wise. There's a chance that I've started to lose my mind, because as well as talking to myself, I'm starting to hear things.

It really sounds like the ghost of my mum is calling me.

## The Next Chapter

'Lily!'

What the fuck? Today of all days *would* be the day I start getting haunted.

I twist round to look back at the path.

Except it's not a ghost.

It's Lola.

Lola is here, in this park.

And she's coming towards me.

# Chapter Twenty-Two

'Lola.' I stand up, realizing how soaked I am. My clothes feel like they're lined with lead.

She's still coming towards me. It would be weird if I started running away from her, and anyway, I don't want to do that.

I'm not used to seeing Lola outside of Skye. It feels wrong, her being here, like the clashing of two completely separate worlds.

'Lola!' I'm having to shout over the rain. 'What are you doing here?'

She answers, I can see her lips moving, but it's hard to make out over the rain. Her plait where it pokes out of her hood is dripping wet, water running down it and onto her raincoat.

'Come on.' I pull at her hand. Mum and Dad's house is just outside the park. I keep pulling her, walking towards it, my brain whirling with the fact that she's here, she came.

We reach the house and I push the door open, dripping my way into the hall. Elton takes one look at us and makes a dash for it, as quick as his arthritic hips can take him.

Lola, who was wearing a coat and so fared much better than me in the freak downpour, takes it off and looks around.

I gaze at her like she's some sort of apparition.

'So, this is where you grew up?' she asks.

I nod. Still not moving.

'I've been trying to picture it for all these years.'

She looks round some more. I need to ask her why she's here. I need to tell her that I was going to come back to her too. But she's wandering now, from room to room.

'I'm going to change quickly.'

I thump up the stairs. My jumper is wool and it's already starting to shrink. I wrestle it off, and my jeans, pulling on fleecy joggers and a hoodie instead. My hair is a tomorrow problem because right now, Lola's downstairs.

I pad down to find her in the kitchen by the kettle.

'I hope it's all right,' she tells me. 'I know that y'all like a cup of tea for these sorts of things.' She has a small smile at her mouth.

'It's fine, honestly.'

The kettle boils and we work together to make two drinks. The air between us feels fragile, like glass that might shatter at any moment.

I don't know what's happening, but I do want to know. 'Why are you here, Lola?'

She looks at me over the top of her mug. She's cupping it with both hands as she blows on it.

'I *want* to make you tea, Lily.' She says it matter of factly. 'I want to be here for you.'

'What do you mean?'

She takes a sip and levels a look at me.

'I gave up on you twice already. I don't want to make that same mistake again.'

I swallow.

'I want to fight for you, Lily. I don't want to give up like I did when you were a baby, or when your pa told me not to call again. And I'm sorry about your letters but—'

'You didn't get them.' I cut her off. 'I know you didn't get the letters. I think Mum and Dad were so scared of losing me, they never passed them on to the agency. I believe you.'

That's one thing I'm realizing in all of this. Sometimes people do hurtful things because of love. Just like Lola all those years ago. And it's up to us to decide whether we can live with those things. Sometimes we can't, and that's okay, but other times, like with Lola and Mum and Dad, forgiving them feels like the right thing to do. There's freedom in forgiveness, I think.

'It's okay, Lola.'

She carries on, looking right at me. 'I walked away from my family. From my life in America. When Jimmy . . . did what he did, I didn't fight it. I never fought for you either. Even Noah was just *there* one day. And I never fought for him to stay. I think half the time he was runnin' from everything that happened to him as a kid. I never told him that leaving isn't the same as escaping.'

'It wouldn't have been fair for you to ask that of him.'

'No, I agree, but sometimes people are looking for a reason to stay.'

'What do you want, exactly, from me?'

Lola puts down her mug on the kitchen cabinet.

'I want a place in your life, Lily, and I'm willing to fight for it. I know I'll never be your parent; you've had two of them already and seems to me like they did a great job. I knew they would and I'm so happy that you had that. I don't think I said, but I'm so sorry, for your loss. This is me, here, fighting for you, Lily. Because I didn't do that before, when I should have done. I didn't fight for the people I love.'

Maybe here there should be a dramatic pause. I should hold my breath a second and let Lola wonder what I'm going to say. I don't do that, though, because I want what she wants. This moment is dramatic enough.

'I want that too,' I rush out. 'I want to fight too. I want to be a part of your life, I mean. Or for you to be a part of mine. Even when it's hard, or especially when it's hard.'

I'm not sure who moves first, or how my drink ends up on the side, but Lola is hugging me then. It's not at all like I expected. She's so strong and wiry, I did not have her pegged as such a good hugger. It feels like relief, that we finally made it here. Despite Lola's anaconda arms squishing me a touch, I can breathe a little easier.

When she pulls back, her eyes are wet again. And being around someone crying always makes me cry, it's just the way of the world.

'Do you think you could ever forgive me? For leaving you back then? I know I had some bad luck, what with Jimmy and . . . but I made the choices I made. I'm not shying away from them.'

I know the answer before she even finishes the question. Forgiveness is a choice. But for me, forgiving Lola, letting it all go, it's as easy as breathing.

'I already have, Lola. How could I not? You gave me all your good luck. Mum and Dad were amazing parents.'

Lola smiles, genuinely happy to hear that.

And then I'm laughing, and Lola is too.

'How did you find me?' I ask, only just realizing that Lola had turned up at a random bench in Manchester.

'Seb,' she answers. 'I turned up at the office this morning. I, er, hope it's all right, but seein' as he's your boss and not your brother, I asked if he might let you come back to Skye. Just for a while now. He said y'all need to look at your phone.'

I fish my phone out of my pocket. It's been on silent ever since my meeting with Mr Vandergilden.

There's a single message from Seb.

**Seb:** Go!!!!!!

I laugh. 'I think he wants me to go.'

And that's how I find myself repacking my bags for the third time in so many weeks.

I forgo the hypoallergenic pillow this time.

Mr Cains is all too happy to have Elton back under his guardianship. I'm thinking, if I'm going to be spending time on Skye, I might suggest some sort of joint custody arrangement.

'The van's by the park,' Lola tells me as I zip up my spare coat. 'It's not far.'

The drive back up to Skye is possibly a test of Lola's newfound motherly love. Eight hours is quite a long time. Grand gestures are bound to lose some of their shine in that time. But actually, this grand gesture doesn't. When my nausea allows, Lola and me, we get to talk about all the things we couldn't before. I field an absolute torrent of questions about my childhood. She wants to know every little detail.

In turn, I ask her everything I wanted to in the sessions. About her childhood, about Baton Rouge and whether she'd ever go back ('Maybe, if I had someone willing to come with me.'). About the hotel.

And between all the talking and the nausea we sing. We sing until my voice is hoarse and I can't sing anymore. Then Lola sings on her own. She really is amazing.

When she begins to hum the tune to 'Eyes Full of Wonder', I nod off. Wake up somewhere in Scotland. Swallow around some nausea.

Scotland makes me think of Lola, but it reminds me of Noah too. Of all the things that I've been trying to ignore this past week. Noah sleeping next to me, his hair over his forehead. Noah eating vegetable pizza without complaint. Clashing teeth in freezing water. Terrible karaoke.

'How's Noah?' I ask Lola.

She taps her fingers on the steering wheel.

'He showed me your plan for the hotel. What did he call it?'

'The three-pronged plan,' I answer automatically because my mind is tripping over the fact of Noah.

'That was mighty kind there, Lily. I don't think anyone ever did somethin' so nice for me.'

'It was mostly Noah. And you can't do it all on your own,' I tell her. My voice still has some far away quality.

In turn, Lola's voice is steady. 'No, you can't.'

It's almost dark as we wind our way to the hotel. The mountains surrounding us are jagged silhouettes against the night sky. It seems almost ridiculous how out of place I was here seven weeks ago. Now, the sight of all the mountains relaxes me.

I'm excited to be here with Lola and to see Noah again. It's that fluttery sort of excitement that feels like a kaleidoscope of butterflies let loose in your stomach. I want to make it right between us. It's like Lola said: you have to fight for the things that you want in life. And I gave up Noah way too easily.

'What on earth . . . '

Lola's pulling into the car park, but something's not right. There's a police car here, its lights flashing. And a bundle of people by the front of the door. I can see Bertie pecking around at their feet.

Lola doesn't pull into a car park space. Instead, she just stops the van and we both jump out. She's taking big strides towards the group and I'm running to keep up. Noah is there, but there's no time for grand reunions.

'What's happened?' I ask him. Even though I think I already know.

'Harper,' he tells me. 'She's been missing all day.'

My brain is lighting up, high on adrenaline. It revisits every interaction with Harper.

'They're saying they might need to look in the loch.' Noah's voice is shaky.

'No,' I tell him. 'She wouldn't go out there.'

God, is this because of me? I left her, didn't I? Just like everyone else has done. Still, I'm running through the places she might be. Where I've seen her. Where we first met.

'The forest,' I say, my voice quiet. But there's so much noise around me.

'What's that, Lily?' Noah asks.

'The forest, I think she's in the forest behind the cottages.' This time, I'm loud enough to be heard.

'I, er, I just think that she liked it in there.'

'We're searching all areas, miss,' the police officer says, not unkindly.

But Lola ignores him. 'Come on,' she tells Noah and I.

We're hurrying through the hotel gardens.

'Later,' I tell Noah.

'Later,' he agrees. Some understanding between us that unless we find Harper, there won't be a later.

Lola produces a torch and Noah and I use our phones to give us some light.

Still, we're marching through the forest in the dark, we trip and stumble over branches on the floor. The thought of Harper out here on her own makes me feel sick.

'Harper!' we call.

'HARPER!'

It's full night now. The darkness thick and velvety.

'Harper,' I shout, tripping and banging my knee. 'Fucking Jesus.' I hop about. 'Harper!'

The thought that I might be wrong here makes me feel queasy.

'Harper!'

Another fall.

'Harper!'

I've no idea how we'll get out of here if we even do find her. It feels like we've been searching forever.

'Harper!' we shout. I don't know exactly when I started to cry.

'Harper!' What if we don't find her? What then?

'Lily.'

'Shh,' I tell Lola and Noah. 'I think I heard something. Harper!'

'Lily.'

'I heard it too,' Lola says.

'Hang on, Harper, we're coming,' Noah calls back.

I want to collapse on the floor with relief. 'Harper,' I shout, 'be as loud as you can. Shout back.'

'LILY.'

'Okay, it's this way.' Noah points to the direction of Harper's voice.

'Keep shouting to us, Harper,' Lola calls.

'Lily!' Harper's voice sounds hoarse.

Eventually, the calls of 'Lily' become louder until we find Harper, arms wrapped around herself sitting at the bottom of a tree.

Her face is puffy with tears, and she's soaked and shaking.

Noah has his jacket off in a second and wraps it around her. He picks her up like a doll and she doesn't even complain. She just tucks her head into his shoulder.

'It's all right, Harper,' Lola says, heading back in what must be the direction of the hotel.

'Yeah, we've got you,' I say, just for something to say. It's been a day, honestly.

'You came back.' Her voice is muffled in Noah's shirt.

'Yeah, Harper, I came back.'

# Chapter Twenty-Three

By the time we get back to the car park, there's an ambulance waiting for Harper. I don't know what worries me more, the fact that she goes into it willingly, or the fact that she endures her foster mum kissing her head over and over.

'We'll see you!' I call to her. 'When you're back.' I don't know if she doesn't hear or if she's ignoring me. And then it's just me, Noah and Lola standing in the car park, shaking.

'Well, I never drink, not anymore, but I think tonight calls for a brandy.'

Lola's day has been even more full-on than mine when you think that she drove to Manchester and back. In a day.

I go to follow her, but she turns around and says, 'Go, your cottage is waiting for you, Lily,' and walks away, leaving me with Noah.

'Come on, you must be freezing,' he says, and I am shaking. Though what exactly is making me shake is quite frankly a toss-up at this point.

I don't argue. My brain is running static. I can't think. I just follow Noah through the gardens and into the cottage. There, I sit on the couch, my back straight and my hands primly crossed in my lap. Noah goes to get some towels from the bathroom. He moves to sit next to me and tilts his knees so that they're touching mine. It settles me, just an inch.

'What a day,' I say, thinking that it doesn't cover everything today has been, not by a long shot. This can't be the same day that I had a meeting with Mr Vandergilden, even if that was eleven hours ago.

'So ... ' I draw it out, thinking that if ever there was a time for honesty, it's now. 'You never knew that she had a baby?' I ask.

Noah shakes his head. 'She told me everything. After you left, she came and told me everything.'

I've started to shake again. It's been an intense couple of hours, but also maybe I am colder than I realize. Noah gets up, switches on the kettle and goes to the bedroom, returning with the duvet. I wrap it around me, like a giant fluffy chrysalis. I look and am ridiculous.

'No,' he tells me, handing me a cup of coffee. Milk and sugar. Fuck my enamel. Oh dear, I've gone insane. 'But it does make sense.'

'How so?' I ask.

'Lola's always been ... how can I describe it? Not cold exactly, but just detached, from life. She's never really let anyone get close to her. I think she missed you, all these years.'

'She was in an impossible situation.'

'I know,' he answers.

'I don't hold it against her. You shouldn't either.'

'I don't, Lily, don't worry. I wondered a lot about why my parents didn't give me up for adoption when I was younger. They obviously never wanted me.'

'I'm so sorry, Noah.'

I hope he knows that I mean for his parents, for lying, for everything.

'I know you said that you didn't see a future for us. And the old me wouldn't have disagreed,' he starts, looking down at his hands. There's a faint flush high on his cheeks. 'But something changed for me. I like you, Lily, I want to try to make this work.'

I'm still shaking, but I nudge a little closer to Noah. He takes the duvet and wraps it around his shoulders too. I'm pressed up against his side. I start talking, thinking that I'm close to maxing out my capacity for unscripted emotional talks. 'I really like you too, Noah. And not just because you're so nice to look at, like, really nice. Lola gave this whole speech about how you have to really go for the things you want in life sometimes and it dawned on me that I'm more like her than I realized. I was running away from everything, from her, from you.'

He smiles and a bit of his hair falls forward onto his forehead, a bead of rain on the end.

And no, nope, I cannot lose my head over a bead of rain.

'But I just need to be honest, because I know I've given the impression that I'm this fun-loving, free spirit,' I carry on, appreciating how his eyes have gone all soft around the edges, 'but Noah, that isn't me, it was all an act. I'm not a free spirit, I'm not even particularly fun unless it's in a very controlled environment. I love to-do lists and adding things to to-do lists that I've already done just so that I get to cross them off. *That's* how I get my kicks. I don't want you going into this believing that we should make a go of it to be based on completely false advertising.'

'Are you done?' he asks at the end of my little soliloquy.

'Yeah, I think so.'

'Good. Because I hate to be the one to break it to you, but you haven't been giving the impression that you're all fun-loving and fancy-free. I mean, sometimes, you are those things – people can be more than one thing at once, I reckon – but a lot of the time you've been you. I've never seen someone eat so many vegetables on holiday. I'm guessing you have health anxiety too?'

I'm taken aback. 'Yes, well, there is that. Several dead parents and abandonment issues. Comes with the territory.'

'I don't care about those things. I know about those things, and I still like you. Who doesn't add things to a to-do list that they've already done?'

314

'I don't know, I always assumed well-balanced people?'

Noah pfts. 'Lily, remember I have a favourite pen.'

'You do have a favourite pen. And a favourite mug,' I remind him. 'That one with the hill on it.'

He laughs. 'It's actually Mt Kilimanjaro, but okay.'

'Shush.' I put a finger to his lips. 'I'm having a revelation here. Do you think we're . . . more alike than we realized?'

'What, because we both like running, and notebooks, and we're both writers? I think maybe you're right! Plus, you did jump out of a plane.'

'Yes, though for the record, that was a terrible idea. I won't be doing that again.'

Noah's smiling and I am a fool for that smile. I shove my wet towel at him. It smacks him in the chest.

'But we're different too. And that's okay. No one is one thing all of the time. It's like the scenery. People are always changing and impossible to describe. There's just too much.'

'I think you understand people better than you think, Noah.'

He smiles, wider this time. 'I'll have to go to Italy still,' he says, stumbling over his words. 'I want to travel. And I don't know how the future might look, not really, but I know, it's like you say, I want to try.'

'I wouldn't want you to not travel, it's what you love.'

Noah looks at me.

'There are things I think I could love more. All this time, I think I just needed a reason to come back.'

It's me. He means me. I'm the thing that he thinks he could love more.

'We can figure it out together,' I say with determination. 'I think that, if you wanted it, I could come sometimes. So long as I see the itinerary ahead of time, of course.'

'Of course,' he agrees.

And then he's holding me close again. I can feel the rhythm of his heart beneath my ear.

I had absolutely thought that this would end with us both naked. I'd hoped that might be the case, to be completely honest. But actually, burrowed under the duvet with Noah, watching the rain splatter against the doors of the cottage and feeling optimistic about the future for once, well, it's just perfect.

\* \* \*

The next morning, (okay, it's closer to midday) there's a tapping at the door to the cottage.

I yawn and Noah shifts in the bed next to me. I don't want to wake up. I'm still tired from the sleepless nights I'd spent with Elton trying to slowly murder me in my sleep.

The knocking gets more insistent, so I pull myself out of bed, wrapping my dressing gown around me. I think I know who this will be.

Harper.

'Harper.' I smile at her. 'You look so much better.' At the edge of the garden, I can see Harper's foster dad watching us.

'You came back,' she says, looking at me like I might be a puzzle in need of figuring out.

I think for a second. 'I did. Do you want to go for a walk?' I look out beyond her to the gardens. It's not raining, but it's not boiling either. The air is fresh and the grass looks impossibly greener.

'You aren't dressed.'

It's not a no.

'Give me one minute.'

I hurry back to the bedroom, rifling through my case.

'I'm going for a walk with Harper,' I tell the back of Noah's head.

'Okay.' He twists around to look at me and I can't help myself. I lean down and kiss him goodbye, feeling unbelievably smug at the fact that I can do that now.

'Come on,' I say to Harper, stepping out into the garden, closing the doors behind me.

'I've got her,' I call to her foster dad. 'I won't let her out of my sight.' He nods and waves, his shoulders hunched and tired.

Harper won't meet my eyes.

'Let's go down to the loch,' I tell her, thinking that we'd better steer clear of the forest.

Harper follows a pace or so behind me and I wonder if she's just here to punish me for going. That she's going to subject us both to a long, stony silence. But then I'm the adult here, I need to go to her.

We reach the loch. It's deserted, now that the summer is technically over. There's a low mist rising off the water, ethereal and mildly spooky.

I sit at the edge of the dock. Harper sits next to me, swinging her feet off the edge.

'I'm sorry I left, Harper. I shouldn't have gone like that, without saying goodbye.'

She doesn't speak for a minute, and I think stony silence it is. Until eventually she says, 'Lola said that she's your mum. Your *real* mum.'

'Is that what Lola said?' I ask.

Harper shrugs. 'She said she gave birth to you and gave you up for adoption.'

I nod. 'That's right. My real mum died when I was eighteen, though. Lola's my birth mum.' I take a deep breath. 'Sometimes, the people who give birth to us, they're not meant to be our parents. It might not be their fault, or it might be, but it has nothing to do with us.' I hope Harper gets what I'm saying. I'm not being particularly subtle about it, so chances are she will.

'It's still fucking shit, though.'

317

'Yep,' I agree. 'It is. I spent a lot of time trying to pretend it was okay when really, I should have just admitted how angry I was.'

'I can't imagine you angry. You're all weirdly nice.'

'I don't get angry much, but sometimes I wanted to scream about how unfair it all was.'

For dramatic effect, I do a small shout across the water.

'It's fucking shit!'

My strange shout makes Harper laugh. I think it's maybe the first time I've ever heard her laugh properly. She sounds so young.

She slaps a hand across her mouth, like she can't believe the noise that she just made.

That makes me laugh and then we're both laughing, our legs still hanging down.

'I feel angry too,' Harper adds, even though she's smiling. I don't tell her that this is news to literally no one, because then she shouts too, louder than I did.

'I'm sorry that I scared everyone.' Her voice is small now.

'It's okay, Harper. So long as you're okay. I know that things can be unfair sometimes.'

I shout again, getting louder still and then suddenly, between laughs, we're both shouting about how unfair life can be.

I'm breathless and my stomach squeezes from laughing so much but it's cathartic, all the shouting. My voice is halfway to hoarse when I say to Harper, 'I really am sorry that I left.'

She shrugs and bumps her shoulder against mine. 'You came back, that's what matters.'

# Chapter Twenty-Four

**The Next Chapter – One Year Later**

'Come on, Lily, step out of your comfort zone.' Harper's face is half submerged in water. It's giving *Jaws*.

'See, that's what I don't get. Why would anyone want to step *out* of their comfort zone? The devil's in the detail. *Comfort* zone,' I emphasize.

My own comfort zone feels about a million miles away right now, but I can't help but smile when Noah laughs, his head bobbing in the water like a bloody buoy.

In fact, they're all bobbing in the water. Lola, Harper, Noah, Ashton, James, Harper's foster dad, Jake. He's friends with Noah now. They're here as often as we are. Even Seb is floating on his back, his sunglasses still in position.

I peer over the edge of the rowboat we'd rowed, for some ungodly reason, into the middle of the deep loch of doom. And even though after extensive googling, I can't actually attribute a single death to its murky waters, someone always has to be the first.

'She doesn't have to come in if she doesn't want to.' Noah splashes a bit of water towards Harper. It's been one of the best things about this last year, watching Harper's confidence grow. She's been, there's no other word for it . . . pleasant at times. We're taking some time to adjust.

Noah had helped a lot too, which is good since she's always been consistently nicer to him than anyone else. Anyway, he doesn't splash her enough to drown her, but enough to encourage her to launch all-out water-based war on him.

While Harper's occupied trying to dunk the love of my life, Lola swims over to the rowboat.

'Are there a lot of fish, do you think?' I ask her, peering over the edge into the darkness.

'I can't speak for the fish, but I know me and Noah, we'd never let anything bad happen to you.'

God, I do know that too.

This past year has been amazing.

No, that's not quite true – parts of it have been amazing. Other parts have been hard because whatever happens, I miss Mum and Dad in the same way that you might feel an old bruise. Constantly aching, no matter what else you have going on.

But having Lola and Noah in my life (and Harper and Blake, for that matter), I have a family. Not the one I expected to have, but they're mine, nevertheless.

Plus, and I can't believe that I'm going to say this, I'm a little bit rich. Apparently, my song, the one Lola wrote for me, well, she's been saving the commission from it all these years in case I ever got in touch. It felt weird, taking her money; after all, she earned it and the hotel needed it.

But Noah's right, Lola can be stubborn, and she promised that she'd never spend a penny of it so it would be there when she died. And then I'd gotten all freaked out about the thought of her dying and had agreed to take it. Let's just say that Your Life has a new partner who was happy to invest in a new business plan (printed and bound, of course).

Plus, unexpectedly, Mr Vandergilden had left a rather large tip.

We didn't sell Lola's memoirs, but we're doing just fine.

'Okay.' I stand up on shaky legs, grabbing the side of the boat as it wobbles. Noah swims closer to the edge, ready to catch me even though I'm the only person wearing a life jacket, because come on, I haven't had a personality transplant this year.

'I'm coming, right now, here goes!' You'd think that I was counting down to launching myself off a cliff, or else shooting along that zip line Noah took me on in Wales (incidentally, I didn't mind that as much. The staff there *did* have a risk assessment and it's nice to see someone taking health and safety seriously.). But instead, I step off the edge of the rowing boat and into the water.

'Got you.' Noah smiles, his hands finding my waist the second I go under the water.

My shoulders don't even break the surface, such is the buoyancy of my life jacket, but still, there is a lot of water in here.

'Don't look down, just breathe.'

I do, because Noah understands me. Maybe it's the ying and yang about us – he's adventurous and I'm not – that makes us balance each other out. Or maybe it's the fact that really, we weren't all that different to begin with. I needed someone to make me feel safe, and he needed a reason to stay. And we get to be that for each other. Plus, we have our shared love of stationery, which seems like as good a foundation for a relationship as any.

'I love you,' he tells me, pressing his forehead against mine. I'll never get tired of hearing that.

'I love you too.'

'If y'all are done, Harper wants to play some game,' Lola interrupts. She's in the water close by, her blonde hair fanning out around her. And though she must be treading water, she's somehow perfectly still.

It's hard to define my relationship with Lola. She's not my parent, but she's more than a friend too. Life, I think, is always more complicated than we might expect it to be. And anyway, I don't really care about defining it, because I like her. I liked her last summer, and I liked her all the times I visited, or she visited me. I liked her when she hosted all of us, including Seb and Ashton, at Christmas on the promise that we help out with some hotel repairs. I'd drawn up a rota.

The game is Marco Polo. I'm awful at it, because my life jacket doesn't allow for much movement, and also, who would want to close their eyes in water?

I only manage to end my turn when Seb accidentally on purpose bumps into me. I smile at him. I'm sure that behind his sunglasses his eyes are rolling. At least we get to go back to shore now. Oh sweet earth.

'Having fun?' I ask Seb as the two row boats we're using bump against the shore and we all clamber (or in my case are hauled) out.

'You're all so unbelievably wholesome.' Seb steps gracefully out of the boat. 'It's nauseating.' Lola is walking a little ahead, holding hands with James.

It's pretty cool to think that this group here, well, we're pretty much the only people in the world who know what happened to Lola Starr.

Seb must be thinking the same thing. Noah now calls it twintuition, even though he knows we aren't twins.

'This happy ending could have made us so much money,' he says, 'so much money.'

Ashton, who's been walking next to Seb (a fact that does not escape my attention one little bit) is looking at him with a puzzled expression.

'Why's that, then?' Ashton asks.

'Because you guys were ridiculously famous,' Seb explains. 'People would have paid good money to hear about what went down with Beyond Baton Rouge.' He looks up at the sky. 'So much money.'

Ashton rubs his chin. He's wearing what look like Gucci swim shorts. They're gold.

'What about if you did me? My memoirs, I mean,' he quickly tacks on. 'Do you think that would make you some money? We could just skip over, you know . . .' He waves a hand towards me.

Seb has stopped walking.

'You want us to write your memoirs?' he asks.

'I don't see why not. I'm not Lola, but there are things I want to say. Stuff I was told to keep quiet, you know.'

I do not see it coming, but suddenly Seb has his hands on either side of Ashton's head. He leans down and kisses him with one big, exaggerated kiss on the mouth.

'Yes!' he says, while Ashton looks at him wide-eyed. 'Finally, some good news for me. My therapist is going to love this.'

Everyone laughs.

'I just need to check on Elton, then I'll get the picnic things ready,' I tell them all, walking a little faster to get ahead.

By some miracle, Elton is still alive. He actually lives with Mr Cains now, and holidays, occasionally, with me. Everyone seemed happier with that arrangement, especially Elton.

I guess, sometimes it's important to know when to let go.

But Mr Cains is visiting his brother, and I didn't want to leave him for the whole summer, so I'd seriously upgraded his travel basket and then given him some cat Valium for the journey. He's formed an unlikely friendship with the blind chicken. It's all very peculiar.

'Is anyone else bringing food?' Harper asks loudly.

'I have some stuff,' Seb answers.

'Thank fuck for that.' Harper high fives him. 'There's only so much grass we can eat.'

'It's salad!' Lola and I call after her.

I make my way back to the cottage, the gardens now much neater since Lola hired a gardener, Noah following behind me. We're sharing a cottage this summer; Seb is in the other one for a couple of weeks.

'You good?' Noah asks into the back of my neck as I work the door to the cottage.

I hum, liking the feel of his proximity. 'I'm *great*,' I tell him as he plants a kiss on my shoulder.

Things with Noah are much more certain than they were last year. It had taken some figuring out, and one giant wall calendar which I don't hate at all, but we have a system now. Noah took the job with the *Guardian*, and while he still gets to travel, it's for shorter periods. The month we spent apart while he was in Italy was enough for us to know we don't want to be apart a huge amount. Sometimes, I even go with him, and – probably unsurprisingly for everyone but me – I always have a good time. I even discovered it's a bit of a skill: Noah says that no one can nail down a three-day travel itinerary as efficiently as me.

'Ready?' I ask, gathering all the tubs of salad in my arms.

Noah tucks a bit of wayward hair behind my ear. 'Ready,' he answers, smiling. 'It's nice, having this little bit of peace before the madness starts tomorrow.'

'Agreed.' I go to follow him.

The race that Noah had wanted to reinstate is happening tomorrow. It turns out that opening a race involves a lot of paperwork and an insane amount of health and safety. It's been heaven. I lost a whole day amidst the hotel archives. There's a display now in the lobby, showing off its history, an addition to the three-pronged plan.

In fact, Lola's pretty much followed the plan to the letter and the hotel is busy again. Except for this week. This week it's just us.

'Come on, then, let's go feed our family.'

Because that's what they are. Seb, Harper, Lola, Noah. They're friends who have become a part of my family.

For some people, the things that they want in life come easily, dropped into their lap like a gift from some higher power. That hasn't been the case for me and Noah, or my parents, or Lola, for that matter. We've all had to fight for the things we want and for the people we love. It hasn't always been easy, and it won't always be smooth. But maybe, just maybe, the very best things never are.

# Acknowledgements

Every time I sit down to write these, I'm in awe of just how many people it takes to get a book from a messy file on my laptop into the hands of readers. It's definitely not something authors can do alone and it's possibly no good for our egos that ours are the only names on the cover!

Acknowledgements keep us humble, but they're also a chance to thank all of the brilliant people we work with, and I'm so fortunate to work with such an amazing team.

Firstly, everyone at Simon and Schuster, thank you so much for championing my books and for your continued and enthusiastic support. Every day, I feel lucky that you're my publishers. Molly, you are undoubtedly the best in the business. It's a huge privilege to work with you. Thank you so much. Thank you also to Harriett (publicist extraordinaire and owner of excellent headbands), Sarah, Clare, Misha and SJ. And thank you India, for the beautiful cover. You really are a fantastic team!

Thank you, Mads, for being an absolutely brilliant agent. I am genuinely in awe of how good at your job you are. I'm only a little bit terrified by your Taylor Swift fervour. Your insights made this book so much better than it was. Here's to many happy years together (not in the married sense, just in the agent – author relationship sense).

Writing can be a lonely affair, so it's important to find the people who make it less so. Emma, even if my writing career bombs, I'll be happy that I got your friendship out of it. Mira, same goes. Jane, you are so funny and supportive! And to writers closer to home, Sam, Lisa, Ailsa, Martyn and all of my MA friends, you all read early versions of this and told me it wasn't rubbish. Mark and Gill, I love working with you both.

Friends of the non-writing variety, Vicky and my NCT friends, Anwen, Hayley, Gemma, Laura and Teresa (a true gold star neighbour). I'm so fortunate to have you all in my life.

To my family, thank you all for your continued support and encouragement. I wouldn't be able to write without you, that's an absolute fact. And my children, Elodie, Hugo and Kit – you are forever my inspiration. It's not even funny how much I love you.

Thank you, Dan, for helping me to heal. Love can be scary for me, but it feels the exact opposite of that with you. And Phoebe and Freddie, you guys are pretty ace!

Lastly, the most enormous thank you to all of the readers, reviewers, bloggers, podcast hosts, event organisers, Waterstones staff and generally anyone in the bookish world who has helped to promote my books. I've said it before, I'll say it again, book people really are the best people, and I never take your support for granted.

# Discover more from Rebecca Ryan

## All available now